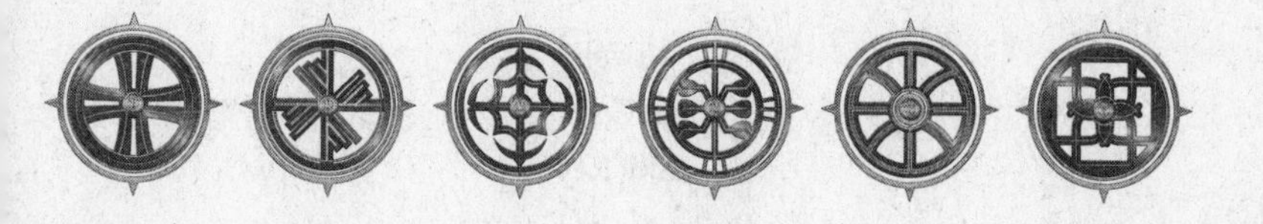

This book is a puzzle.

Decipher, decode, and interpret.

Search and seek.

If you're worthy, you will find.

ENDGAME SERIES

Novels:
The Calling
Sky Key
Rules of the Game

Digital Novellas:
Endgame: The Training Diaries Volume 1: Origins
Endgame: The Training Diaries Volume 2: Descendant
Endgame: The Training Diaries Volume 3: Existence
Endgame: The Zero Line Chronicles Volume 1: Incite
Endgame: The Zero Line Chronicles Volume 2: Feed
Endgame: The Zero Line Chronicles Volume 3: Reap
Endgame: The Fugitive Archives Volume 1: Project Berlin
Endgame: The Fugitive Archives Volume 2: The Moscow Meeting
Endgame: The Fugitive Archives Volume 3: The Buried Cities

Novella Collections:
Endgame: The Complete Training Diaries
Endgame: The Complete Zero Line Chronicles
Endgame: The Complete Fugitive Archives

RULES OF THE GAME

AN ENDGAME NOVEL

JAMES FREY

AND

NILS JOHNSON-SHELTON

HARPER

An Imprint of HarperCollins*Publishers*

NO PURCHASE NECESSARY. Contest begins 9:00 a.m. EST, January 9, 2017, and ends when the puzzle has been solved or on July 10, 2017, whichever is earlier. Open to ages 13 and older. Void where prohibited. Aggregate value of all prizes: approximately $251,000.00. Sponsor: Third Floor Fun, LLC, 25 Old Kings Hwy N, Ste. 13, PO Box #254, Darien, CT 06820-4608. For Contest details, prize descriptions, and Official Rules, visit www.endgamerules.com.

HarperCollins Publishers is not responsible for the design or operation of any contests related to Endgame, and is not the sponsor of any such contest. All such contests have been designed, managed, and sponsored by Third Floor Fun, LLC, which is solely responsible for their content and operation.

Rules of the Game: An Endgame Novel

Puzzle hunt experience by Futuruption LLC.
Additional character icon design by John Taylor Dismukes Assoc.,
a Division of Capstone Studios, Inc.

For information address HarperCollins Children's Books, a division of HarperCollins Publishers, 195 Broadway, New York, NY 10007.
www.epicreads.com

Library of Congress Control Number: 2016952952
ISBN 978-0-06-233265-3

17 18 19 20 21 PC/LSCH 10 9 8 7 6 5 4 3 2 1
❖
First paperback edition, 2017

KEPLER 22B

Ansible chamber on board the Seedrak Sare'en, active geosynchronous orbit above the Martian North Pole

kepler 22b sits in a shiny chair in the center of a black, low-ceilinged room. His seven-fingered hands are woven together, his platinum hair bound into a perfect sphere perched on top of his head. He reviews the report he is about to give over the ansible to his conclave, many light years away. The game taking place on the blue-and-white planet in the next orbit has experienced hitches and unforeseen developments, but it progresses nonetheless. Most of what has transpired is not terribly worrying, with the notable exception of the destruction of one of Earth's 12 great monuments. This was the one that belonged to the La Tène Celts, the one called Stonehenge, and it is now utterly gone and useless. kepler 22b is deeply disturbed by this. At least one of these ancient structures—ones that were erected many millennia ago, when his people walked alongside the young humans of Earth—at least one is required to finish Endgame.

And this, more than anything, is what he wishes to see happen.

For a Player to win.

A Player.

He turns his attention from the report to a transmission hologram projected into the air not far from his face. A dim real-time blip moves over the map of a city on the Indian subcontinent. A Player. Judging by the speed, he uses some kind of vehicle.

This Player is not the one that kepler 22b expects to win, but it is the one he has been most curious about.

He is a shrewd and incautious Player.

Unpredictable. Excitable. Merciless.

He is the Shang, An Liu.
And kepler 22b would continue to watch but then the ansible hums and the hologram flicks off and the room fills with pitch blackness and the temperature drops to -60 degrees Fahrenheit. Moments later the blackness pricks with drifting motes of light and the room glows bright and there they are, their projections surrounding him on all sides.
The conclave.
kepler 22b would prefer to watch the Shang, but he cannot.
It is time to give his report.

AN LIU

Beck Bagan, Ballygunge, Kolkata, India

The Shang.

SHIVER.

blink.

SHIVER.

An Liu rides a Suzuki GSX-R1000, trying to gain speed but getting thwarted by the Kolkatan throng.

He twists the grips. The wheels spin over the uneven pavement.

No helmet, teeth gritting, lungs burning, eyes like slits. Chiyoko's remnants press into his chest. Next to the necklace of his beloved is a SIG 226 and a small collection of custom-made grenades. All of these are hidden from view by a cotton shirt.

He pushes north for South Park Street Cemetery. Pushes, pushes, pushes.

The cemetery. It is where he is. One of the Players who Chiyoko had nicked with a tracker. One of the Players that An is now tracking.

The cemetery is where he will find the Nabataean. Maccabee Adlai.

Who has Earth Key and Sky Key. Who is winning.

Or believes he is winning.

Because there is a difference between these.

If An gets there soon, there will certainly be a difference.

If An gets there, Maccabee will not be winning. Not at all.

He will be dead.

And An is less than two kilometers away.

So close.

But the streets are full. Kolkata has poured her citizens out of doors this evening, all of them clamoring for information, for loved ones, for a decent cell signal. An dodges businessmen and spice wallahs, brightly dressed women and stray dogs, crying children and stalled Ambassador taxis, rickshaws with reed-thin men pulling their carriages along haphazard streets like fish working upstream. He curls the bike around an oblivious Brahman bull. Some people get in An's way. These either get nudged by the bike or get a swift kick from An's foot.

Out of *SHIVERSHIVER* out of the way.

In his wake are screams and bruises and cursing and shaking fists.

There are no cops. Not a single officer of the law.

Is it because the world is on the cusp of lawlessness?

Is it because of Abaddon, even now, before it has struck?

Could it be?

Yes.

An smiles.

Yes, Chiyoko. The end is near.

Two large men appear at the intersection of Lower Range Road and Circus Avenue. They point and shout. They recognize him. They saw his video—everyone in the world has seen his video by now—and they want to stop him. They may try to *kill* him, which An finds preposterous. He revs the bike and people scatter, but the men hold strong and lock arms.

Fools.

An rides straight for them, through them, knocking them aside and running over one, tearing skin from an arm. The men yell and one produces an ancient-looking pistol from nowhere. He pulls the trigger, but instead of firing properly it explodes in his hands.

He falls, screaming.

The gun was faulty. Old. Broken.

Like this BLINKBLINKBLINK this world.

An might feel sorry for the man and his mangled hand, but he is the Shang and he doesn't care. He jams the throttle and rises out of the saddle and weaves the bike's rear wheel back and forth and scuttles away, one of the men screaming as his leg is momentarily caught under the rubber and made bloody and raw.

An's smile grows.

He leaves the men behind. Passes a barbershop, a sweetshop, a mobile phone shop, an electronics shop crowded with people. On the screens in the windows of this store An catches the image of kepler 22b.

The alien outed himself when he gave his announcement about Sky Key. kepler 22b began to show his true colors. Endgame is real for everyone now. It is real for rich people and poor people, the powerful and the impotent. The brutal and the kind. Everyone.

And An loves it.

Now the whole world knows that the first two keys are together. That Maccabee has them. That Endgame continues despite some of the other Players' misguided attempts to stop it. That it continues despite fear and hope and murder and even love.

Best of all, kepler 22b told the people of Earth that Abaddon can't be stopped. That the giant asteroid will fall in less than three days and there is nothing anyone can do about it.

That millions will die.

An loves it.

The bike churns. The street widens. The crowds part and An moves a little faster, up to 60 kph now. He glances at Chiyoko's watch. Sees the tracker's display screened over the numbers.

Blip-blip.

There. Maccabee Adlai.

So *BLINK* so *SHIVER* so close.

So close that An can smell them.

An screams across Shakespeare Sarani Road and goes two more blocks and spins northwest on Park Street. He looks at the watch again and sees it.

Blip-blip.

Blip-blip.

Only blocks away.

BLINKshiver

Chiyoko Played for life.

SHIVERblink

But I

SHIVER

I Play for death.

COMSTARCHAMBER·KEPLERFUTURIST
ICS·C

SARAH ALOPAY, JAGO TLALOC, AISLING KOPP, POP KOPP, GREG JORDAN, GRIFFIN MARRS

The Depths, सूरय को अन्तमि रेज, Valley of Eternal Life, Sikkim, India

"Everybody chill the fuck out!" a man yells. He's mid-40s, weathered, drenched in sweat, a little chubby. He stands in the middle of the hallway that is crowded with Players and their friends.

Sarah and Jago are at the far end, their backs to an open doorway. The Donghu, the Harappan, the Nabataean, and both Earth Key and Sky Key were in the room beyond the doorway not minutes before. Baitsakhan was very alive and very intent on killing Shari Chopra out of a psychotic sense of revenge, but Maccabee felt sorry for the Harappan, and he stopped the Donghu. He was about to take sole possession of both Earth Key and Sky Key when Sarah and Jago surged into the room. As Baitsakhan lay dying, the Olmec jumped forward and attacked Maccabee, and while the fight was close, Jago won. Sarah had a chance to kill Little Alice Chopra, the girl who is Sky Key, a death that should have put a stop to Endgame.

But Sarah couldn't do it.

And Jago couldn't do it either.

Aisling's squad arrived moments after the fight ended. The Celt had a chance to kill Sky Key too, and she tried to take a shot with her sniper rifle, but at the last moment Sky Key reached out and touched Earth Key and in a flash of light the little girl disappeared, taking an unconscious Maccabee with her, and the mutilated body of Baitsakhan as well.

The only living person left in that room is Shari Chopra, knocked out, with a large lump on her head courtesy of Maccabee. He could have killed her too but, perhaps out of mercy or righteousness or empathy, Maccabee let her live.

Where Maccabee and the keys are now, none of them know. It could be that they went to Bolivia, or to the bottom of the ocean, or are in an Endgame-finishing audience with kepler 22b himself.

All that is left here, in the routed Harappan fortress carved out of the Sikkimese Himalayas, are these Players and Aisling's friends.

All that is left is their fear and their anger and their confusion.

And their guns.

Most of which are pointed at one another.

"Just chill out," the man implores again. "No one else has to die today," he says.

You might, Sarah thinks, her pistol trained on the man's throat. Sarah refused to kill the Chopra girl, but she wouldn't think twice about shooting this man, or the people with him, if it means escape.

The man steps around Aisling, places a hand on the barrel of her rifle, forces it down two inches. It's now aimed at Sarah's chest rather than her forehead. The man's other hand is empty and palm forward. His eyes are wide and pleading. His breath quick.

A peacemaker, Sarah thinks.

The man licks his lips.

Sarah says, "I'll chill out when none of you are standing in our way." Her voice is calm. Sarah notices that Aisling Kopp is flushed. She has a smear of blood on her skin—maybe hers, but probably not.

Blood. And sweat. And grime.

Aisling asks, "Where's Sky Key?"

Sarah's gun is light. One bullet. Maybe two.

"Move out of our way," Jago insists. His pistol is aimed at Aisling's head. Aisling looks different from when he last saw her. Older, harder, sadder. They must all appear so. Endgame was simpler in the early stages, before any of the keys had been recovered. Now it is vastly more complicated.

"We're not going anywhere," Aisling says, her eyes not moving from

Sarah's. "Not until we find out where Sky Key is."
Sarah says, "Well, she's not here."
Shoot her! Sarah orders herself. *Do it!*
But she doesn't.
She can't.
Aisling tried to do what Sarah couldn't. She tried to kill the little girl.
Aisling tried to stop Endgame.
Which means that Aisling and her friends can't be all bad.
Sarah glances at the other men in the room, the ones who haven't spoken. One is old but formidable-looking, an eye clouded and white. Maybe a former La Tène Player. The other is middle-aged, a contemporary of the Peacemaker. He has a bandanna tied over his head, wears round eyeglasses, and is strapped with a heavy-looking pack spilling with communications equipment. He also carries a sniper rifle, which he doesn't bother to aim at anyone. Instead, he reaches into his shirt pocket and pulls out a hand-rolled cigarette. He puts it in his mouth but doesn't light it.
Both men look spent.
Long day, Sarah thinks.
Long week.
Long fucking life.
Sarah figures she could jump backward and fire simultaneously, killing Peacemaker. Aisling would instantly return fire, but since Peacemaker has his hand parked on her rifle, this shot would miss. Jago would kill Aisling. Then they would finish the old Celt and the hippie walkie-talkie. Provided no one else is hidden nearby, she and Jago could let their guard down and fall into each other's arms and exhale. They could walk out unscathed. They could continue their mission to stop Endgame. Sarah puts their chances of killing these four people at 60 or 65 percent. Not bad odds, but not great.
"Don't do it," Peacemaker says, as if he can read Sarah's thoughts.
"Why not?" she asks.
"Just hear me out." He glances at Aisling. "Please."

"Here it comes," the man with the cigarette mumbles, breaking his silence. The old man with the white eye stays mum, his gaze dancing from person to person.

The man says, "My name is Greg Jordan. I'm a retired, twenty-plus-year vet of the CIA. I'm associates—no, *friends*—with Aisling here. I know all about Endgame. Maybe more than any of you know about it, believe it or not." He glances at Aisling. "More than I've been letting on," he says apologetically. Aisling's left eye twitches. The old man exhales loudly. "Anyway, I've seen my share of Mexican standoffs, and this qualifies big time. One wrong move and we all die in this hallway pretty easily. Like I said, no one else has to die today. A lot of people already have." Sarah doesn't know what he's talking about. She doesn't know that Aisling and Greg and the other two men—and also a woman, now dead, named Bridget McCloskey—spent the previous day marching into the mountains and killing everyone they met. Killing, killing, killing. By the end of the day many, many Harappan were dead. Well over 50.

Too many.

The man sighs. "Let's not add to the body count."

Aisling's shoulders slump, her burgeoning guilt palpable. Greg Jordan's words so far make some sense. Bullets remain in chambers. Feet remain planted on the ground. Sarah's and Jago's faces say, *Go on.*

Greg Jordan continues. "I'm going to go out on a limb and say that I think we can *all* be friends. I think we all want the same thing—namely, to put a stop to this madness. Am I right? Whadya say, guys? Friends? At least until we've had a few minutes to chat and are out of this Himalayan fortress?"

Pause.

Then Jago whispers, "Screw these guys, Sarah."

And a part of Sarah is inclined to agree, but before she does anything rash Aisling asks, "Why didn't you kill her, Sarah? Why couldn't you do it?" As she speaks she lets her rifle fall to her side. Aisling is now completely defenseless, and that counts for something.

The Celt steps past Greg Jordan. "Why?" she repeats, staring intently at Sarah, her voice barely above a whisper.

Aisling wants the game to end badly. She wants to stop it. She wants to save lives.

Just like Sarah and Jago do.

Sarah's forearm pounds, reminding her that in the fight with Maccabee and Baitsakhan she suffered a gunshot wound that needs attention. Her head spins a little. Her grip on the pistol loosens. "I know I should have . . ."

"Damn right you should have," Aisling says.

"I wanted it to stop. I *needed* it to stop."

"Then you should have pulled the trigger!"

"You're . . . you're right. But I needed it to stop," Sarah repeats.

"It's not going to stop until that girl is dead," Aisling points out.

"That's not what I mean," Sarah says, her voice dropping half an octave. "I want Endgame to stop too, Aisling, but I needed—what did you say, Greg? Madness? I needed the madness to stop. The madness in my head. If I'd pulled that trigger, then it would've . . . it would've . . ."

"Destroyed you," Jago says, also letting down his guard a little. "I also tried, Celt. I couldn't do it. It may have been selfish, but I think Sarah was right not to kill Sky Key. She was a child. A baby. Whatever happens, she was right."

Aisling sighs. "Fuck." No one speaks for a moment. "I get it. Truth is, I was praying the whole way up here that I wouldn't have to do it up close and personal. That I'd have a clear and long shot with this." She jostles her rifle and peers around Sarah into the dark room at the end of the hall. "But I guess I missed, right?"

Sarah nods. "She's gone. She was repeating 'Earth Key' over and over and I think she touched it and—"

Jago clicks his tongue. "Poof."

"What do you mean, 'poof'?" Jordan asks.

"They just disappeared," Sarah says. "It's not that crazy when you consider that about thirty minutes ago Jago and I and the other two Players were in Bolivia."

"Bullshit," Aisling says.

"What, you didn't teleport here too?" Jago asks, trying to make a joke, even while he still aims at Aisling's temple.

Aisling doesn't care anymore. It's not the first time someone's aimed a gun at her and it won't be the last. "No, we didn't teleport," Aisling says. "Just good old-fashioned planes, trains, and automobiles . . . and feet. Lots of feet."

"But Sky Key—she *is* gone, right?" Jordan asks.

Sarah nods. "Her mother's in there, though."

Aisling double-takes and tries to peer into the room. "Who—Chopra?"

"Yeah," Sarah says.

"Alive?" Aisling asks, her voice a little too desperate.

"Sí," Jago answers.

"Shit," Jordan says. "That's not good."

"Why not?" Sarah asks.

Aisling says, "We uh . . . we just killed her entire family."

"¿Que?" Jago says.

"This is a Harappan stronghold," the old man explains from the back of the room, pride lacing his words. "Except it wasn't strong enough."

"She's not going to like me too much when she wakes up," Aisling says. "I wouldn't like me, either."

"Shit," Sarah says.

"Sí. Mierda."

"We should kill her," the old man says.

But Aisling raises a hand. "No. Jordan's right. It's been too much today. Marrs"—Sarah and Jago realize that Aisling is talking to the man with the walkie-talkie—"you can keep her all Sleeping Beauty, right?"

"Sure, no problem," Marrs answers, his voice nasal and high-pitched.

Jordan says, "Hey, we all sound cool. We're cool, right?"

"Cool*er*," Sarah says. But she gets where he's going and lowers her gun. Jago does the same.

Aisling lays her rifle on the floor. "Listen, Sarah, Jago. I'm done Playing. I thought for a while that I would try to win, but there's no winning here. We're all losers—maybe the one who wins will end up being the biggest loser of all. Who wants the right to live on Earth if it's ugly and dying and full of misery? Not me."

"Not me either," Sarah says, thinking again of how she set the whole thing in motion when she took Earth Key at Stonehenge.

Thinking again of Christopher and her guilt.

Aisling drifts toward Sarah, holding out her hand. "When me and Jordan and Marrs teamed up I told them that if we couldn't win Endgame then we would try to find like-minded Players. We'd give them the option of teaming up with us so we could stop this whole fucking mess. For instance, if I ever find Hilal, I want to fight with him. He was right, way back at the Calling. We should have worked together then. Hopefully it's not too late to work together now."

Sarah steps closer but doesn't take Aisling's hand. "How do we know we can trust you?"

Aisling frowns, the corner of her mouth turning up. "You don't know. Not yet."

"Trust must be earned," Sarah says, as if she's quoting something out of a training manual.

Aisling nods. She's heard that. They all have. "That's right. But you can have some faith. I didn't shoot you when I tried to kill Sky Key. I didn't shoot you in the back in Italy when I had the chance, though I arguably should have. Pop over there certainly thinks so." The old man grunts. "And a few days ago I thought the same thing. But maybe I didn't do it so we could meet right now. Maybe I didn't because the three of us aren't done yet. What will be will be, right?"

"*Sí.* What will be will be," Jago mutters.

Aisling says, "If we try to stop this thing together, really try, then I won't hurt you. None of these guys will. You have my word."

Sarah cradles her injured left arm. She stares at Jago and tilts her head. Suddenly all she wants is to fall asleep in Jago's arms. She can tell that he wants the same thing. He snaps off a quick nod. Sarah leans into his body.

"Okay, Aisling Kopp," Jago says for them. He puts out his hand and takes the Celt's. "We'll put our faith in you, and you will do the same with us. We'll kill Endgame. Together. But one of my many questions can't wait."

Aisling smiles. It's as if a gust of air has blown into the hallway. Sarah feels it too, and relief washes over her. No more fighting on this day.

Jordan makes a low whistle and Marrs lights his cigarette. He crosses the hallway, mumbling something about checking on Shari Chopra as he passes Sarah and Jago. The only one who stays on edge is the old man.

Aisling ignores him and gives her full attention to her new allies. Maybe her new friends. "What question is that, Jago Tlaloc?"

"If Sky Key survived and we missed our chance, then how do we go about stopping Endgame now?"

Aisling looks to Jordan. "I'm guessing that's where you come in, isn't it?"

Jordan shrugs. "Yeah."

Aisling sighs. "I know you've been holding something back since the day we met, Jordan. So, you ready to get on the level here?"

Marrs laughs loudly from the next room. Jordan straightens. He says, "Friends, it's time you met Stella Vyctory."

$$ds^2 = -c^2dt^2 + dl^2 + (k^2 + l^2)(d\theta^2 + \sin^2\theta\, d\phi^2).$$

MACCABEE ADLAI, LITTLE ALICE CHOPRA

South Park Street Cemetery, Kolkata, India

Maccabee thumbs a Zippo lighter. The flame pops and flickers. They are in a small and pitch-black chamber, one that Maccabee doesn't recognize. Apparently, Maccabee has been teleported somewhere beyond his control yet again.

He lowers the flame and there, yes, is Sky Key. She trembles before him. Big eyes, beautiful dark hair. Fists balled at her chest. A terrified child.

All the girl can manage is, "Y-y-y-y-y-you."

"My name is Maccabee Adlai. I'm a Player, like your mother." His words are muffled, his voice twangy from the beating he took from Jago Tlaloc before he woke up here in the darkness. He reaches up and shifts his jaw back into place with a loud *snap!*

"Y-y-y-y-you."

His whole body hurts, especially his groin, the pit of his stomach, his left pinkie, and his jaw. The pinkie is bent completely backward. At least he has his ring. He flips the ring's lid shut so the poisoned needle is covered, then he cracks his finger straight by pushing it against his thigh. A line of pain shoots up his arm and into his neck. The finger won't bend at the knuckles, but it's not sticking out at an odd angle anymore.

When I do win this thing there'll hardly be any of me left, he thinks.

"Y-y-y-y-y-you," the girl says again.

He moves toward her. She recoils. Color drains from her face. She can't be older than three. So young. So innocent. So undeserving of what's happened to her.

The game is bullshit, Shari Chopra said. And in that moment Maccabee agreed with her. He realizes that this sentiment was probably the one that saved Shari's life—the one that prompted him to knock her out instead of gun her down. Looking at Alice now, he doesn't regret this decision.

So young.

"Your mother lives," Maccabee says. "I saved her from a bad person. He came for her and I . . . I stopped him." He almost said *killed*, but that would be inappropriate, wouldn't it? With a child? He says, "She lives, but she's not here—wherever we are."

"Y-y-y-y-you," she repeats, her eyes widening.

Maccabee shuffles forward another foot, his chin tucked to his chest, the back of his head grazing the stone ceiling. The air is damp. The only sound is their breath. Maccabee wiggles his fingers at her, the unmoving pinkie like a stick growing out of his hand. "It's okay, sweetie. I won't hurt you. I promised your mother I wouldn't and I meant it." He stumbles over something. Looks down. A clump of cloth.

"Y-y-y-y-you. From my dream. You-you-you *hurt* people. . . ."

"I won't hurt you," he repeats. He lowers the lighter and pushes the thing on the ground with his foot. It's heavy. He looks. A limb. A leg. A hole burned in the cargo pocket on the thigh. He sweeps the Zippo through the air, illuminating the blood-spattered face of Baitsakhan, his eyes vacant and staring, slack-jawed, the throat torn open by the bionic hand that still clutches the cervical section of his own spine.

Baitsakhan.

Take.

Kill.

. . .

Lose.

His Endgame is over.

Good riddance.

Maccabee spits on the floor as the girl gasps and points. "No! Not you! *Him! He* is the one! *He* took Mama's finger! *He* hurt people! *He* is the one! *He* is the one!"

Maccabee kicks the Donghu's body so that it flips facedown. He steps between Sky Key and Baitsakhan. She shouldn't see that. No child should see that.

"It's okay. You're okay. He can't hurt you."

"Mama."

"He can't hurt her either. Not anymore."

Maccabee is suddenly afraid that Shari also made the trip to wherever they are. And the Olmec too, and maybe the Cahokian. He spins, searching the rest of the chamber, but no one is there. It is just him and Sky Key and—

"Earth Key!" he says.

WHERE IS IT?

The girl shudders. She jumps up and then her body stiffens as if she's possessed. Her right hand falls to her side, her left hand juts out, palm up. Maccabee leans closer. She doesn't move. It's like her fear has been spirited away and replaced with emptiness. *Shock,* Maccabee thinks. *Or maybe a force more powerful.*

He peers into her hand. A little ball. Earth Key.

He swipes it from her. Her eyebrow twitches but otherwise she's expressionless.

"I'll keep that." He slips it into a zippered pocket on his vest and pats it.

"Earth Key," she says.

"That's right," he says. He inspects the small room. *Where the hell are we?* The floor is earth, everything else is featureless stone. There are no windows, no doors. No way in or out. As he looks around he runs a hand over his torso, checking to see what he's got to work with.

No guns, but he has his smartphone, a pack of gum, and his ancient Nabataean blade.

A wave of pain crashes over him as the adrenaline fades from his system. He realizes that everything that's happened recently—finding Sarah and Jago in Bolivia, tracking them through the Tiwanaku ruins, getting teleported somewhere through that ancient portal, fighting, killing, fighting some more, and then getting knocked clean out by the live-wire Olmec, who is 20 or 30 kilos *lighter* than him, and then getting teleported yet again—all of that probably happened in only the last couple hours.

He needs rest. Soon.

"Earth Key says that . . ." the girl says in a monotone.

His pant leg vibrates.

". . . says that one is coming."

It vibrates violently. He touches his leg—*the tracker orb!*

Another Player!

He looks left and right and up and down and can't figure out where to go. Is another Player going to appear in this small room? Is he going to have to fight with a broken-down body in this box? This, this—sarcophagus?

He whips around, the lighter's flame blows out. He thumbs the flint. *Flick, flick, flick*—the sparks don't take. But in the total darkness something catches his eye. Right before his face. A thin white line. He follows it, tracing a faint square on the ceiling. He stuffs the lighter in a pocket and places both hands on the stone overhead and pushes. It's heavy and he strains and grunts as his panting mingles with the scraping sound of rock on rock. An opening. Light. Hot air pours into the small room as he gets his fingers around the edge of the six-centimeter-wide slab, heaving it away. He gets on his tiptoes and looks over the edge.

They are in a hole in the ground. The hole is covered by a pillared gothic cupola like one that might cover a grave or a monument. A point of orange light from a streetlamp somewhere, the muted glow of dusk in the sky beyond the cupola, the black boughs of leafy trees hanging over everything like a curtain. A dove coos and then flaps away. The muted jostle of a city—traffic, AC hum, voices—in the near distance.

Maccabee grabs Sky Key and pushes her out of the hole. He jumps out. They're in the middle of a vast cemetery from a bygone era, every grave marker grand and significant and carved from stone—domed Victorian tombs that must hold entire families, and seven-meter-tall obelisks and basalt pedestals that weigh thousands of kilos. Many are covered in moss and lichen and all are splotchily weatherworn. Plants grow in every available nook and patch—grasses, palms, hardwoods, weeds, sprawling banyan trees with their air roots diving down to the ground here and there. It's one of the most impressive cemeteries Maccabee has ever seen.

Sky Key steps onto the path, her arms glued to her sides, her legs moving like a robot's. She's completely zoned out but manages to say, "One is coming. He is close."

Maccabee gets out the orb with his right hand and pulls his knife with his left. His unbending pinkie sticks out. As when Alice Ulapala closed in on his hideout in Berlin, the orb simply glows its warning, not giving any intelligence as to who is coming or from which direction.

Maccabee knows that for the first time in his life he is going to have to run. He's too hurt and too unarmed and too disoriented and too vulnerable with Sky Key to stand his ground.

He stuffs the orb in a pocket and snags the girl, tucking her under his arm like a parcel.

He takes off along a dirt path, the cemetery dark and claustrophobic, until the trees and massive graves give way to an open area. A three-meter-high stone wall rises in front of them, plain concrete buildings beyond it on the street side.

Where the hell am I? This doesn't look like Peru or Bolivia at all. Or even South America!

He goes to the solid wall, peers left then right. It's rough enough to scale, but not while carrying Sky Key. He turns left and trots along, keeping the wall on his right. The orb in his pocket has calmed a little, so maybe whoever's coming got thrown off the trail.

Sky Key weighs about 15 kilos. He holds her sideways, her head forward and her legs flopping behind him. It's like he's carrying a life-sized toddler doll.

Near the interior corner of the wall Maccabee comes across a cache of gravediggers' tools: a shovel stuck in a pile of sand, a pickax, a coil of sturdy rope. He carefully puts down Sky Key and cuts a four-meter length of rope. He lashes it around his waist and shoulders and then works Sky Key onto his back and loops the rope under her butt and twice over her back. He pulls her tight, tying a hitch in the X of rope that crosses his chest. She's secure in this makeshift child carrier, and he has the use of both hands. He feels her quick breath on his neck. She remains zoned out, likely from the trauma of being taken from her mama, and from coming into contact with Earth Key.

He wants to climb the wall and get out onto the street of whatever city he's in, but the wall is smoother here and there's nothing for him to grab. He's about to double back to where he can climb but then freezes. The rope! The pickax!

He ties the rope to the wooden handle and hurls the pickax over the wall, creating a kind of grappling hook. He gives it a hard tug and it holds. He places his feet on the wall and starts up.

But then, at the same instant, the orb in his pocket jostles like a tiny earthquake, and Sky Key shakes off her zombie-like state and grabs a handful of his hair and yanks it. He loses his footing and swings a half meter to the side. The air cracks around him. A chunk of wall explodes next to his face, followed by a pistol report.

"He's here," Sky Key says.

Maccabee dives behind a stone grave marker as three more rounds tear by them, each barely missing. Maccabee kicks the shovel into the air and snatches it. He spins to his right, but Sky Key yanks his hair again and says, "Other way."

That would take them across the line of fire, but Maccabee trusts her. He quickly guesses that the male Player must be the Shang, An Liu. Marcus and Baits are dead, Jago's with Sarah, and Hilal is probably recovering from his wounds back in Ethiopia.

And if it is Liu, then he's probably got some bombs.

That means that Maccabee has to *MOVE!*

He takes a shovelful of sand and throws it into the air, creating a smokescreen, and sprints behind it. He hears a muted clunk, and he spins around a thick tree trunk and throws his hands over Sky Key's head and *boom!* An explosion from where they just were, debris showering all around, leaves whipping along on the shock wave, bits of wood and rock pinging here and there. It was a small explosion but big enough to have hurt them if he hadn't moved.

"Turn right here," the girl says calmly.

He's blind in this place and his body aches from everything that's happened but she *did* save them, so he listens.

"Left here. Straight. Left. Left. Straight. Right. Left, left, left."

He follows every instruction, even if it feels like they're going in circles. They bob and weave, pivot and fly. They're narrowly missed by several more shots and one more small explosion. She's transforming the dense cemetery into a maze, and it's working. Somehow she knows where An is. Maccabee realizes that this girl, at least in this moment, is vastly superior to the mysterious orb that he's been using to track the Players.

Finally they round a black stone block and find an arched break in the wall big enough for a car. Two small buildings flanking it are painted pink. A wrought-iron fence is on the far side. Past that a wide street, cars moving along, a late-model motorcycle parked on the curb.

The exit. It's 10 meters away, a straight shot. But those 10 meters are completely exposed.

"It's too far," Maccabee says. The orb in his pocket moves back and forth so fast he's afraid it's going to jump out. "He'll kill us."

Sky Key scratches the side of his neck. "Here," she says.

"I see the exit, but it's too far!"

They don't have more than a few seconds. She scratches harder, begins to claw at his flesh. "Here!" she whispers into his ear.

Then Maccabee understands. Something is in his neck: *a tracker*. One that An and who knows how many other Players have been using to follow him!

He whips up his knife and expertly carves a lump of skin from his neck. He's careful not to nick anything important or shred a muscle or

tendon. The pain isn't too bad, but there's a lot of blood.
"That's it," the girl says.
Maccabee pulls the knife away and stares into the lump of flesh and, yes, there it is. A small black blob.
He balls up the flesh and chucks it away. The bloody projectile sails over a gravestone and disappears. He gets ready to run, but the girl digs a nail into this latest wound and whispers, "Wait."
He stifles a cry and does what he's told. One second. Two. Three.
"Now. Straight."
He drops the shovel and runs as fast as he can for the exit. No shots come. They were waiting for An to take the bait of the discarded tracker, and apparently he did.
The exit gets closer and closer and they're going to make it. A person walks by outside, a woman wearing an orange sari. A bus drives past and Maccabee sees a cigarette ad on the side. The writing is Hindi.
India. We're in India.
They're going to make it. The orb in his pocket is going crazy now. He reaches down to secure it but then it pops out and he skids to a stop.
"Leave it!" the girl says.
Maccabee backtracks, the orb glowing bright and yellow and bouncing around on the ground like a living thing.
"No!" she says.
Something catches Maccabee's eye. There, on the path, is An Liu, a dark pistol in his fist. He hasn't seen them yet, he's swinging back and forth and Maccabee almost has the orb but then—too late. An Liu locks onto Maccabee and Maccabee dives sideways and the orb glows so bright that its light eats up the wall and the path and An too. Shots come but all miss since An is blinded by the light and can't see Maccabee anymore.
"Leave it! I am using it! Go!" the girl implores.
Once again he does what he's told. He vaults toward the street. He sees the motorcycle and breaks open its ignition switch and hot-wires it in

the blink of an eye. He jumps on. It zings to life and they take off, fast. The light from the orb chokes out everything for 20 meters now and people on the street are yelling, pointing, running.

"I am using it," the girl repeats in a soft voice, her head slumping onto Maccabee's shoulder. "I am using it." Her body feels limp. She is exhausted too.

A block later the light gives way to a high-pitched whine and then it's snuffed out and then—*FFFUHWHAM!*—the entire street puffs up in a ball of smoke. Maccabee dips the bike around a corner, its rear wheel skidding and his foot planting on the ground as a pivot. Bits of buildings and cars and trees whip through the air at their backs.

The girl passes out, the Indian city is a blur, and for the moment An Liu is no longer hunting them.

For the first time in his life Maccabee ran from a fight. And it worked. With the help of this small, remarkable, maybe possessed Sky Key, it worked.

I won't let anyone hurt you, he thinks.

And he means it.

AN LIU

South Park Street Cemetery, Kolkata, India

An kneels. He shakes his head, trying to get it clear.

Almost got them.

SHIVER.

Almost.

BLINK.

That was a big blast.

An had thrown a grenade into the light at the last second, but that explosion was from something else. The Nabataean must have planted that glowing thing and set it off in order to create some space and some time. It was successful. The Nabataean is gone now. With the first two keys.

Gone.

BLINK.

An peeks under his shirt at the Chiyoko necklace. Like everything around him it's covered in a fine dust. He pulls the necklace over his head and shakes it gently, wipes it with his fingertips, blows on it. When it's reasonably clean he slips it back on.

He brushes himself off, finds his SIG. He loads a new magazine. Sirens in the distance.

Shivershiver.

The world knows about Endgame, and Abaddon is coming, but the law isn't all the way gone. Not yet.

He trots to the exit. The Nabataean is gone, and An's bike is gone too.

An spits, the stream thick with black ash.

The Nabataean is gone.

AISLING KOPP, GREG JORDAN, GRIFFIN MARRS, POP KOPP, SARAH ALOPAY, JAGO TLALOC, SHARI CHOPRA

Heading south along the Teesta River near Mangan, Sikkim, India

Aisling looks over her shoulder into the back of the jeep. Shari Chopra slumps in her seat, an IV bag pinned above the window, a tube running into a spike in the back of her hand. Dripping into that line on a regulator is a small dose of BZD, keeping her good and asleep for as long as necessary. All the way to Thailand, where Jordan is taking them and where Stella Vyctory awaits.

The jeep bumps along the road, mountains looming all around. Aisling thinks about Shari. After the standoff with Sarah and Jago, Aisling followed Marrs into the deepest chamber of the Harappan fortress and saw the raven-haired mother of Sky Key, alive and more-or-less well. This is a wrinkle that has Aisling feeling very conflicted. On one hand, Aisling suspects that Shari is one of the decent Players, one who doesn't deserve a meaningless death at the hand of a psychopathic Player. She's glad that Baitsakhan and Maccabee didn't kill her. But on the other hand, as far as Shari's concerned, Aisling probably *is* that psychopathic Player. If it weren't for Aisling, Shari's family would be alive. Sure, her daughter would probably still have been taken by the Nabataean, but all the Harappan who'd taken refuge in the mountains would be breathing if it weren't for Aisling and her ragtag death squad.

Aisling tries to reason out of this by blaming Endgame for what happened—Aisling didn't make Shari's daughter one of the fucking keys, Endgame did. Aisling was only doing what she thought she had to do to stop Endgame, and Shari, for her part, was only doing what any mother would do.

All of which makes Aisling want to stop Endgame—and punish the Makers, especially kepler 22b—all the more.

Aisling knows in her bones that when Shari wakes up she won't be in a very forgiving mood. All Shari will want is revenge, and Aisling knows that revenge is a soul-gnashing affliction that operates completely outside the realm of logic. Sure, Aisling could wave her hands at Chopra and plead for reason, insisting that Endgame killed all of Chopra's people, but Aisling also knows that's bullshit. *She* killed those people, along with Jordan and Pop and the rest of her team. And for better or worse, Chopra is now slumped behind Aisling in the jeep.

Jordan drives, Aisling wedged between him and Marrs in the front seat. Whenever Jordan shifts gears he reaches between Aisling's legs. He half apologizes each time until Aisling tells him to shut up. He does. Sarah's in the middle of the backseat, between Shari and Jago, her body folded awkwardly into Jago's lap, her injured arm, which Aisling patched up, bent into a sling. Jago is awake and mostly silent. His hand rests on top of Sarah's head, his fingers entwined in her hair. He's said very little, but when he does speak he's been even-tempered and friendly.

Pop is a different story.

He's in the wayback, jigsawed into the gear they couldn't leave behind—mainly guns and a mobile satellite uplink that Marrs uses for internet access. Pop has not said a single word since they forged this latest alliance. He hasn't asked about Sky Key or spoken to Sarah or Jago at all. He hasn't said if he's on board with the plan to meet Stella, and he hasn't said he's against it.

To Aisling, his silence is the same as a full-throated scream. She knows that Pop hates the course they're charting. It goes against every one of his beliefs. It is not what Endgame is meant to be.

Aisling is not sure how she's going to handle Pop, but she knows that it will fall on her to handle him when the time comes.

The others don't seem as concerned. Especially Jordan and Marrs. Ever since getting into the jeep, Marrs has been tearing around the internet, going from news sites to encrypted government forums to deep-web hovels full of rumor and intrigue, providing an account of recent world events and bantering with Jordan on pretty much every point.

"The space agencies have been scrambling since the kepler's announcement. At the moment, NASA's got Abaddon falling in the North Atlantic," Marrs says in his nasal monotone. "South of Halifax. Gonna wipe out a lot of land. A *lot*."

"Fucking hell," Jordan says. "What's DC doing?"

"Moving. Lock, stock, and barrel. Looks like to Colorado."

"NORAD?"

"Naturally. Gold's going through the roof, New York's under martial law but seems pretty tame. Boston is coming apart at the seams, though. One of the New England Patriots did a murder-suicide with his wife and kids—dog too."

"Any flags on other Players?" Jordan asks.

"There's some indication that the Shang is in Kolkata, but it's pretty tenuous, and my Bengali is shit. No sign of the Nabataean yet. Oh—and looks like someone's destroying monuments."

"Besides Stonehenge?" Jordan asks incredulously.

"Yeah. This morning while we were trekking from the fortress, a group of nongovernmental operators that remains anonymous, at least to our guys, blew up the ziggurat at Chogha Zanbil. That was the Sumerian one."

"Stella won't like that."

"No, she won't," Marrs says.

Jordan whips the jeep around a slow-moving truck, guiding them into oncoming traffic, which is de rigueur for India. A motor scooter buzzes out of the way into the shoulder and passes them.

"What the hell are you guys talking about?" Jago demands.

Aisling nods. "Yeah, what *are* you talking about?"

"Your line has a monument that is more sacred than any other—right, Aisling?" Jordan asks.

"Jordan, you know it was Stonehenge." *Asshole,* Aisling thinks.

Jordan says, "And you, Tlaloc?"

"We do. It's on the Yucatán Peninsula in Mexico."

"La Venta," Marrs says.

Jago looks a little surprised, and thinks that maybe these guys really do know more than he thought they could about Endgame. "*Sí.* That's what we call it."

Jordan asks, "And your girlfriend?"

"I wouldn't know," Jago says. He's lying, though. He knows the exact location of the prime Cahokian monument. It's called Monks Mound, and it's in southern Illinois, not far from St. Louis, Missouri. He knows this because it's where the Cahokian Rebellion of 1613 occurred. The rebellion that the Olmec oracle, Aucapoma Huayna, told him all about. The rebellion that branded the Cahokians as unworthy of winning Endgame, which was precisely why Aucapoma had implored Jago to end his alliance with Sarah Alopay. No, more than that—the Cahokians were so dangerous that Aucapoma had ordered Jago to *kill* Sarah so he could prove to the Makers that he'd not been poisoned by the Cahokian Player.

Too late for that.

As much as he might want, Jago isn't about to start talking about all of this. It would be too revealing, too . . . *complicating.* So he plays dumb, and they believe him.

"Well, her line has one," Marrs says. "Called Monks Mound. Big tourist attraction now, kinda like Stonehenge but not as well-known."

"Never heard of it," Jago says.

"I have," Aisling says. "Used to be the center of some huge Native American city."

"Once upon a time it was the largest city in all of the Americas, long before any Europeans outside of Vikings even knew about the New World," Jordan says.

“All right,” Jago says, “but why are these places so important to finishing Endgame?”

“What he said,” Aisling adds, sticking a thumb in Jago's direction.

“I’m going to let Stella fill you in on the details,” Jordan says as he works the jeep through a series of accordion-like turns, “but we're certain that Sun Key is hidden in one of them.”

Jago leans forward, nearly pushing Sarah's head off his leg. “No shit?”

“No shit,” Marrs says. “And if they all get toasted before the Player with the first two keys finds it, well . . .”

“No one will be able to win,” Aisling says.

“Bingo,” Jordan says.

“Who *is* this Stella woman?” Aisling asks.

“You’ll find out soon enough,” Jordan says.

Jago leans back in his seat, resettling Sarah's head across his thigh. “Whoever she is, you've gotten my attention, Mr. Jordan. I look forward to meeting her.”

“I can promise that the feeling is mutual. She has been waiting to meet you—*all* of you—for a very, very long time.”

SARAH ALOPAY, JAGO TLALOC

Heading south along the Teesta River near Mangan, Sikkim, India

Sarah is not asleep. She hasn't slept at all. And while Jago has been friendly with the others, and truly does want to meet this Stella Vyctory, he's not convinced. Not by a long shot.

Sarah slumps across Jago's lap, her hand resting under her hair and on Jago's thigh. She taps out messages to him in Morse code, and he answers in the same code by squeezing her scalp so softly that the movement can only be felt by her and not seen by anyone else.

Their conversation has been long and a little testy, and it revolves around one question, which in this moment Sarah asks for the seventh time: *Should we really trust these people?*

And Jago answers, *We have to for now. If what Jordan says is true, then maybe we now know of another way to stop this thing. Even if Abaddon hits, and the world is changed, we might have a way to prevent a Player from winning. And if Jordan isn't right, it seems that these people really do want the same thing. They can help us, Sarah. We can help them.*

Help us so that we can stay together.

Yes. So that we can stay together.

We stick with them, then.

Yes.

All right, she taps. *I only wish . . .*

What?

I wish we were alone, Feo. I wish it were just you and me.

This is the first time she's said it all day.

And Jago squeezes back, *I do too, Sarah. I do too.*

HILAL IBN ISA AL-SALT

Ayutthaya, Thailand

Hilal is also headed to Stella Vyctory, except he is much, much closer. He hustles out of the Phra Nakhon Provincial Railway Station, turning this way and that, slicing through a mass of people. He went directly from the Bangkok airport, where he last spoke to Stella, to the central Bangkok train station. He got on the first train to Ayutthaya and now he makes his way on foot to Stella, who is a short four kilometers away. He goes south from the station through a platoon of food carts, smelling fried things and salty things and sweet things. Squid, mushrooms, pork, onions, garlic, sugar, basil, citrus, peanuts. His large rucksack claps his shoulders as he jogs. It contains his twin machetes, a change of clothing, a first aid kit for his wounds, the device from the ark (which has ceased working since the kepler's announcement), and the incomprehensible book he took from Wayland Vyctory's hotel suite in Las Vegas.

A few blocks from the station a large group of worshippers blocks the street and forces him to detour into the Wat Pichai Songkram temple complex. Monks are everywhere. Bald and saffron-robed and busy. Devotees wearing conical shade hats and carrying parasols surround the holy men, pleading for mercy and praying to Lord Buddha. Hilal does the same in his mind as he rushes past the gilt icon covered in marigolds and lotus blossoms and surrounded by a pyre of incense. He searches for a way out of the complex so he can pick up the pace again and get to Stella as soon as possible.

After a minute he finds himself on the banks of the Pa Sak River. He turns south and resumes running. Longtail boats ply the cloudy water and schools of huge catfish boil to the surface to eat bread being thrown by children. It is nice to see young people doing everyday things, to witness innocence.

It is also nice to feel the sun.

He is afraid that, thanks to the impact winter that is likely to shroud the skies after Abaddon, sunlight will be something of a luxury soon. He is very afraid of this.

He tilts his disfigured face to our star as his feet carry him toward Stella.

The sun. Earth's life force. The photons that bounce off his skin and everything else around him left the solar surface eight minutes and 20 seconds ago. Eight minutes and 20 seconds! They hurtled through the void of space and entered the atmosphere and made a beeline for this spot, right here, on Earth, in the continent called Asia, in the country called Thailand, in the city called Ayutthaya, onto the man and Endgame Player named Hilal ibn Isa al-Salt. A great cosmic accident that happens over and over and over again to everything the sun's light touches. Over and over and over again.

Stella.

He quickens his pace.

Stella. Her name means "star," like the sun.

May she give us light, Hilal thinks.

He turns east onto the wide Rojana Road. He jogs now, passes car dealerships and beauty salons and tourist offices and convenience stores and Thai motorcycle cops in brown uniforms who give him suspicious looks but who don't do anything. He passes a two-story stupa right in the middle of the six-lane road. He passes a group of teenage boys loitering on souped-up scooters, smoking filterless cigarettes, whistling at girls, laughing.

Hilal slows to a brisk walk when he sees these young men. Four of them wear makeshift masks of a face that everyone has seen and everyone has memorized and everyone is confused by and many are terrified by.

The pale face of kepler 22b.

There were Meteor Kids throwing raves and partying after the twelve meteors that announced Endgame, and now there are kepler Kids.

The teens are loud as Hilal approaches, but when they notice him the silence hits. They see his scarred face and his discolored eyes and his lack of hair and his missing ear. Two of the kids pull the masks from the tops of their heads and over their faces, as if to hide.

Hilal doesn't break stride. *"Krap,"* he says, dipping his chin and raising his hand.

None of them say anything in return.

He resumes running. Another kilometer and he reaches the Classic Kameo Hotel, a collection of glass and cement blocks, all white and modern and clean. Hilal imagines it caters to upscale tourists and Asian businessmen.

This is where he will find Stella.

He goes inside. The air conditioning slaps him in the face. He moves through it, crossing his arms for warmth. Nice lobby, big chairs, front desk, clerk, elevator, hallway, room.

Its number is 702. He is about to knock when he is overcome with nerves. He is going to see her again. Stella. The woman who beat him in a fight, who helped him, who claimed Wayland Vyctory as her father. Hilal trusted her in Las Vegas, and he trusts her still, but now that he is on the edge of whatever comes next in Endgame he pauses.

Breathes.

Knocks.

He hears the soft pad of footsteps on the far side of the door. The world turns some more.

The door opens. The woman smiles.

"Hilal," Stella says. "Come in. It is so good to see you again."

AN LIU

Shang Safe House, Unnamed Street off Ahiripukur Second Lane, Ballygunge, Kolkata, India

An walks from the cemetery back to his safe house. He walks briskly, angry and red-eyed and oblivious to the world around him.

He had them. The Nabataean and Sky Key and Earth Key too. Right in his sights. He had them and his shots missed and they *outplayed* him! And they got away.

They are gone.

"Gone, Chiyoko, gone! How could I let it happen?" he curses *BLINKshiverBLINK* he curses himself as he marches through the choked streets, and when he finally reaches the secluded side entrance of his hideout his emotions are a tempest.

He opens the door and bolts it shut from the inside and punches a code into the security system. He stalks toward the bathroom, stripping off his clothes as he moves, letting his garments fall to the floor in heaps. He rants the whole way. "I had"—*BLINKBLINK*—"I had them! I could have killed"—*shiverBLINK*—"killed"—*shivershivershiver*—"killed"—*BLINK*—"them." *SHIVERshiver.* "Could have"—*SHIVERshiver*—"Could have"—*SHIVERshiver*—"Could have stuffed a grenade in his mouth and stepped back and laughed and watched the whole thing burn!" *BLINK.* "No"—*BLINK*—"No"—*BLINK*—"No"—*BLINK*—"No winner could be"—*shiverSHIVERshiver*—"no winner could be"—*BLINKBLINKBLINKBLINKshiverBLINKBLINK*—"No winner could *be*!"

He's in the bathroom and naked except for Chiyoko's necklace. He puts his hands to it but they shake too much. She can't calm him right now, she can't, and he lets go of the necklace because he's shaking so much that he's afraid he'll break it, that he'll *hurt* her, and he raises his arm and bites it and clamps down, gnashes, grinds. It hurts and stings and a little blood comes and he stops shaking. He turns on the hot water tap, and his hands calm. He removes Chiyoko and sets her gingerly on the edge of the sink and steps through the curtain and into the stall. It is scalding and his skin turns red and he winces and holds his breath from the shock of the temperature.

He calms some more. His arm throbs. He ducks his stubbly head under the water stream. It burns.

"The world would have gotten what it deserves," An says.

And in that moment there is a small sound deep in his mind and he knows it is her and she's trying to speak to him but he can't hear. He strains and concentrates but he can't hear her.

"What it deserves. All because of me."

He feels better. He washes, dries, cleans the necklace, gets dressed, eats, and then moves to a control room and settles down. He checks the tracking program that marks the Olmec's position, and then turns on several monitors at once and watches the news.

The news. The news. The news. It is glorious and beautiful and amazing.

BBC, CNN International, Al Jazeera, Fox News, TASS, France 24, CCTV. Fear is rampant. Martial law in every Western country. Police forces thinning out as their members flee to be with family. Full military battalions being repositioned to minimum safe distances. Nuclear energy facilities being put on lockdown. Chemical plants following emergency shutdown protocols. Municipal airspaces the world over thick with helicopters and drones. Astronauts and cosmonauts on the International Space Station initiating emergency sequences and preparing for a prolonged isolation from Mission Control. The destruction of the ancient monuments of Stonehenge and Chogha Zanbil—the former of principal importance to the La Tène Celts, the latter equally as essential to the Sumerian line. No one knows who is obliterating them, or if they do know, no one is telling. Are other such monuments slated for destruction as well? Will those belonging to the Olmec, the Cahokian, the Nabataean, the Harappan, the Shang, and all the others be destroyed in time? Is the kepler destroying them? A consortium of the world's militaries? Some group as yet unknown? An is unsure. He watches a dozen segments about the alien called kepler 22b. Interviews with people who revere him or hate him or want to befriend him or kill him. People who want to subjugate themselves to him. People who want to enslave him. But mostly people who want to run away from him, even if there is nowhere *to* run.

Don't tell the leaders of the world that, though. Don't tell the rich. An watches stories about presidents and prime ministers and scientists and educators and MPs and the wealthy, all fleeing, all bunkering, all burying themselves. Trying to disappear. Everyone else looting or taping up windows or trying to get inland and for the most part failing. Shoot-outs on clogged highways up and down the American East Coast. Throngs of people at churches and mosques and temples and synagogues praying to their gods. The Vatican, the Dome of the Rock, the Western Wall—all three so crowded that worshippers at each are being trampled and crushed.

An falls asleep to this beautiful chaotic dance at around three in the morning.

He wakes 2.4 hours later. The television screens are still full of fear and confusion and questions. When will Abaddon hit? How big is it and what's it made of and how many will die?

And some answers.

Abaddon is a dense nickel-and-iron meteor that will strike soon on the edge of the Nova Scotia shelf, 300 kilometers south of Halifax. The asteroid is spherical with a diameter of just under three kilometers. It will punch a hole in the atmosphere and the sky will light up, snuffing out the sun's light. The initial blast will vaporize everything around it and underneath it and over it for hundreds of miles. The impact will trigger a massive earthquake to ripple across the globe, which will even be felt on the other side of the world. After the quake comes the airborne shock wave, destroying everything for hundreds and hundreds of miles. And last but certainly not least will be the tsunamis, affecting every North Atlantic city from San Juan to Washington, DC, to Lisbon to Dakar.

In the hours and days that follow, the secondary effects of Abaddon will wreak havoc over the entire planet. These are less certain. They could include eruptions of long-dormant volcanoes as they are shaken from their slumbers. The Big Island of Hawaii could crack and calve a huge section into the Pacific, causing massive tsunamis up and down the Pacific Rim. Acid rain could fall everywhere, but especially within a few thousand miles of the crater, poisoning the sea and all drinking water in the vicinity. Electrical storms and hurricanes could whip up and ravage the land and sea around the crater.

An flips through the channels. There will be tornadoes, floods, landslides, ash, fear, depravation, suffering, death. There will be firestorms. Impact winters. No more internet in a lot of places. No more air travel for a long time. And on and on and on and, yes, soon, very soon, a lot of things are going to die.

At around six in the morning the first report of a visual comes on air. Spotted in the sky over the South Pacific. A dark speck skirting across the sun's disc. A video plays on CNN International in a GIF loop: fishermen in small wooden boats hoisting Mylar-covered binoculars to the sky. They're surrounded by blue water and white sand and green trees and the sky as clear as ever, and the men point and scream and yell.

That's when everyone knows that it's really true.

That's when An knows it's not a dream.

It's better than a dream.

He will miss the internet, though. Sorely.

An turns from the news and hops up and moves. He needs to get back on the road, to get out of this city before it goes completely insane. The asteroid will hit on the far side of the globe, but he wants to be in the countryside for Abaddon, not in Kolkata or anywhere like it.

He has a quick breakfast of fish cakes and warm Coke. In the garage he loads his bulletproof Land Rover Defender with his go box and the cans of extra gasoline and his guns and bombs and Nobuyuki Takeda's katana and the other box too, the precious box that contains the vest should he ever need it. The 20-kilo suicide vest that is his fail-safe.

By 9:13 he is ready to go.

But now that he's sitting in his Defender and looking at the monitors that show what's happening outside his safe house, he's a little worried.

An didn't expect this.

Not at all.

Hundreds of people choke the alleyway outside. All men. All crammed into the narrow street that is his Defender's sole egress. They sit on the ground, lean against walls, mill around. Someone must have followed him from the cemetery and called their friends, and then they called friends, and *they* called friends. The men have sticks and pipes and machetes and a few have semiautomatic rifles. Some have dogs on ropes. Many are shirtless and rail thin and wear the ubiquitous loose cotton pants seen all over India. Some carry placards. Most of these are in Bengali or Hindi, which An can't read, but some are in English. They say, WE SEE YOU! and BROTHERHOOD OF MAN! and EARTH IS OURS! and NO TO ENDGAME! NO TO THE PLAYERS! NO TO KEPLER 22B! More than a few have blood smeared over their faces and arms. Blood from chickens or goats or dogs, sacrificed in ceremonies at local temples.

An understands. These men know who he is—the Shang, An Liu, Player of Endgame—and they want his pain. His life. His blood.

He understands perfectly.

BLINKshiverBLINK.

An pounds something into a laptop mounted in the center of the car. He hits enter. Like all Shang safe houses, this one is wired to blow, and blow dirty, irradiating this section of Kolkata. But the bomb will only detonate when his system detects that he and his vehicle have

reached a safe distance.
He flicks the laptop closed.
"Are you ready, Chiyoko?"
And then he hears a small sound deep in his mind.
"Chi"—*BLINK*—"Chi"—*SHIVER*—"Chiyoko?"
The sound grows a little louder, like a hum in the distance.
"Are you ready?"
SHIVERSHIVERSHIVER.
And then—*I am*, she says in the voice she never had.
The quality of her voice doesn't surprise him. Calm but firm. It is her. It is perfectly, succinctly, fully her.
He's been expecting her.
He says, "You are always ready and I love you for it."
An taps a button and the garage doors crack open.
"I love you." An repeats. And she says it too, at the exact same moment, his voice mingling and weaving with hers.
He smiles.
Chiyoko and An. The Mu and the Shang.
They are the same.
The mob outside stirs and crackles.
Those who were sitting stand.
He hits the button again and the doors swing wide. A Kalashnikov fires. Shots explode across the Defender's bulletproof windshield.
BLINK. SHIVER.
He flips the key in the ignition. The engine comes to life. He jams the gas and the engine roars. The men howl and gesticulate, wave their arms and sticks and their ridiculous placards, as if An cares for any of what they have to say.
This is not a protest, it is a war.
And he will fight it with his beloved.

SARAH ALOPAY, JAGO TLALOC

Gulfstream G650, Bogdogra Airport, Siliguri, West Bengal, India

Sarah and Jago recline in very comfortable seats in Jordan's very comfortable private jet trying to figure out what to do. It took them a long time to get down from the Himalayas, and now they're stuck waiting for permission to take off.

The wait is agonizing.

Aisling and Jordan are in the cockpit going through preflight stuff. Marrs is outside dealing with airport personnel. Pop sits in a seat alone near the bulkhead, staring out the window, his rocky knuckles white with tension. Shari is unconscious in the rear of the plane, already seat-belted in place, an IV bag hanging from the overhead compartment. Her chest rises and falls evenly.

Sarah is envious of Shari. Being knocked out would quell the hate and guilt and doubt and fear roiling inside her. Being knocked out would quiet her mind, her soul.

She leans into Jago's side and whispers, "I wish we were fighting, Feo. Right now. I wish we were moving—*Playing*."

"I know," he says. "Me too."

Action or oblivion, she thinks. *Those are the only options right now.*

Aisling emerges from the cockpit, interrupting Sarah's train of thought.

"How long till we're outta here?" Jago asks.

Aisling drops into the nearest seat. She reaches for her Falcata and lays it over her thighs. She runs her fingertips over the sword.

"At least an hour," she says. "Maybe less if Marrs can bribe the right air traffic controller. But for the moment we're holding." She pulls a stone from a pocket and runs it over her blade's edge. It's razor sharp and doesn't need the attention, but she needs something to do.

Also restless, Sarah thinks.

Sarah straightens and asks, "All right if Jago and I take over the lav for a little while?"

Jago snickers.

"Really?" Aisling's eyebrows spring upward. "Now?"

Jago flashes his glittery smile and strokes Sarah's knee. "*Sí.* No time like the present, *¿sabes?*"

Sarah jabs him with her elbow. "Don't listen to him. Jago picked up a dye kit back in Peru. I'm gonna be raven-haired from now on. Since Liu's video came out and we can all be made, I don't want to take any chances."

He runs his fingers through his platinum hair. "I'm sure you couldn't tell, Aisling, but I'm not a natural blond."

Aisling shakes her head and tilts the blade in her lap, eyeing a miniscule nick. "Go for it. It's all yours."

Sarah and Jago move to the rear of the plane. The lavatory is very nice. There's space between the toilet and the sink, and the sink is normal-sized, not a tiny bowl wedged into the corner. The towels are real, the toilet paper plush and soft.

Jago closes the door behind them. He helps Sarah out of her shirt, being careful with her wounded arm. She leans over the basin, face down, and Jago washes her hair using a plastic cup and the liquid soap on the counter.

"Rosemary," Sarah says. "And lemon. Smells nice."

"Mmm," Jago says. He massages her scalp, rinsing out the soap. He runs his fingers along her nape and lets them trail down her back and over the band of her sports bra.

"Give me a towel," she says.

He does.

She wraps it around her head and stands. They're face-to-face. Her bra brushes his shirt and a shot of electricity races up her back. She smiles. "Can you dry my hair?" she asks.

"Sí."

But instead he immediately leans forward and they kiss. She holds his head tightly between her strong hands and pulls him closer.

And they kiss.

And kiss.

They stop.

She sits on the closed toilet seat. He dries her hair. She brushes it, working through the tangles, while he preps the dye. When she's done brushing, Jago separates her hair into sections and fastens a towel over her bare shoulders. He puts on latex gloves and gets to work, moving methodically from the back of her head and over the crown.

"Feels good, Feo."

"I know." He pushes his leg into hers in a show of affection. She pushes back. "I'm glad we're alive," he whispers.

"Me too. We shouldn't be, though."

Jago pauses so she can speak.

"Baitsakhan had us dead to rights back in the Harappan fortress," she explains. "You were out and I was pretending to be. He had the opportunity, the motive, and the gun. Would've taken a second. *Pop, pop.*"

Jago's hands resume working. "Why didn't he?"

"Who knows. Arrogance? He was messed up from the teleportation? Who cares?"

The plane's hydraulics and servos make some preflight music. Jordan says over the PA, "Just got word that we're close, amigos."

Sarah looks up at Jago, his ugly scar, his stern eyes. "Know what we should do, Feo? Steal a plane first chance we get," she jokes. "Run away and make babies and teach them how to fight and survive and love."

"Sounds great."

"It will be."

They both chuckle at the impossibility of all that.

They are silent for a while.

"If we want to do that someday—and I do—then we really need to stop Endgame," Jago says seriously.

"Yes, we do."

"And you think these people will show us how?"

Sarah shrugs. "I hope so." Then, very quietly, as if she's worried they're being listened to, she says, "Do you believe Aisling? Do you trust her people?"

Jago shrugs. "They haven't tried to kill us."

"No. And I guess we haven't tried to kill them, so we're even there."

"True." He removes some clips from her hair, places them carefully in the sink.

"Okay. Done." He drapes another towel over her. He opens the door and angles his head into the cabin. "Sarah, I have to tell you something."

Sarah frowns, takes his hand, and he leads her to the closest pair of empty seats. Aisling is near the front, sitting next to Pop in silence. Shari is across the aisle, the closed window shade by her shoulder illuminated by the dawn's early light.

Sarah laces her fingers into Jago's. "What is it, Feo?"

"I couldn't tell you before. It was too much. It was Aucapoma Huayna. My line's elder. She told me that . . . she told me that you needed to die."

Sarah releases Jago's hand. *"What?"*

Aisling turns to look at them for a brief moment. Sarah and Jago lower their voices.

"And she said that I was the one who had to do it."

Sarah clenches his hand tightly, painfully. "Why would she say that?"

Jago looks her directly in the eye, not wavering, not showing any signs of being dishonest. He wants her to hear. He needs her to. "It had something to do with your line. She said the Makers would never allow the Cahokians to win, nor would they allow my line to win so long as I walked alongside or Played with you."

Sarah winces. "That's nonsense."

"She said your line did something extraordinary. She said that back in

the sixteen hundreds the Cahokians actually *fought* the Makers!"
Sarah shakes her head. "What do you mean?"
"According to her, before the very last group of Makers left Earth—back in 1613—They asked the Cahokians to fulfill an old bargain. You had to give up a thousand young people in a grand and final sacrifice, I guess for Them to take with them on their ships."
"And?"
"And your people *refused*. She said that by then the Cahokians understood that the Makers were mortal and that they appeared to be godlike simply because they possessed more knowledge and technology than humans. She said your people fought, using an old Maker weapon against Them, and that as a last resort the battlefield was iced from orbiting ships, killing everyone there, Maker soldiers included."
"A Maker weapon?"
"Yes. And she said your line received *more* punishment. She said you were made to forget your rebellion and much of your ancient past, even the original name of your line. 'Cahokian' is apparently what you've called yourself since this battle. Before that you were known as something else."
Marrs bounds back into the plane and closes the door behind him. He plants his hands on the bulkhead and leans forward. "Buckle up. We're flying in five."
Sarah pulls the seat belt over her lap. "I don't know what you're talking about," she says a little more loudly as the plane's engines come to life. "The Cahokians have plenty of documents going way past 1613. I've seen them. We have plenty of language and knowledge, Jago. Plenty of *history*. And I have never heard anything like what you're describing—"
Jago raises a hand. "I'm merely telling you what she said. It's been eating at me. Obviously I'm not going to kill you, Sarah. And obviously I don't care what the Makers think or want for themselves. I want you, and I want to stay alive, and to save my family if I can, as fucked up as they are. I want to fight—and fight hard—for what's right." He

shrugs as the plane lurches backward. "Who knows," he says. "Maybe she didn't expect me to kill you. Maybe she wanted me to doubt you—doubt *us*—so that I'd leave you at my parents' estate. So *they* could deal with you."

"We're number one for takeoff," Jordan announces on the PA. The plane pulls around a turn and jerks to a stop. "Flight attendants, cross-check, and all the rest. Sit down and do a crossword."

Aisling peers around the edge of her seat at Sarah, smiling at Jordan's lame joke.

Sarah smiles back, not letting her expression relay the seriousness of the conversation she's having with Jago.

"You didn't let me finish," Sarah says, thankful for the sudden hiss of the engines as the jet throttles down the runway. "I don't know about this battle, but I *do* know about the weapon. I've never seen it, of course. No Cahokian Player has since—get this—*1614*. But I know where it's hidden."

"Where?"

"A little south of Monks Mound. The Cahokian monument Marrs was talking about earlier."

"A place that someone, for some reason, might try to destroy."

Sarah shakes her head decisively. The plane jostles through a small cloud, sunlight lancing the cabin as soon as they clear it. "Maybe, Feo. But not if we can get there first."

AN LIU

Shang Safe House, Unnamed Street off Ahiripukur Second Lane, Ballygunge, Kolkata, India

An Liu's Defender moves into the daylight to meet the mob. His Beretta ARX 160, specially modified with a powered picatinny rail, fires through a slot below the windshield. The report is loud inside the vehicle and he likes it. The bullets sail into the crowd. The casings pitter onto his lap. A few men are hit. They dive and scatter to the side but the mob doesn't dissipate. He gives the rifle four more long bursts, swinging it side to side. Red sprays of blood and small clouds of dust as bodies fall and feet scamper. An puts the car in second and lets out the clutch, and the Defender jumps forward. Another volley. He hopes the men will thin enough for him to escape to the wider street at the end of the alleyway.

And for a moment this is exactly what happens. But then the men yell and turn back all at once like a school of fish, surging toward his car. They throw rocks and pipes, and the soldiers with rifles fire at will. These projectiles bounce off his car without causing any real damage, but now things are about to get trickier.

They're blocking his escape.

He'll have to run them down like dogs.

Which is fine with him.

An yanks his rifle into the interior, the flap under the windshield closing immediately. He flips open a panel on the dashboard. Two covered switches and a pistol grip with a trigger are built into the console. He snaps open the switch covers. Presses the left button. It glows red. He takes the grip and angles it up and pulls the trigger. A white arc traces from the front of the car, the projectile rainbowing over the crowd, sailing 30, 40, 50 meters before hitting the ground at the end of the alley and detonating. The air there turns orange and black as the grenade does its job.

An feels giddy.

He slams the clutch, puts the car in the third, and grinds forward.

He meets the men. The sound is sickening, lovely, unusual. Yells of defiance turn to screams of pain and terror, but still the men press in on him. The Defender rides over a body. Faces mash into his windows, their flesh going flat and pink and brown and white against the glass. A pair of men grabs the door handles and tries in vain to work them open. The car slows a little. An drops it into second gear. The men beat the car and grab at it and jump on top of it. The car rocks side to side as An jogs the wheel, pinning men on the sides between the car and buildings, blood smearing across the hood and then the windshield. Some men with the kepler masks get caught and crumple under the rear wheels. The car is a four-wheel-drive beast. He lets out a little laugh. He flicks the wipers. Bad idea—the blood smears and obscures his view. The car moves forward more slowly now, the men treating it like a drum, but it's useless. It's too heavy for them to topple and they can't get in or breach its armor. An is sure that he'll make it out and get away.

But then a giant man jumps from a low building onto the hood. He turns and sits on the roof, facing out, his feet planted wide. An peers through the arcs of blood swiped across the glass and sees that he's almost reached the street where the grenade went off. A burned-out car, a few bodies, a dying cow. A strangely dressed woman—cropped hair, a stick tied to her back—darts across the street. A matted stray dog limps from left to right. The grenade cleared a path and if he can get there then he should be able to gain some speed and get away and then, once he's three kilometers distant, *poof!* His bomb will detonate and that will be the end of the mob and the end of this safe house and the end of this dank little corner of Kolkata, India.

But then, *BAM!* An is rattled. The man on the hood has swung a heavy maul into the windshield. The bulletproof glass holds. The men outside whoop and yell and—*blink SHIVERSHIVERblink*—An's heart nearly stops as a trio of men heave a thick metal bar across the end of the alleyway and bolt it into place. It's a meter off the ground, and there's no way he'll be able to drive over it.

An pulls the car to within five meters of the barricade and stops.

SHIVERSHIVERSHIVERblinkSHIVER.

"This can't be it, Chiyoko, can it? Do we abandon the car?" He turns left and right and looks into the cargo area for ideas. His equipment, his weapons, the sword. His vest.

It would be a waste to use that now.

The street.

The barricade.

"We have to at least try."

BAM! The maul again and the car shakes.

BAM! Again. A small spiderweb in the glass. A chink in the armor.

An puts the car in reverse and guns it. The mauler falls onto his hands and knees, his weapon sliding off the hood to the ground. The mob at the back folds under the car as it rides over them. More mashing. More popping. The mauler looks over his shoulder, stares right at An. Anger, menace, stupidity. An slams the brake and the mauler slides up the hood and into the windshield, his legs bunching under him. An grabs the rifle and sticks it back into the hinged flap, and he fires directly into the mauler's thigh and buttocks. The mauler rolls to the side in agony. An puts the car in first and it jumps forward and the mauler tumbles off the hood.

Clutch, second, gas, clutch, third, gas. He's up to 55 kph in no time, the men flying away from the car, gunshots hitting the rear window. He takes the wheel with both *blinkblinkblink* both hands and peers at the barricade. Will it hold? Will it buckle? Will he make it?

An squints, readying for impact. And then—what is that? A head sailing through the air?

Whatever it is, it rolls under the barricade, and then another head-like

ball, and then, at the last second before impact, the barricade is unlocked and the grille slams into it and the bar swings violently away and into the street. He hits the brakes. The car swerves and stops.
The street ahead is clear enough for him to complete his getaway. But before he leaves he looks back down the alley, full of bodies living and dying and dead. What is left of the mob comes for him.
But another comes for him too. The woman with the cropped hair. She's wiry and fast and strong. A stick—no, a *sword*—in her hand.
And her face.
Her face.
It looks like Chiyoko's, except 20 or 30 years older.
SHIVERSHIVERSHIVERSHIVERSHIVERblinkblinkblinkblinkSHIVERblink SHIVERSHIVERSHIVER SHIVERSHIVERblinkblinkblinkblinkSHIVERblink SHIVERSHIVERSHIVERSHIVERSHIVERblinkblinkblinkblinkSHIVER blink BAM! BAM! BAM!
"Go, go, go!" the woman yells in Mandarin. She stands on the running board, right next to An on the outside of the car, slapping her hand on the roof. "Go! They'll kill us!"
"Who are you?"
"I am Nori Ko. I am Mu. I knew Chiyoko. I can help you. Now, *we have to go*!"
And An's heart fills and he feels light and free and he wonders how many has he killed today and how many more will die when the bomb goes off and *ChiyokoChiyokoChiyokoNoriKoNoriKoChiyoko* and he feels free and light and An's heart fills.
He drives. Half a kilometer later he stops. He lets her in. "Watch," he says, and she says nothing. He drives some more and a short while later the sky behind them lights up, and they are free.

MACCABEE ADLAI, LITTLE ALICE CHOPRA

Road SH 2, Joypur Forest, West Bengal, India

Maccabee runs a straight razor over his bare scalp. He swishes the blade in a copper bowl half-filled with a stew of water and black stubble and soap. Next to the bowl is a pair of scissors covered by a pile of thick hair. He squints at his reflection in a clouded mirror that's propped against the wall. He's never shaved his head before and he likes the way it feels. The smoothness, the lightness. Also, with his bruises and his crooked nose and his physique, the baldness makes him look like a real badass.

Which of course he is.

"What do you think, Sky Key?"

The girl sits next to him. She leans into his side. Her body is warm, and he feels comforted by it. He wonders if she is comforted in turn.

Probably not.

Her legs are tucked up and her arms are wrapped over her knees. She doesn't answer his question. He briefly touches her hair. It's thick and soft, the hair of a girl who's been well cared for.

If he's going to get her to the end, he'll have to take good care of her too.

He passes her a bowl of rice and lentils, a stiff circle of dal balanced on top. "Here. Have some more food."

She digs in with her bare hands and eats. Her appetite is strong and, so far, insatiable.

They are in an abandoned roadside hut 130 kilometers west and north of Kolkata. It's midmorning. The landscape outside is lush and verdant. Jungle surrounds the hut, but fields of jute and potatoes lie less than a kilometer to the north. Sporadic cars and buses pass on the road, but other than that there are no signs of people here.

Which is good. Early that morning he and Sky Key wandered through a shopping center west of Kolkata buying supplies. Rice, soap, candles, batteries, towels, a sewing kit, a small butane camp stove with a liter of fuel. Baby wipes, pull-up diapers for Sky Key to sleep in, a blanket, and three changes of clothing for the girl. He also lucked into finding one of those cloth child carriers that straps over the shoulders and holds the kid tightly on the back. At a pharmacy he bought generic ibuprofen, amoxicillin, Cipro, zolpidem, and a small first aid kit with an extra bottle of iodine. Back at the hotel he packed all of this into a new knapsack as well as into the stolen Suzuki's touring panniers, one of which blessedly contained a SIG 226 and two magazines.

The same kind of gun An Liu had fired at them back in the cemetery.

It was then that he realized he'd had the good fortune to steal An Liu's bike.

He checked the SIG's decocker and stuffed it into the top of his pants.

Throughout the morning he'd dealt with merchants and for the most part they were nice to him. He had to pay a small fortune for everything, though—prices were going through the roof under the threat of Abaddon, even here on the other side of the world where the effects of the asteroid would be less urgent. The fact that he wasn't Indian didn't make things any cheaper. Regardless, none of the shopkeepers recognized him as a Player, which was fortunate.

But then they stopped for breakfast at a dosa stall, and as they sat at a plastic picnic table the owner turned up the news on the small television mounted over the counter. He gabbed on in Bengali with one of his workers, no doubt talking about all the craziness happening in the world, while stills from An Liu's video clicked past one by one on the screen. And that's when Maccabee saw his own face, clear as day.

He didn't worry about it at first. He was banged up from all the fights he'd been through and he didn't think that the shop owner was paying close enough attention to make the connection. But he was. He turned on Maccabee and Sky Key in a flash, pointed a finger, started yelling.

Maccabee stood, his mouth half-full of curried potatoes, and hoisted up the girl. The man stepped around the counter with a long kitchen knife. Maccabee backed away, swallowed his food, lifted his shirt to reveal the butt of the pistol, and said, "You don't need to get hurt, my friend. None of us do."

Stunned, the man quieted for a few moments as Maccabee and Sky Key left. He resumed yelling as soon as they were out on the street, and people began gawking, but the pair made it onto the bike in front of the hotel and Maccabee got Sky Key into the child carrier and they whisked out of there.

They rode all morning, stopping once to buy some rice and lentils at a food stall. Not long ago he caught sight of this hut flickering through the trees. Sky Key had been squirming for the previous 10 kilometers, and Maccabee had to piss, so he pulled over. He hid the bike in the bush and crept toward the corrugated metal building, the SIG pistol in hand. The hut was empty of people. It contained some basic items like bowls and a mirror and a few bedrolls and a low table. Maccabee figured it was a crash pad for itinerant farmhands, but it didn't look like it had been used in a while.

They went in and he fed Sky Key some already cooked rice and lentils that came in simple plastic bags. Then he got going with the scissors and the straight razor. And now he is done. It isn't a perfect disguise, but he doesn't look anything like he did in the video.

It will do.

"Well, I like it," Maccabee says of his new look.

Sky Key chews and manages a grunt. One of the first noises she's made all morning.

Maccabee scoots over so that he's sitting opposite the girl. A warm breeze pushes through the windows. The leaves outside rustle, a tree trunk creaks.

So young, he thinks.

Too young.

He dips his fingers into the bowl of rice and lentils and takes a handful in the Indian fashion and brings it to his lips. For food purchased from a roadside hawker, it's surprisingly good.

Sky Key's face is wind worn and streaked with grime. He reaches across the bowl and uses his thumb to wipe her cheek. She doesn't move away. Her eyes are locked forward, staring at Maccabee's chest.

"I'll steal a car soon. You shouldn't ride like that. Too exposed."

She chews. Stares. Swallows.

"Good," she says, breaking her silence since the day before.

"So you *are* going to talk?" he says, trying to sound kind.

"I don't like it. The motorbike."

"We'll get rid of it then."

"Good," she repeats. She takes another mouthful of food.

"The problem is—once we get a car, where do we go?"

She doesn't say anything.

"I mean, we should probably wait out the impact before we keep going," he says, thinking out loud more than talking to her. "But where will we be safe? And how will we find Sun Key?"

"We'll be safe, Uncle," she announces emphatically.

He frowns.

She takes another bite of food in her fingertips, pushes it into her mouth.

Strange girl, he thinks.

"Please, call me Maccabee. Or Mac."

"All right, Uncle," she says, as if she's agreeing to a different request.

He ignores it. "How do you know we'll be safe?"

The girl swallows her food before answering. "The Makers won't destroy me or Earth Key. Mama said. The bad thing will happen far from here. From me. From who is with me. What we need to be afraid of are the others. Like the man from yesterday. That's what Mama said too."

"Your mama," he says slowly.

"Yes. Thank you for killing the bad man, Uncle," she says in a smaller than usual voice. "Thank you."

Very strange girl, he thinks as pangs of guilt shudder through him. Baitsakhan was absolutely bad, but that didn't make Maccabee a saint. Not by a long shot. After all, he nearly killed Shari Chopra too.

But he didn't. And this girl, she does not need to know otherwise.

"You're . . . welcome," he says. He wonders if she's always spoken beyond her years. He wonders if touching Earth Key made her this way, or if she was like this before.

He can't know that she was.

That Little Alice was always precocious, always special.

He says, "All right, let's assume we are safe from the asteroid. I still don't know where to go. How do I win? Where *is* Sun Key?"

She chews. Swallows. Then she sticks out her arm and points a few degrees south of due east. "I know, Uncle."

Maccabee frowns. "You *know*?"

"Two two dot two three four. Six eight dot nine six two."

He gets his smartphone, launches Google Maps, and punches in the coordinates. A pin over water pops up, a short distance from the coast of the western Indian port city of Dwarka. He shows it to Sky Key. "This? Is this where we'll find Sun Key?"

The girl nods.

"It's not that far at all!"

Giddiness wells in his heart and works into his throat.

"Yes, Uncle. Sun Key is there."

"You're certain?"

"Yes."

He fumbles with the smartphone and his smile grows. Two thousand four hundred thirty-four kilometers. Thirty-six or 37 hours of driving. Maybe faster if he can find a plane to steal.

He can win Endgame, he can guarantee the survival of the Nabataean line after the cataclysm, he can see the new Earth and live on it until he is old and frail. Maybe he *can* save this young girl and fulfill the promise he made to her mother.

Maybe he can win *and* right some wrongs.

He jumps to his feet, intent on going outside and flagging down the next decent-looking car that comes along the road and carjacking it. He can hardly contain himself. “Sky Key, this is amazing!”

“I know, Uncle.” The girl takes another bite. “They call me Little Alice.”

“I could win, Alice! *The Nabataeans could win!*”

She chews. Swallows. “I know.”

AN LIU, NORI KO

HP Petrol Pump, Baba Lokenath Service Station off SH 2, Joypur Jungle, West Bengal, India

An's heart is full.

After the explosion Nori Ko moved to the Defender's backseat. She said in Mandarin, "Drive west."

He did.

He watched the road slip under the car and continue to unfurl before them and he watched her in the rearview mirror and he watched the road and he watched her. The road and her. Road and her. He did not speak. He did not need words. He did not speak for over three hours. She did not bother him with words either.

Chiyoko would have done the same.

ChiyokoChiyokoNoriKoChiyoko.

Now they've stopped to refuel. He's outside. She's in the car, her head propped against the far window. He's in the stifling heat, a gas pump in his hand. The paved highway lies to the north. A few kilometers earlier they entered a jungle reserve and now trees rise all around, making the air a couple of degrees cooler than it is out by the open fields of jute and corn. Behind the filling station is a low concrete building, a white bull lolling under a jackfruit tree, its leafy boughs heavy with oblong fruit. Aside from the attendant in the air-conditioned booth, no people are around.

An finishes and pays and gets in and drives.

"West?" he asks.

"West."

He merges onto State Highway 2, headed for Bishnupur. They drive through the jungle. An doesn't see any buildings or signs of people except for the road they're on and a brief glimpse of a derelict metal hut hiding behind the trees. He thinks nothing of it.

After another quarter hour, An says, "I'm ready"—*blink*—"I'm ready"—*blink*—"I'm ready to talk." *SHIVER.* "We have to talk."

"We do," Nori Ko says. She moves An's rifle from the front passenger seat and climbs forward. "You have questions."

An nods. "Why did you find me?"

"I found you because I also loved Chiyoko."

His skin crawls at hearing another person say her name. Even this one, who comes from her stock and looks so much like her. He's reminded of the British interrogator on the destroyer who insisted on saying it. That one who wielded the name like a blade. Drove it into An's ears and twisted it. An almost tells his new ally that she should not say Chiyoko's name either, but he knows he doesn't have the right. Whoever Nori Ko is, she was someone to Chiyoko. That counts for something.

"Chiyoko," Nori Ko says quietly.

Yes, it counts for something. But . . .

The name is mine now, he thinks. *Chiyoko. Chiyoko Takeda.* My *name.*

Nori Ko reaches across the inside of the car, her fingers yearning for the necklace that hangs around An's neck, breaking his train of thought.

SHIVER.

He moves away from her.

"It's okay," she says. "I want to touch her. Like you do."

BLINKSHIVERBLINK.

She touches the necklace. After a moment Nori Ko returns her hands to her lap. Her fingertips rub together, the residue of Chiyoko on them.

"I *love* her," Nori Ko clarifies. "After what happened I couldn't sit idly by. That's why I found you."

"After what happened?"

"I am Mu. A high member of the training council. I know much about Endgame." She pauses, and then says quietly, "I saw a recording of your

conversation with Nobuyuki. I saw how you killed him."
SHIVERSHIVER.
"Yes, I saw it, Shang. There was a black box containing surveillance recordings that survived the fire in Naha. I heard what you said, what he said. I thought Nobuyuki was unfair to you. Under no circumstances would he have allowed you to Play for the Mu, but I thought it not right of him to test you like that."
"He deserved what he got," An says.
"No, he did not."
SHIVER.
She says, "You didn't need to honor his request for Chiyoko's remains. You did not have to respect Nobuyuki the way you respected Chiyoko. But for that same reason, you should have spared him. Not for his sake, but for hers. Killing him dishonored Chiyoko, An. As well as yourself. It did nothing to tarnish the honor of Nobuyuki Takeda."
BLINKBLINK.
Her voice is cold.
SHIVERBLINKblink.
"You speak like him," An finally says.
"I *can* speak like him. But I am not him."
An wrings the wheel in his hands. His knuckles whiten. He pushes the gas a little more. The car accelerates.
Her voice is cold.
Her words cut.
"I loved Nobuyuki too," she says. "But don't worry, I'm not interested in honor like he was. I'm not here to punish you for his death." The thought of this woman punishing him almost makes An laugh.
She continues. "I chose you precisely because I've seen what you're capable of."
Death, he thinks. *She wants death.*
"What were you to her?" An asks.
"A trainer. Bladed arts, karate, acrobatics, evasion, disguise. She was my best student. I've never met anyone faster or more ruthless. She was—"

"She should not have died."
"No. She shouldn't have."
Silence. One kilometer. Two.
"You love her," An says. "I love her. This doesn't explain why you're here."
"Because I want the same thing you want."
"And that is?" He's glad to be wearing Chiyoko right now. She gives him strength. Allows him to speak without too many glitches or tics.
So glad.
She is like you, love, Chiyoko says to him.
Nori Ko says, "What you want is as plain as the nose on your face, An Liu. Love multiplied by death—by *murder*—has only one solution."
Pause.
"Revenge," An says.
"Revenge," Nori Ko says.
More silence. The sky is bright. They pass a multicolored Tata truck laden with rebar.
She doesn't lie, love, Chiyoko says. *Her anger makes her strong.*
I know, An thinks. *It is the same with me.* Chiyoko doesn't say anything to this.
"How did you find me?" An asks.
"I've been on your trail since Naha. I was going to approach you the other day, right after you arrived in Kolkata, but then Endgame caught us by surprise, didn't it?"
"It did. Things happened quickly. Very quickly. We were so close."
"To Adlai?"
We were so close to killing the Nabataean, love, Chiyoko reminds him.
He nods. "Yes. We were *very* close," An says to Chiyoko and Nori Ko.
Nori Ko ignores An's use of the first person plural and says, "I tried to reach the cemetery, but I was too late to help you. Believe me, I would have."
An thinks of what she did to the mob in Ballygunge. He says, "I believe you."
"Good."

Silence again. They pass roadside things. A group of women in bright clothing, a flock of pigeons rising from the treetops, a road crew patching potholes in the oncoming lane.

The other side of the world faces the apocalypse, but in India life goes on.

"What do you think of when you think of revenge, An?"

"Blood. Ashes. Swollen things."

Nori Ko shakes her head. "No. I mean, *who* do you think of?"

The answer is quick. "The Cahokian. The Olmec. They were there when she died. If they hadn't been, she would've lived."

A brief silence before Nori Ko intones, "Then I want their deaths too, An Liu."

SHIVERshiverSHIVERshiverSHIVERshiver.

"But tell me, An Liu—is there someone else you want dead?"

The car jounces over a bump. Neither speaks for a moment. He looks at the instrument panel. The Defender whips along at 123 kph. The engine hums at 2,900 rpms. It is 37 degrees Celsius outside.

"Yes," he answers.

Nori Ko says, "The kepler."

An nods. "Him. *It.*"

Nori Ko grunts. "I'm also in the mood for his blood. And I will see that you have it. That we both have it."

An says, "You're not like Chiyoko."

"I'm older than she was. Age does things to a person, and people who know of Endgame age even faster and in different ways." She waves her hand as if to bat away a fly or an unpleasant memory. "I had ideals once, if that's what you mean."

BLINKshiverblink.

"It is."

"I've learned a lot about Endgame over the years, An. From a lot of different people, not all of them Mu. Not all of them *wanting* Endgame the way the Players did. My ideals, such as they were, suffered the more that I learned." Pause. "They were dashed for good when Chiyoko was killed."

Hearing her name again hurts. *She shouldn't say it,* he thinks.

Chiyoko whispers, *It's all right. She will help you. Don't be hard on her. She will help you. She will help us.*

An shakes his head—not a tic, just a hard shake to quiet her voice, which echoes in his brain.

A car appears in the rearview mirror, driving very fast.

"So tell me—where *are* we headed, Mu Nori Ko?"

"You've been watching the news?"

"Yes."

"And seen that someone's destroying monuments from Maker-human antiquity?"

"Yes. Do you know who?"

"I have a hunch, but that's not important. What *is* important is that we get to the next closest monument—which happens to be the Harappan one in western India. Odds are that is where the Nabataean is taking the first two keys. It is where he thinks he will win."

"Where exactly?"

"A sunken temple near the Gujarati town of Dwarka."

An jams the brakes and holds the wheel tightly and Nori Ko braces herself on the dashboard and the tires squeal and they come to a lurching halt.

The car that is driving fast so fast overtakes them. A small late-model sedan, one driver, bald and in a hurry. No passengers. The driver looks nothing like Maccabee and there is no one else in the car so An doesn't pay it any mind. Everyone drives like a speed demon in India anyway.

"Why is Adlai going there?" he asks urgently. "Is it because of Sun Key?"

"Yes."

"Is it there?"

"I don't know for sure."

"But you think it's at one of these monuments? The ones that are being destroyed?"

"Yes. It is. Although I don't know which one."

He pauses. Squints. The car disappears around the next turn. He says, "Then Sun Key could also be at the Mu monument? Or the Cahokian? Or the Olmec? Or—the *Shang*?"

"Yes. It could."

An puts the car back in gear, whips the wheel around, pulls a tight U-turn, and heads back in the direction from which they came, going fast fast fast.

"What are you doing?" Nori Ko demands.

BlinkSHIVERSHIVERblinkBLINKBLINKSHIVERshiverBLINK.

She reaches out and puts a hand on his arm. He yanks it away.

China, Chiyoko says.

Yes, he answers.

"The Nabataean could already be halfway to Dwarka!" Nori Ko protests.

"I know. And if he's lucky enough to find Sun Key there, then he's already won, and we are already too late," An says through clenched teeth. "Nothing we do will matter. We need to get the keys to see the kepler face-to-face. If he wins, then we will have lost our chance to meet and then kill the Maker. *But* . . ."

And then Nori Ko understands. "The pyramid of Emperor Zhao."

"Yes. We start at the Shang monument. If Dwarka doesn't have Sun Key—and the odds are decent that it won't—then Adlai will go to the next closest monument. *Mine*."

"China," Nori Ko says. Accepting. Approving.

"Yes. We're going home," he says, thinking of all the things he hated about it, of all the pain he endured during his training, of all the suffering. "My hellish home."

SHARI CHOPRA

Mercedes Sprinter Van, Ayutthaya, Thailand

Shari Chopra is not in her home, although that is where she would rather be more than anything. In her home, smelling cooking food, watching her child run through the garden, holding her husband's hand.

But her husband is dead.

She is not home, but she is awake, and none of the others know it yet. Her eyes remain closed but her reawakening senses tell her much. She is bound, in the rear of a vehicle, probably a van.

She came around 15 minutes ago. She's been counting slowly in her mind, partly to keep calm and focused, partly not to cry out for her daughter, partly to get her bearings. She pictures the numbers instead of saying them in her mind. Some of the numbers are made of green leaves, some are simple lines like the strokes of pen on paper, some are made of sticks, some are made of blood.

Shari is careful that none of these images remind her of Little Alice. No peacock feathers, no pakoras, no toys, no numbers scrawled in crayon by a child's hand. Of course Little Alice is there in Shari's memory. She always is. But right now, in order to keep up her subterfuge, Shari has shifted Little Alice to the wings of her consciousness. Because if she brought her to center stage now it would be too painful and dangerous.

She counts.

984.

985.

987.

No. I skipped one.
986.
She is still groggy.
She hears the voices of others talking. She hears Aisling Kopp and Jago Tlaloc and Sarah Alopay. She remembers each of their voices from the Calling. She remembers their accents. She remembers the sharp and tinny edge of Jago's voice, the throaty innocence of Sarah's, the sanguine twang of Aisling's.
Aisling Kopp. The Celt. The Player who killed the Harappan.
The Player who Shari will kill someday in turn. Hopefully sooner than later.
My enemies.
987.
988.
989.
My enemies are so close.
There are other voices she doesn't recognize. Two men. Middle-aged. And a third man behind her in the van who doesn't speak, but whose breath is plain and audible. He has a rattle deep in his throat. Perhaps he sleeps. Perhaps he's angry. Perhaps he too is a prisoner.
The vehicle comes to a stop. Everyone but the silent man gets out. The air wafting into the van is hot and humid. They're not in the mountains anymore. The voices talk outside. "*This* is the place?" "Where is she?" "Are you sure your friend will help us?" "Will she be able to stop Endgame?"
Yes, yes, yes, yes, one of the unknown men answers.
They move out of earshot.
Shari considers opening her eyes now, springing to action, getting revenge.
But she stays. She is bound and she can't trust her body yet, its responsiveness, its strength. She doesn't know where she is or why these three Players are together and not trying to kill one another. Have they called a truce? Have they come to an understanding, like

she and Alice Ulapala did? Are they working together? She doesn't know.

She stays. She needs to be sure that if revenge is the tonic she seeks, she will get it.

The others move back into earshot and then climb into the van and restart the engine. None talk. Shari feels the tension between them.

Did one mention trying to stop Endgame?

Yes. One did.

Is that possible?

She wants to serve her revenge, but she also wants to sate her curiosity over what these people are up to.

She stays.

She stays.

Most of all she wants to live, and acting now would not guarantee that.

She *has* to live if there is any chance that Little Alice is safe.

The van moves forward. Makes a tight turn, rides over a bump in the pavement, and feels as though it moves inside. The ground pitches downward five or six degrees. They drive for several minutes, making twisting turns like one would in a multistory garage. Then the ground levels and they stop.

She counts.

1,009.

1,010.

1,011.

Doors open. People get out. "Don't forget the Harappan," one of the men says. Jago Tlaloc grunts as he works Shari out of her seat and heaves her over his shoulder. A shot of pain in her side. She wants to call out but she doesn't.

She welcomes the pain.

It means she is alive.

That her senses are returning.

By the sound she can tell that they move into a hard-walled room. The smell of food, spicy and oily and salty and peppery and doughy and fresh. Her stomach turns. She hopes it won't call out and grumble.

She counts.

She concentrates on severing the connection between her gut and her woken brain.

She counts.

Jago places her on a chair. She keeps her body limp. He props her up.

The zip ties on her wrists, which are not terribly tight, dig at her flesh.

Her legs are not bound.

If it comes to it, she can run.

She counts.

Some eat. The three Players sound unsure of why they're here. They talk in short bursts, their tension palpable. They're waiting for someone. Someone Shari has never heard of.

Someone named Stella Vyctory.

She counts.

1,050, made of white feathers.

1,051, made of water droplets suspended in space.

Please live, Shari thinks. *Let my child live.*

1,052, made of blood and bones.

AISLING KOPP, SARAH ALOPAY, JAGO TLALOC, SHARI CHOPRA, HILAL IBN ISA AL-SALT, STELLA VYCTORY, POP KOPP, GREG JORDAN, GRIFFIN MARS

Bunker beneath Classic Kameo Hotel and Serviced Apartments, Ayutthaya, Thailand

They are assembled in a brightly lit conference room 103 feet underground. Its northern and southern walls are made of concrete, the eastern and western ones of thick structural glass, each with a high-tech sliding door set in it. At the moment, both of these doors are closed.

Beyond the westernmost glass door is a large garage containing a late model Mercedes sedan and a Sprinter Van that they drove here in from the airstrip northeast of town. The van was courtesy of Stella Vyctory, and it's full of weapons and supplies and a cooler of ice-cold Cokes, and they are thankful for all of it. Especially the Cokes.

Behind the vehicles is a steep driveway that leads to the surface. The only other obvious way in or out of the bunker is a stairway behind a metal door just outside the easternmost glass partition. This stairway, Jordan says, is the one that Stella will use to join them from the hotel above.

She is almost here.

As they wait they sit around a large teak table set with food, though only Jordan and Marrs bother to eat. The others are clearly anxious. Jago has ejected the magazine from a new Glock 20 and plays with the slide. Sarah and Aisling, who also have new pistols from the van, are motionless. Aisling watches Shari. Shari, who everyone assumes is

unconscious, keeps her eyes shut and tries to keep her mind calm.
And then the doorway swings open and Stella appears. She is Caucasian, tall, dark-haired, muscular, confident, late 20s or early 30s, and she strides into the conference room accompanied by a dark-skinned man whose face has recently been hideously burned, his hands clasped easily at his waist. He wears loose cotton clothing and carries a heavy rucksack by the shoulder straps at his side. Stella is dressed in black jeans and a gray V-neck T-shirt and dark running shoes. She has no jewelry and no visible weapons. The man with her also does not appear to be armed.

Jordan rises to greet Stella, grabbing her by the shoulders and pulling her into a hearty hug. "It's good to see you again," he says. "I'm sorry we parted ways for a while."

She shrugs it off. "It's good to see you too, Greg." Then she gently pushes him aside and says to the room, "I am *so* glad to see you. I've been waiting my entire life to be in a room full of Endgame Players." The relief and joy and gratitude in her voice are palpable and a little infectious.

A good first impression, Sarah thinks.

Aisling and Jago think the same.

Shari thinks, *Where am I? Who is this new stranger? Is she an enemy too?*

Stella addresses each of them individually. "Aisling . . . Sarah . . . Jago. Thank you for agreeing to trust Greg. I know it hasn't been easy. I'm sorry you couldn't kill the little girl that is Sky Key, as terrible as that sounds. I'm sorry you couldn't stop the Nabataean from taking her."

Little Alice is alive!

Little Alice is alive!

Little Alice is alive!

Shari wants to scream for joy and relief, but her training controls her body, not permitting her to move even a centimeter. Her chest doesn't heave, her fingers don't twitch, her eyelids don't flutter.

Little Alice is alive, Shari thinks.

And then something terrible strikes her: *Could it be that my captors and these strangers are also my . . . my friends? That like me, they know that Endgame is amoral? That it is wrong?* Her stomach turns at this thought and it takes all her concentration not to vomit all over her lap.

"And you must be Mr. Kopp," Stella says, interrupting Shari's train of thought.

Pop, at the far end of the table and half turned away from Stella, grunts disapprovingly.

So that's the silent one, Shari thinks. *A line member of Aisling's. He must have been with her in the mountains.*

He also will have to die for what happened to my line.

And then Stella says, "And Shari Chopra is here too. I'm happy to see her."

How does she know all of our names?

Stella continues, "But does she need to be kept unconsc—"

She's cut off as Aisling and Sarah blurt in perfect unison, "Who the *hell* are you?"

The two Players look at each other and almost smile.

Shari thinks, *Yes. Who?*

Stella makes a small curtsy. "Well, as Greg has told you, my name is Stella Vyctory. And I am very interested in Endgame."

"Why?" Jago demands. "You're no Player."

"What line are you with?" Aisling asks.

And Sarah says, "How do you know *anything* about Endgame?"

Stella pats the air in front of her. "I promise, I'll tell you everything the more we get to know one another. But we're short on time, so for now I'll say that my adoptive father taught me about Endgame. He wasn't with any of the lines, but—"

"Your father?" Sarah says.

"Why isn't he here?" Jago asks.

And Aisling says, "I trust Jordan, but how do I know I can trust you?"

"Please," Stella pleads. "You *can* trust me. You *must* if we are going to stop Endgame. I can tell you how."

"The prophecies say nothing about non-Players intervening," Sarah says. "Least of all to stop Endgame."
Stella shakes her head. "No. They don't. But the prophesies are false. And the rules—"
"The rules of the game have changed," Jago says gravely.
"That's right, Jago Tlaloc," Stella says.
"Or rather, there are no rules," Aisling reminds them. "That's what kepler 22b said. If we really are going to stop Endgame, then I guess we're finally going to have to embrace that, completely."
"I understand your concern, Sarah," Stella says. "If I were in any of your shoes I wouldn't trust me at first either. And after what I tell you about my father I would probably trust me even less."
Jago leans forward. "And that is?"
"My father knew a lot about the Makers. More than any of the lines do, more than *all* of the lines put together. He knew a lot because, well, because he was one of *Them*."
What? Shari thinks.
Looks of doubt dominate the Players' faces.
"It's true," Jordan says quietly.
Pop grunts again, barely masking his dislike for Jordan or Stella or anything either has to say.
Finally Sarah says, "So—you're a Maker too?"
And in case the answer is yes, Jago quietly slides the magazine back into his Glock and gets ready to fire.
Stella stays cool. She keeps her eyes locked on Sarah. "Absolutely not. All I want is to stop Endgame."
The man with the terrible burns steps forward. "I beg you, my fellow Players. Listen. Ms. Vyctory is sincere. I trust her completely. I implore you to do the same."
Sarah claps her hand over her mouth.
Jago blurts, *"Aksumite?"*
"What . . . what happened?" Aisling asks.
Shari yearns to open her eyes, to see what is so disturbing about Hilal

ibn Isa al-Salt. She wants to see the Player who revealed the location and identity of her daughter, the man who enabled the decimation of her line.

She wants to see him and she wants to kill him.

Hilal says, "I was attacked by the Donghu and the Nabataean after the Calling. Sadly, both survived."

"One's dead now," Sarah whispers. "Baitsakhan. Jago and I saw his body."

Goose bumps rise on Shari's nape and along her forearms at the mention of the Donghu's name. She hopes no one notices.

"I am glad he is dead, at least," Hilal says. "But I am also ashamed to say that I am sorry the girl lived."

"I couldn't do it," Sarah says after a moment. "She was so young. So vulnerable. It was too much."

"I couldn't either," Jago says quietly.

Hilal sighs. "I do not think I could have done it myself."

They are *friends,* Shari realizes. *They are my enemies* and *my friends. Hilal and Aisling too. Or if not friends they are at least human beings, like I am. Like we are.* Once more she pushes back the urge to retch.

Hilal looks to Stella. "May I?"

Stella nods, holding up a hand for Hilal to speak.

"If you remember, in China I asked us to pause before we began to Play. I asked that we pool our knowledge of Endgame and work together. I ask you now to do the same. Everything I have learned since Endgame began has led me to believe that it is an evil endeavor, one that we and our forebears have been tricked into preparing for and prosecuting. This is our chance to make amends, not only for ourselves, but for our lines. I do not know the motivations of the kepler and nor does Ms. Vyctory, but if we can stop Endgame from progressing any further, then that is a good thing for the world. I for one wish never to see the Maker again, unless I am looking down on his death mask." He clears his throat. "Barring a miracle, Abaddon will arrive on the other side of the globe in a matter of hours. It will kill untold millions and will make the world a hard place in which to live for a very long time. Be that as it may, we *can* live in it—together. But first we must put aside the prejudices, hate, and myopia of our separate heritages so that we can fight back—*together.*"

There is a long pause. The lights flicker. Stella frowns briefly before deciding it's nothing.

"What do you want us to do?" Jago finally asks.

Stella places her hands firmly on the table and leans forward. "We must find Sun Key before either the Nabataean or the Shang does. As Greg has told you, I know that Sun Key is hidden at one of twelve ancient monuments scattered across the world. As you know, two have already been destroyed."

"You know who's doing this?" Aisling asks.

Stella nods. "They are a brotherhood as old as the lines—maybe older. And its members work against us. Luckily, this brotherhood also works against the Makers, otherwise we'd be totally fucked. Unluckily, in addition to destroying your lines' most sacred monuments, they're also trying to destroy *me.* And if you accept my help, they will also try to destroy you."

"But who *are* they?" Jago asks.

"That's simple. They're people loyal to—"

A snappy hiss followed by a small biting sound and Stella Vyctory gasps. She brings her hands from the table to her throat. Hilal reaches over and grabs her arm to steady her, but her breath cuts short and the veins in her temple pop and the capillaries around her nose darken and her eyes bulge and water. She doesn't look afraid or angry so much as disappointed and sad.

"Pop!" Aisling yells, spinning to her grandfather.

Stella's knees buckle. Hilal catches her, supporting her full weight, while everyone else stands at once. Pop spits a metal tube from his mouth and it clinks onto the table. He's standing too, one hand a fist and the other reaching for the pistol resting on his hip. "Blasphemy!" he hisses as he backpedals, Aisling quickly advancing on him. She has her sheathed

Falcata in her hands and she whips it at her grandfather, simultaneously knocking his hand from his gun and the gun off his belt. The lights flicker again, plunging the room into complete darkness for nearly a second, which feels like an eternity. When they come back on, Sarah and Jago look all around, trying to make sense of what's happened, their shoulders touching as they guard each other before helping anyone else. Hilal stands over Stella, cradling her head. Jordan is on her other side, gripping her arm and cursing. Stella sputters and begins to turn pale green. Shari risks half opening an eye to witness all of this. No one notices. Marrs has his pistol up and he's pointing it at Pop.

He shoots as Pop surges toward Aisling. The shot misses. "Traitor!" Pop yells, raising his arms and crashing forward to head-butt Aisling. She's shocked by this attack but her training kicks in and she moves by rote, grabbing one of Pop's wrists and pirouetting around him and twisting his arm painfully. His knees crumple. With his free hand he reaches for a long knife on his thigh. Aisling mashes her foot on top of his hand, and it crunches to the floor. The knife comes free, Aisling flicks it with her foot, and it slides across the room.

Aisling doesn't notice that it stops at Shari Chopra's feet.

"Christ, Pop!" Aisling exclaims.

Marrs takes careful aim now. He has a bead on Pop, except that the line of fire goes right through Aisling's thigh. Still, he doesn't hesitate. He pulls the trigger.

But he does not see Jordan sliding around the table, his eyes wild. He tackles Marrs full-tilt and the second shot rings out as the slug bounces off the floor next to Aisling's leg and embeds in the underside of the table.

Jordan says, "Damn it, Marrs! Not like this!"

Marrs protests but Jordan is much stronger and better trained for this sort of thing, and he brings his friend and colleague under control.

At the same time Aisling says, "Someone help me!"

Jordan eyes a bag on the table. "There's a tranq in there, Jago. Brought it for Shari. Use it!"

Jago glances at Sarah. "Go on," she whispers. Jago jumps onto the table and runs over it, grabbing the bag as he moves.

He reaches Aisling in seconds. She's grinding her knee into her grandfather's back, his vertebrae cracking audibly. Aisling looks up to call for help again, but Jago's right there, a syringe aimed for exposed flesh. He puts it in Pop's neck and presses the plunger and Pop Kopp relaxes.

"Christ, Pop," Aisling repeats in a whisper. "Why the fuck did you do that?"

Pop passes out.

She stands and looks across the room. Hilal is on one knee now, Stella Vyctory draped over his thigh, her arms hanging limp and lifeless at her sides, her legs crossed under her hips at an uncomfortable angle. The bright fletching of a small dart sticks out of the center of her throat. Her face and neck are coated in saliva and mucus as these stream out of her mouth and nose. Her chest rises and falls quickly, a few bubbles forming on her swollen lips, and then this stops.

Stella Vyctory is dead.

Then the lights flicker once more and a sound like an explosion rattles down the tunnel that leads to the surface and the lights go out for good. All that is left is blackness and the sudden silence and the uncertainty.

Hilal says, his voice now hard and bitter, "It is too late. They have found us—*together*."

SHARI CHOPRA, HILAL IBN ISA AL-SALT, AISLING KOPP, SARAH ALOPAY, JAGO TLALOC, POP KOPP, GREG JORDAN, GRIFFIN MARS

Bunker beneath Classic Kameo Hotel and Serviced Apartments, Ayutthaya, Thailand

Shari doesn't hesitate. She can't think about whoever it is that's coming for them. Because she's *not* one of them. She is the Harappan, and her daughter is out there somewhere. And in order to get to her Shari needs to be free.

She slides out of her chair and feels around on the floor, her fingertips searching, and she finds it. Pop Kopp's blade. She snags it and flips it around and slips it carefully between her bound wrists and then snaps the blade up, cutting the zip tie that binds her hands together.

The zip tie falls to the ground. She bites the blade between her teeth like a pirate and hunkers down and waits for her chance to run.

A flashlight's white beam pierces the dark. It belongs to Sarah. The beam skirts around the room as she asks, "Who's coming, Hilal?"

"The people destroying the monuments. The people who want—*wanted*—to kill Stella," Hilal explains, Sarah's light illuminating the side of his face and that of a very dead Stella Vyctory.

While they talk Shari takes advantage of the flashlight's shifting ambient light to get her bearings. Aisling stands over her grandfather, near the sliding door that leads to the cars. Shari'll need one of those to escape. This door opens as Jago slips into the garage. She moves her eyes over the floor, searching for Pop's gun, and yes—there it is—a shadowy lump near the same sliding door.

Jago bounds back into the room. "People are coming down the ramp.

They're trying to be quiet but I can hear them."

Sarah racks her pistol and moves toward Jago. "I'm coming. We'll cover the tunnel. Won't let anyone down it alive."

"Good," Jordan says through clenched teeth. "Go!"

Sarah sprints out of the room, brushing past Aisling.

Marrs uses the hem of his T-shirt to clean off Stella's face. "Goddamn it, why did your grandfather do this?"

Aisling flicks on a flashlight and watches Marrs wipe the corners of Stella's eyes, her mouth, the bridge of her nose. "I should have known better. I should have left Pop in the van," she says.

"I want to know too," Jordan says. "Stella is like—*was* like . . ." He trails off. Their grief and confusion is cut short by the sound of two gun reports from the tunnel.

"Now is not the time, my friends," Hilal says.

Jordan straightens. "No. It isn't."

Aisling shakes off what Pop has done and forces herself to concentrate. "We need to get out of here. The stairs!"

Jordan points at the van in the garage. "But all those guns. All those supplies."

"There are more where they came from," Hilal says, unzipping the top of his rucksack. He reaches in and draws out a single machete, the word *LOVE* engraved on its hilt. "Stella briefed me after I arrived last night. She has another supply cache here in Thailand, though it is a few hours away."

"She also brief you on who exactly these people *are*, Hilal?" Aisling asks, taking a few steps away from her unconscious grandfather.

Shari senses an opening. She creeps toward the cars. Another flashlight goes on, this one belonging to Marrs. Hilal says, "They are people loyal to her adoptive father—to the man named Wayland Vyctory."

"The hotel guy?" Aisling asks incredulously.

"The same," Hilal answers.

Aisling doesn't understand. Everyone has heard of Wayland Vyctory—

everyone in America at least. He's one of the richest and most successful men in Las Vegas. His business is casinos and showgirls and five-star restaurants and golf courses, not Endgame. She says, "Why the hell would a hotel billionaire have anything to do with End—"

But she's cut off by another loud blast, this one much, much closer. The whole bunker flashes brightly, and the glass doors on the eastern side of the conference room push in with the shock wave but don't break.

Jordan runs to a keypad by the glass doors and enters a code. Behind the doors is a cloud of white billowing smoke. This cloud lights with muzzle flash as hidden shooters let loose with semiautomatic rifles. Jordan winces as the shots strike the bulletproof partition and bounce away next to his face and chest. He hits enter. The doors lock shut. They are safe from the men coming down the stairs, at least for a few moments.

Aisling leaves her grandfather and joins Jordan, Marrs, and Hilal.

This is Shari's chance. She doesn't wait. She's in the middle of the action but everyone is preoccupied. She slips across the floor. She takes the gun and stuffs it in her waist and hooks her hands under Pop's shoulders and drags him toward the vehicles. She works quickly, silently, reaching the Mercedes in under 20 seconds. There's enough light from the flashlights for her to operate. She opens the passenger door quietly and gets in the Mercedes and drags Pop into it. She slides over the center console, working Pop into the passenger seat. Once he's in she pulls the door shut, locks it, and gets belted into the driver's seat.

She runs her hands over the steering column and yes, there is the key. The van's on her left, Sarah and Jago out of sight on the far side. The others are in the conference room on her right. There's a concrete wall directly in front of the car. The only way out is the way they came in: the tunnel.

She looks over her shoulder at it. Lights dance some distance up the ramp. A man appears around the corner, his rifle up, and Jago and Sarah fire on him. He falls and rolls down the incline.

They are coming.
She can't think about this shitty situation they're in.
She has to act.
Shari takes a deep breath. She'll take the tunnel. She'll run over whoever she finds in it, probably taking fire the whole way. She hopes the car is bulletproof. She expects it is but won't know until someone's shooting at her. She grips the wheel with one hand and holds the other over the ignition and takes a deep breath and gets ready to turn the key.
She just waits for the right moment.
Meanwhile, Aisling, Hilal, and Jordan stand shoulder to shoulder as four men—tall and athletic in head-to-toe tactical gear, their faces covered by helmets and goggles—emerge from the cloud obscuring the stairwell. They move into position, only a few feet from Aisling and Jordan and Hilal, behind the locked and very well armored glass door. They open two duffel bags containing explosives and detonators and get to work.
One of the men flips up his goggles. Jordan shines a light on his face. The man blinks. His skin is pale and his eyes are set a little wider than they should be. His mouth is open, and Hilal can plainly see that he has no tongue.
A mute. Like Wayland's guards in Las Vegas.
"Nethinim," Hilal says quietly.
"Shit," Jordan says.
Hilal twirls his machete. "They are not so tough. I took down two in Las Vegas. But when those doors open we cannot wait. We must strike at once."
Aisling doesn't have a clue what they're talking about, but now isn't the time to ask.
"We can take them," Aisling says.
"We *will* take them," Hilal says.
"Maybe we won't have to," Jordan says. He spins to Marrs, Stella draped over his shoulder. "Get her to the van, Marrs. See if there's another way

out of here. Stella wouldn't blind alley herself like this."

Marrs answers by double-timing it to the Sprinter. He's so shocked to be carrying the dead body of Stella Vyctory, and the darkness is so complete, that he doesn't notice Shari or Pop is gone. He walks around the sedan and doesn't see Shari sitting in the driver's seat, staring at him hard, waiting for the moment to make her run for it.

Marrs opens the van's side door and gently lays Stella across the backseat. Then he jumps in and fires up a laptop mounted on the dashboard. He pounds the keyboard furiously, trying to access the bunker's security system to see if it will divulge any of its secrets.

In the conference room Aisling, Hilal, and Jordan watch one of their ambushers spray aerated C4 on the glass door in a starlike pattern. Another points a rifle at them, its muzzle dancing between their heads, a smile on his face.

Jordan sticks up a meaty middle finger at him before saying, "I'm sure we can take these guys, but I think we should get in the van too. It's our best cover. It's bullet- and bomb-proof and full of guns." Jordan takes a half step toward the garage. "Come on!"

The beam of Jordan's light bounces between Aisling and Hilal's faces. Aisling looks ready to follow Jordan, but Hilal is less certain. It's hard to read his expression because of his injuries.

After a beat, Hilal says, "You are right." He picks up his rucksack and swings it over his shoulders. He hasn't told them what else is in this bag of his—the Maker book from Wayland Vyctory's hotel suite. He hasn't told them how important it could turn out to be, and how essential it is that Wayland's Nethinim do not, under any circumstances, regain possession of this book.

Hilal holds out a hand for Aisling. "We should fight these men on our terms, not theirs. Come, Aisling Kopp."

Aisling doesn't need to hold his hand or anyone else's. She bats it away and takes the lead, running toward the garage, but at the far end of the table she stops short. "Give me a hand with Pop, will you? Wait. What the—?"

Hilal continues for the van while Jordan bumps into her. "What is it?"
Aisling points at the floor. "Where the hell is he? Marrs!" she yells. "Did you get Pop?"
"No!" Marrs answers from the van.
"What the fuck?" Aisling says, moving the flashlight all over the ground. "He was knocked out." And then she remembers.
Shari.
The beam of light whips to Shari sitting in her chair.
Except that now it is empty.
Jordan grabs her roughly by the arm and tugs her toward the van.
"Come on, Aisling! We don't have time!"
But Aisling ignores him. She shines the light here and here and here.
The cut zip tie. Pop's missing gun. A scuff mark on the floor leading to the cars.
She raises the light and shines it directly at the Mercedes sedan, a circle of white light on the dark window. On the other side of that window is Pop, slumped in the passenger seat. And next to him, gripping the wheel and staring murderously at Aisling, is Shari Chopra.
"No!" Aisling yells, wriggling free of Jordan's grasp. She is about to sprint for the car and save Pop but at that very moment Aisling and Jordan are lifted off their feet and sent sailing through the air. They slam painfully into the side of the sedan. The men have blown open the glass door at the far end of the conference room. The blast is large and deafening, its shock wave rattling around the bunker with great force. Both vehicles rock, and inside the sedan Shari braces herself and catches the sun visor, knocking it open. Something falls into her lap. She shakes off the ringing in her ears and reaches between her legs and picks up a small remote with two buttons. One green, one red.
The blast also knocks Sarah and Jago off their feet, but they're the farthest from the explosion so they don't suffer too much. They dive into the van as Marrs starts the engine, steeling himself for a rough drive back up the tunnel and through who knows how many enemies.

"Come on, Aisling!" Hilal yells.

Jordan scrambles to his feet, his ears stuffed by a high-pitched whine, grabbing Aisling. Gunfire *rat-a-tats* from the tunnel. Shari turns on her car's engine. Marrs revs the van. Aisling follows Jordan reluctantly—she so badly wants to get Pop away from Shari. Jordan and Aisling move between the vehicles and now Aisling is less than a foot from Shari, the sedan's closed door between them. Aisling reaches for the door handle and yanks it but it's no use.

Locked.

Shari eyes Aisling contemptuously, shaking her head. *He's mine*, Shari mouths.

More gunfire, this time on their other flank from the men who've breached the conference room. Bullets zing off the armor and whiz past Aisling. Jordan yanks her hard as slugs crackle all around and then she's inside and the door's closed and she's safe.

Everyone is out of breath. "I couldn't find anything," Marrs says, pointing at the laptop. "We're trapped."

The pitter of bullets bounce off the outside of the vehicles like frantic music. Aisling stares at Shari. Marrs stares at Jordan. Jordan stares at Stella's feet hanging off the backseat, the shock of her death grabbing him. Sarah and Jago stare at each other, holding hands. Hilal says, "What now?"

Shari remembers the object that fell in her lap. She takes it back up.

Green button. Red button.

She picks red.

As soon as she pushes it the concrete wall in front of the vehicles slides down in a flash, revealing a subterranean road wide enough for two cars.

Again, Shari doesn't hesitate. She jams the gas and squeals away, her car's high beams illuminating a long, straight tunnel.

"Go, go, go!" Jordan shouts.

Marrs punches it too, fishtailing into the void, the red taillights of Shari's much-faster car already receding into the distance.

Shari is so happy she doesn't know what to do except drive as fast as she can. She knows the others are behind her, but so what? This car has 280 kph on the speedometer. Even if they've also escaped, she'll surely outrun them.

Then, to see what happens, she presses the green button.

She can't see from her vantage point and distance, but the door that so serendipitously opened for them closes, sealing the men hunting them into the bunker.

And then the bunker and the hidden tunnel and the ground shake and shake and shake.

The men aren't hunting them anymore.

The men are dead.

All of them—Shari, Aisling, Jordan, Marrs, Hilal, Sarah, Jago—are in disbelief. They escaped an ambush. They made it out and they are not being chased anymore.

Shari thinks, *I'll find you,* meri jaan.

And Aisling thinks, *Fuck, fuck, fuck.*

Please don't kill him.

Fuck. Fuck!

SHARI CHOPRA, POP KOPP

Subterranean tunnel, Ayutthaya, Thailand

Shari drives like a hellcat, one eye on the road and one eye on the unconscious man bouncing in the passenger seat. She drives with one hand on the wheel and her other hand on the knife she took from the floor.

"I know what you did," she says to Pop, thinking of all the Harappan he helped to kill. All of them so beautiful and true and loyal.

Paru and Ana and Pravheet and Peetee and Varj and Ghar and Brundini and Boort and Helena.

Shari remembers the hate that filled her heart when Helena died. When the Celt said to her, truthfully, that they were both already in hell.

Yes, this is *hell.*

She looks at the man. "I know what you did."

The road curves left. She handles it expertly.

"I should kill you right now."

She holds the knife to his throat.

She rounds a wide turn and the lights of the van disappear behind the curving wall.

She pushes the blade forward and it touches his neck and makes a thin depression. The man's skin is wrinkled and loose and it folds over the metal a little.

The wrinkles make her think of Jovinderpihainu.

Shari wonders if Jov was killed too. Perhaps not. There could have been survivors at the Harappan fortress, people who hid and waited and lived. Jov could have done this. If Jov—all 94 years of him—was anything, he was a survivor.

What would you do in my place, Jov? she wonders.

The road straightens and a few moments later the van's lights appear behind her.

She looks at the instrument panel. They have traveled 0.9 kilometers. The car is humming nicely at 126 kph.

She thinks, *Jov would spare him. Vengeance doesn't run in his blood, certainly not when there is a chance to be strategic. I must be strategic to have the best chance of finding Little Alice.*

She slowly pulls the knife away from his neck and then stabs it onto the dashboard out of frustration and anger and grief, above everything grief.

I can't kill you.

The headlights reveal a change in the road ahead.

A fork.

She hits the brake. The car stops. She looks to Pop. She grabs the knife's handle again, its blade a good four centimeters in the leather and plastic console.

"I should kill you right now," she says one last time.

The van gets closer. She doesn't want to see them. She picks a passage and guns the engine again, taking the left-hand tunnel. When the van reaches the fork, it follows.

I can't kill you.

I have to hold the hate back. I have to let it go as much as I can.

MACCABEE ADLAI, LITTLE ALICE CHOPRA

Unnamed road near Shree Dwarkadhish Temple, Dwarka, Gujarat, India

Little Alice is strapped to Maccabee's back in the child carrier. Men all around yell and throw up their hands and warble in half a dozen languages, a mélange of Gujarati and Hindi and English and Urdu and Punjabi. Maccabee and Little Alice get swept up and are funneled through an alley of concrete buildings. A 2,000-year-old Hindu temple is on their right, its main feature a towering cone of carved stone, weather-beaten and grandiose. A multicolored flag stands at attention in the stiff wind coming off the Indian Ocean only a stone's throw to the west.

They turn a corner and the alley opens onto the ghat, a concrete walkway with stairs leading down to the Gomti River. It's low tide so the river is in retreat, exposing sand and silt mixed with refuse, the water's dark surface a few more meters away. The far bank is also man-made but looks more industrial. A few people are scattered here and there on its rocky slope.

The walkway here is narrow and crowded, however. Everyone is turned to the southwest, to where the river ends and the Indian Ocean begins. Many either talk into cell phones or hold them up to take pictures or shoot video.

Maccabee shoves his way to the top of the steps. He stops next to a man nearly his height wearing a perfectly tailored western business suit. Maccabee's briefly envious of the clothing. He misses the way a good suit feels, the way a perfect shirt hugs his shoulders and arms, the touch of fine cotton and wool against his skin.

He misses the order and neatness of the world before Endgame.

Splotches of sweat stain the neck of the man's yellow dress shirt.

Maccabee asks, "What's happened?"

The man looks him up and down. His nose wrinkles at the sight of Maccabee's bald head and his busted nose and the black rings under his eyes, but mostly at the small Indian child fastened to his back, her head peeking over the top of Maccabee's shoulder. "There was a large blast not far off the coast," he answers. "Some think it was a small meteoric companion to Abaddon, but rather one falling on this side of the globe," he says with a poetic lilt. He points. "Do you see that?"

A dense swarm of dive-bombing seabirds confettis the air less than a kilometer away.

"Yeah."

"It was there. The birds are picking off chum, it seems."

Maccabee peers at the birds.

Little Alice says, "That's where it is. The underwater temple. Two two dot two three four. Six eight dot nine six two."

The businessman squints at Little Alice. "What did she say?" He leans close to her. "How old are you, pakora? Two? Three?"

She shakes her head furiously. "Not *pakora*. Only Mama calls me that."

Maccabee angles her away from the man, but he persists. "Where *is* your mama? Is this your child, my boy?"

Little Alice says, "Two two dot two three four. Six eight dot nine six two."

"Thank you, sir," Maccabee says, shuffling away. The man reaches for Maccabee and asks again how old Little Alice is, but the crowd closes around the man and he doesn't follow.

A little farther on Maccabee stops next to a slight man sitting on a burly friend's shoulders. The man on top presses a worn brass telescope to his eye. Maccabee holds up his hand. "Mind if I have a look?"

The man barks at Maccabee in a language he doesn't understand.

"Friend, I *need* to have a look," Maccabee says forcefully in English. "I'll give it back."

The little man protests again but hands it over and then cups his hands over his eyes to ward off the sun. The larger man stares at Maccabee's profile.

Maccabee holds the glass to his eye with both hands.

Little Alice says, "Two two dot two three four. Six eight dot nine six two."

"Quiet, sweetie," Maccabee says. "I'm trying to see if another Player beat us here," he says quietly.

He doesn't see how it would be possible, but maybe An Liu, or a different Player altogether, knows that this is where Sun Key is. Maybe someone has narrowly beat him to it.

He scans the sky and finds the birds. White gulls and dark cormorants and masked boobies teeming as one. He moves the telescope to the water's surface, which is roiled by the wind but otherwise unexceptional. The crowd hoots and ahs.

Little Alice bats the telescope. "Look, Uncle."

He pulls the telescope away and sees a large, dark object rising vertically above the birds. Maccabee recognizes it immediately as a medium-sized four-rotor drone. It shoots up 30 or 40 meters and stops, tilting into the stiff wind in order to stay in place. He peers through the telescope and catches sight of the thing before it zips away, moving toward the shore.

The little man shakes his hand for the telescope. The larger man nudges Maccabee's shoulder. Little Alice says, "Two two dot two three four. Six eight dot nine six two." Everyone but Maccabee watches the drone. He looks to the ocean again.

And then the ground shakes violently.

The crowd crouches all at once, but not Maccabee. He merely winces and turns his head. Little Alice barely flinches at all.

"Two two dot two three four! Six eight dot nine six two!"

An explosion much larger than the previous one has just detonated under the water. A thick column of water grows skyward, instantly rising 50, 75, 100 meters. Many of the birds are swallowed by it, the rest are scattered and cast away. A halo of water rises next, ringing the bottom of the column, and almost immediately afterward black spikes of debris arc through the foam. It reminds Maccabee of a grand fireworks display, but far more impressive, as this is not a show of light but an explosion moving weight and mass, displacing anything near it. Within a few seconds the crowd is pelted by debris, some chunks as big as a fist slamming here and there. Maccabee deftly unfastens Little Alice's carrier and swings her into his arms, shielding her with his body. The crowd panics. Feet and legs and hands push on Maccabee, but he is like a rock. The bombardment doesn't last long, and when it's over he asks, "Are you all right?"

"Two two dot two three four. Six eight dot nine six two," Little Alice says.

"Yeah, you're all right."

The crowd thins out quickly. A few people lie on the ground, moaning and bloodied. Little Alice points. Maccabee sees it. The drone is headed back out to the water. It flew in to take cover, and now it's returning to the site of the explosion. He shifts Little Alice into his left arm and lifts the telescope. "It's taking readings," he says frantically. "Little Alice—do you think Sun Key is . . . gone?"

Before she can answer, the telescope's owner appears and tugs at Maccabee's shirt. The man holds out his hand.

Maccabee shakes his head. "Not now, friend. I'm keeping it."

The large companion steps next to the small man, a toothless grin on his face. Maccabee knows that look. The man likes a good fight.

So does Maccabee, but these two aren't worth the trouble. He stashes the telescope in a pocket and whips out the SIG, leveling it on the little man's face. "I said I'm keeping it. Move along. Now!"

The men backpedal. *"Acha, acha, acha,"* they say. They head back to the streets of Dwarka and disappear.

Maccabee reholsters the gun and returns to the telescope. The drone makes the blast site. For a minute or two it zips there and there and there, rising and lowering and rising. It finishes its work and begins the short trip back to the city, again headed directly toward the river. "Someone's running that thing. Someone close by." He scans the tops of the buildings and the length of the ghat but doesn't spot anyone suspicious. "Tell me it isn't gone, Little Alice."

"The place where it was is gone," the girl says slowly.

"What?" he demands. "You mean . . . ?"

"We have to leave here, Uncle."

"But how will I win if—"

"Move, Uncle!" the girl yelps, and Maccabee gets an overwhelming sensation of something bearing down on him. He dives to the steps of the ghat, being careful not to land on Little Alice, and a chunk of concrete explodes less than a meter above them. He rolls onto his back, the edges of the stairs digging into his spine, as the report sounds in his ears. In his periphery he sees the drone coming in low, and on the far bank he sees two things and knows instantly what they are. The long line of an RC antenna and the glint of a sniper's scope. He makes them for 120 meters. A very long shot for a pistol. He's flat on his back, Little Alice lying across his chest. He sights over Little Alice's head and down his arm with the SIG. He throws his left arm over Little Alice, who at this moment is his human shield, a situation he can't abide. He pulls the trigger on the shooter, three times quick, making micro adjustments for recoil and the wind coming from the ocean. The glint of the sniper scope blinks out and a dark figure pops up and falls sideways. Hit. The one with the RC controller moves quickly for cover and Maccabee fires twice more, striking the hip and the flesh above it. The person falls and disappears behind the opposite embankment.

He zips the gun left and right, searching for others, but finds none. "You okay, sweetie?"

Little Alice dips her chin. Her hands are cupped over her ears. She's shaking.

"I'm sorry," he says. "But you're okay?"

"Yes, Uncle."

"Who the hell was that?" Maccabee was listening to the news as they tore across India, and he heard all about the other monuments. He says, "First Stonehenge, then Chogha Zanbil, now Dwarka. Who's destroying these places? Not the kepler. Not another Player. Right?"

"Look, Uncle." She points at the drone, hovering practically overhead, 30 or so meters away. Maccabee pops up and aims. "Cover your ears again."

She does. He fires twice. The casings bounce off the concrete. Two rotors are hit, and the thing loses altitude. Half a minute later it hits the walkway along the ghat, now absent of any other people. He works Little Alice into the back carrier and goes to the drone. It whines like a winged housefly bouncing on a stone floor. He stomps out the other rotors. He flips it over and sees the camera and the sensors and the portable drive hooked into the frame. He unplugs the drive, pries it free, and slips it into a pocket. "Maybe this will have some answers." He looks back to the ocean. The water churns from the explosion. It was massive. Waves wash into the river's mouth like a fast moving tide. "It's gone," he whispers. "Isn't it?"

How will I win?

"Yes. The temple is gone, Uncle . . . But Sun Key . . . Sun Key." She is quiet for a moment. Her eyes flutter as if she's been struck with some new information. She points to the northwest and says, "Three four dot three six two two six. One zero eight dot six four zero two six two."

"I don't understand, Alice." Maccabee frowns.

"Three four dot three six two two six. One zero eight dot six four zero two six two."

"Are you saying it—it moved?"

"Yes, Uncle. Three four dot three six two two six. One zero eight dot six four zero two six two."

"That's in . . ." He runs through the basic coordinate system seared into his brain. "That's in China, Alice. Near Xi'an."

"Three four dot three six two two six. One zero eight dot six four zero two six two."

Maccabee nods. "Xi'an. We're going back to where it all started."

AN LIU, NORI KO

Nathula Border Crossing Station, India-China Border, Sikkim, India

Nori Ko bribed their way up to Nathula, one of three overland trading posts on the Sino-Indian border. At over 4,300 meters it is extremely remote, with the mountain state of Sikkim on the Indian side and, after the trip down the Himalayas, the Tibetan Plateau on the Chinese side. The land around is desolate and rocky and steep and tufted by rough alpine grass. It is a little past noon, and the gray sky hangs low. The air is damp and cool and very out of place for midsummer.

Legally only Indian citizens are allowed this close to the crossing, requiring a permit and registration with the Indian Army. But legal concerns have "gone the way of Abaddon," as Nori Ko put it aptly after bribing the last soldier with a measly 10 American dollars and a cheap ballpoint pen. The soldier assured them there were no more men at the gates.

No more Indian men, anyway.

They've stopped a few jagged switchbacks below the pass. The mountains' teeth disappear into the clouds. Weatherworn prayer flags whip in the wind on plastic poles.

Nori Ko lights a Golden Bat cigarette. Her window is rolled down and she props her elbow on the edge of the door. "This place is too far-flung for people to care about now," she says, staring at the tidy red-roofed administrative buildings surrounding the pass.

An strokes Chiyoko's hair. "I would love to see a place where people *do* care," he says. "I would love to see New York City. It must be terrifying. It must be beautiful."

She blows a stream of smoke. The wind catches it and takes it out of the car, away from his nose and his senses. An is happy for this. He does not like the smell or taste or the sight of cigarettes. His father smoked them. His uncles.

The men who hurt him.

Who broke him.

The men who put their cigarettes out on his skin.

The men who singed him and burned him and scarred him with joy and glee.

She is not one of these men so he lets her smoke.

She says, "Trust me, An. You don't want to be in New York City right now. It must be hell on earth."

"But I want to see hell, Mu. Like a God would see it. Like a Maker."

"Like a devil."

"Yes. Like a devil. I want to smell it. Hear it. Touch it."

Pause.

A gust of sweet air slices into the car.

"Let's go," Nori Ko says, changing the subject. She points the cigarette's ember up the road. An puts the car in gear and after a few meters she adds, "I know what I see in you, An Liu—opportunity. But sometimes I'm not sure what Chiyoko saw."

An whips his head to his passenger, about to spit, *Don't say her name! It's my name now!*

But instead *shiverBLINKshivershiverblinkshiverBLINKBLINKblinkSHIVER SHIVERSHIVERblinkBLINKSHIVERblink—*

Nori Ko snags the wheel with one hand and slaps him hard across the cheek with the other. "Snap out of it, An!" she says, the cigarette dancing between her lips.

He does. He pushes the brake. The car stops again. His cheek stings. It feels good. He takes the necklace in both hands and brings it to his face and buries his nose in it. There is so little of her smell remaining that it might as well be odorless, but it does the trick. His body quiets. His heart pounds.

"She didn't see me like that," An says. "She never saw that. I was whole around her. I was . . . better."

Nori Ko takes a deep drag and flicks the hot filter out the window. She almost says, *So she pitied you,* but thinks better of it.

Instead she says, "Chiyoko eschewed relationships—mutes tend to do that—but she always liked a project."

An tightens his grip on the wheel. It's all he can do not to lash out at this woman. He could kill her, but he needs her.

For now.

Thankfully Chiyoko says, *I love your vulnerability, An. I love your broken heart. I love your buried tenderness, like you showed me on our one night together. I love that you're a Player, like me, but one completely unlike me. I love you because I shouldn't. Because it is impossible.*

He loves the sound of her voice. Why couldn't she have shared it with him when she was *BLINK* alive?

"That's not how it was," An says after a few moments. He will not share these feelings with Nori Ko. They are too personal, too revealing. He says, "I was not a project. She loves—loved—me, Nori Ko. That's all you need to know."

Nori Ko releases the steering wheel. "Well, love *is* mysterious." Pause. "Sorry. I'm just on edge. You might want the world to end but, believe it or not, I prefer if it didn't." She lights another cigarette. "Nothing I can do about Abaddon now. Nothing except make sure that kepler bastard dies one way or another."

"Yes."

"Let's both shut up for a while and get to China."

"Yes."

He resumes driving. As they wind up the mountainside Chiyoko says over and over, *China. You're going home. China. You're going home. China. You're going home.* Her voice is soft and flowing and sweet. Like the water in the painting that used to hang in her room in Naha.

You're going home.

The road squeezes between a set of buildings and these give way to walls that rise on either side, hemming them in. The trade route is literally a passageway cut from the mountain pass. A tall white gate hangs between the walls like a curtain. Above the gate is a red sign with white lettering in Chinese and English. Both read NATHULA BUSINESS CHANNEL FOR CHINA-INDIA BORDER TRADE.

And now there *is* a man. A solitary Chinese soldier on the far side of the gate, parading back and forth. He has the dark green uniform and the wide-topped green military cap with the red band and the stiff black visor and the red star on front. His breath is visible in the cool air.

A bolt-action service rifle leans on his shoulder. His feet go high, he spins, he paces, his feet go high, he spins, he paces. Repeat.

The Defender is plain for him to see, but he doesn't acknowledge it. He just keeps pacing.

"I'll handle this," An says. He opens the door, pulling the Mu katana from under the driver's seat.

"You won't need that. He's a boy," Nori Ko says.

An pauses before closing the door. "Some would say the same of me."

She gives him a look that says, *You have a point,* but doesn't speak.

An's feet and legs move in hurried, stabbing steps. His shoulders hunch around his chest. His eyes stare at the ground. He holds the sword in his left hand. He pulls the hood of his thick sweatshirt over his bald head, now speckled with black stubble.

He stops at the gate. The soldier really is a boy. All of 15 or 16. The uniform barely fits him. It's cuffed at the ankles and the wrists, and the hat is too big.

He continues to pace.

"Open the gate, soldier," An orders.

The boy passes less than a meter in front of him. The gate—easily climbed, and so porous that it would serve as more of a channel than a barrier to a sword or any other slender weapon—remains closed. The soldier remains silent.

He paces left to right, hits his spot, spins on his heel, and paces back.

An unsheathes the katana and slides it through the gate, blocking the boy soldier's path. He stops. He has pale skin and rosy cheeks from the chill. An guesses by his features that he is ethnically Han. Black peach fuzz lines his upper lip.

"Open the gate," An says. "This is not a request."

"I know who you are," the boy says, his Mandarin thick with a Qinghai accent. "My father showed me. You're the Shang. You're in Endgame."

"Who's your father?"

"My father's dead."

"So is mine."

"He sent me up here before he died. To do his job when he no longer could. To protect the homeland from . . ."

This boy isn't even an official soldier. He's a pretender. A misguided patriot. "Open the gate. I won't say it again."

The boy half spins and brings the rifle to firing position, aiming for An's chest. An hears the door of the Defender click open behind him, but he doesn't look. Nori Ko is undoubtedly aiming a Beretta at this child.

But his old rifle is rock steady. "You're calm. It's impressive," An says.

The boy moves the muzzle from An to Nori Ko.

An pulls the sword back half a meter and angles the tip so that it presses the flesh of the boy's stomach. It does not cut. Not yet.

"Keep the rifle on her. Put it on me again and you're dead. Like your father."

The boy doesn't move.

"She's Japanese. You know what they did to us in the war, yes?" An says, trying to stoke his nationalistic ire. An doesn't want Nori Ko to die, but he's curious to see what this one might do.

He does nothing. The rifle stays.

"What are they saying about me?" An asks.

The boy doesn't speak.

An pushes the sword forward a centimeter. It effortlessly slides through the first layer of the uniform.

The boy says, "The government says you should be killed on sight, but the generals say you should be captured. Some people say you are a monster. Others say you will save all of China from Abaddon's coming winter."

"What do *you* say? What did your *father* say?"

He says nothing.

"Answer. I am a Player of Endgame, and I am coming home. You can facilitate that, or you can die."

The boy shakes his head ever so slightly. "You can't come home. No one can. Father said. 'The borders are sealed. No one is allowed in or out. Guard them, son. Keep them.' The border is sealed."

No it isn't, An thinks. He thrusts the sword forward in a flash. The hilt's hand guard clanks into the metal gate. The boy lurches forward. He convulses and squeezes off a round, but the slug hits the pavement and bounces away harmlessly. The blade juts out of the boy's back and drips thick blood. An slides his hand through the gate and lifts a small box off the boy's belt. He pulls the sword free. The boy crumples to his knees. Blood pools on his lips. "The border is sealed," the boy says before pitching onto his side.

An presses the button on the box. The gate creaks and clatters as it slides open.

"No it isn't."

An goes back to the car. His steps curt. His shoulders slumped. His sword dripping. He wipes a flat side of the blade on his palm, transferring some of the blood to his skin. The liquid is warm and comforting, like an old glove.

Nori Ko utters her disbelief in Japanese. An can't understand her exact words but he doesn't need to and he doesn't care.

Chiyoko says, *China. You're going home.*

An smiles.

He is glad to be going home with blood on his hands.

SHARI CHOPRA, AISLING KOPP, HILAL IBN ISA AL-SALT, SARAH ALOPAY, JAGO TLALOC, POP KOPP, GREG JORDAN, GRIFFIN MARRS

En route to hidden airstrip, Thailand

Shari emerges from the escape tunnel six klicks north of the hotel. It opens onto a paved road hidden between a pair of jute fields. She drives fast for a few minutes, wanting nothing more than to drive and keep driving. Away from the people behind her. Toward her daughter. But where *is* Little Alice?

She looks from the road to Pop to the road to Pop. *I didn't kill him because it was the strategic thing to do. The strategic thing. What else would be strategic?*

She's so far in front of the van now that she can't see it in the rearview mirror, but she knows they're following her.

She knows they might have information about Little Alice.

Much as she hates it, she knows she could use their help.

She slams the brakes, coming to a screeching halt on the side of the road. She exits the car and stalks to the passenger door and opens it. She takes Pop by the collar and pulls him out, letting him fall onto the ground in a heap. She goes to the back of the car and sits on the trunk and waits, reminding herself every few moments that not killing Pop Kopp is the smart thing to do.

Even if she wants to do the not-smart thing very, very badly.

The van appears in the distance. It is not being pursued. Shari can see that they're several kilometers west of Ayutthaya now, a tendril of smoke rising above the city's skyline. This must have been where the hotel was. Where the people hunting Stella were.

The van is closer.

Little Alice. You're doing this for her.

Closer.

Close.

Here.

Shari pops off the trunk as the Sprinter screeches to a halt in the middle of the road. Before the van comes to a complete stop Aisling opens her door and jumps out.

"Where is he?" Aisling demands, jogging to a stop a few meters away from Shari.

"He's fine," Shari says.

Aisling marches toward her. "But *where*?"

Shari points toward the front of the car. Aisling stops for a moment, glaring at Shari. Shari glares straight back. "I'm telling you, he's fine."

"He better be," Marrs says from inside the van. "Because I'm going to fucking kill him."

Aisling shoots Marrs an angry look before checking on Pop. He's been dragged into the dirt and there's a bloody nick on his neck, but Shari's telling the truth. Aisling props Pop into a more comfortable-looking position and slowly walks back to the Harappan, eyeing her warily.

"Listen, Shari," Aisling says, intending to offer some explanation as to why so many Harappan had to die.

But Shari's head twitches. "No. *You* listen. There are things I need to say to you." She points at the van. "You too, al-Salt. All of you, in fact."

The van's doors open and everyone files out. Hilal takes a spot next to Aisling. His head held high but his eyes forlorn and contrite. Jordan and Marrs stand behind them, their faces red with anger over Stella's death and shame over the death of Shari's family. Sarah and Jago, sensing this has little to do with them, stand off to the side.

Shari asks, "First—are we being followed?"

"I don't think so," Marrs says.

"Did you set that bomb off?" Jago asks.

"Yes," Shari says. "I found a remote detonator in the car. I got lucky."

"You mean *we* got lucky," Sarah points out.

"Yes," Shari says reluctantly. "We did. But that's not what I want to talk about. I want to talk about what I heard in that place. What I heard this Stella say. I want to talk about *you*." She bites her lower lip. "I want to kill you," she says, squinting at Aisling. "For what you did to my family and what you wanted to do to my daughter."

Aisling takes a breath to speak but Shari cuts her off again. "No. Don't talk. I can't hear your voice anymore. It's too painful. The same goes for you, Aksumite."

Hilal nods. Aisling is stock-still.

"I know Endgame is amoral," Shari says. "I know that the Makers are amoral. I know it must be stopped. I think I knew this the moment I understood who—*what*—my daughter is. My child, Little Alice. She is the *only* reason I didn't kill your line member, Aisling. The only reason I have not tried to kill you right here and now."

"Can I ask something?" Sarah says.

"Yes."

"What if we were to help you? What if we promised to help you find your daughter? Would you help us? Because I think we're going to need all the help we can get."

"Sarah speaks for me as well," Jago says. "I'm truly sorry we intended to kill your child. But you heard us. We couldn't do it. We wouldn't."

"I think I speak for Aisling and Hilal too," Sarah says. "And for these men. Their names are Greg Jordan and Griffin Marrs."

Smart of her to name them. Humanizes them, Shari thinks.

"I'll consider it," Shari says slowly. "But Hilal, I have a question. You said Stella had another supply cache in—we're in Thailand, right?"

"We are," Hilal says. "And yes, she does. At an airstrip in the north. This place is at least three hours away."

Shari bites her lip again. "All right. Then let's go. I'll follow you. And I'll think about your offer while we drive. Is this acceptable?"

"Sounds good to me," Sarah says.

"Me as well," Hilal says. The others nod silently.

After a moment Shari says, "If I do agree, I'll have two conditions. First is that if we split up I cannot go with Aisling or her men. You have hurt me too much. Second is that we make saving my daughter a priority. We don't place it above stopping Endgame, but we do place it above everything else, including our own lives. Little Alice is special, and if this world is to survive I believe it will need her. If you think that's a bunch of nonsense, then at least agree to this condition because of what you've done. You owe me at least this much." She takes a deep breath. "Little Alice is three years old. Every child who survives Abaddon will inherit this world. But it will be *hers*." She points to the sky. "Not the Makers'." She pats her chest. "Not mine." She points at them. "Not yours." She lets her hand fall to her side. "If I agree, then I ask you to help me deliver it to her."

Afternoon crickets in the brown field. The growl of a generator in the distance. The smell of a brush fire upwind.

Defying Shari's order for silence, Aisling says, "I swear I will help you, Shari Chopra." But her voice is so low and so small and so heartfelt that they all understand that she's really saying, "I'm sorry. So sorry."

Jordan and Marrs swear it next, their voices equally contrite, before helping Aisling retrieve Pop. They take him to the van and put him in the back and then get in themselves.

Sarah and Jago promise their help and also go back to the Sprinter.

Finally, Hilal says defiantly, "I swear she will live. On my life."

Then he climbs into the van and closes the door.

They move out, Shari following them alone in the car.

Hilal is wrong. It takes them *five* hours to get to Stella's airstrip. They loop west toward Sai Yok National Park, then head north on small roads through hilly jungles. Jordan insists on this circuitous route to make sure no one follows them. They eventually link up with a main road in Tak and head north-northeast for Lampang, turning west again before reaching the city center and then leaving it to detour deep into the jungle.

As they drive Hilal briefs them on Stella's plan. He says that the airstrip has three Bombardier Global 8000 jets, each modified for extended range and equipped with enough food, weapons, and supplies to last them weeks. "She wanted us to form three teams that would go out into the world in search of Sun Key. Stella and I were to be one such team. We were to go to the Koori monument in Australia and then to the Mu monument in the South China Sea."

"I assume Sarah and I would be another?" Jago says.

"Naturally. She wanted you to go to the Cahokian and Olmec monuments. You know where these are, yes?"

"Of course," Sarah says.

"*Sí.* I know La Venta. *No problema.*"

Hilal points to the sky, which is now clear and dark, a few stars here and there. "What *will* be a problem for you is Abaddon. It is due to hit very soon. Your side of the world will be very . . ."

"Different," Sarah says dejectedly.

"Yes. Your lines' monuments, even though they are thousands of miles from where the asteroid is supposed to hit, may not survive."

"One way to find out," Jago says. "We go to them."

Hilal strokes his arm—the same arm that's wrapped with the wooden ouroboros from his fight with Wayland Vyctory back in Las Vegas—and shrugs.

Sarah gets the impression he's not telling them something.

Before Sarah can ask what this is, Aisling says, "And what about us? Obviously we're not heading to my line's monument, since Stonehenge is long gone."

Hilal tilts his head. "Stella suggested the Donghu monument in Mongolia followed by the Shang one in China."

"I'm game, Hilal, but by my count you're leaving four out," Jordan says. "The Nabataean, Minoan, and Harappan monuments—and *yours.*"

Hilal holds up a finger. "You are right, Mr. Jordan. I can assure you that the Aksumite monument has already been searched and is being guarded by my master and our line members. Sun Key is not there.

Categorically. And Wayland's people will not be able to breach it or destroy it."

"And the other three?" Sarah asks.

"We will be in contact as we finish searching these places, and will decide who will go to them after this first phase. With any luck, we may not have to. Hopefully we will have found Sun Key and thereby prevented Adlai or Liu from winning."

"About that," Aisling says. "Based on the way it's gone so far, I'm pretty sure we can agree that the Shang isn't interested in winning."

"So you would consider him an ally?" Hilal asks incredulously.

Aisling shakes her head vehemently. "Fuck no. He's got his own agenda, whatever that is. I'm only saying I don't think he wants to *win.* That doesn't mean he wants to stop Adlai from winning or stop Endgame or make sure the Makers don't get whatever it is they want. It simply means that, well, he's unpredictable."

"Honey," Sarah says, "we're all unpredictable at this point."

"True," Aisling says with a snicker.

"We're almost there, guys," Marrs says from the wheel. "Another klick or two up this road, if your coordinates are right, Hilal."

The van dips through a large bump in the road as Hilal says, "They are correct, Mr. Marrs."

They fall into silence for this last leg of their trip. The road they're on is not much more than a dirt track, and the jungle is tight on all sides, including overhead. Each of them is preoccupied with what's coming—the concerted search for Sun Key, yes, but also the impact of Abaddon. How will it alter their world? They know it will be big, but will they feel it on this side of the planet? Will it be a geologic-level extinction event like the one that killed the dinosaurs 65 million years ago? Will the entire planet be shrouded in darkness for months or years, or will they be spared an impact winter? Will all the plants and all the animals that depend on them die? If the sun is blotted out, how long will it be until they can stand on the earth and look up and see the life-giving solar disk again?

And what of humanity? Will nearly everyone die, as promised by the Makers? If Adlai manages to win, will his line really be the only one to survive? How will the Makers ensure that everyone else perishes?

None of them can answer these questions. No amount of training or studying has changed this fact. All they can do now is act, and do this in good faith, with hope in their hearts. The truth is that no matter what the prophecies say, life must be lived to be experienced. The rules of the game may have changed, but this rule is immutable.

Time will tell.

What will be will be.

Shari thinks of these things too as she follows the van into the jungle. She doesn't know the details of their plan, but she does know that the reckoning promised by the Makers is imminent.

Finally, at a little after midnight, they stop at a chain-link fence running right through the jungle's undergrowth. Shari watches as Hilal jumps out of the van and moves to a kiosk hidden under a thick-trunked tree. A few red lights flicker here and there and then the fence starts to slide open. Hilal—stark-looking in the halogen glow of her sedan's headlights—gives Shari a little salute.

She doesn't salute back.

He wouldn't have been able to see her anyway.

As Shari follows the van through the gate she notices several guns mounted on swivel turrets and a few cameras here and there. She concludes—rightly—that when the gate closes behind her, the perimeter of this hidden airstrip will be guarded by a computerized sentinel system.

Shari follows the van down the length of a smooth runway. It is well hidden. Nearly the entire length of the strip is covered by jungle canopy, with an opening in the trees at one end for takeoffs and landings.

They stop near three private jets parked on the side of the tarmac. Shari stays behind the wheel while the others get out and form a semicircle near her car. They're waiting for her.

"My enemies are my friends. For now. My enemies are my friends," she repeats, trying to convince herself. "I'll use them to get Little Alice. Then . . . then I don't know."

She gets out and joins them. They stand in silence for a moment.

Friends.

Enemies.

No. The Maker is the enemy right now.

"Well?" Sarah asks. "You in?"

"Yes," Shari says. "I'm in."

They will leave at first light.

Right after Abaddon falls into the ocean on the other side of the world.

But they don't talk about Abaddon. It's too much. They can't.

Instead they get ready, spending the night taking care of business.

They clean off Stella's body and dress her in fresh clothes and bind her in a stark-white sheet from one of the airplanes. Hilal wraps a bullet and the red bloom of a local flower he does not know the name of in a piece of cloth and tucks this package into Stella's rigor-mortised hand.

They bury her in an unmarked grave under a tall rubber tree, Jordan and Marrs pushing back tears, Hilal giving a brief but heartfelt eulogy for this remarkable woman he knew for less than a week.

They swear to be true to her memory by doing everything in their power to stop Endgame.

They also check weapons, go through preflight routines on the planes, establish channels of communication. They charge satellite phones and radios, and Marrs sets up an encrypted closed channel designated Alpha Romeo Five Seven. They agree on check-in times over the coming days. Jordan shares a string of clandestine clearance codes used by spy planes so that they can safely navigate restricted airspaces.

Aisling and Marrs tend to Pop, placing him safely in the plane, binding his wrists and ankles and hooking him up with the same IV cocktail they had in Shari to keep him unconscious and harmless.

Most importantly they bring Shari up to speed on their plan. They ask her who she'd like to go with and, to their surprise, she chooses Hilal. "It can't be Aisling," she reasons, "and I think Sarah and Jago should go to their places alone. That leaves you, Aksumite."

"I happily accept," Hilal says.

"I can't say the same. But I won't try to kill you. I promise you that."

"Understood. And all the same, I am pleased."

At around four in the morning Sarah and Jago gather wood from the jungle and make a fire. Hilal and Shari join them, while Aisling, Jordan, and Marrs retire to their plane for some much-needed rest.

Sarah, Jago, Hilal, and Shari pass the rest of the night talking. Each tells of where they've been, who they've fought, who they've lost. Shari is reluctant to speak at first, but Sarah moves next to her and puts an arm over her shoulders and says, "It's okay. We want to hear." Shari takes a breath to speak but instead of words come tears, fast and hard, and for eight solid minutes she bawls and shakes and clings to Sarah because Sarah is the only one there is and she needs to cling to someone.

When she's done crying she says weakly, "I can't talk about them, my family. So let me speak about Big Alice Ulapala."

She tells them about seeing Alice on the bus after the Calling, about how Shari delivered a baby right there, about how Alice helped. She told them about Alice's special connection to Shari and about a thing Big Alice called the Dreaming. She told about how Big Alice rescued her from the Donghu, and about how Big Alice had also figured out that Little Alice was Sky Key.

She said, "I don't know how she died, but Big Alice shouldn't have. She should be here now, with us. She would have wanted to stop all this needless suffering too, I think."

The other Players believe her.

When she's finished, Sarah and Jago speak about how they escaped the Calling and decided to Play together, about meeting Chiyoko and watching her free Christopher from Maccabee and Baitsakhan, about Stonehenge and An Liu, and of course about Renzo. Jago briefly eulogizes his friend, pointing out that both he and Sarah would be dead if it weren't for him.

As if waiting his turn, Hilal goes last. He speaks carefully about his belief in the goodness of man, and about how he came to realize that there's something wrong with Endgame. He talks about the Ark of the Covenant and Master Eben and the men who perished when the ark was opened. He talks about the device he found in the ark. He talks about meeting Stella, and how he came to believe her. He talks about how he confronted and killed her father, Wayland Vyctory, an ancient alien also known as Ea.

And, at long last, he tells them about the book. "According to Stella, it is ten thousand years old at least, and is one of a very few artifacts here on Earth that came from the Makers' home planet."

"Will it help us?" Sarah asks.

"It already has," Hilal says, before remembering that Shari is sitting right here. He looks down to the ground and says, "I used it to discover . . . to figure out why your daughter is important to Endgame."

An awkward silence drifts over the fire. It cracks and glows. The creatures of the jungle click and whoop, and the birds call and sing, as the sky brightens with the dawn.

"Let me show it to you," Hilal says. He goes to his plane and comes back with a large silver tome held out in both hands. He sits on the ground and places it on his lap. He traces his dark fingers over the fine cover, pointing out a coin-sized glyph tucked into the lower left corner. A pair of snakes twisted in a figure eight and devouring each other, set over an eye shape inside a circle.

"The mark of Endgame," he says.

Then he opens the book and beckons them to come and look.

Sarah and Jago move to either side of him while Shari stands off a little. She's not sure she wants to see the thing that exposed her child and her family to ruin. In her mind it is evil and not to be trusted.

But she *is* curious.

Hilal leafs through the book's vellum-like pages. They see diagrams of ancient monuments, an alphabet of lines and dots, pages full of things that appear to be mathematical formulas, constellations and spirals and webs of complex systems that describe who-knows-what. They see long passages of indecipherable glyphs. They see graphs and line plots and sweeping arcs that describe orbits or light-year parabolas through time and space. They see a few things they recognize—monuments, details from stones and hieroglyphs, shapes like pyramids and obelisks and spheres laced with coordinate systems.

But mostly it is mystifying.

As they peruse the book's pages Jago asks, "Stella could read this?"

Hilal shakes his head. "No. Hardly at all."

"But you read part of it, right? To figure out what Sky Key was?" Sarah asks.

"Correct. The device I told you about translated that section, and only that section, when I pointed it at the book."

"The device that's busted now," Jago says.

"Unfortunately."

Sarah puts a finger on a passage. "And this is Maker language?"

"Yes. It is."

"And it's about Endgame?"

"That and much more, I would presume," Hilal says.

"So it *could* help us—if we could figure out what it says?" Sarah asks again.

"Yes. Do you have an idea of how we may accomplish this?"

She shakes her head. "No, I'm just thinking out loud."

"It's useless, then," Jago says.

And here Hilal holds up a finger. "Ah. It is not at all useless. Look."

He flips to a section at the back of the book and then goes through it page by page until he stops. He plants a forefinger in the middle of the page. "Do you recognize this drawing, Sarah?"

She leans closer. The jungle animals continue their dawn symphony all around.

"Well, it's a little different—less eroded, newer looking—but I think it's Monks Mound."

"That is correct." He flips a few more pages. "And here is my line's monument—the Temple of Yeha." It is a stonework tower with an ornate, pyramidal roof.

He flips through more pages. They recognize the monuments for the Olmec, Nabataean, and Minoan lines, and they see other, unknown monuments for the other lines. After looking at one that looks more like a garden than a building, Hilal stops. The drawing on this page has been blotted out by an orderly series of lines.

"What's that?" Jago asks.

"That was Stonehenge. As soon as it was destroyed, this page flickered and changed into what you see now." He flips to another. "This was the Sumerian monument. It also was snuffed out the moment Wayland's people destroyed it. This is a living book. Somehow connected to Earth's innate energy. Even if we cannot understand its words, it is useful, Jago Tlaloc. It will tell us what monuments survive Abaddon, and which may fall to further destruction at the hands of Wayland's brotherhood."

"Good for preventing wild goose chases," Sarah says.

"I have not heard that expression before, but if I understand, yes. No wild gooses."

Shari leans closer too. "Where's the Harappan monument?"

Hilal flips through a few more pages. "Dwarka, of course. It is the last one. Here—oh!"

He stops on another page that has been crossed out and effectively erased.

Shari's shoulders slump. "I've lost that too, it seems."

Hilal glances at her sideways. "Yes. I am sorry for this as well. Wayland's men continue their work, apparently."

"We'll have to be ready for them as we look for Sun Key, won't we?" Sarah asks.

"Sí. Muy listo," Jago confirms. He likes the idea of fighting. In fact, he *loves* the idea of fighting.

He's tired of talking.

He imagines the same is true for Sarah.

Shari sits back down. Jago takes the book from Hilal and pulls it into his lap and he and Sarah look through more of its strange pages. Hilal sits and looks at the sky. The morning is here now, the sky clear and bright.

He wonders what the sky looks like under threat of Abaddon. Black. Red. Torn asunder.

On fire.

And then, at that very moment, all the birds and insects and small creatures go silent, as if a predator has drawn too close. Sarah looks at her watch. Jago closes his eyes. Shari hums a prayer to herself.

The silence is deafening.

A barely perceptible tremor shakes their bodies.

A piece of wood topples over in the fire.

"That was it," Sarah says. "That was Abaddon."

"Sí."

A bird of prey screeches in the jungle.

Hilal says, "It is a new and terrible world."

And the second angel blew his trumpet,
and something like a great mountain, burning with fire,
was thrown into the sea.

AN LIU, NORI KO

Provincial Road 204 near Wakang, China

An Liu and Nori Ko wind their way out of the Himalayas, catching glimpses of the Tibetan Plateau between peaks and valleys. The geography they're headed toward is limitless and barren. Sky and land, sky and land, sky and land.

An loves its emptiness.

Nori Ko has on a pair of headphones and fiddles with the dials of a field radio. She searches the Chinese state-run media for any news of Abaddon, but it's useless. Most of what she finds are stations playing nationalistic songs on a loop or news programs discussing air quality and water rationing in the western half of the country. China has sealed her borders, restricted her airspace, and declared martial law in many cities until the post-impact dust clears.

"It's like they're plugging their ears and singing la-la-la!" Nori Ko says. "They're treating Abaddon like it's a Western problem that the East can simply ride out."

"They'll be"—*SHIVERblinkblink*—"They'll be"—*BLINKblink*—"They're wrong."

"I hope they're not. But yes—they're wrong."

She rolls down her window. The air is warming as the sun rises and they lose elevation.

They round a turn in the mountains and the land below opens up. Tan and brown and gray and as wide and limitless as the sea. *I could stay here,* An thinks.

I know, Chiyoko says. *We could.*

He bites his lip, trying hard not to converse with her out loud. It's not easy. Because as far as he's concerned, she's here.

Next to him.

With him.

Always.

If anyone bothered us we could kill them, he says to her in his mind.

Yes, love. We could do that. Chiyoko's voice is supple and inviting. *We could be alone. We could be . . .*

Happy, he thinks, finishing her thought. *No people, no trouble. I could stay right here if I didn't have to kill the Players who killed you. If I didn't have to kill the kepler.*

I know, love.

But I do.

I know, love.

ShiverBLINKBLINKBLINK

"I do," he says out loud.

"What was that?" Nori Ko asks, pushing the headphones from her ear.

"Hmm? Oh." He sweeps a hand over the dashboard, indicating the landscape. "Was only saying I do like this place. So empty."

"Ah," Nori Ko says. "It's very—" She cuts herself short. "The channel went dead." She spins the dial this way and that, searching more. She finds nothing at first, but then hears a few stunned voices in the studio, a producer saying, "No, no! Play the anthem!" Followed by the first bars of "March of the Volunteers."

"I think . . . I think it's happened, An," she says.

"Good," he says.

And he means it.

MACCABEE ADLAI, LITTLE ALICE CHOPRA

Hotel Shivam, Railway Station Road, Dwarka, India

Maccabee and Little Alice are in a dark hotel room in central Dwarka. Maccabee sits on the foot of the bed. Little Alice is curled up, her back pressed to his thigh, her chest rising and falling in sleep. He rests a hand on her shoulder. He watches the news on NDTV, which is about to air a live broadcast from the Indian prime minister.

The screen shows nothing more than the NDTV logo. It dips to black and the Indian governmental seal fades up. Three clocks pop up in the corner. The first reads GMT 02:26:08. The second reads IST 07:56:08. The third reads simply PA 0000 00:00:00.

The clocks tick.

Then a crackle and some voices and yes.

Here he is, in a spare wooden chair against a patterned backdrop. He looks straight into the camera and begins speaking. "Friends, Indians, fellow humans. Abaddon is down."

The clock labeled PA begins to count forward. Maccabee understands. Post-Abaddon.

A new age of human existence on planet Earth.

Little Alice tosses in her sleep, her lips part, her eyes dart back and forth beneath her eyelids. Maccabee mutes the television and shakes her gently. "Come on, sweetie."

Her eyes bat open. Wet and dark.

He says, "We have to leave. Now. If we're lucky, we'll get to China before any of the others."

She rubs her eyes. "Okay, Uncle." She takes one of his large hands. She smiles. The smile of someone decades older. He can't help but marvel at this small creature yet again.

This Sky Key that he will give to the kepler.

And when he does this, he will break his promise to Shari that he would take care of her.

Because the kepler will most likely take her. And then, who knows what he will do with the child?

Maccabee turns away. He can't look her in her eyes.

She doesn't seem to notice his remorse. She squeezes his hand and says, "Yes." And then, "Let's go."

AISLING KOPP, SHARI CHOPRA, HILAL IBN ISA AL-SALT, SARAH ALOPAY, JAGO TLALOC, GREG JORDAN, GRIFFIN MARRS

Hidden airstrip west of Lampang, Thailand

Aisling is woken by the staccato burst of small arms coming from the jungle, followed immediately by the wail of an air horn echoing through the trees.

She pops out of her very nice bed on the very nice plane that Stella left for her and runs to the door near the cockpit. She leans out and sees the others—Hilal, Sarah, Jago, and Shari—standing at attention around a small campfire.

Another burst of gunfire.

"What was that?" Aisling yells to the others.

"The security system has been activated," Hilal exclaims. "Wayland's men must have followed us. It is time to fly. *Now.*"

Jago kicks out the campfire as the others move toward their planes, their weapons already drawn, their feet already running, their brains already coursing with adrenaline.

Aisling spins inside her plane and yanks the door shut. Jordan appears right next to her as Marrs whisks past a slumbering Pop, moving into the cockpit.

"Go time," Aisling says.

"Good," Jordan says, his eyebrows drawn across his forehead in a grave and unwavering line.

Outside, Jago and Sarah sprint side by side, Sarah pulling ahead with each step. She bounds up their plane's steps and pirouettes into the cockpit, Jago right behind her. He shuts the door and seals it and joins her at the controls.

Shari follows Hilal into their plane and both plop into the flight seats, Shari in the copilot chair.

Aisling sits next to Marrs in the cockpit of her plane and pulls on the headphones. "We're ready," she says. Their plane is first in line. Marrs is already pulling it onto the runway.

"You are clear, Aisling," Hilal says. "We will talk to you at the first check-in in twenty-four hours."

"Roger that, Hilal. Good luck."

"And to you."

Aisling peers out the window and sees Sarah at the controls of her plane, her hand whipping off a quick salute. Aisling returns the gesture as Marrs pushes the throttle. Their jet wash obliterates what's left of the small campfire as the plane hurtles forward, the jungle canopy rushing overhead like an inky blur. At the midway point Aisling sees the gate they drove through the night before, its sentinel system going full bore, the swivel-mounted rifles flashing and spraying bright casings onto the ground. As they pass, there's an explosion that takes out one of the guns, but it doesn't matter to Aisling or Marrs or Jordan because a few seconds later the canopy breaks open to reveal the blue sky. As they hit 128 knots Marrs pulls the stick and the nose tilts up and they shoot through a hole in the jungle and they're free.

Sarah spins up her engines and says, "Ready to fly—copy back, Hilal. You first or us?"

"You first, Sarah," he says, and she can't help but think that even now Hilal's manners are impeccable. "Get on your heading as soon as possible."

Jago takes the controls and the engines hum and their plane rounds onto the runway, the ribbon of concrete laid before them. He engages the throttle and the aircraft jolts forward. As they zip past the break in the trees that leads to the road they see lots of muzzle flashes and another explosion and Sarah catches sight of two men cutting a hole in the wire fence, each working fast with bolt cutters.

Sarah yells into her headset, "Hilal, the gunmen are going to make the runway! I repeat, *they are going to make the runway*!"

Before the trees break overhead Jago pulls up on the flight controls. Their jet spits out of the fringe of leaves hanging over the open end of the runway. As soon as they're over the jungle they bank hard to starboard. And then Jago pulls up and punches the throttle and they climb fast on a steep angle and they're free too.

But the last plane—Hilal's—is not.

Shari yanks off her headset. "Get us airborne, Hilal, but don't go full speed until I give you the all clear." She clicks out of her seat belt and stands up.

"Where are you—"

"Fly the plane, Hilal!"

Shari exits the cockpit and heads to the storeroom in the tail section, going right for the guns. She grabs a stock M4 with an extended clip and an undermounted M203 grenade launcher preloaded not with incendiaries but with smokers.

Then she bounds back to the front of the plane and does something very inadvisable for taking off.

She opens the door.

It flops open below her, the steps on the inside of the doorway leading to the ground below.

"What are you doing?" Hilal asks as warning lights ping across the flight console.

"Making sure we get out of here," Shari says, pulling the cockpit door shut so she can concentrate better. "Just fly!" she commands.

Hilal yells something in a language she's never heard, but he listens. The plane lurches forward and begins its turn onto the runway. Shari drops to the floor, a gust of warm morning air coating her face. She peers down the runway and sees the fire and the outlines of three men—no, four—taking cover near the gate. She smells the cordite from the firefight. She braces her feet against the bulkhead and quickly fires the grenade launcher. *Fwomp! Fwomp!* The projectiles travel on low arcs before hitting halfway down the runway, exploding in a dense blue haze that instantly obscures the gate.

"Go!" she yells, but Hilal doesn't need to be told. The plane surges, the bottom of the door scrapes noisily along the concrete, sparks flying. They take fire, but due to the smoke and their rapid acceleration, these shots all miss to the aft of the tail. As they trundle down the runway, her hair stiffening in the wind, her eyes squinting and watering, Shari pulls the assault rifle into her shoulder. She lays down cover fire as the plane goes faster, faster, faster, the blue smokescreen getting closer, closer, closer, and then they are through it. The men stand and Shari holds her breath as she fires three-shot bursts, her body pivoting as the plane passes her targets. Seven quick bursts, four of them finding their targets. Two heads, one chest, one leg. All four men fall and the one with the leg injury screams but she can't hear because the wind is so strong now.

After a few more seconds the trees give way to the sky and Hilal pulls up. A few stray shots come from behind them as one of the survivors fires, blindly and pointlessly.

Shari carefully gets to her feet, bracing herself in the galley as air whips around her and screams in her ears. She grabs the top of the door's handrail and pulls with all her might, but it's useless. The force of the air holds it open and she can't get it to close.

She picks up the closest handset. "I can't shut it!" she yells.

Hilal says something but she can't understand him over the deafening whine of the wind.

"What?" she asks.

He says it again and then the plane accelerates and jerks violently to port and before Shari can get ahold of something she's falling over and cradling her head and she feels momentarily weightless. Her shoulder mashes into something hard and her rifle flies out the open door and to the greenery below. The plane straightens and she looks up but instead of the ceiling she sees the floor and she understands. They're inverted, flying in an arc. The door remains open and she's not sure what Hilal is doing or if they've been hit and he's lost control of the plane, but before she can think about any of this the plane flops over and is suddenly right-side up. The door obeys the laws of physics and hinges shut with a loud *clap* and Shari doesn't waste a second as she springs to her feet and grabs the lever and pushes it hard into the closed position.

Shari spits hair out of her mouth. Her shoulder stings. She smiles.

"It worked?" Hilal asks from behind the cockpit door.

"Yes, Hilal!"

She falls to her bottom and sits there and begins to laugh. The plane pitches up and accelerates more.

It worked.

They are free too.

They can Play the way they want.

They can go and find Little Alice Chopra.

51.397742, 84.676206

KEPLER 22B

Ansible chamber on board Seedrak Sare'en, active geosynchronous orbit above the Martian North Pole

He sits in the chair again. The dark room pinpricks to life and grows incredibly cold, then glows brightly. His brothers and sisters on the Heedrak mother ship, more than 600 light-years away, surround him on all sides.

Five men, six women.

The 11 members of the conclave speak as one entity. Sentences start in one mouth and are finished in another. This is the way his people communicate when they are near one another. Unfortunately, the ansible transmits sight and sound but not thought, so in this chamber it's like receiving only part of what's being said. This cuts in their direction too—they cannot hear his thoughts either, and all struggle against this.

He takes their voices in—drinks in their tones and timbres—as they go around the room with their obligatory salutations. Their speech—low resonant warbles punctuated by high-pitched coos and rhythmic clicks—is like music in his ears. It is far more gracious than Earth humanspeak, and he is eager for the day when he can sit among his own kind and be woven into discussions with both thought *and* vocalization. His Nethinim are serviceable telepaths, and he has had many fine conversations with them, but as mutes they lack the ability to convey nuance and feeling through their voices. Conversing in one mode—either purely through speech, as with the conclave, or purely through thought, as with his Nethinim—is like speaking with half his vocabulary.

Once the salutations are over, they turn to the business at hand.

The conclave says, "Give us the news, Sare'en Gamerunner."
"The asteroid has impacted," he says. "The Nabataean Player is close to presenting the three keys at the Shang monument. We are confident that completion of this game is imminent." He speaks in the first person plural, as is their custom.
"Were any primary monuments destroyed after impact?"
"Unluckily, the Minoan was lost to a stray bolide accompanying Abaddon, and there are some fluctuations at the Olmec monument. We are monitoring this. We may lose it as well."
"Pity. But we merely need one for the game to end. What of the other Players?"
"Most have banded. It is our belief that they wish to stop Endgame from progressing. The Shang Plays, though. He alone chases the Nabataean Player in pursuit of the keys."
"Have we considered direct intervention?"
"We have not as yet, but it is an option."
"We may order you to pursue this option. Tell us, who is destroying the monuments?"
"This is our main concern, Heedrak. They are people loyal to the old member of our race. The one we abandoned so long ago."
"Ea?"
"Yes."
"But you previously reported that the Aksumite killed him."
"We did, and this is true. But his brotherhood lives on. And they are not pleased. As you know, Ea did not wish for Endgame to occur. His loyalists are trying to carry on in his absence. They are trying, in their own crude way, to stop what has begun."
"This brotherhood cannot succeed. Are we tracking them?"
"Yes, but Abaddon has severely stressed Earth's surveillance systems. We will not be able to follow their movements as easily. Having said that, we surmised that after destroying the Harappan monument they were on course for the Donghu monument."
"We are concerned."

"We are as well."

"We have a notion. We encourage you to follow it."

"What is this notion?"

"It would require two things. The first is that we channel Sky Key as soon as we can. In order to help speed the Nabataean along."

"And the second?"

"That the Nethinim on your Seedrak descend to the surface for a brief time."

"To do what?"

"To stop this brotherhood."

"They can go to Mongolia and do this as soon as our session ends."

kepler 22b half rises out of his chair.

"Wait. One Nethinim can do this in Mongolia. The other one *must* go to the Cahokian monument."

kepler 22b sits back down. He frowns. "Why?"

"We left an object there a long time ago. We have never told you about it. You need to know about it now, though. This thing could be dangerous to us."

kepler 22b leans forward, intrigued. "I am listening," he says, intentionally using the first person to indicate his high level of interest. "Please. Do go on."

MACCABEE ADLAI, LITTLE ALICE CHOPRA

Boeing 737, en route from Ahmedabad to Xi'an, China, crossing 90° E

Maccabee sits in a first class seat, Little Alice awake and silent next to him, in an otherwise empty Air China 737. There were precious few flights after the impact, but he'd found one persuadable Chinese pilot in Ahmedabad willing to take them to Xi'an, and all Maccabee had had to give him was $300,000 worth of gold.

A bargain, if it will guarantee that he wins Endgame.

They fly north and east. A laptop sits on the large fold-out table afforded to all first class passengers. Little Alice's hand rests on his thigh. His hand rests on hers.

This tenderness almost makes him sick. He hasn't spent more than a few days with this girl, but she is so fragile, and the forces that have made her important to Endgame seem so craven, that he cannot help but care for her.

And he thinks that, despite everything, she cares for him too.

What will be will be.

Maccabee opens and closes a few windows on his laptop. The hard drive he took from the drone in Dwarka is hooked up to it. He looks from the girl to the clock in the corner of the computer screen and then out the window. The flight is halfway over. They have crossed the Himalayas.

The sky outside is unlike any he's seen. They're cruising at over 40,000 feet. Sooty, gray clouds are everywhere. The dark blue arc of the upper atmosphere stretches above the aircraft, but the horizon is an odd gradient that, moving from top to bottom, goes from blue to white to brown to orange to the gray floor of the clouds. The air is thick and poisonous looking.

This is the first sign he has seen of Abaddon.

Soon, he assumes, soot will blanket the earth. Winter will come, and it will stay for a long time.

But he is not too concerned about this. He's too excited. He can barely contain his anticipation. His happiness.

He is so close to winning.

He turns back to the computer. He types away. He's accessed the innards of the drive, finding curious things. Vestiges of names and organizations. Instructions. Locations. Timelines. Names. Ea. Rima. Stella. Lists of coordinate locations. An organization called the Brotherhood of the Snake.

"Who are they?" he wonders out loud, not expecting Little Alice to say anything.

But she does. "They are people who want to stop Endgame. Who want to stop us."

"That's why they blew up the Harappan temple?"

"Yes. And no."

"I don't understand. Sun Key was there, wasn't it?"

"It would have been if you'd reached the temple's star chamber, but as you didn't, it was not there. Sun Key is safe."

"How do you know this, Little Alice?"

"I am not Little Alice. Not right now. I am kepler 22b."

"*kepler 22b?*"

Her face snaps to him and her black eyebrows rise but otherwise she maintains her blank expression. "Yes. And no. I am mostly Little Alice, daughter of the Harappan Player. But I can also speak as kepler 22b at certain locations on Earth. We are riding along the ninetieth eastern meridian right now. This is one such location, Nabataean."

Maccabee's heart quickens. "Where are we going?"

"The girl knows all of the locations where we can conclude Endgame. The next closest is near Xi'an, China."

"Sun Key will be there?"
"Yes. Sun Key is always moving, Player. It is not merely one thing, and not merely in one place."
"It has a quantum component?"
"You will find out when you reach Emperor Zhao's burial temple, Nabataean."
"It'll materialize when I get there, then?"
Little Alice/kepler 22b tilts her head. "In a manner of speaking. Patience, Nabataean. Endgame is the puzzle of life, and the reason for death. You will see when you reach the Shang temple."
Pause.
Maccabee asks, "Will other Players be there?"
Sky Key frowns as if she's trying to peer through a mist. "Uncertain. But you should be prepared."
Maccabee actually laughs at this one. "I *am* a Player of Endgame," he says by way of explanation.
"Good."
"One more question."
"Yes?"
"The girl—what'll happen to her? Will you . . . hurt her?"
"No."
Maccabee breathes a sigh of relief. "I'm glad for that at lea—"
But Little Alice/kepler 22b cuts him off. "Her death will be painless, Nabataean. In fact, she'll barely be aware of it at all."
Maccabee expertly hides his emotions—shock, anger, disgust, guilt—when he says, "Good."
"You are moving off the meridian, Nabataean. Do not tarry when you land. Go to the temple. Find the star chamber within. Call to me and claim your prize. Win Endgame. For you and for your line."
And then the plane bumps over a patch of rough air and Little Alice's face goes slack and she blinks four times. Her head cocks to the side. Maccabee holds his steely expression, afraid that the Maker can still see him. He only relaxes when Alice says, "What is it, Uncle?"

kepler 22b is gone.

"Nothing, Alice." He turns away in shame and reaches for a bag of chips. "Hungry?"

She shakes her head. "No. Thirsty."

"Let me get you something." He stands and walks past her. "What do you want?"

"Chai if they have it."

She wraps her arms around a pillow. Her wrists are chubby with baby fat. He smiles weakly. "I'm sure they do. I'll make it special for you."

"Thank you, Uncle."

He walks to the galley. He has never felt more empty or full of self-hate in his life.

I am sorry, Shari Chopra. I lied.

I cannot protect your daughter. Not from him.

Not at the end.

This is Endgame.

AN LIU, NORI KO

G310 National Road, 313 km west of Xi'an, China

Nori Ko drives.

An Liu lies in the rear seat, keeping out of sight.

He cradles his Beretta rifle and Nobuyuki's katana. His fingertips grace Chiyoko's hair.

It's midday but the sky is dark and covered with ponderous clouds.

Light rain lashes the windshield. The wipers dance. The tires hiss.

BLINKSHIVERBLINK.

"How will I find your murderers now, Chiyoko?" He whispers so that Nori Ko won't hear.

Patience, Chiyoko answers. *They will show themselves.*

He stares at the watch on his wrist. The same one that used to belong to Chiyoko. The blip-blip marking Jago Tlaloc was there two days earlier. But as he and Nori Ko drove through the bleak desert of western China, as the Olmec moved over northern Saskatchewan, he disappeared in a poof and hasn't come back.

Dead? Crashed? Shot down? Did he finally remove the tracker? He better not be dead. I need to be the one to kill him.

He isn't, love.

"He better not be."

"What's that?" Nori Ko asks, an unlit Golden Bat cigarette dangling from her lips. She knows by now that An hates the smoke, so she's refrained from lighting up.

"Nothing," he says.

"You said *some*thing."

"I said that Maccabee better not"—*blinkBLINKshiver*—"better not get there before us."

Nori Ko swipes at a phone mounted on the dashboard. A map pops up, tracking their location faithfully. She smiles, pleased that things still function on this side of the planet. Abaddon triggered a few serious earthquakes on the Kazakh border, but they didn't buckle or rend any of the roads An and Nori Ko have taken. She can only imagine what's happened in the United States—did the San Andreas finally trip? Did the Mid-Atlantic Ridge buckle and rage? Is the rain falling there poisonous and acidic? She doesn't know and she doesn't want to know.

Because that side of the world is screwed.

They've driven nonstop since Kolkata, taking turns in six-hour shifts. The car stinks of body odor and socks and empty food containers. She inhales sharply, enjoying the sweet smell of the unlit cigarette below her nostrils. "We'll find out about the Nabataean soon enough. Less than four hours to go."

"Good," An says. He runs a finger over Chiyoko's hair, and then over the cool metal of his rifle's receiver.

Patience, love, Chiyoko says again.

They drive in silence. An listens to the rain and the wind. He listens to his heartbeat. He listens to Chiyoko hum a traditional Japanese song he can't recall ever hearing before. When she is finished he whispers, "That was nice."

Thank you.

Nori Ko says, "I have a question."

"Yes?"

"If—*when*—we get the three keys and you see the Maker again, how are you planning on killing it?"

An doesn't hesitate to answer. "You've noticed the metal box in the back?"

"Yes."

"It has a suicide vest in it."

"Dirty?"

"More." *BLINKSHIVERBLINKBLINK.* "Nuclear."

"Ah. The Maker shouldn't be able to survive a point-blank explosion that big."

"No. Even I have faith in some things."

"The Church of Immaculate Demolition."

An cracks a smile but doesn't laugh. "That's right. I Play for death."

"And I do too," she says.

"I know," he says.

They don't talk for a quarter hour. The road is mostly straight here, but then they round a turn and Nori Ko taps the brakes. "Shit. Checkpoint. About half a kilometer."

An thrusts his head next to hers. "How many?"

Nori Ko squints. "Four cars. At least as many officers."

"Police or army?"

"Looks like police." She downshifts the Defender. "You'll have to hide under something."

An climbs into the passenger seat. "No, I won't." He counts five—no, six—officers. All standing around in slick rain gear. They look bored. One is on a radio. Two others smoke, their hands cupped over the orange ends of their cigarettes. One officer looks up, throws his cigarette to the ground, moves to the center of the road. Waves a hand back and forth demonstratively.

An flips open the panel on the dashboard that hides the car's grenade launcher. He presses the left button and slides his fingers over the pistol grip. He grabs the steering wheel with his other hand and jerks it from Nori Ko.

"Hey!" she protests. The car snaps left. An pulls the trigger. He releases the wheel as a white arc traces forward, the projectile clanking into one of the police cars and then rolling in a tight spiral on the pavement. The cops scatter as they anticipate the explosion, but the one in the middle of the road plants his legs and draws his pistol and begins firing.

"Speed up," An says calmly, the slugs glancing off the bulletproof glass, none of them hitting the wipers that swish back and forth.

Nori Ko does as she's told.

The grenade goes off. But it doesn't explode in a ball of fire like the one in Kolkata. Instead it lights up brightly and falls open and the police cars' twirling cherry lights go out. In fact, all of the cars' lights go out—the white headlamps, the red taillights, the yellow parking lights.

"EMP?" Nori Ko asks.

An doesn't say anything, but Nori Ko sees his head snap in the affirmative.

Nori Ko chuckles. "I suppose they won't be calling for backup, then."

"No," An says. "They won't."

The police peek from behind cover. The Defender isn't more than 100 meters away.

An opens his window. Air rushes in. "Slow down," he says over the sound of the wet road.

He casually hoists the Beretta to his shoulder and sticks it outside. Rain splashes onto the weapon and his arm. He aims quickly and pulls the trigger. A casing sails into his lap, a police officer twirls and falls, the back of his head gone. The cop in the center of the road adjusts his aim to get a bead on An, but Nori Ko turns slightly so the front of the car shields the Shang. An fires three more times at the scrambling officers, and three more officers die. The only cops left are the one in the road and another who's abandoning her post, running as fast as she can south across a field of waist-high grass.

"Stop," An says.

Nori Ko hits the brakes. The Defender swings 90 degrees, rocking to a halt and straddling the centerline of the road. The officer fires at will, aiming directly for Nori Ko's stoic face. He empties his magazine into the glass, not understanding why his bullets aren't doing anything.

Nori Ko almost feels sorry for him.
An exits on the sheltered side of the Defender, rifle in hand. He drops to the ground and, shooting below the undercarriage, lets off a burst. The bullets hit the man above his feet. He falls into a heap, screaming, reaching for his shredded ankles. His hands come up soaking red.
Nori Ko shakes her head.
What a Player, she thinks.
An swings his rifle to the field. The fleeing officer is about 50 meters away, the swaying grass above her hips. A torso and a head and pumping fists bobbing up and down, up and down. Alive and scared.
Fool, An thinks. *She should drop and hide among the greenery.*
But fear clouds her mind and she runs instead. He flips open the scope's covers. Sights through it. Tucks the rifle into his shoulder. She moves in and out of the crosshair. He exhales.
Let her go, Chiyoko says.
A *SHIVER* rattles his stomach but doesn't rise into his arms or hands. His eye is unblinking. He presses the trigger. The officer is thrown forward with the shot. A bloody mist pops in the rain like a firework and then is washed away.
No one gets away, An thinks.
He turns to the downed officer in the road. Walks forward. Nori Ko puts the Defender in first and creeps along. An reaches the officer, a fresh-faced young man not much older than he is. The officer's mouth is drawn shut in a tight line. His eyes are red and full of anger. His eyelashes are clumped together from rain and tears. The man spits, but the gob of phlegm misses An's pant leg and lands in a puddle. An smiles. He places the muzzle on the man's forehead. The skin turns pink around the metal. Water runs down the barrel and onto flesh.
"You!" the man says.
"Yes."
Nori Ko honks the horn. "Come on!" she calls from inside the Defender.

"They'll find you," the man says.
"No, they won't."
"I see you. Someone else will too. They'll find you and—"
The final shot rings over the countryside.
Nori Ko honks again.
An gets in and they leave.
Nori Ko wants to light the cigarette, and badly. *Screw it,* she thinks. She digs in her pocket and pulls out a lighter and flicks it on and holds it to her sweet-smelling Golden Bat. Her cheeks glow orange. She smokes noisily, making a show of enjoying it.
"Open your window," An says, but Nori Ko already is. Fresh air whisks the smoke away.
"Can we take back roads to Zhao's pyramid?" An asks, releasing the Beretta's magazine and checking it.
"I think so," Nori Ko answers, swiping at her phone's map once more, trying to hide that her hand is shaking.
"Good." An opens the glove compartment and takes out a box of ammunition. He snaps new rounds into the cartridge one at a time. *Click, click, click.*
"I don't want any more of that today." He holds a single brass-colored round between his thumb and forefinger. "I want to save these for the Nabataean."
He pushes it into place.
Click.
"He better not be there before us, Nori Ko."
And she understands perfectly. *Because if he is, then An Liu is going to try to kill me too.*
She takes another pull off the cigarette. She blows the blue smoke out of the side of her mouth, aiming it at An.
She says, "Don't worry. He won't be."

SARAH ALOPAY, JAGO TLALOC

En route to Monks Mound, Collinsville, Illinois, United States

Sarah and Jago fly out of Thailand on an initial heading of 009° 35' 26". After double-checking to make sure their plane didn't get hit during takeoff, they spoke to Hilal and Shari and Aisling to make sure they got away safely too. They did. They synchronized their watches to Zulu time and reițerated when they would check back in. They wished one another good luck and said good-bye and that was it.

For at least the next two or three days, Sarah and Jago will be on their own.

And they couldn't be happier.

They pass over Laos, China, Mongolia, Russia. The Asian air is empty of other aircraft and, in the immediate aftermath of Abaddon, still normal-looking. They enjoy clear skies and unlimited visibility. They encounter very little turbulence and virtually no communication from ground controllers, all of whom accept Jordan's top-secret clearance codes without question.

Their heading turns easterly as nighttime settles in. They trace over the Arctic Ocean and see signs of life on the surface below—the orange twinkle of far-flung Siberian settlements and the white glow of ships plying the cold, dark waters. Signs that things perhaps are not so bad on the surface below.

Both Players remember that night at the Calling, when kepler 22b showed them an image of a scarred and ravaged Earth, promising that this was what their planet would look like at the conclusion of Endgame. And both Players think: *Maybe, just maybe, Abaddon won't be that bad. Maybe the kepler was wrong.*

The plane's navigation system works as it's meant to—meaning that the GPS satellites orbiting 20,000 miles above Earth haven't been swept away by the asteroid—so nine hours into the flight they activate the autopilot and go to the spacious cabin. The chairs are huge. The tables are wide. The bathroom is stately, there's no other word for it. And, best of all, there's a bed.

Sarah is exhausted and teeming with nerves, but she also wants to feel what it's like to forget. Jago wants it too. They stand shoulder to shoulder and hand in hand, staring at the bedcovers for a few moments.

"Action or oblivion," she whispers, lacing her fingers into his. "Those are the only things I want now, Jago. To stop Endgame, or to have my memory wiped clean."

He wraps an arm over her shoulder. His lips touch the curl of her ear as he whispers, "I could say maybe the cheesiest bedroom line ever right now, Alopay."

"What's that?" she asks coyly.

"I can't. It would ruin the mood, what little there is."

He helps her out of her shirt and peels her legs out of her jeans and she sighs when he inexplicably fumbles with her bra's clasp and then he takes off his own clothing eagerly and clumsily and she sees how young he really is, how young she is, how for all their experience—with each other, and Jago's with other women, and hers with Christopher—even with all they know about the world and their bodies and their physical limits, she sees and she feels and she knows just how young they are, and how foolish. While he's on top of her, being careful of her arm, and deliberate with his movements, while she's enjoying the attention and the sensation and fulfillment of her immediate desire, she realizes why it is that the Players are required to be young. Until then she thought it was so they could have long leaderships as they helped to guide and repopulate a broken planet, but the real reason must be because only young people are so sure of themselves and so willfully foolish. *Especially* the young Players of Endgame, who are taught from the beginning that they're special—no, *unique*—as if all of their received wisdom and training could wring their foolishness out of them. But now Sarah sees that really, it's their foolishness that is exactly what's being counted upon by the perpetrators of Endgame. She wonders if the Makers were likewise as foolish at some point in their cognitive development. She wonders if true wisdom runs through their veins now. Because for all of her own foolishness—which led her to kill Christopher, which allowed her to believe that she was responsible for finding Earth Key, which drove her so quickly into Jago's arms—she also sees in her heart some wisdom. Baitsakhan, he was foolish. But he was also 13. Jago, Hilal, Aisling, Shari—probably Chiyoko too—these are not foolish people. Not necessarily wise, but not *only* foolish, and each of them is proof that the Makers have miscalculated.

Maybe they should have started Endgame sooner.

She wonders if kepler 22b thinks something similar. She wonders if he might possibly be *worried* about whether Endgame will go the way he wants it to go.

These thoughts fly through her mind in rapid succession, but then she refocuses on Jago. She kisses him fully and clumsily and tugs at his lower lip with her teeth. Jago, who is so humanly unpretty and so strong and also so tender. He kisses back, and keeps moving, and within moments she's gone.

There it is.

Oblivion.

Sweet, sweet oblivion.

She stays gone—*they* stay gone—until they're finished. Probably not more than a few minutes, but while they're there it feels stretched out and all-encompassing and timeless.

Afterward she pulls a sheet over their bodies and she falls into a deep sleep. She's shaken awake as the plane passes through some rough chop and Jago sits bolt upright.

She rubs her eyes. "How long was I out?"

"Not very long. Maybe an hour."
"You sleep at all?"
"Mmm, no." The plane flies smoothly again and he lies back down. "Mainly I was doing more cheesy things."
"Like?"
"Watching you."
"Creepy."
"Sí."
Pause.
"What were you going to say before?"
"¿Cuándo?"
"Before. The bedroom line."
"Ah. I was going to say, 'I can give you action *and* oblivion, Sarah Alopay.'"
"*Super* creepy!"
He shrugs. "Would've said it in Spanish at least. *'Yo puedo dar acción* y *olvido.'* Everything sounds better in Spanish."
She pushes her hip into his thigh. "Yeah, it does."
The plane jostles again but this time it doesn't stop. Jago bounds out of bed in a T-shirt and underwear and zips to the cockpit. Sarah goes to the bathroom. She has to hold onto the handle as she pees. She removes a robe from a hook and pulls it over her shoulders, keeping her injured arm underneath the plush terrycloth. She works her way through the cabin, her good hand grasping for things to help her stay upright. When she reaches the cockpit she plops into the copilot chair and buckles in, shoulder belts included.
What emerges in the distance is bewildering.
They're well over 3,000 miles away from the eastern United States, but it doesn't matter.
It's there.
Abaddon *is* as bad as kepler 22b said it would be.
There is no horizon in the east. The entire expanse from top to bottom is black, like a hole punched through the sky and earth. The only

light comes from high-altitude lightning flashing constantly and everywhere over the reaches of Canada, and while it's a ways off, they're going to be flying through this storm soon.

"It's going to get rough," Jago says, flicking switches and punching commands into the touch screen, disabling the autopilot.

"I know. We can handle it."

For the next several hours they fly through or over a succession of terrible storms, each growing in intensity. They stay in the cockpit and don't sleep as they white-knuckle it across Canada. Somewhere over Saskatchewan they lose contact with the external GPS systems and are forced to fly by instruments alone, hoping that by the time they reach the small airport Hilal marked for them, everything will be working again, otherwise they're not sure they'll be able to find it. As they cross the US border they manage to reconnect to the satellites overhead, but for the rest of the flight this connection remains erratic and unreliable. They get a few automated pings from ground control systems in North Dakota, and they answer these with Jordan's codes, but otherwise they have no indication that anyone on the ground is tracking or even aware of them.

Dawn arrives but the sun does not. The sky barely brightens. A little light leaks through the gas and ash directly overhead, but otherwise it's as if the world has been dipped in smoky ink. Sarah expected the eastern side of the country to be like this but not the western too, and for a while neither she nor Jago can figure out why it's happening. The jet stream should be blowing everything Abaddon has kicked up over the Atlantic, not over the plains.

And then, somewhere over Nebraska, they understand.

The plane flies into a pocket of decent visibility, and when they look west they see the contours of a massive plume of ash, several hundred miles across, billowing from the Rockies like it's being vented from the depths of hell. The plume rises so high that it looks as if it reaches into space itself. Every now and then crooked streaks of blue and purple lightning web through it, or the plume glows with a fiery orange light that's quickly snuffed out.

"The Yellowstone Caldera," Sarah says. "It blew. Jesus Christ, it fucking blew." She turns to Jago, her face pale. "My family's down there somewhere, Feo."

"Countless other families are relying on us right now, Sarah."

She ignores this. "I want to see them."

"You can't. Not yet."

She almost protests—they went to his family, didn't they?—but he's right. They can't take a detour. *Action or oblivion,* she thinks. *Running to Mom and Dad is neither.*

"All right, but I *do* want to see them eventually."

Jago can't argue with that.

Her thoughts of home are interrupted when their visibility returns to zero and they slam into a wall of turbulent air that lasts the rest of Nebraska. The jostling reaches a crescendo over a corner of Kansas that throws the plane 20 feet in all directions over several minutes. The air settles again over Missouri, which they pass over at a relatively low 25,000 feet, flying under a high-altitude storm and over a low-slung bank of ash carried on the wind. Not since the far north of Canada have they seen the ground. As they approach the small Creve Coeur Airport near St. Louis, Jago puts the plane into a virtual dive to get below 2,000 feet, trying to keep the engine intakes from jamming full of particulate. Communication with the GPS system is blessedly functioning and they find the airport—really nothing more than a runway and an array of private hangars—to be completely empty. They touch down at a little after 11 a.m. local time, and as they taxi to the hangar Hilal marked for them, the plane's tires cut through a thin layer of Yellowstone ash that coats everything. The windshield wipers swish back and forth, pushing the stuff to the side and making streaks on the glass. The sun is nearly at its zenith, but the sky is stuck in a constant state of dusky twilight, and with the exception of the airstrip's emergency lighting, including that on the runway, nearly all power in the area appears to be out.

After a couple hours spent getting the plane inside and packing bags with weapons and supplies and changing clothes and putting on respirators and goggles and firing up a vintage Harley-Davidson XLS Roadster, they hit the road.

They don't bother with helmets.

No point. Not like anyone's going to pull them over and write them a ticket.

There are hardly any vehicles moving around. Sarah guesses that the blast from Abaddon, while devastating to large areas of the eastern seaboard, had the added effect of washing at least half of the country in a giant electromagnetic pulse, frying nearly every circuit east of the Mississippi. And she is correct. This is why no one's out driving around—their cars simply don't work. The motorcycle works because its engine is purely mechanical—including its kick-starter. As they take their ride and begin to get a ground's-eye view of what Abaddon has wrought—even over a thousand miles away way from the point of impact—it dawns on Sarah that if people could go somewhere, they wouldn't know where *to* go. Most of them must be holed up at home, taking stock of food, water, batteries, fuel, clothing, pets, livestock, and, this being America, guns and ammunition. People are hunkering down and waiting, trying to get news from the radio or neighbors or whatever authority figure they can find.

People are *scared.*

Sitting on the back of the bike and using a paper map, Sarah navigates them around St. Louis to the north, crossing the Mississippi River on a completely dead I-270, which cuts over Chouteau Island. The four-lane highway is peppered with derelict cars, abandoned right where they died. Many have their doors open. Many overflow with personal items and things that will soon be thought of as supplies.

Might as well be zombies out here, she thinks as they motor over the short causeway into Illinois.

After a short ride on the Illinois side Sarah squeezes Jago with her legs and they exit the highway, taking local roads that wind east and south.

Monks Mound is very close. She sees it on the map, but more than that she feels it in her skin.

They turn onto Horseshoe Lake Road. Jago goes right down the double yellow line. No cars, abandoned or otherwise. A wall of hardwoods and power lines on their right. A grass tract on their left abutted by a line of modest two-story homes. A few people run into their houses when they hear the prattle of the motorcycle engine. One man doesn't run. He has a long hunting rifle, the butt parked on his hip. He waves them down. Jago brakes to a stop.

Sarah pulls the respirator from her face. "Need any help, mister?" she yells.

"Sure I do! Can you clear the skies and turn the power back on?"

"Wish I could."

"Yeah, well . . . I was flagging you 'cause you probably shouldn't go that way, less you want trouble."

Sarah runs a finger over her map, scanning it for the name of a nearby town. "Unfortunately we have to go that way. Got a big sister over in Shiloh with two little ones," Sarah lies. "Haven't heard from her since before. Need to make sure they're all right."

"I hear you, then. You know where all this ash is coming from, by the way? Ain't nothing on the radio. Can't be that Abaddon, can it?"

"Nah. I heard that Yellowstone blew up. Abaddon probably triggered it or something. There's a huge volcano under there."

"Yellowstone? Old Faithful Yellowstone?"

"That's the one."

He runs a hand through his hair a couple times, clearly distressed. "Goddamn. I mean, I know this is Illinois and all, but we ain't in Kansas anymore, are we, miss?"

Sarah nearly laughs. She's happy to be home, if only for a short visit. "No, we're not."

Jago says quietly, "What's he mean?"

"I'll explain later," Sarah says.

The man says, "Well, be careful out there, you two." He leans to the side and squints, eyeing the pistols on their waists and the rifle-shaped duffels strapped to their bike. He says something to himself that Sarah can't hear, but she can read his lips: "Looks like you're being careful."

"We will, mister. You too."

They wave to one another and Sarah and Jago take off.

But not more than half a mile away they stop again.

A black Ford police cruiser is ditched on the right side of the road. Its front doors and trunk are open. The communications console mounted to the dashboard is shot to pieces, probably by a shotgun blast. But far more disturbing is the taut rope that leads from under the car's rear bumper, angling toward the crossbeam of a nearby telephone pole, and over it, to the lifeless body of a uniformed cop hanged 15 feet above. They can't see his face. He's missing his shoes, and a black sock is bunched around the arch of his right foot. His gun holster is empty. His hands are purple. One is clenched in a fist.

Jago bounds off the bike to inspect the car. Sarah slides forward in the saddle and draws her pistol. *"Nada,"* Jago says. "Weapons are gone. Handcuffs, ammo, pepper spray, all of it."

She stares at the dead man. "Bad omen, huh?"

"Bad for him, anyway."

"Yeah. We should cut him down."

Jago rummages through the trunk. "There's a tarp in here. We could cover him, no?"

They work together to get him on the ground and laid out and covered at the base of the telephone pole, which takes on the double purpose of a grave marker. Sarah makes sure to close his swollen and bloodshot eyes before laying the tarp over him. She lays stones around its edge to keep the wind from blowing it off. She says a quiet prayer for him in her old Cahokian tongue.

They carry on.

They turn right onto Bruns Road, a meager strip of frost-heaved asphalt, and head south. The land is flat and dark, the road straight. The soybean plants on either side of the road are, like everything, covered in a thin layer of volcanic ash. They pass a farmhouse and a huge willow tree. They turn right onto another farm road and then left. The land begins to roll. More trees. Sarah looks at her map.

Closer now. The road passes over I-55/I-70. They see more abandoned vehicles on the highway. One car creeps along in the distance, its yellow hazards flashing and its headlights cutting eerie beams through the dusty air.

A scavenger who, like them, lucked into finding a functioning vehicle.

Sarah looks to her left. If her memory serves her, it should be there.

And yes, over the tops of a stand of trees she makes it out. A flat-topped earthen pyramid covered in grass, about 92 feet high and 951 feet long. Sarah knows from her studies that it's also 836 feet across, meaning that at its base it's a little larger than the Great Pyramid of Giza.

Jago banks the bike onto Collinsville Road. And then they slow down abruptly.

Yes, Monks Mound is there, waiting for them. Maybe Sun Key is hidden in its depths. Maybe not. And to the south is the Maker weapon Sarah wants to find.

But first they have to deal with the danger that the nice man warned them about.

Sarah twirls her finger next to Jago's face, asking if he wants to turn around to avoid trouble.

He answers by gunning the throttle and rushing toward it.

A hundred yards later he pulls to a stop, the bike angled across the road at 45 degrees. He cuts the engine and kicks down the stand.

Neither gets off.

They stare straight ahead.

"This is gonna get ugly, Feo."

"*Sí.* Stay sharp."

"You know me."

Eight motorcycles are pulled to the edge of the fields. As many men in leather vests and dirty jeans and dark leather boots are nearby. A car, apparently still functioning, is hemmed in by the bikers. One bike has a pair of black boots tied to the bitch bar. An argument is well underway.

"Hey!" a towering man built like a castle yells to Sarah and Jago when he notices them. He points. "Whose bike's that?"

"Ours, amigo," Jago says through his respirator.

"I ain't your friend." The biker walks toward them to get a better look at the Harley. "And that ain't gonna be yours for much longer, hombre. Like the look of that gas mask too."

"Es bueno," Jago concedes.

Sarah gets off and rests her good hand on her pistol. "Not to point out the obvious, but by my count each of you already has a bike. How do you plan on taking ours also? You use some pixie biker dust to ride two at once?" While she talks she peeks past the biker at the car. It's an early 2000s silver Ford Taurus, a lot like the one they keep at her family's Niobrara River compound in western Nebraska. This one is dinged up badly, as if it's taken a few direct hits with baseball bats or, as is more likely, falling debris. It has no plates. There appears to be a single occupant, a driver, probably male. She can't tell if he's speaking to the bikers surrounding him, but she can tell that he's locked himself in and that the bikers are growing frustrated.

"Hey, Curly," the large biker shouts over his shoulder, "we got us some more smart-asses."

Curly leans from behind a man much bigger than him and says, "Who's that, Misty?"

Misty? Sarah thinks.

Jago laughs quietly.

"These two. Got a nice ride. Eighty-something XLS." Curly gives the giant an order and extracts himself from the car situation. Curly isn't much taller than five feet. He's as thin as rope and moves like it too, in a loose, boneless gait. He carries what is clearly the hanged police officer's shotgun in his left hand and in his right a buck knife, which he twirls expertly.

"Howdy, travelers. Name's Curly. And you are?" He addresses Jago.

Jago shrugs. He slouches nonchalantly in the saddle. "*Sólo hablo un poco de inglés*. Sorry." He makes a point of rolling his *R*s.

"We're just passing through," Sarah answers for them.

Curly turns to her. "Friend's a spic, eh? Guess I'm talking to you then." He spits a thin stream of clear saliva onto the road. "Maybe you are passing through, miss. But it'd have to be after we make a little trade. You give us that bike, and I'll let you keep your pretty little face. I assume there's a pretty face under all that. Best offer you're gonna get today, I'm sorry to say."

Sarah's eyes are hidden behind her goggles, so Curly can't tell that she isn't bothering to look at him while he talks. Instead, she watches the giant brandish a tire iron in the background. "Last warning!" he yells to the man in the car, his voice a high-pitched whine that completely contradicts his stature.

Sarah points. "Can we help you with anything back there, Curly?"

Curly half glances over his shoulder. "That? Nah. Nice motorist got lost and needs some directions. Funny thing is, he won't take 'em." He spits again. "Can you believe what the world's come to? Aliens on TV, killer asteroids, teenage assassins playing some kind of apocalypse game, and now this guy who won't talk sense with us simple road warriors. Folks are losing their minds these days. Along with lots of other things."

"And here you are to shepherd them to sunnier pastures," Sarah says, raising the riding goggles onto her forehead. "Figuratively speaking, of course."

Curly raises an eyebrow. "I like that. Mind if I use it? In the future like?"

"It's all yours."

"Say, you *are* pretty. Pretty eyes, anyway."

Sarah fakes sounding scared when she says, "Thanks."

"Speaking of using something that isn't mine . . ." He raises the shotgun and rests it across his right forearm. "Sorry for pointing this at you, miss, but I can see you're armed, so—nothing personal."

Sarah holds up her hands. "All right, all right." She nods at Jago. He puts his hands up too. "The bike's all yours. I'm just going to take the key out of the ignition. So I can slide it over to you. Cool?"

"Cool." Curly tilts toward the other biker without taking his eyes off them. "I like this one, Misty."

"Me too."

Sarah pulls out the key and wraps her gloved fingers around it. The giant raises the tire iron and takes a step away from the Taurus's passenger-side window. She sees the driver's eyes in the rearview mirror, wide and intense and, oddly, looking straight at her instead of at the man who's about to attack his car. Sarah waits for the right moment, and then instead of sliding the key to Curly she tosses it directly at him.

He fumbles as he instinctively tries to catch it with his knife hand. He fails. At the exact moment that the key hits the ground, the giant smashes the glass and it shatters and rains down onto the pavement. Misty glances at Curly. Jago jumps backward off the bike and draws his blade in one motion. The giant leans into the car and, to his surprise and Sarah's as well, he is *pulled* halfway inside. Something causes the back of his leather vest to tent upward and then it quickly falls, and the giant's legs lift off the ground and shudder and shake. He's dead, his nervous system just doesn't know it yet.

Meanwhile, away from the car, Sarah drops and rolls, her bad arm stinging, as Jago flings his knife, hitting Curly square in the neck. Curly twists away and squeezes the shotgun's trigger, but the blast sprays harmlessly into the air. Curly drops in a heap. The men around the car hoot and yell, and Sarah hears more glass breaking and a lot of cursing from the bikers and she pops up right in front of Misty with a short knife in her hand. He swings a meaty paw in her direction but she ducks under it and jams her fist toward his neck, catching it full bore with the blade. It sinks in four inches, severing everything Misty needs to eat, breathe, and deliver blood to his brain. Sarah whisks the knife free. Misty falls to his knees and brings his hands to his throat and blood spills over them.

Sarah and Jago rush toward the car and draw their pistols. The five bikers on the driver's side have retreated a few steps and hold up their guns. Not aware of what's happening with Sarah and Jago, they fire freely at the car, peppering its side with bullets and, unfortunately for them, masking the sound of the shots that are simultaneously being fired in their direction. Within three seconds Sarah and Jago hit each biker in his unprotected head—they're not wearing helmets either, not that it would matter—the last two facing them, their eyes full of disbelief and a little bit of terror.

Keeping their guns in the ready position, Sarah and Jago advance on the car, Sarah in the lead and Jago half a step behind her. His gun dances from biker to biker, making sure they're well and truly down. Holes perforate the car's side panels and the glass is broken and scattered on the pavement and the seats inside. The giant's head lies across the center console. It took a few shots and it does not look pretty or very head-like. Both tires on this side are flat. The air reeks of cordite. The driver's seat back is fully reclined. A large black mound of cloth takes up what's left of the rear seat.

There's no sign of the driver.

Sarah looks at Jago quizzically.

Where could he be?

But before Jago says anything a voice from under the black mound says, "Sarah?"

She knows that voice. She'd know it if it were whispering under the screams of thousands.

"D-dad?"

The black mound, a bundled pair of ballistic vests, is pushed away. And jutting above these is the beaming face of Simon Alopay.

KEPLER 22B

Teletrans chamber on board Seedrak Sare'en, active geosynchronous orbit above the Martian North Pole

His large hands are immersed in plasmastone—a molten rock-like substance—all the way to his forearms. A three-dimensional map of Earth spins before him, midair. The two Nethinim are at the far end of the room, occupying the transpots. Each has a svelte pack with supplies strapped to his back and each is dressed in a paper-thin jumpsuit that bends and reflects all light, rendering the Nethinim virtually invisible. These suits extend over their long hands and fingers, and are pulled tightly over their heads and silvery hair. A see-through flap can be pulled down to cover their faces, but these are up for now. He looks at their faces. The trace of their braided hair moving back from their foreheads. Their flaring nostrils. Their obedient eyes. He makes final adjustments with his fingers in the plasmastone.

Go, he telesays.

He twists his arms, the far end of the room grows unspeakably frigid, the portals open, shimmery yet dark, like the one that took them to the Great White Pyramid for the Calling. Their suits activate, and the Nethinim all but disappear, their faces floating seven feet above the ground.

Return as soon as you've achieved your objective, he telesays.

Each nods.

Each takes a step backward.

And each disappears completely from the room, and the ship that sits idly in space.

AISLING KOPP, GREG JORDAN, GRIFFIN MARRS

Approaching 45.1646, 98.3167, Govi-Altai Province, Mongolia

"Bum-fuck nowheresville," Jordan says, his feet packing the loose earth one step at a time, his gaze wandering over the high Mongolian desert.

"Yeah," Aisling mutters. "This place is *dead*."

More than anything it reminds her of pictures of Mars she's seen over the years—the planet, not her adopted CIA case officer. She suspects that the sloping land in this part of Mongolia is carpeted in stout green grasses at the end of the wet season—and she sees little clumps of dried plant life here and there to support this—but right now it's reddish-whitish-grayish dirt and pebbles and rocks that culminate in a range of stark but beautiful mountains in the near distance.

Nowheresville, like Jordan said.

Yet, here they are. While Sarah and Jago and Hilal and Shari are all airborne, Aisling and her team have already touched down in Mongolia and are hoofing it to the Donghu monument to search for Sun Key.

The flight from Thailand took a few hours. It was completely uneventful. There was no turbulence, no sign of Abaddon's aftermath, no problem with ground control systems. The only rough things were landing the plane, which they had to do on a long flat expanse of desert a few miles south of a mountain range, and this hike they've embarked upon to get to the target hidden in said mountain range.

Oh, and dealing with Pop.

Aisling had Marrs wake him up before they shoved off. She expected Pop to be groggy and disoriented, but as soon as his eyes opened he pulled at his restraints and his neck muscles trussed his skin and he screamed through his teeth, "Traitor! Traitor! Traitor!"

"Pop!"

"Traitor!" he shouted, picking up right where he'd left off in the bunker in Ayutthaya.

"Hit him with another dose, Marrs," Aisling said quietly. Marrs did and Pop's eyes flagged and his neck relaxed and he slouched. "Shesatraitor, Ais. Donbeonetoo. Dontrussherfriends."

Aisling took one of his hands. "I have to. It's the only way to stop Endgame. Won't you help us?" And then more quietly, "Won't you help me?"

He blinked before saying no.

Aisling hung her head. "I want you to help me, Pop," she said quietly.

"No."

"What else would you have me do?"

"Win."

She looked at the top of Pop's head. Thin white hair, tan scalp, age spots. "Enough of that already, Pop. Abaddon hit. Our home is probably gone. Shit, all of New York City is probably gone. Who knows how many are dead. No one's winning this thing . . . except maybe the kepler."

"Win. win . . . er try to beat tha Maker but on yer own."

She shook her head and held out her hand. "I'll take it," she said to Marrs. He passed her the syringe that was plugged into Pop's IV. She cradled it in her fingers.

"I know wha yer doin, Ais. Why yer doin it."

"No, you don't, Pop." She put her thumb over the plunger. "I'm doing this for everyone. But mostly I'm doing it for you and for Dad. For Declan."

"Fugh me and fugh Declan. Whadideeno?"

She pushed the plunger all the way in. "He knew more than either of us. I'll see you later, Pop. Sweet dreams."

"Fugh Declan an fugh yoo . . ." And then he was gone once more.

They left him belted down in the plane and took off on foot.

According to Hilal, the Donghu monument is located in a cave at

45.1646, 98.3167, 4.3 miles from where they landed. They walked uphill over mostly open land, and then through a crooked arroyo leading up the mountain like a witch's finger. Aisling enjoys the movement, the sweat, the dry and fresh air in her lungs. She enjoys the desolation, too. The sky is grayish blue, undoubtedly filling with some of the ash and gas and water vapor that Abaddon has thrown to the heavens. On the ground there are no scampering animals, no yurts, no horses or riders, and absolutely no regular people trying to figure out what to do after the impact. No people at all as far as she can tell.

It occurs to Aisling that the men and women who live nomadically in this place—including Baitsakhan's line members—might not be affected by Abaddon at all. They're resourceful, they know hardship and deprivation, and they have a long and unbroken history of survival in a harsh environment. So long as Abaddon doesn't completely cover the sky in clouds for years, these Mongolians and others like them across the Eurasian Steppe and down into the 'Stans should be fine.

After about an hour she stops and checks the GPS. "Got a mile left. How do you think we should approach? If Wayland's men are bent on destroying these places, we have to assume they could be here too." She glances across the otherworldly landscape.

Jordan points. "Get on that knoll and see what you can see through the scopes. I'll cover."

"Got it," Aisling says.

She and Marrs drop their packs and scramble up a rocky hill. Aisling sights through her sniper's scope as Marrs works with the range finder and his GPS, scouring the mountainside for the cave's exact position. It takes a few minutes, but then he says, "There. A little to your left . . . two degrees higher . . . That's it."

Aisling peers at Marrs's spot. It doesn't look like much. A fold in the side of the rock face about 10 feet above a shallow canyon floor. Marrs says, "A little farther up the canyon are some steps cut from the stone. They're kind of worn, but they're definitely steps."

"Oh, yeah. I see them." Aisling brings her eye away from the scope. "Doesn't look like anyone's there."

"No."

"Guess there's only one way to find out, huh?"

"Yep."

They keep walking.

They make the cave in under an hour, encountering nothing but more rock and dust and the cool air rolling down the mountainside. In spite of the emptiness Aisling scans the surrounding country the whole time, looking for movement, tracks in the dirt, reflections, any pattern that's out of the ordinary. She sees none. But she knows how easy it would be to camouflage oneself in this place.

Too easy.

Before taking the steps up to a ledge-like path, Aisling pops two canisters of tear gas into the cave mouth—a rough and low semicircle whose sides curve inward like an old man's toothless mouth. The gas pours out of the cave and into it at the same time, the canisters hissing.

No one screams, no one runs out.

Aisling pulls on a gas mask. "All right, let's go." She leads them up the steps, a beige FN SCAR pulled to her shoulder. She walks along the narrow ledge, scanning the walls, the ground, the cave's entrance.

Something catches her eye. A bright silver hairline near her feet. She drops to one knee. Jordan stands over her. "What is it?"

Aisling runs her fingers over the dirt. "I swear I saw something," she says. "Trip wire, maybe."

"Where?"

"Right—there!"

It flashes again. It's curled over the ground, not more than a few inches long. "Not a trip wire. Looks like . . . hair." She picks it up and inspects it. "It *is* hair. *Silver* hair."

Jordan pokes his rifle into the cave.

Aisling stands. "The kepler has silver hair," she says slowly.

Neither Jordan nor Marrs says anything to that. None of them want to run into the alien prematurely.

Aisling stands. "Stay loose and let's move."

She ducks into the entrance, which is less than five feet high. Jordan comes next and then Marrs. They walk through the tear gas in an awkward semicrouch for 15 feet before the cave opens up. Light here is scant, so they flip down the goggles on their helmets and activate their night vision.

The chamber is large and round. There are no prehistoric paintings like in the cave in Italy, no signs of previous occupants like a fire pit or footprints, and no seven-foot-tall aliens waiting for them.

It's just a cave.

Except for the perfect and narrow rectangle cut from the stone 34 feet away.

Aisling hoists her rifle and walks to it carefully, testing each step before putting her weight down, eyeing the ground for booby traps or wires.

She reaches the doorway. The ground slopes sharply on the other side through a passage that's the exact dimensions of the door—8 feet high and 2.5 feet wide. Her eyes run up one side, over the top, and down the other. And there, near the ground, she sees two things that nearly stop her heart.

She kneels. Brushes away a pile of dirt collected in the corner.

And yes. There. A small rune of two snakes twisted together, devouring the other's tail.

"The mark of Endgame. Like on Hilal's book," Aisling says. She points at the other thing. The faintest outline of a shoe print. "Looks like we might not be alone after all."

"Let me see," Jordan says.

They switch places while Aisling scans the rest of the floor inside the chamber. "I don't see any others. Whoever it was was good at erasing tracks. No sweep marks . . . no telltale craters or anything."

"Maybe it was a ghost," Marrs says.

"Maybe," Jordan says.
Aisling pushes forward and disappears through the doorway. This time Marrs is second, and Jordan covers the rear.
Down, down, down, 50 feet, 100, 150. As they descend the air gets cooler and damper. The sounds change, as if the walls are sponges soaking up noise.
At the bottom the tunnel makes an abrupt left turn. Aisling stops. She pulls a small pen-sized periscope from her breast pocket and slides it past the edge of the wall. She looks inside.
The tunnel goes a few more paces and then opens into a hard-angled room. It appears empty.
She stashes the periscope and brings the rifle back up and turns the corner. She steps carefully, never letting her heels touch the ground. She checks her corners. Clear. She steps forward again.
Jordan squeezes her shoulder. She stops. It is very cold here, and the night vision shows that the room is somehow illuminated. She risks flipping her goggles up, and yes, the room's walls glow with a faint blue phosphorescent light. There's a round, bowl-shaped depression in the center of the room, its surface covered with shiny metallic leaf. She pulls out a flashlight and shines its white beam into the bowl.
Gold.
They split up and look around.
The room is shaped like a six-pointed star, with one of the inward-facing points blunt and flat. Another doorway—a portal, it appears—is surrounded by more mysterious glyphs, though she recognizes some as Egyptian and Sumerian and an old version of her line's written language as well. She runs her hands over these. Her breath hangs thick in the air. This portal reminds her exactly of the one set into the Great White Pyramid in the Qin Lin Mountains.
She touches the jet-black stone in the middle of the doorway, half expecting her hand to pass through it.
But it doesn't.
It's rock hard and freezing and her hand recoils from the cold.

"What do you think? Twenty degrees in here? Less?" Aisling asks.

But no one answers. Marrs is too busy searching the opposite side of the room and Jordan inches toward something tucked into one of the corners.

"Come here," he whispers, his voice slithering around in a bit of acoustic gymnastics. "You should see this."

Jordan stares at four tubelike objects. They're the size of people and they're stacked like logs, one on top of the other.

"Holy shit," Aisling says. She tiptoes past him. She shivers. The air near the tubes is well below zero. "kepler 22b stacked us up in these shroud things at the pagoda in Xi'an. He's been here recently."

"What're you talking about?" Jordan asks.

Using the muzzle of her rifle Aisling catches the edge of the nearest tube and lifts it away. The other side of the material is covered with a dark, glittering surface, like a star-filled night sky. Inside the tube is the face of a corpse, his skin blue and pale, his eye sockets large and set farther apart than most people's.

"That looks like one of the guys who stormed Stella's bunker," Aisling says.

Jordan slips the knife between the man's lips and pries his jaw open. He has no tongue.

"A Nethinim. Definitely one of Wayland's guards." Jordan peels back more of the shroud. The man is dressed in full tactical gear, his hands resting on the receiver of a Bushmaster ACR.

"I meant to ask before—why do they not exactly look . . . human?"

"They are human, but Wayland messed with their genetics to make them appear more like Makers. These men were here to destroy this place, Aisling. Like they destroyed Stonehenge and the other monuments too."

"To wit," Marrs says from across the room. "Check it out."

Aisling and Jordan quickly cross the chamber to find Marrs tucked into a star-point near the portal. He's hunched over something, his rifle slung at his side, his hands working in front of him.

"What is it?" Aisling asks, her eyes glancing all around nervously.
"A bomb," Marrs says casually.
"What?"
"Don't worry. It's been disarmed. Strange design. Looks like PETN is the main explosive, but I haven't seen one configured like this before. And here—" He points at a metal panel on the side.
The same glyph that marked the threshold in the room above.
Jordan points at the bomb. "So 22b came down here from wherever he is, killed Wayland's guys, and broke up their bomb. I thought he was only supposed to come back to wrap up Endgame?"
"He was," Aisling says. "Apparently the rules of the game have changed for him too."
Marrs stands and faces them. "Why would he do any of that? Seems risky."
"Because Sun Key is here?" Jordan asks.
Aisling shakes her head slowly. "I don't know. It doesn't look like it. Maybe he took it with him?"
"But why go through the trouble is what I mean," Marrs says.
"It's like Stella and Hilal said—one of these places has Sun Key, therefore 22b can't sit on his thumbs while they're getting blown up by a band of Maker-looking humans loyal to Stella's dead father. So he decided to come here and put a stop to it."
Marrs snaps his fingers. "Aisling—what if Endgame has run so far off the rails for him that he's getting *nervous*?"
This feels like a revelation. Aisling says excitedly, "Yeah . . . What if he feels squeezed by Wayland's demolition crew on one side and us on the other? What if he thinks Endgame won't have a winner, and for some reason that's not acceptable? He could be out there doing whatever it takes to make sure Maccabee is crowned the winner, since Maccabee is the only one interested in winning the way he's supposed to. 22b could be bringing Maccabee Sun Key *right now*, killing whichever other Player he comes across along the way, killing Wayland's men too, interfering even more than he did when—"

Her jaw drops open.

"What?" Jordan asks.

"Fuck."

"What?"

"What if 22b finds our plane? What if he finds Pop? I thought he was safe out there, but . . ."

Aisling doesn't wait. She bolts out of the chamber, Jordan and Marrs following. Up, up, up through the tunnel, outside, off the ledge, double-timing it down the arroyo toward the plane. Aisling is in much better shape and she wants to get her legs into a dead run and Jordan yells, "Go!" and she takes off and within 15 minutes she's not much more than a speck to Jordan and Marrs.

Her pack digs at her shoulders and bounces painfully on the base of her back. Her rifle is heavy and after an hour and 20 minutes her arms are leaden and she has to slow down, but she's a lot closer. She stops for a moment behind a boulder and checks the GPS: 0.74 miles to the plane.

Have a look first, Ais. Fools rush in.

She gets on top of the boulder and surveys the flat section of desert where they landed. The scope zips over the Bombardier and her nerves ease up. It's there. It isn't a smoldering pile of scrap metal. She moves the scope back and finds it and zeroes in.

And then her heart nearly jumps out of her chest and through her shirt.

The plane is where they left it. It's not engulfed in flames. Its tires are fully inflated. Its door is closed.

But its wings are lying on the ground. They have been cut off clean and neat by who knows what and they are lying on the ground.

Aisling spits a string of curses. She puts her eye back to the socket and looks everywhere for 22b but sees no sign of anything. She scans and scans and scans.

She slides down the boulder and paces and breathes and tries to calm her heart and finally after 15 minutes she hears the noisy footsteps of

Jordan and Marrs approaching. She tells them the news.

"And Pop?" Jordan asks, badly concealing his disappointment at losing the plane.

"Don't know," Aisling says, her voice shaking. "I've been waiting for you before going down there. I think you should stay here and cover with the long guns. I'll go alone. You can run if things go south."

Marrs quickly says, "Not alone, Aisling." Jordan charges a round into his rifle in agreement.

She doesn't argue. They strip their gear to the essentials and a few minutes later, as the sun begins to cradle into the horizon, they take off.

They triple-time, guns up the whole way. When they're 500 feet from the plane they fan out, Aisling in the center and Jordan and Marrs 30 feet on either side. She moves up a little so they form a three-point wedge. She looks and looks in the late evening twilight.

Nothing.

They reach the plane. Aisling's heart has never beaten so fast. Marrs gawks at the wings, thinking, *It's as if lasers cut them.*

Aisling indicates the plane's door with her rifle, signaling that she'll cover Jordan while he opens it.

Jordan nods. Marrs moves into a cover position too. The door swings down and the stairs fold out.

More nothing.

Aisling forces her legs forward, her heart in her throat, and bounds silently up the stairs and clears the cockpit and pivots into the cabin. Empty.

Empty except for Pop Kopp. She slides to him, checking behind seats. Clear. She kneels next to him. Feels his arm. Warm. The pulse is there. His breath is good. Yes, he's against everything she's trying to do in Endgame, but he's alive, and that's what matters.

She goes back to the door. "He's all right," she says.

A chill wind blows from the south.

Marrs says, "Good."

And then it gets very cold and a ring-shaped pulse tears the air between the three of them and it hits Marrs in a millisecond and he gets pushed back a few feet as if he's been punched in the chest and then he kind of disappears, leaving a few shreds of cloth and metal and probably skin too but no blood, and all of these pieces blow away and are gone.

Aisling and Jordan fire at will at the spot where the pulse came from. The rounds bounce away and some seem to be absorbed into the air itself, or the dirt, or the rocks, Aisling can't really tell. She breathes out and sees her breath in the chilly air and Jordan shouts, "Fire in the hole!" and he pumps out one, two, three grenades from his launcher, and somehow all three are caught by a huge invisible hand, and they explode, and Aisling hears the explosions, but it's like they went off miles away or underwater, and she can't see them. Not at all.

And then another pulse, this one aimed at Jordan, who fires a fourth grenade at the same moment, and this one does explode as expected and Aisling is thrown backward into the plane and she can't see what's happening to Jordan, if he was vaporized too or blown up or knocked on his ass like her. She kicks her feet in front of her and scoots backward. Her back hits the far side of the cabin and the open door is in front of her and her heart booms all over now, in her temples and toes and armpits. The air shimmers and her feet are like ice and only then does she realize that 22b is invisible and right in front of her!

She presses the trigger and holds it down and the bullets simply hit 22b and slide around him and continue off into space, as if he's Teflon coated.

Her magazine is empty. Her trigger finger aches. Firing the grenade would be suicidal.

But if she's going to die anyway, she might as well try to kill this fucker too.

She applies pressure to the grenade's trigger as the pale face of an alien—not 22b, but one of his kind—appears in front of her like a phantom. And before she can squeeze all the way, the world goes light and dark simultaneously and she's gone.

All she's aware of in that last moment is the cold.

The terrible, terrible, freezing cold.

19h 16m 52.2s[ii]

HILAL IBN ISA AL-SALT, SHARI CHOPRA

Approaching -21.6268, 129.6625, Yuendumu Hinterland, Northern Territory, Australia

Hilal and Shari walk southeast through the red sand grassland of the Australian outback. Nighttime. No people. No moon. No breeze. They weave through stands of mulga trees and creep around mounds of grassy spinifex, some of which look like earthbound corals. They walk silently, listening to the clicks and coos of insects and bats and other small animals plying the night for food and shelter.

The stars are out, and they are brilliant. The duo's eyes have adjusted from the inside of the plane, which they left 4.7 kilometers to the north, and the starlight is all they need.

Hilal has been to the southern hemisphere many times—to the bush of Zimbabwe and Mozambique and Botswana—but he has never seen stars like this.

He would talk to Shari about the stars if she had not ordered him to be silent before they set out for the ancient Koori monument. "I am angry beyond angry at you, Aksumite."

He did not argue with her. If he were in her position it would take every ounce of his will not to slaughter him where he stands.

But the stars. If he could talk he would point out Achernar, a few degrees above the horizon, the final star in the wandering constellation of Eridanus. Next to it, rising from the earth itself, the Phoenix takes wing. And to their right is Acrux, the bright white star that anchors the Southern Cross. From this constellation he arches his head back and follows the glowing swath of innumerable pinpricks and pink and blue and yellow clouds that stitch the heart of the Milky

Way together. There is the Centaur, and Lupus the hound, and Norma and Circinus and Ara, and directly overhead are Scorpius and the archer, Sagittarius. Between these are the thickest and brightest star clouds, marking the center of our galaxy, 26,092 light-years away. If he were speaking to his companion he would spin around and point his machetes toward Vega, which glows brightly, even through the Abaddon dust that begins to sully the northern and western skies. This star belongs to the constellation Lyra, and flying next to it is the long-necked swan, Cygnus.

He would talk about all of them.

Of course Shari is probably equally enthralled and knowledgeable. Maybe she looks up and places her departed loved ones among the stars. Certainly she hopes that she can save her Little Alice from returning to these stars.

For that is where they will ultimately return, just as it is from where they ultimately came.

To the stars. From the stars. Like every atom of every thing.

Shari is 10 paces in front of him and she comes to a sudden stop. Hilal cocks an ear but only hears the same thriving nocturnal buzz of the bush that has accompanied them since the plane.

Before leaving their Bombardier Global 8000, they consulted Wayland's book to see if any ancient monuments had been destroyed or otherwise affected by Abaddon. The book showed that the Olmec monument had indeed been damaged, as well as the Minoan monument, which was curious since it was so far from the impact zone. Hilal reasoned that perhaps Wayland's brotherhood had reached it and converted it to ruins.

Shari didn't appear to care.

"All I want is to see my daughter and hold her in my arms."

Again, Hilal could not argue with that.

But he is not thinking about that right now. He wonders what Shari senses as they stand stock-still in the Australian outback. She carries a holstered Glock 20 and pistol-grip Mossberg 500 Cruiser tactical shotgun. Hilal clutches a suppressed Colt M4 Commando in his right hand and the machete named *LOVE* in his left. The other machete is sheathed on his hip. He also carries Wayland's book in his pack. It is too precious to leave anywhere.

Shari kneels and runs her fingers over the dirt. She inches forward without standing. Hilal doesn't move. The ground underfoot slopes toward a dense thicket of wanderrie wattle that they can't see past. Shari points at the ground, running her finger in a straight line.

Hilal sees it. Two grooves etched in the parched dirt, joining in a point at Shari's feet. The grooves run as straight as arrows, the angle between them appearing to be exactly 60 degrees. Inside these lines is the gnarled and dense shrub, outside is sand and earth.

"It is in there," Hilal whispers. "We need to find the entrance."

Shari holds out her shotgun, indicating that she wants Hilal to take the lead. He does this without thinking twice. He knows that a large part of Shari wants him dead, and he will not fault her at all if she decides to strike him down.

He will accept it as a price paid.

But she does not strike him down.

He walks due south, toward the Large Magellanic Cloud seeping over the horizon like a milk stain. The two Players curve around the edge of dense wattle. Hilal sees that the grooves in the ground depict a star, such as one would find on the Seal of Solomon, roughly 30 meters in diameter. As they reach the northern side of this star the earth rises on their left to head height, forming an amphitheater for the star shape, and when they reach the northern star-point they find a low but clear path through the plantlike wall.

They will have to crawl.

Hilal takes off his pack and disappears into the thicket. Shari follows him immediately.

Half a minute later they emerge not in a star-shaped interior, but in a 15-meter circle created by the foliage. They stand on the edge of this circle, shoulder to shoulder, and Hilal is almost afraid to step forward.

Both he and Shari know that they are in a sacred place.

Luckily, they appear to be the only ones there. No members of Wayland's brotherhood. No Koori men and women guarding it.

Strangely, the sounds of the outback that were so present outside the thicket are nonexistent here. The breeze that brushed over their faces from the west is gone. The fine sand underfoot is pebble- and rock-free and has recently been swept by a rake, making a pattern of centimeter-wide concentric circles whose center is the ancient and gnarled trunk of a dead tree. This rises two meters from a bowl-shaped depression. The inside of the bowl appears to be coated in a metallic substance.

"This is the place Stella told me about," Hilal whispers. He steps forward. The ridges and valleys of the circles drawn in the ground are flattened and rearranged into a bootprint. Hilal adjusts his grip on the machete named *LOVE*. Shari stays rooted to her spot.

A sudden sound overhead, like the wind has picked up. The air grows perceptibly colder. A dark flicker like a bird taking wing at eye-level. Hilal raises his machete and wheels, and Shari spins in a semicircle, flashing her shotgun, but both are caught off guard as the bush itself comes to life.

Hilal is grabbed at each wrist and his arms are yanked outward, like Christ on the cross. He tries to kick, but a snare has jumped from the dirt and encircled his ankles. Strong hands twist his weapons backward, forcing him to release them. His other machete is lifted out of its sheath, and just like that he is unarmed. He is bound, his back brushing up against the coarse leaves of the shrub.

He would call out to warn Shari, but he can see that she is already similarly incapacitated.

All of this happens in less than three seconds, and all of it without a sound save that of a few rustling branches and their leaves.

Hilal feels a warm breath on his neck. A blade—one of his own—flashes below his face and he feels the hairline metallic edge grace his Adam's apple.

"Wait," Hilal says.

The metal pushes into his flesh.

"Kill me if you must, but please spare the other. Shari Chopra is her name. The Harappan. She was friends with Alice Ulapala, your line member. Shari is mother to Sky Key. She deserves the chance to see her daughter again."

The metal pushes in more. Hilal feels a bead of warm blood trickle down his neck and settle in his suprasternal notch.

"Stop," a raspy female voice says.

The blade is removed. Hilal would fall if the hands restraining him did not prop him up.

A diminutive elderly woman in jeans and a dark windbreaker stands next to the tree trunk, her hands thrust into her jacket's pockets. Her head is wrapped in a white bandanna, her face is pudgy and round, its skin crumpled, her nose turnip-like, her eyes bright and beady. Flanking her are two large figures, presumably men, dressed head to toe in branches and leaves. They look like living bushes. Hilal scans the circle and now understands that the entire interior was lined with these unspeaking sentinels. Three stand around him, and two around Shari, who kneels on his right, her arms also pulled wide, a knifepoint dimpling her temple.

The old woman waves at Shari. "Easy," she says. The knife retreats.

"Show me Chopra's face," the old woman says with a broad Australian accent.

A light shines on Shari. She blinks.

"That's her." The woman pokes out her blunt chin. The light goes off. "I seen you in the Dreaming. Seen your daughter too," the old Koori says. "Been watching yours since Alice zoned in on her. I seen both you and your daughter when Alice died."

"Where is Little Alice?" Shari demands.

"Dunno. Wish I did. Truly."

Pause.

"I was there," Shari says slowly. "In that dream. I saw Alice die, too."

"That's the Dreaming all right. You and yours were there like me. Difference was I went there on purpose, whereas you two ended up there on account of, I'm thinking what I'll call your *innate* abilities. That or luck."

"It is never auspicious to see a friend die," Shari says as much to herself as to the old woman.

"Good words," the elder says approvingly.

Shari shakes her head. "You've seen me before, then?"

"Yeah."

"I haven't seen you, though."

"Nope."

Shari says, "I . . . don't understand . . ."

"You tried to save Alice from that little Donghu brute—remember that?"

"When I saw her die?"

"That's right, Shari. But while it looked and felt like a dream, it also happened to be—"

"Real," Shari says, her eyes cast to the ground.

"Yeah," the old woman says, her voice low and sad.

"I'm sorry. I tried—"

"Weren't nothing you could do. Me neither. We were like ghosts. That's the Dreaming for you."

"I would have helped her if I could," Shari says quietly.

"And me too. Like I said, that's the Dreaming for you."

Hilal says, "Madam, I am sure that I do not understand any of this."

The old woman says, "No, you wouldn't."

"She's related to Alice," Shari explains to Hilal. "I'm guessing."

"You're guessing right."

Shari continues, "Alice and I had a connection. I can't explain it, but it was there. It was real."

Hilal says, "I see. Madam, may I ask your name?"

"Sure you could *ask*." She snickers. "Don't have to answer, though.

But since Alice and Shari were mates, I'll tell ya. Name's Jenny. Jenny Ulapala. Gram to Alice, among a couple dozen others. Elder scion of the Koori line, even out here in Yuendumu, where our Warlpiri sisters and brothers keep themselves and the land."

"My name is Hilal ibn Isa al-Salt, the—"

"I know—the Aksumite. And she's the Harappan. The one who lost her daughter for no damn good reason that I can fathom."

"Don't kill me, Mrs. Ulapala," Shari says a little out of the blue.

"Not planning on it," Jenny says.

The guards release Shari's restraints. The knife that was pressed to her head disappears into a sheath.

The old woman says, "Not sure about you, though. What do you say, Shari?"

Hilal's heart skips a beat. Shari has found a new ally. She might not need him anymore.

Hilal would plead for mercy, but he knows it would be unbecoming. He also understands that, from Shari's perspective, he more than deserves her wrath. He was the one who revealed her line's secret fortress to the other Players, who used that information to kill nearly all of them.

"He . . ." Shari says. "He . . . I want him dead."

"All right," the old woman says.

The blade returns to Hilal's neck and presses into the nick that was made moments before. More blood trickles down his skin.

He closes his eyes. He does not want death, but he will accept it.

"But you should not kill him," Shari says at the last moment.

Hilal's eyes shoot open, Jenny flicks her hand, the knife moves away, his life is spared.

For now.

"I suppose I will need all the help I can get to see my daughter again," Shari explains. "I would rather use your guilt to that end, Hilal, than succumb to base revenge."

Hilal lets out a quiet sigh of relief. "Understood. And I am grateful, Shari."

A moment passes. The stars turn.

Jenny says, "I'm curious. Abaddon is down. My Player is gone. Why are the two of you here, together?"

"Because we have seen enough of Endgame," Shari says. "We do not want it anymore. The lines don't deserve it, and the people of Earth don't deserve it either."

"And we are here because we want to find her daughter," Hilal says with as much sincerity—because he *is* sincere—as he can muster. "We want to stop Endgame, Mrs. Ulapala. Shari and the Cahokian and the Olmec and the La Tène want this as well. We are working together. We do not Play for what the Makers wanted us to Play for. Not anymore."

Jenny frowns but she has clearly listened carefully. "What do you Play for, then?"

"Many have gone to the stars today," Hilal says. "I do not know the magnitude of Abaddon's destruction, but I feel that it is great. Now we Play to save lives. To prevent more from returning to the stars. Together we can achieve this. We have power and we have knowledge. We even have something that belonged to the Makers."

"Whachya mean?"

"It is in my pack," Hilal says.

"He's telling the truth," Shari says.

"If there's something in your pack you'll have to get it yourself, Aksumite." One of his machetes whips down on the cord around his left wrist and it is free. A guard gingerly holds open his pack at arm's length. "No malarkey," Jenny says. Hilal feels the cold ring of a gun barrel pressed to the back of his head, behind where his ear used to be.

"None," Hilal says. "I swear it."

He reaches, feels the cold edge of the book, and slowly pulls it free.

"It is merely a book. A Maker book from the first days. I invite you to inspect it." He holds it by one of the covers and lets it fall open. "It is harmless."

Jenny leans forward. "Bring it here."
The guard drops the pack, takes the book, and walks to Jenny. The gun stays pressed to Hilal's head. His skin warms the metal.
The guard holds the book open in both hands. Jenny turns its pages slowly. She leans forward. Squints. Shines a light on it. After a few moments she glares at Hilal. "Where did you get this?"
"From a man named Wayland Vyctory."
Jenny grunts. Hilal guesses that she knows who this man is. "You read this book already?" Jenny asks.
"What? No," Hilal says. "I cannot."
"And you, Shari?"
Shari shakes her head.
"Can *you*?" Hilal asks.
Jenny takes the book from the guard and shoos him aside. She continues to leaf through the pages. "You have all heard of the Mu, have you not?"
"Of course," Hilal says. "Their Player was exemplary by all accounts."
"They like to claim their line's the first, only 't'ain't true. Oh, their line is old—going back twenty, twenty-five thousand years and more than any of yours. But my line, *we're* the oldest. My people been walking these lands on foot and in the Dreaming for forty, fifty, sixty thousand years. That's when the Baiame—the Makers—first came down and met with *us*. *We're* the original line. We just don't like to brag about it."
"Chiyoko did not brag," Hilal points out.
Jenny says, "Good on her . . ." Uneasy silence falls as Jenny continues to peruse the pages. "Flames above, do you know what this is, Players?"
"What?" Shari asks.
Jenny smirks. "It's an instruction manual. Called *Domination*, roughly translated. Here are some section headings, and these are only guesses, because their language is very odd: 'Explaining Flight to Earth Beings,' 'Modern Deification,' 'Images and Idols,' 'Metals Primer,' 'Genetic Lines of Establishment,' 'Fear for the Sake of Good.' It goes on and on."

Hilal brims with excitement. That there is a person alive who can decipher this text is magnificent.

He can tell by her voice that Shari feels the same. "Mrs. Ulapala," she says respectfully, urgently, "*will you help us*?"

Jenny closes the book and tucks it under her arm casually. She takes a step back. "Let 'em go, boys. Keep their weapons. One false move and kill, no questions."

Their bindings come free, the gun is removed from Hilal's head. Shari is pulled to her feet. Jenny retreats another step into the shadow of the old tree trunk.

"What're you here to do?"

"Try to find Sun Key before the Nabataean does," Shari says.

"He alone Plays the way the Makers want," Hilal says. "He has the first two keys. He is close to winning."

Jenny nods slowly. "I know. I seen as much in the Dreaming. It's why we're here guarding this place now. To make sure the Nabataean didn't claim his prize."

"We're also here to save my child," Shari says, her voice measured and firm.

Jenny smacks her lips. "There are no guarantees there, Shari. Like any of us, your daughter could die a thousand different ways in the next day or week. But I am glad to hear you're lookin' for her. Big Alice would be glad too."

"Thank you," Shari says.

Jenny's shoulders slacken. "Too much violence these days, if you ask me. Since I got properly old I kinda soured on Endgame. I been telling the Koori about it for a while, but I've always been a bit of an odd bird." The bush-covered guards retreat to the edge of the circle as if on cue and seem to disappear. "Listen, now. I have a proposition like. And it will require a thing much more hard to come by than violence."

"Trust," Hilal says.

Jenny dips her head in his direction. "Trust, Aksumite. Line to line, human to human." Then, her head slowly turns to Shari. "And, most importantly, mother to mother."

The stars turn overhead. The Milky Way pulses with an untold amount of life, even if it is cold and distant and unobservable. Hilal can feel it.

"I'll help you. And together we'll try to Dream Little Alice Chopra right on back into her mother's arms."

The air grows warmer, and Hilal again hears the breeze, where before he heard nothing of the world.

Jenny grins kindly at Shari. The old woman only has a few teeth left.

"We'll get you your girl, mum," Jenny says. "Promise."

SARAH ALOPAY, JAGO TLALOC, SIMON ALOPAY

Monks Mound, Collinsville, Illinois, United States

Sarah holds on to her father so, so tightly. She can't breathe.

Excitement. Relief. The improbable—no, the *impossible*—good fortune of crossing paths with him.

And judging by how tightly Simon holds on to her, he feels exactly the same way.

After several moments Jago clears his throat. Sarah eases up on her embrace and Simon pulls away from his daughter, holds her by the shoulders. Jago looks this way and that, watching for any movement on the horizon, his gun reloaded and ready.

"What did you do to your hair?" Simon whispers, staring into his daughter's eyes.

"Disguise. After the Shang showed us in his video."

"Of course. With Abaddon and Yellowstone and everything else, I'd actually forgotten about that video."

"It's all kind of overwhelming, isn't it?"

"I can't imagine what it's like back east," Simon says.

"Me either. Don't want to, frankly."

"It is hell, we all know it," Jago interjects.

Simon's gaze shifts to Jago. His eyebrows scrunch. "And you are?"

"Jago Tlaloc. The Olmec. Sarah's . . . friend."

Simon steps back defensively and puts a hand on a black pistol holstered to his hip. Jago doesn't flinch. Sarah claps her hand on top of Simon's gun hand, squeezes his knuckles. "It's all right. He *is* my friend. He's saved my life more than once. He's here to help."

Simon's eyes dart back and forth—Sarah, Jago, Sarah, Jago—as he tries to decipher what's happening. "Why are you *here*?" Simon asks Sarah. "Do you have the keys? Are you ready to end it?"

"No. It's a long story, but basically we're here because we need to find the third key. According to some people who seem to know, it could be hiding in there." She points at the grass-covered hill that is Monks Mound.

"Sun Key's in there?" Simon says. "I've been in there a hundred times. Sun Key is not in there."

"We still have to look," Sarah says. "If we have any chance of stopping Endgame then we have to find it. It's the best chance we have at surviving. And by 'we' I mean humanity, Dad. All of us. You. Me. Jago. Pricks like these," she motions to the bikers littered around their feet. "Mom . . ." Her face goes white.

"She's fine, Sarah."

"Omaha?" she asks.

"No. The farm. She's there with your uncles and Aunt Millicent and also a few neighbors from home. We couldn't leave them behind to fend for themselves. We brought the Smithsons and the Nixes and the—"

"Vanderkamps?" she asks, a big part of her hoping he'll say, *No, not the Vanderkamps.*

"Yeah, the Vanderkamps too," Simon says. "I thought they would hole up at one of their ranches, but they didn't want to be alone. Especially not after, well . . ."

"What?"

"It's Christopher. He . . . disappeared. Not long after you left. I'm sorry, Sarah."

She falters. Jago reaches out and touches her arm.

I'm going to have to tell them. His parents. I'm going to have to tell them what I did to their son.

"I'm sorry," Simon repeats. He can tell something isn't right, but he doesn't press.

"It's okay," Sarah says.

Jago peers to the east. "A car's coming. We should move."

"Yeah, of course." She holds out her hands. "Dad, will you come with us? Will you help?"

"Search the mound for Sun Key?" he asks.

"Yes," she says. "But before that, we need to do something else."

"Sarah, come *on*," Jago says urgently. He points through the haze. A pair of bright halogen lights is headed right for them, but not with any apparent urgency. "Probably nothing to worry about, but we *are* standing in the middle of a murder scene. No point in asking for more trouble."

"Agreed. We didn't come here to kill people," she says, as much to herself as to Jago. *That was so easy,* she thinks of killing the bikers. *Too easy. If I really am going to get back my humanity, I need to work harder at sparing people. Even people like these.* Especially *people like these.*

"Are our line members at the welcome center?" Sarah asks her father.

"No. I told them to be with their families before the impact. I told them I was on my way here and that they weren't needed anymore."

"Good," Sarah says. "Get the bike, Jago." He pivots and runs to the Harley. "Let me help you with your passenger, Dad."

She moves around the Taurus and takes one of the giant's ankles with her good hand. Simon takes the other. They heave in unison, pulling hard on over 270 pounds of dead weight. But Sarah and her father are strong, and they get the giant out of the car. What's left of his head makes a sickening *smack-pop-hiss* when it hits the pavement.

Jago pulls up next to them. "Go to the welcome center," Sarah shouts over the bike's engine, indicating a building off the main road to the south. Jago guns the bike and leaves them. Simon slips around the front of the car and gets behind the wheel while Sarah climbs into the backseat, where the seats are blood-free.

"We're going to stop Endgame, Dad." She speaks quickly, hoping Simon won't interrupt her. "We're working with other Players and some CIA guys. A woman named Stella Vyctory was helping us too, but she was killed. The Makers may have been gods to us once, but not anymore. They're frauds. Maybe we all are."

She takes a breath and holds it. *Here it comes.* She expects him to rail against her, to remind her of their history, of her training, of the honor of being named and molded into a Player, of her dead brother, of her dead friends, of her destroyed school, of the old stories and the rituals and the rites and *ahama muhu gobekli mu, ahaman jeje, ahaman kerma.*

And while she waits for it she remembers what she said on that commencement stage in the sun, right before the meteors came, when she was still young and innocent as well.

I choose to be the person that I want to be, she'd said. Those words felt so meaningless after finding Earth Key, and then again so true as she chose not to kill Sky Key.

What a fucking ride it's been, she thinks, waiting for Simon to light into her.

Except he doesn't.

She looks in the rearview mirror and finds her father's eyes. He looks at her, not the road. Jago banks the bike into a parking lot in front of them. Simon blinks. He follows the Harley.

Sarah leans into the front half of the car. "Dad, why are *you* here?"

"Because I'm scared, Sarah."

"Of what?"

"Maybe of what you're hinting at."

"The Makers . . ."

Simon shrugs. "At the worst, yes. But also of people. Of uncertainty. Of *that.*" He tilts his head to the east, to Abaddon. "Let's not kid ourselves. None of us ever thought we'd see it. No Player or trainer really does, and now that I *have* seen it I understand why we thought we never would."

He pulls next to Jago in a handicap spot right next to the entrance. Jago is already off the bike and stalking to the welcome center, gun up,

to clear it of anyone else who might be hanging around.
A crack of bright lightning near the mound. A loud clap of thunder shakes the car. A gust of cold wind.
Simon runs his hands nervously over the top of the steering wheel. "Why am I here? Because once Abaddon happened all I could think of was keeping what's left of my family and my friends safe, and—" The corners of his mouth crumple. His eyes well. "You look so much older, Sarah."
She touches his cheek. "You too, Dad."
"Grown-up, huh?"
"I guess. Mostly just fucking exhausted, mentally and physically."
"Me too. Maybe that's all it means to be grown-up."
Pause.
"I'm so glad I found you," Simon says. "Me and your mother, not an hour has passed since you've left that we haven't spoken of you. We think about you always. Hoped you were alive, hoped you were Playing, or at least surviving."
"You trained me well."
"I know. Now I understand why. It wasn't because I wanted Endgame or even cared for the prophecy, if you can believe it. It was because I wanted to protect you. You'd been chosen and I wanted to give you the tools you'd need to survive, whether the prophecy came true or not. But lucky us . . ."
"Yeah, lucky us."
Jago emerges from the welcome center, giving a thumbs-up.
Simon grabs one of Sarah's hands. "I came here to get the weapon, Sarah. The one the stories tell of, the one the Makers gave us and showed us how to use. If I'm going to continue to protect the ones I love, then your mom and I thought we should have it."
"No shit," Sarah says.
Simon doesn't understand.
"I'm not being flip, Dad. The weapon? That's why we're here too. If

we're going to ever cross paths with a Maker—and before this thing is through, we might—then we want it too."

Simon smiles wanly. "I really *did* train you well."

Jago raps a knuckle on the passenger window. Simon rolls it down.

Jago leans in. "Done catching up?"

"More or less," Sarah says.

Jago looks at Simon. "You going to help us, Señor Alopay?"

Simon reaches for Sarah's shoulder and kneads it lovingly.

His thin smile melts away as his eyes darken. "Let's get our gun."

Event 17[iii]

AISLING KOPP, POP KOPP, KEPLER 22B

Seedrak Sare'en, active geosynchronous orbit above the Martian North Pole

Sssssup!

Aisling can't see but she can hear.

Her head swims, her eyes flutter, her quads twitch, her fingers clench into fists. She feels light and upside-down and twisted and her stomach turns and she strains forward to let it out but her entire body—stretched long from head to toe, her arms pressed to her sides—is locked in place.

The vomit comes anyway. Her last meal and some cashew nuts and water and bile. Mostly bile. The vomit doesn't fall onto her shirt or her shoes or across her face. It doesn't linger on her lips, she doesn't have to lick it away, it doesn't get stuck in her nose or entangled in her hair. She realizes that that sucking sound has whisked the vomit away. She realizes that her face is covered with something—a mask, a skin, a device, she's not sure what. She tries to turn her head but can't. She tries to move her legs but can't. She tries to scream but can't. The intent is there, the neurons are firing, the synapses are transmitting, the axons and dendrites are twinkling, the brain is converting her disorientation into fear, but there is no release, no flight, no fight.

Because she can't.

There is only her body, and her clouded mind, and the darkness, and her fear.

And more bile.

Sssssup!

Gone.

An electric pulse shoots through her body, from bottom to top. She senses it most in her toes and behind her knees and under her triceps and at the base of her neck and then at the tip of her tongue. In a fit of synesthesia she experiences the pulse as color and taste. Blue at first, bursting and bright, imploding from the edge and flying toward the center and consuming everything. The blue spikes with fingers of red then purple then orange and then a blob of green that eats all the other colors away. While these kaleidoscope through her visual cortex, her taste buds are subjected to an onslaught of milky sweetness, to the point of being disgusting, and she retches again and vomits whatever might be left in her stomach into the tube.

Sssssssup.

She flicks her tongue and finds that it's blocked by something, that it can't reach her teeth or her gums, and in this instant she realizes that a tube has been inserted into her mouth, and her tongue is inside the tube. She swallows and feels an extension of the tube in her throat. And then a thought forms—the first not dedicated to her body or her senses or to her primal fear.

Where am I?

For some indeterminate amount of time she is unsure. She remembers Mongolia perfectly—Marrs's vaporization, Jordan's last volley, the cool face of the kepler who wasn't 22b, the frigid air that enveloped her—but there is nothing after that. She is a prisoner, of that she has no doubt, but where, and what exactly, is her cell?

An inkling of an answer comes when she finally discerns something. Several feet from her face the light changes, and she makes out the hazy contours of a ceiling. It is curved and reflective and liquidy. Wisps of white and yellow trace across it, and a tuft of red and a fun-house mirror blob of blue. A reflection. She squints through the film covering her face and understands that the red is her hair, and the tube is her body, shrink-wrapped in an unknown material.

She tries to move again but can't. It's not so much that she's being restrained as it is that her body simply doesn't work. Her toes and her tongue and her eyeballs in their sockets can move when she wills them to, but none very well.

She strains to look in as many directions as possible. She eventually sees that another form is some distance to her left, topped by white instead of red. This must be Pop. Her fear is nearly all-consuming, tinged with a small offering of relief in this moment. She is not completely alone. Pop is not dead. Or if he is, his body is intact.

Maybe I am dead, she half thinks. *Certainly as good as dead.*

There is nothing else. Seconds or minutes or hours or days pass. She can't tell. The slivers of color on the ceiling change now and then, like a psychedelic dream. Something shoots through the tube and passes tastelessly over her tongue and passes directly into her stomach. Food. The electrical pulses tickling her body come and go. She is powerless, and afraid, but she settles into her predicament as best she can. What else can she do?

She drifts here and there and in and out and then . . .

Then . . .

Then . . .

Her eyes tear up and shoot open and in front of her is not the ceiling or the wall but the unmistakable face of kepler 22b, lithe and blue and cold.

The alien busies its hands over her body, tending to unseen controls. His dark eyes are blank, his mouth slightly agape. She tries to make a noise but it's useless. kepler 22b certainly doesn't make any noises. He does whatever he does and lifts away, apparently satisfied. Aisling's mind begins to cloud again. She's been injected with something. The sickly sweet taste returns. kepler 22b spins away and speaks—no, he doesn't speak, he thinks. Aisling can hear his words not as language but as ideas, clear and completely comprehensible.

She is strong, and the grandfather holds on. Both survived the transport. We hope the other two will survive as well. We hope we can retrieve our weapon.

It cannot hurt that we have more Player-hostages, Nethinim. More will be better.

SARAH ALOPAY, JAGO TLALOC, SIMON ALOPAY

Monks Mound, Collinsville, Illinois, United States

Sarah and Jago follow Simon along the groomed walking paths that loop around the smaller hillocks south of Monks Mound, and then beat a track through a stand of leafy hardwoods. Each wears a respirator and goggles and carries a compact M4—Jago's with an M203 grenade launcher—and a blade.

Simon consults a small laminated map the size of a credit card.

Although it's midday it looks and feels like a cloudy evening, one where a storm is on the horizon or has just passed. And while they know the sun is high overhead, the yellow disc is blotted out by the ash and gas choking the atmosphere. The lights of houses and buildings in the middle distance are extinguished, the power still out. People are somewhere out there, huddled inside and confused, but for now these three Endgamers are alone.

Sarah is glad for that. She's had enough of other people for one day.

They head south for half a mile and hit the Conway rail tracks running east to west. No train cars block their path. They skirt over the steel bands and leave the boundary of the state park, jogging over an open and rough field, the settled Yellowstone ash padding their footfalls.

They don't speak. Jago watches the countryside like a hawk, and Sarah watches Jago. She trusts him to safeguard them, but she's not sure what he might say about this Cahokian rebellion that the Olmec elder told him about. She hopes he says nothing. They're here to do a job, not to talk fuzzy ancient history.

They pass a few squat maples and round some overgrown bluffs that belonged to the ancient pre-Columbian city that once flourished on this Mississippian flood plain. Taken with Monks Mound, the 109 mounds of this city formed the heart of a thriving Mesoamerican metropolis that was as large and populous as any in the Americas, from the Bering Strait to Cape Horn. In fact, the city that grew around the mounds, with as many as 40,000 people at its height, was *the* largest city in North American history until Philadelphia surpassed it in the mid-1780s, long after any cultural trace of the Cahokian people had disappeared from the record books.

Long after their line's secrets were moved and dispersed and hidden from the prying eyes of Europeans and other Native American clans. Long after the Cahokians retreated in order to stay better prepared for Endgame.

"A little over half the mounds are in the state park," Simon says, pulling to a stop in a patch of thigh-high switch grass. He turns in a semicircle and tucks his map into a breast pocket. His voice is muffled and hollowed out by his respirator. "The rest are scattered. The one we're looking for is so eroded that you wouldn't recognize it as anything significant." He slides a metal bracelet down his arm, folding his hand through its circle and yanking it off. He swings it in an arc, like he's using it to dowse for water.

A dirty drizzle falls, a chill wind blows from the north. Rain streaks their goggles and clothing. Sarah shivers as the wind touches an exposed section of her neck. Another lightning strike near Monks Mound. They swing around to look, but it's lightning, nothing more.

Simon resumes his search for the hidden mound. He walks slowly, heel to toe, measuring distance. The bracelet guides him.

Sarah and Jago inch along a few paces behind. Out of the blue, Jago says, "Obviously Sarah's told me of this weapon, Señor Alopay. But I'm very curious."

"Yes?" Simon says, concentrating on his search.

Shit, Sarah thinks. The tops of the trees on the other side of the tracks bend and sway in their direction. The drizzle turns to light rain. She unclips a ball cap from her belt and puts it on over her raven-dyed hair, pulling the brim tight to the goggles to keep them dry. *Please don't say it,* she thinks.

"What does it do exactly?" Jago asks. "And why did your line hide it? Why not keep it and use it? That's what the Olmec line would've done if we'd been given such a gift."

Simon pauses. He tilts toward Jago. "Our people buried it because it's powerful, Jago Tlaloc. The books say that it can light the heavens, and that it can kill Makers. Did my people ever try to do that? Not to my knowledge. To be honest, I don't know if it's real, or if it'll work. It's been buried for a long time. As to *why* we hid it, I assume it was because my ancestors were afraid of it. It is a weapon that belonged to Them. And the Makers were to be feared. Surely your people share this fear."

Jago says, "Of course. But how did the Cahokians get it in the first place? Did they steal it?"

Sarah reaches up and flicks the back of Jago's ear. He flinches and gives her a look that says, *Okay, okay!*

Simon stops again. "All I know is that it's supposed to be buried . . . here!" Simon does a little prestidigitation with the metal ring, and right before their eyes it's standing on its narrow edge in the palm of his hand, as if propped up by invisible forces.

He goes on one knee and works his fingers through the thick grass, parting it like hair. "Help me look," Simon says. "The marker's an oblong stone in the shape of an eye and about the size of a fist. This ring is a kind of key. It will open any important chamber in this ancient city. This one, and the one up there." He tips his head toward Monks Mound to the north.

Sarah gets on the ground several feet away from Simon. Jago picks a spot and does the same. Sarah's goggles are fogging, so she lifts them from her eyes and pulls them over the top of her hat. She works the fingers of her good hand through the grass and over the dirt.

They search for a couple minutes with no luck.

Jago straightens, scanning their surroundings. No sign of anyone. Just more dirty rain, probably acidic and toxic, and more cold air blowing in from the north. "You sure it's here, señor?"

"I'm sure," Simon says. "When I lapsed, my father brought me to this very spot and showed me the rock. He didn't know much about the weapon either, except that it was buried and that it should only be unearthed in extreme circumstances."

"You mean if Endgame actually began," Sarah says.

"That was the gist of it, yeah. We saw the rock and went back to the park. Had a picnic by the train tracks. Counted empty coal cars as they lumbered by, headed back to West Virginia."

Sarah crawls forward and is surprised when her left knee digs into something hard. She moves over and uses her hands and, yes. "Here!" she says.

A black and smooth stone—completely out of place in this non-volcanic part of the world—shaped like an Egyptian hieroglyphic eye.

"That's it!" Simon exclaims. He puts the bracelet next to the stone and works his fingers around its edges and pries it free. The dirt underneath is wet and buggy, worms corkscrew and writhe as they dive into the safety of the earth. Simon ignores them and digs in, pushing the dirt away and severing some unlucky worms with his fingernails. After a minute another hunk of sleek black rock is revealed at the bottom of a 12-inch hole. The rain intensifies. The ash coating everything washes from the leaves and the grass and their clothing. The water also helps Simon clean off the rock, and now Sarah sees that in its surface is a rounded indentation about two inches deep.

An indentation that is a perfect match for the bracelet.

Simon fits the bracelet into the slot. It slides into place and he wraps his fingers around it and turns it 37 degrees. A click and a hiss. He lets go and pulls away.

But nothing happens.

A flicker in Sarah's periphery and she hoists her rifle reflexively, aiming north toward the tracks and beyond at the rain-lashed trees.

"What is it?" Simon and Jago ask.

Sarah squints through the rain. "Thought I saw something but it's . . . Eh, it's only the wind in the trees."

They return their attention to the vessel peeking from the ground. Jago says, "Why isn't—" but is cut short by a rumble underfoot. All three dance defensively. Sarah and Jago think anxiously of Stonehenge, of how it morphed and grew around them after the disk activated the monument, of how Chiyoko was crushed by accident.

But this time nothing so dramatic happens. The rumbling lasts a few moments and instead of a glass-and-stone monstrosity rising from the ground it is nothing more than a simple black pillar, seven feet tall and three feet in diameter, the bracelet rooted to the top.

From where they stand the thing appears solid, with no recess or door that might hold this ancient weapon.

Simon walks around the pillar, letting his fingertips trail over its glassy surface. When he gets to the far side his eyes widen and he makes a sound that's equal parts relief and wonder.

Sarah and Jago join him. The pillar has a recess covered by a clear glass panel. Simon touches this and it swings open, revealing a fist-sized metal object shaped like a lump of malformed clay. The only indication that it might have any purpose are three finger-sized holes running through one side and a cradle for a thumb on its top.

Simon takes it, carefully inserting his fingers through the holes. It fits in his hand perfectly.

"It looks like a paperweight, not a death ray," Jago says.

Simon points the thing away from the Players and angles it toward the ground and taps his thumb into the cradle, expecting it to act as a switch or trigger. But nothing happens.

Jago shrugs and reaches on top of the pillar, popping out the bracelet. "We got it, whatever it is," he says dismissively. "Now let's look for Sun Key and get out of here. We need to check in with the others soon, Sarah."

As he speaks the spindle of stone drops back underground.

Sarah is about to agree with Jago when the air gets very cold. An invisible presence brushes past her, and Simon twists violently and is thrown to the ground, the Maker "weapon" is knocked out of his grip and tumbles into the grass. Jago and Sarah lift their rifles but don't know where—or what—to shoot. They twirl and search and Sarah calls out, "Dad!" and Simon moans and Jago shouts, "There!"

Sarah looks, not knowing what to expect, and Jago taps his trigger, firing three shots. The space between them ripples and then darkens and a thing like a net appears from nowhere and catches Jago's bullets. It surges toward him and then sucks up his arms and his chest and his face. His skin turns blue and within a fraction of a second his entire body is wrapped in this gossamer shroud and he's unconscious and teetering to the ground like a falling tree.

The Maker! Sarah thinks desperately.

Simon moans again, straining toward Sarah.

She dives sideways as another net-shroud hurtles overhead, missing her by inches. She skids over the dirt, her respirator catching the ground and twisting uncomfortably around to the side of her head and crunching her ear. She sees the clump of metal less than a foot away and scrambles toward it. She gets it, her fingers fit perfectly, her thumb grows almost unbearably hot as it settles into the imprint. Her arm locks at the elbow and her shoulder feels like it's being used as a pincushion by a thousand needles. Her bad arm, tied to her stomach in a sling, aches. She rolls onto her back and points the weapon defensively, sighting along her arm. She blinks at the thing in her hand. It isn't a little mound of metal anymore but an elongated spike extending from the pinkie side of her hand for about three feet. Despite its sudden length it's featherlight. The air shimmers and another net-shroud opens from a small point above her and spreads into the air like an ink stain. She squeezes her entire hand around the weapon and keeps her eyes open and thinks of what she wants it to do—reveal the Maker and cut it down—and the spike glows yellow and gray and a thin disk of light appears from the tip. It flashes for a millisecond, a blade of light extending to the clouds and beyond. The net-shroud is shredded into a thousand pieces. It blows away on the wind. And behind that, about seven feet above the ground, a melon-sized object flips through the air and thumps onto the ground close to Sarah's feet.

A form appears before her in streaks. Whatever it's using for camouflage fritters and malfunctions. She sees a body, skinny and pale, headless and falling. When it hits the ground it's completely visible, and she knows for certain that it's dead.

"YEAH! *Yeah!* Fuck you!" she spits. "Fuuuuuuuuhuuuuuck yoooooouuu!"

She sits up hastily and yanks her bad hand from the sling and tears the respirator and goggles and cap from her head. She zips the weapon all around, getting to her knees, covering every angle while she looks for another target, but there isn't one and the thing in her hands is already morphing back to its innocuous state.

She pants, her breath quickened by adrenaline and joy and disbelief but mostly joy.

I killed him.

I killed kepler 22b.

She lets out a laugh, full and hearty, and crawls to Jago. She tugs at the shroud, which is bitterly cold to the touch. It crinkles and cracks as she frees him from it, and as soon as he's out his eyes flutter and he's back with her.

She wraps her arms around him and kisses his face all over: his lips his scar the bridge of his nose his blinking eyes. They embrace awkwardly on the ground, the weapon that is very much a weapon there in her hand.

The rain falls ever harder. She doesn't care.

"I killed him," she whispers, her lips on the soft skin of his ear. "I killed him, Jago."

He smiles, but his eyes dart to the side. "And your father?"

Sarah peers over Jago's shoulder. Simon works his way onto his elbows as he gets his bearings. "He looks fine."

Sarah kisses Jago one more time, a smile plastered to her face. She jumps up and bounds to Simon. He *is* fine. He laughs. They hug. They regroup over the next several minutes, drink water and check their guns. They are entranced by the alien body and its severed head. Sarah and Jago argue about whether it is actually kepler 22b—it doesn't look exactly the same—but Simon giddily asks, "Does it really matter?"

No, it really doesn't.

They have the weapon. And it works, and it can kill Makers.

They take the alien head, slipping it into a plastic bag and tucking this into Jago's large pack. They firebomb the body with an incendiary grenade, making sure it burns, and as the fire rages at their backs they return north, a sense of victory in their throats. Within the hour they enter the Cahokian monument and find the central star chamber and search for Sun Key. It isn't there. Simon is convinced. They will have to move on and search the next monument. They leave and go up, up, up, outside and to the vehicles. Sarah and her father get in the old Taurus, bloodstained and bullet-riddled. Jago gets on the Harley.

They go back to the plane. They will talk to the other Players. Get new orders. Maybe rendezvous with them somewhere else. Maybe head to La Venta, as planned.

Or I can go home and see Mom, Sarah thinks as they board the plane after refueling. And as it hurtles up the runway and bumps into the air, Jago at the controls, her head resting on her father's shoulder in the main cabin, her good hand holding his hand, she says quietly, "Or I can go home . . ."

Within minutes she is asleep, the smell of Simon's hair in her nose, dreaming of what could be.

AN LIU, NORI KO

Approaching 34.36226, 108.640262, Huzhucun, China

Nori Ko turns off an empty six-lane highway, bouncing the Defender onto a dirt service road. Both roads cut through flat farmland, the fields green with corn and soybeans and potatoes. To the east and south is the semi-industrial sprawl of Xi'an—water towers and a tangle of wires over electrical substations and soulless buildings and tall concrete chimneys spewing smoke and steam.

Countering these, and watching over the farmland like half-asleep dragons, are the pyramids. Unlike the hidden Great White Pyramid, these structures sit out in the open. There are dozens scattered around Xi'an, making this area a vast graveyard for China's ancient emperors. The tomb that An Liu and Nori Ko are headed to belongs to a Han emperor named Zhao, who only lived until the age of 20 and ruled for a mere 13 years between 87 and 74 BCE. At least this is the pyramid's nominal purpose. Its other purpose, and one that is much more important than that of resting place for a forgotten child-king, concerns Endgame.

Nori Ko drives a few hundred meters north to the nearby pyramid, although it doesn't look like much of one anymore. It's more like a slump-backed hill, crisscrossed with worn footpaths through clumps of wild grass. The site is culturally significant, and technically protected by the Chinese government, but there is no welcome center, no ropes cordoning it off, no formal parking lot for visitors. Instead there's a shabby patch of open dirt at the western base of the hill littered with plastic bottles and bags and food wrappers. A cornfield full of leafy stalks grows right next to the hill.

No other cars are here, and An is glad for it. He almost says as much to Chiyoko, who speaks often now, saying annoying things like *Stay* and *Honor life* and *Let it be* and then things that contradict these niceties like *No quarter* and *Take the keys* and *Seek blood, love. Seek blood for me.*

An *SHIVERblink* An *SHIVERSHIVER* An and Nori Ko exit the Defender. He bites his lower lip in order to keep quiet. He wants to talk to Chiyoko, but he knows that doing so would make Nori Ko ask questions.

He glimpses his reflection in a car window. His stubbly head, his tattooed tear, his deep-set and sleepless eyes, his thin purple lips.

We're nearly there, Chiyoko, he thinks.

She doesn't respond.

He checks his weapons and his supplies. He checks his string of homemade bombs. He slings Nobuyuki's katana over his shoulder.

Nori Ko's movements mirror his. She clicks metal on guns and sheathes blades and makes sure that clothing is not loose. Her face is hard and cold. He has grown used to her over the course of their drive from India, and while it hasn't been more than a few days he's already begun to take her for granted.

"I am glad Chiyoko sent you to me, Nori Ko," An says.

Nori Ko pauses. This is the first time An has said something that sounds grateful, even kind. She smiles a little as she says, "I'm glad too." She slaps a magazine into her rifle and snaps the charger. "Now let's go get those keys." She winks and spins away from the car and slams the door.

She leads, he follows. They pass a tidy shrine at the base of the pyramid, a small plaque inside naming Emperor Zhao and giving the years of his truncated reign. A bouquet of wilted flowers and the butt ends of a few sticks of burned incense are inside, no doubt left by some superstitious farmer who believes in the grace or ire of local spirits.

An and Nori Ko march up the dirt track. An notices for the first time that the northern face of the hill is covered in a stand of dark pagoda trees. A perfect place to hide an entrance to this forgotten relic from another age.

It's a short climb—the hill is only 30 meters high—and Nori Ko reaches the summit first.

But when she does she freezes and drops to the ground, swinging her rifle in a 45-degree arc. An checks their flanks. A truck cruising north on the wide highway to the west, and another ancient pyramid rises over the farmland another mile past that.

He gets on his belly and military crawls behind Nori Ko. "What?" he whispers.

"There's a car parked at the bottom of the opposite slope."

"People?"

She shakes her head.

An slithers next to her and peers over the lip of the hill. The car is a dark-blue late-model Fulwin, unremarkable in every way except that it's shiny and not road-worn. "Rental," he says. "From the airport." He points to the northeast.

"Let's move," Nori Ko says. "Crossing cover, four meters apart. I'll lead. I know where the entrance is. No more talking."

SHIVERBLINKSHIVERbilnkblinkSHIVER.

Nori Ko rises to a crouch and points her rifle to the trees. An rises too. They move forward until they're a few meters apart. He angles his rifle so it covers her front and she points hers so that it covers his. If someone pops out and tries to surprise Nori Ko, An will kill him. If someone tries to surprise An, Nori Ko will kill him.

BLINKshivershiver.

An sees movement and he swings his weapon in her direction, his finger hovering over the trigger but not firing. Nori Ko mistakes this motion, thinking for a brief moment that he's aiming at her, and she also swings her rifle in his direction, momentarily sighting him before tipping her Beretta to the ground and mouthing, *Sorry.*

Blinkblinkblink.

A squirrel chitters and spirals around a trunk and then disappears into the branches above. An follows it with his weapon and then repositions to cover Nori Ko. He takes a step forward. She mouths another apology and they continue to advance.

They walk downhill now, weaving through trees. After 10 meters Nori Ko puts up a fist and both stop in their tracks. They're on the edge of a patch of grass, a large tree blocking An's line of sight. Nori Ko signals him to stay put. She slips into the trees and he catches slivers of her as she flits around, clearing in every direction with her rifle.

Nori Ko reappears, her gun pointed down and held tight to her chest, her face wrinkled with concern. She motions him closer.

He stalks to her. A curved obsidian spur rises from the clearing to waist height. Broken and discarded earth is thrown to the side as if the stone has grown up from the ground below. An cranes his neck and sees that one side is cut away, revealing a hole big enough to slip into.

"There're stairs," she says cautiously. "I'm sorry, An. But I think the Nabataean is already here."

An shudders, he quakes, his knees begin to falter, his head begins to pound, but through the riot of his body he hears her voice:

It's all right, love.

SHIVERshiverSHIVERshiver

It's all right, love.

blinkblink BLINKblink

It's all right.

shiverBLINK

Love.

An bites the side of his tongue. The tics stop. His eyes water. The pain feels good. "It's not all right, An," he says.

Nori Ko regards him with a confused look and says nothing. She doesn't like the tics or the fact that he's speaking to himself.

SHIVERblinkblink.

You can still kill him, love.

shiver.

Move! Chiyoko implores.

"It's all right," he says calmly. He looks to the sky, the tops of the trees silhouetted against it like spear points. "He hasn't won yet. We would know."

"Okay, but let's find out for sure," Nori Ko says.

An hoists his rifle and brushes past her. "You can still kill him," he says.

"Good," Nori Ko says. "But won't *you* kill him?"

"Yes. That's what I meant." He steps around the stone and into the ground. Nori Ko follows.

And then he says, "You can still kill him, love."

Nori Ko doesn't know what to think of that. Is he coming undone, now that they're so close to the end?

She very much hopes that he is not.

She needs him. He needs her.

He can't come undone.

Not yet.

KEPLER 22B

Teletrans chamber on board Seedrak Sare'en, active geosynchronous orbit above the Martian North Pole

He stands alone in the room, staring at the blank archway of transpot 2. One Nethinim is dead—*dead!*—and the other is safe in stasis. The La Tène and her grandfather are interned and semistasised. He wanted to bring back the Cahokian and the Olmec too as extra insurance, but they remain free on Earth.

But worse than this—much, much worse—they have the weapon.

"More Players would have been better," he says. "But no matter. We have one. And we may not require her in the end."

Because here, twinkling in the darkness of the transpot, he sees the form of the person he waits for.

The Nabataean. With the first two keys, and on the verge of discovering the third. He is entering the Shang monument's star chamber.

kepler 22b has not felt such excitement since he first arrived in the quadrant over 15,000 Earth years ago. Since he saw the lush sweep of the blue planet and the barren expanse of the red one.

It is nearly over.

A winner approaches, and in a few moments, kepler 22b will crown him.

Crown him with the prize of death.

HILAL IBN ISA AL-SALT, SHARI CHOPRA, JENNY ULAPALA

-21.6268, 129.6625, Yuendumu Hinterland, Northern Territory, Australia

Hilal and Shari stand shoulder to shoulder at the heart of the Koori monument. It is evening. The sky is dark. It is less than 24 hours since they met Jenny Ulapala but it might as well be weeks. Jenny likes them, and while they've not yet had their weapons returned, they like Jenny. Jenny and Shari and Hilal have spent the better part of the last 20 hours in a simple hut immersed in Wayland's book, deciphering as much as Jenny can about this last stage of Endgame. It hasn't been easy. The book is organized in a manner that defies logic, so her understanding of the specifics of Endgame is incomplete, but nonetheless it is greater than it was the day before.

They have learned many things.

First, Jenny confirmed that at least one of these twelve ancient monuments is needed to finish Endgame, as Stella believed. But Jenny also learned that in the hearts of these monuments are "star chambers," which serve a secondary and, especially in the old days when Maker ships orbited Earth by the hundreds, essential purpose. They were transportation hubs.

The Makers had a technology with an unpronounceable name that harnessed something they called "Earth's intrinsic energy lines," Jenny explained early that morning. "These are the same things we use to work through the Dreaming. We use the Dreaming in spiritual or mental capacities, not in physical ones. But the Makers—They *can* use this energy to get about."

Jenny learned that while They had flying machines that could travel at great speeds and deliver material around the globe in the days of human prehistory, the Makers preferred to get around using their teleporters. There were many hundreds of these all around Earth in the old days—in places like the pagoda in Xi'an and at the Gateway of the Sun in Bolivia and in the Depths of the Harappan fortress—but these portals just linked places on Earth.

They did not posses the ability to move Makers to and from orbit.

"But the portals in the star chambers of the world's most ancient monuments *did* possess this ability. And they still do today," Jenny said.

After breakfast Jenny kept reading the book, Hilal and Shari helping her to take notes. Their other discoveries were far-ranging, concerning things as varied as gold extraction, genetic modification, neuropathology, advanced bioengineering, religious indoctrination, and, of course, the implementation and execution of the thing the Players have always known as Endgame.

Jenny needs more time—months or perhaps years—to fully understand why it's happening and how, but after a few hours she was convinced that the ultimate goal of Endgame as espoused by the Makers and accepted by the lines was false.

As Hilal observed, "Endgame is merely another tool designed to exert control over an alien race. *Us.* It is coercive in nature, designed to get us to act against our best interests."

"The Makers are like bloody politicians, then," Shari quipped.

Jenny chuckled at that one.

As the sky darkened that afternoon, the sun hidden behind gathering clouds, Jenny said, "Here's what we're looking for." She stabbed a section of the book. Hilal and Shari huddled closer to her. "It's about the keys."

"Does it say anything about my daughter?"

"It says her genetic code contains something essential to finishing Endgame. Seems like they hid some bit of information in the lines' genes, and that certain children are born with the section of code they need. Your Alice, unfortunately, has that running around her little system."

Shari said, "We *need* to get her, Mrs. Ulapala."

"Call me Jenny, mum."

"All right, Jenny."

"We will get her, Shari. A promise is a promise," Hilal said. "But I want to know, Master Ulapala: What about the third key?"

"It's all right here," Jenny said. "And it's simple as simple can be, Aksumite. It's you. Or Shari. Or one of your mates—Jago or Sarah or Aisling. Or Adlai."

"Sun Key is a Player?" Shari asked urgently.

"It's the Player who's got the first two keys. There's also a code in your genome, one you all got. That's why Players are chosen. You don't have this code, you can't Play. Anyway, when it's all said and done this code links with Sky Key's, and when these are combined with Earth Key in one of these star chambers, then the Maker gets whatever it is he wants out of Endgame."

"I wish we knew what exactly that was," Hilal said.

"And me too. This book'll show us sooner or later. Need more time to study it is all. But right now we got to act. Sky Key is in grave danger, mum."

Shari frowned. "More than we already know her to be in?"

"Yeah. Says here that at the end, she'll die," Jenny said. "Player will too."

Shari clapped Jenny's wizened hand. *"Jenny."* That was all she said.

Jenny nodded. "I know, mum. We'll save her. And I got an idea how. Bit risky, but I think we can use the Dreaming to figure out when Little Alice comes into one of these star chambers. Once we see her I open the portal at the Koori monument—I've done this before, but I was always too scared to go through since I didn't know where it let out. But now I do. You can stay in the Dreaming and hold the connection to Little Alice while Hilal and some of my Koori mates go and whisk her away. We get her here, I close the portal right quick on our end,

and that's it. Endgame over—or effectively over, anyway."
"We can define what it means to win," Hilal said.
"That's right," Jenny said.
"Is it safe?" Shari asked.
"That I don't know, mum. We definitely need to try it first. Don't want to hurt your girl out of rash stupidity."
And so here they are, back at the heart of the Koori monument, doing a trial run of a Sky Key rescue mission.
Now Jenny and Shari sit cross-legged near the tree in the middle of the circle. The Koori guards stand at intervals around the circle.
Hilal watches and waits.
"Ready, mum?" Jenny asks Shari.
"Ready."
"Take my hand and close your eyes and follow my lead," the old woman says.
Shari does.
"You see your girl, don't jump, understand? You're just a passenger for now."
"I understand."
Jenny squeezes Shari's hand. "It's going to be fine." Shari nods nervously. Over her shoulder Jenny says, "Hilal, when the connection is solid I'll come out and we'll test the door. Shari, you stay in the Dreaming. Your presence will hold our connection to the other portal in place."
"I'll try," Shari says.
"It'll be easy for you. You'll see when you're there, mum. You've already done it in your dreams, you just didn't know it."
"All right. Let's give it a go."
Jenny clicks her tongue. "Close your eyes now, mum. Here comes the Dreaming."

SHARI CHOPRA

With those words her world goes dark and silent. It is not so much dreamlike as it's simply no longer there, like any person experiences as she gives way to sleep and is not yet delivered to her dreams, whether these end up being banal, strange or, as it often happens, simply forgotten.

Time does not exist. Space does not exist. The desire to see her daughter, the wreckage of Endgame, the vast Australian desert beyond her physical body—none of these exist.

In many ways she does not exist.

She spends some time here. Seconds or hours—she doesn't know and she doesn't care.

But then, after an interval, a form comes to her through the darkness. The form is small and her steps are childlike and her hair is dark and straight. Shari can't see her face, but she knows who it is. She would know who it is from any distance by the way she swings her arms and stands on her toes when she walks. It is Little Alice Chopra.

She seems to walk to her forever, never getting closer or bigger, yet increasing in presence. The front of her body and her face are cast in shadow, and Shari reaches out and calls for her but the girl doesn't do anything. She just keeps walking easily toward her mother.

When the little girl finally comes into view Shari is shocked to find that it's not Little Alice but Jenny Ulapala. The old woman holds out both hands. Shari is overcome with sadness, and then fear, and then she remembers why she's here. Where *here* is.

"The Dreaming," she says.

"Stay with me, mum," Jenny says. "Don't act. Follow."

Shari takes her hand and they walk, side by side, over the darkness. The ground beneath is not hard or soft. The air is not cold or warm. The void is not limitless or pressing in on them. Jenny swings her hand joyfully, and Shari can't help but swing it too, like a child would do with her mother or father.

Like Little Alice would do.

Eventually they come to the circle of dirt and shrubs in the desert, the same one their physical bodies occupy. It's early evening. They keep walking, getting incrementally closer to the tree and the portal carved in its trunk. Hilal and the guards are nowhere to be seen.

"Will it work?" Shari asks, her lips and tongue tingling, her voice echoing through her skull.

"Quiet, mum," Jenny answers.

Shari becomes aware of a shade passing next to her, or perhaps also following. It's tall, substantial, and with a head of twirling black hair. Whenever she looks directly at it, it disappears, but she doesn't need to see it to know who it is. Shari's just happy she's here, in some form. It's Big Alice.

And she has something to say.

"They're all behind you, Shari. You won't see 'em, you can't, but they're all here. An unending parade." At that moment Jenny and Shari reach the tree in the Dreaming, and the space in the doorway shimmers and turns black like ink. Jenny squeezes Shari's hand reassuringly. Alice says, "All of 'em. Jamal and Paru leading the line, back through the centuries. They're all smiling, Shari. The entire line. *Your* line. All of 'em."

Shari's heart fills, and her gut empties of sadness, and she smiles with them.

"They're all here, mate. They're all here."

HILAL IBN ISA AL-SALT, SHARI CHOPRA, JENNY ULAPALA

-21.6268, 129.6625, Yuendumu Hinterland, Northern Territory, Australia

"By the Makers," Hilal says, staring at the portal. It changes before his eyes. It reminds him of the door in the pyramid at the Calling, except that this one is darker and not reflective. It is black and empty save for the faint twinkling of lights like those of intermittent stars.

"Wait here, mum," Jenny whispers to Shari. "Stay present and hold the link."

Shari doesn't speak.

Jenny releases her hand and rises, her old body creaking upright. She walks halfway to Hilal.

Jenny says, "Time to see if this portal links with another star chamber. You have the markers?"

Hilal holds up a pair of flat red stones the size of large coins. Both come from this patch of Australian desert, and both are easily spotted. They walk to the tree together. Jenny says, "I'm going back to Shari for a sec. The link to the other portal is there, but it's like on old window jammed in its frame. Needs unsticking before it's all the way open."

"When will I know?"

"You'll know." She sits back on the ground gingerly and takes Shari's hand.

Hilal watches as Jenny's eyes roll forward, revealing the whites, and then her lids flutter shut. For several moments nothing happens. The portal stays dark and inky and Shari and Jenny remain motionless and silent.

But then the surface of the portal changes again. Hints of faint blue light stream from it, and a line here and there like the edge of a wall, and a shiny thing set in the ground on the other side like a large salad bowl. It is a star-shaped room, and he knows that it is real and right there, even if it is thousands of miles away.

"Now!" Jenny blurts.

Hilal hurls one of the stones at the portal. Its surface ripples exactly like when a rock disturbs a glassy lake, but the stone sails through to the other side. It slides over the floor, dipping into the bowl and shooting into the air on the far side, finally stopping in one of the room's pointed corners.

"It worked!" Hilal says.

"I see it, Aksumite," Jenny says. "We should be able to cross in either direction when the time comes."

Shari grunts. Hilal assumes she is speaking in the Dreaming but is unable to make the words here in the world.

But then an epiphany. The world includes the Dreaming. This is so spiritually pleasing that he cannot help but smile. Whatever has happened with Abaddon, this world remains, and it is wondrous.

"We're gonna try another chamber, Hilal. Gotta make sure we can get to wherever Little Alice shows up."

"Understood, Master Ulapala."

Jenny hums a low tune. Hilal watches the image of the room recede and fall out of focus and disappear, the surface turning placid and black once more.

"It'll take a while to navigate through the Dreaming," Jenny whispers.

"I will wait," Hilal says excitedly. "With pleasure."

MACCABEE ADLAI, LITTLE ALICE CHOPRA

34.36226, 108.640262, Huzhucun, China

Maccabee and Little Alice descend a narrow spiral staircase carved from a tube of slick black stone. The staircase is less than a meter wide, forcing Maccabee to angle sideways. Little Alice, who becomes more afraid and unsure the deeper they go, holds his hand. The cramped tube, along with Little Alice's increasingly tentative steps, causes them to move slowly. Maccabee's pistol is in his right hand. He has a blade on his hip and the poison ring on his pinkie. Earth Key sits securely in the zippered pocket of an ill-fitting windbreaker he bought at the Ahmedabad airport. Between his teeth he holds a cheap and weak-beamed flashlight, also bought at the airport. Its batteries are already failing.

These are the things he carries to the end.

These are the things he carries to win.

These are the things he carries to meet kepler 22b, and to see how this girl will die.

He squeezes Little Alice's hand. She squeezes back.

"I'm scared, Uncle."

"Don't be, sweetie," he lies, his brow covered in a cold sweat.

He feels awful. He feels sick. He feels elated. He feels nervous.

He feels.

After 21 minutes and three seconds of descent the ground levels and the tube opens into a room. The air is a few degrees below freezing. He zips his jacket to his neck.

The walls glow, and his breath visibly plays in the flashlight's beam. He pinches his teeth and the light clicks off. Little Alice shivers.

“We’re here,” she says.

“We are.”

The room is high ceilinged, its hard-angled walls laid out in the shape of a six-pointed star. At the far end of the room, blunting one of the in-facing points, is a tall and slender alcove, its edge surrounded by glittering runes, a few of which he recognizes. The interior of the alcove is jet black and liquefied, a limitless pool set on end. In the floor in the middle of the room is a gilt, bowl-shaped depression.

Maccabee steps forward, but Little Alice clutches his leg and won’t budge. “I’m scared,” she repeats.

“It’s all right,” he says.

“I . . .”

“Yes?”

“I want my mama,” she says weakly.

For a moment he can’t move. He swallows hard. If he were her, he would want his mama too.

KEPLER 22B

Teletrans chamber on board Seedrak Sare'en, active geosynchronous orbit above the Martian North Pole

kepler 22b hears this conversation from his ship above the red planet. He sees the girl. Knows her fear. It is real and well-founded. He almost steps through to reveal himself in this moment, to speak, but he wants them to come closer. There can be no doubt that this Player will claim his prize.

None.

He wants them to come closer.

AN LIU, NORI KO, MACCABEE ADLAI, LITTLE ALICE CHOPRA

34.36226, 108.640262, Huzhucun, China

An Liu moves quickly but silently. Maccabee is close. The girl is too. He can smell both.

Don't rush to the kepler, love. Have patience.

BLINK

Quiet!

SHIVER

They'll hear you!

SHIVERSHIVERBLINKBLINKSHIVER.

Patience. Don't hurt the girl.

They'll hear you!

He bites the edge of his tongue so hard that the tips of his teeth meet and grate. His eyes water. He wants Chiyoko to shut up, to let him work.

To let him kill.

But she won't.

Don't hurt the girl, she insists again, not hearing An's thoughts. *You'll need her if you want to kill the kepler! Don't hurt her!*

He moves, one foot grapevining after the other, one after the other, in the utter darkness. Nori Ko has fallen farther behind.

"Shush!" he hisses.

Spill Adlai's blood, not hers!

"SHUSH!"

He stops. That was too loud. He waits for a response from below, hears nothing. Nori Ko comes to his shoulder. She nudges him with her knee.

They have been descending for nearly 10 minutes. He estimates that they're more than 100 meters underground, the air getting colder and colder as they go.

He cocks an ear to the darkness. No sound from Maccabee. The hole must be that much deeper.

ShivershiverBLINKshiverBLINKBLINKblink.

An releases his rifle's hand guard and takes one of Chiyoko's shriveled ears and slips it between his lips.

It tastes like paper.

SHIVERblink.

Like nothing.

blink.

But it works.

She is quiet.

He moves his feet, faster now.

Much faster.

"It's all right," Maccabee whispers. He kneels before Little Alice, holding her gently by the shoulders.

"I want my mama."

Maccabee looks at her feet. He's too ashamed to meet her gaze. "When we're done here, I'll take you to her," he lies again. "We'll find her and I'll take you to her. I promise."

"After you win?"

"Yes. After I win."

"Promise?"

If she's going to die, he doesn't want her to be stressed. It should be peaceful. Painless.

Like the Maker promised it would be.

Maccabee raises his face and stares at her intently, tenderly. "I swear it." The sincerity in his voice surprises even him.

You fucking monster, he thinks.

Little Alice blinks. "Okay." She peeks into the middle of the room. "Okay."

Maccabee runs the back of his hand over her cheek. "Do you know what to do over there?"

"Yes, Uncle."

"Show me. The sooner we're done, the sooner we can see your mama."

"Okay."

She walks to the bowl in the middle of the floor. He follows, unzipping the pocket that contains Earth Key. He wraps his fingers around the small stone ball, its surface unusually warm, and pulls it free.

I am going to win, he thinks, he rationalizes.

Little Alice stops at the edge of the depression, her toes hanging over it. She holds out her hand. Her small body shakes.

"Okay," she says. "Give me your hand, Uncle. Give me Earth Key."

KEPLER 22B

Teletrans chamber on board Seedrak Sare'en, active geosynchronous orbit above the Martian North Pole

kepler 22b steps to the edge of the transpot. He pulls his cloak of armor around his body. He slips the hood over the topknot perched on his head. The hood's edges adhere to his cheeks and then grow and meet, covering his face.

Endgame is over, and he is glad for it.

He takes a breath. It is slightly tentative, shaky.

What is this odd feeling? The one he hasn't had in such a long time?

Ah, yes.

Nervousness.

Slowly, he steps forward.

HILAL IBN ISA AL-SALT, SHARI CHOPRA, JENNY ULAPALA

-21.6268, 129.6625, Yuendumu Hinterland, Northern Territory, Australia

Hilal watches as Jenny and Shari work through the Dreaming.

He watches the portal.

After a while the black surface changes, as before. A line here, a line there, the faint light.

He starts to see another room.

And then Shari screams. Jenny throws both arms around her, half pinning her to the ground.

Hilal squints at the image in the portal.

The room pulls into focus.

This room is not empty like the other one. In the middle stands Maccabee Adlai, and clinging to his leg is Little Alice Chopra! The Nabataean is seconds away from winning!

"Do you see kepler 22b?" Hilal asks desperately.

"No!" Jenny shouts. "But—"

"The Shang!" Hilal yelps, pointing past Maccabee. "There is the Shang!"

AN LIU, MACCABEE ADLAI, LITTLE ALICE CHOPRA

34.36226, 108.640262, Huzhucun, China

An reaches the bottom of the steps. He is as silent and cold as the air enveloping him. Nori Ko could not keep up with his pace, and she is at least a minute behind.

The Nabataean and Sky Key stand in the middle of the room. Adlai looks shorter than An remembers, but then An notices that Adlai is in a small hole in the ground. On the far side of the room is a dark doorway, its surface black and opaque. An calmly adjusts his aim for the back of Adlai's neck, right below the skull. He puts the slightest pressure on the trigger. A couple more millimeters and the Nabataean's spine will explode and his throat will collapse and his face will be torn away and flung into the star-shaped room and he will be instantaneously killed.

Sky Key says, "There, Uncle!" She points. An can't help but look. A play of light on the far side of the room causes him to ease off the trigger. The blackness in the doorway stirs, like an invisible stick has swirled its surface, and near the floor An sees something foot-shaped begin to step out of it.

HILAL IBN ISA AL-SALT, SHARI CHOPRA, JENNY ULAPALA

-21.6268, 129.6625, Yuendumu Hinterland, Northern Territory, Australia

"Gun!" Jenny orders. "Give Hilal his blades!"

Shari writhes and calls out for Little Alice, her eyes shut, her hands outstretched, her legs kicking.

Hilal sees Maccabee and Sky Key and An, but none of these people appear to see him. If he can make it to the star chamber on the other side of the portal he will have the element of surprise.

He skids to a stop in front the threshold. A Koori guard throws a pistol at him and Hilal snatches it from the air. He tucks it under his chin and holds out both hands as his machetes arrive, *LOVE* in his right hand and *HATE* in his left. He hastily slips one under his belt and takes the gun.

"Go!" Jenny yells. "Go and get her!"

AN LIU, MACCABEE ADLAI, LITTLE ALICE CHOPRA

34.36226, 108.640262, Huzhucun, China

The kepler! Chiyoko screams. *Stop him, An! Adlai will win if you don't. Stop him now!*

An releases his Beretta. It falls to his chest, making a muffled sound. Maccabee hears this and he whips around. In a single motion An yanks a ball from the strand of explosives hung around his body and slings it through the room. It arcs over Maccabee, who stabs one of his massive hands into the air, missing it by a few centimeters. Maccabee drops to the ground, covering Little Alice with his arms, shielding her with his broad shoulders and back.

The tiny bomb lands in the middle of the archway on the far side of the room.

It is rigged to explode on impact.

And it does precisely that.

HILAL IBN ISA AL-SALT, SHARI CHOPRA, JENNY ULAPALA

-21.6268, 129.6625, Yuendumu Hinterland, Northern Territory, Australia

Just as Hilal steps through the portal, its surface crackles and shivers and the room on the other side shatters and snaps. The blackness returns and he almost slams headlong into it, but someone strong snatches his belt and twists him to the side and he whiplashes into the tree trunk, mashing his cheek on its rough bark.

The person holding him is Jenny Ulapala.

"It's no good. There was a blast. You go through that now and you'll end up in the void, Aksumite." She winks. "Trust me."

He does.

"Shari," he says.

Shari lies on the ground, her eyes blinking, her stomach spasming in fits of sadness and pain.

"I pulled her out of the Dreaming," Jenny says.

"I saw her!" Shari wails.

"You did," Jenny says gently.

"Why couldn't we save her?"

"You saw," Jenny says.

"The Shang," Hilal says quietly.

"Shut up, Hilal!" Shari spits through her tears. "I saw her. *You saw her.* I was so close I could smell her hair, her skin."

Hilal casts his eyes to the ground.

"You couldn't smell her, mum," Jenny says, trying to calm her. "Those were your memories. They get tied up with what you experience in the Dreaming. She was there but you weren't. Not really. Not in body."

"I could smell her," Shari insists, her tongue razor sharp.

A moment. The hiss and whorl of the wind. Crickets. A snapping branch.

"What happened?" Hilal asks.

"An Liu threw one of his bombs," Shari whispers. "The Maker was coming. An stopped him."

"Shari, that's good," Jenny says. "It means the game ain't over. It means your daughter lives."

"No it isn't! I don't have her!" She points at the blank portal in the tree trunk. "One of them has her! Or one of them is killing her! Or . . . or . . ."

"Easy, mum," Jenny says. "The Maker doesn't have her. That's what counts."

Another moment.

Jenny starts to speak again but Shari raises a hand. She gathers herself, sits and wipes her eyes with the back of her hand. "The explosion was concentrated," she says quietly. "Adlai smothered her. They were alive when you pulled me out, Jenny. I saw. Adlai was rising to fight, and Alice . . . she was curled up. Like a little bug. Like a cat. Curled up and scared."

"So she does live," Hilal says, trying to sound encouraging. He moves toward Shari. "Until it is proved otherwise, that is what is true."

"Hilal's right," Jenny says.

The sky is dark and featureless. The clouds cover the stars, the same that were so brilliant the night before.

"She lives!" Hilal insists. "And if I must die to deliver her safely into your arms, then I will." He gets on his knees right next to her. He stretches his fingers for her arm but doesn't touch. "Our plan will work. All we have to do is execute it again. She lives!" he repeats like a refrain, like a prayer. "You *will* see her alive again, Shari Chopra. This I swear."

AN LIU, MACCABEE ADLAI, LITTLE ALICE CHOPRA, NORI KO

34.36226, 108.640262, Huzhucun, China

The portal is destroyed.

Little Alice cowers as Maccabee rushes An Liu. Maccabee's gun rises. He pulls the trigger, aiming for An's chest. The shot echoes harshly throughout the room. An is felled by the force of the first shot and twists into the entryway, disappearing for a moment.

Maccabee is there in a flash. An's chest heaves, his hands clutch at his throat. The shot hit armor and he gasps for air. Maccabee reaches down and grabs An's rifle strap. He yanks the gun awkwardly around An's side where it's impossible for him to reach it.

But An has other things.

Like a sword.

It flashes and cuts across the muzzle of Maccabee's pistol, slamming it to the wall and crunching the Nabataean's knuckles into the stone entryway. The pistol fires uncontrollably as it's knocked free. The slug hits the stone and bounces around but doesn't hit anyone. An draws a deep breath and holds it so he doesn't have to fuss with his struggling lungs. He bounces to his feet. Maccabee, relieved of his pistol, backpedals as the tip of An's sword zips past Maccabee's face.

Maccabee draws a tactical knife, double-edged with a hilt.

The Nabataean parries the sword with the knife, catching the edge with the hilt and pushing the sword away. The knife might be short next to the sword, but Maccabee's superior strength more than makes up for it.

They parry and attack and counterattack for a few seconds as each sets his feet. An exhales and surges forward and Maccabee leans to his left to avoid An's steel. He stabs for An's exposed neck and is certain he'll strike but then An steps into the bowl in the middle of the room and shrinks by a foot. The knife scratches the top of An's head, but it doesn't draw much more than a few drops of blood.

Where is Sky Key? Maccabee thinks. She was in the bowl, terrified and curled up like an insect, but now she's gone. *Did the Maker get her? Is she safe?*

Maccabee slices his knife down hard, cutting An's rifle strap. He grips the side of the stock and pulls it free, but An zips a backhand at the weakest section of the gun, where the receiver meets the barrel. The rifle is actually cut in two. The top half twirls away and the bottom half falls to their feet as Maccabee folds himself backward like a circus acrobat, narrowly avoiding the rest of the blade. An sets his feet and grips the sword two-handed and is about to smash it into Maccabee's leg when another shot rings in their ears, a bullet grazing the Shang's ear and causing his strike to miss. Maccabee clambers to his feet. Both Players search desperately for the shooter, and both are shocked to see Little Alice Chopra clutching Maccabee's pistol like a giant deadly toy. An is between the girl and the Nabataean. She aims at An again and pulls the trigger, pulls it pulls it pulls it. She fires all the bullets left in the gun, and all miss badly, the recoil nearly knocking her over. The gun clicks. Empty. An runs toward her, Maccabee follows, yelling, "Leave her alone!"

Chiyoko yells, *Don't hurt her, love!*

An can't help himself. Not now. Sky Key is going to get hurt.

She's going to die.

An reaches the girl—terrified and crying and shaking so badly she can barely hold the gun—in less than two seconds. Maccabee is right behind him but he'll be too late. An is going to strike.

But before he can, An's face lights in pain and the world goes silver and then black.

Maccabee skids to a stop. An's knocked halfway across the room, hit hard in the head with the butt of a rifle. He splays across the floor, flat on his back. A woman steps from the entryway behind Little Alice, and also behind the rifle that knocked An Liu to the floor.

Maccabee has never seen the woman before, but there is no doubt that she resembles the Mu, Chiyoko Takeda.

Maccabee holds out his hand to Little Alice. "Come here." The girl sprints to him, slams into his leg, grabs it, digs her nails into his pants, his flesh. His hand clutches the top of her head, his fingers in her hair. He can smell it. Rich and sweet and powdery, like a baby's.

"I want my mama," she says.

"I know, sweetie," he says.

He gently—lovingly—squeezes her scalp.

"I'm sorry," she says.

He thinks, *No, I'm the one who's sorry.*

The woman steps all the way into the room. She's three meters away, her rifle tucked to her shoulder. Her eye is in the sight. Her finger is on the trigger. It is aimed for Maccabee's crooked and bruised nose.

Maccabee smooths Alice's hair. He tilts his head in An's direction. The rifle moves incrementally. "Don't let him hurt—"

His back goes straight as a board. His neck snaps. He falls.

He doesn't hear Little Alice cry out. He doesn't feel any pain.

He didn't even hear the shot.

KEPLER 22B

Teletrans chamber on board Seedrak Sare'en, active geosynchronous orbit above the Martian North Pole

Transpot 2 ripples and shatters like broken glass, blasting debris into the teletrans chamber and throwing kepler 22b to the floor. He became aware of the Shang at the last moment, when it was too late to stop him from detonating a bomb inside the star chamber of the Shang monument.

kepler 22b scrambles backward. His armor protected him and he is uninjured, but transpot 2 is plainly damaged beyond repair. He jumps to his feet and rips off his hood. He hastens past the holographic map of Earth. He stops in front of transpot 1 and sinks his arms into the plasmastone control panel. It shouldn't take more than a few seconds to link transpot 1 to the portal in Xi'an. His fingers dance furiously and the liquidy stone grows over his bare arms and past his elbows. His eyes flit between transpot 1 and the map, transpot 1 and the map, and yes, there, he sees the link and yes, transpot 1 is powered up and yes, there, it is activated!

He can go to the Nabataean! He can still finish Endgame!

His eyes rest on the empty space of the transpot, expecting it to fill from the edges with the dark medium that will enable him to move instantly to Earth's surface.

But the dark medium does not appear.

His fingers work faster, and his mind too, and the transpot lights around the edge. He checks and double-checks the switches and connections and they're all correct but nothing happens.

He swings to the map. The dot marking the Shang monument changes color, indicating that the portal in that room so far away—that room that contains the three keys—is no longer functional. It is utterly destroyed.

He will have to wait until a Player gets the keys to a different star chamber now.

He will have to simply wait.

Unless he can finish Endgame on his own!

He tears his hands from the plasmastone quickly, peeling a thin layer of skin from his forearms. He curses aloud and stomps from the room, crossing the ship's hallway and entering the medbay where the La Tènes are interned. He rips the Player free from a web of wires and bindings, checks her consciousness level, yanks the mask from her face, pulls out the tubes that snake around her mouth and down her throat to her stomach and her lungs. She remains unconscious but her body reflexively gasps for oxygen, of which there is little on the Seedrak. He pulls a bag from the wall and slips it over her head, and it filters the nitrogen- and methane-laden air. She breathes. He drops her on the floor and takes a storage shroud from a far corner and wraps her body in it.

He picks her up with one arm and moves back to the teletrans room. He looks at the map. He has a Player. All he needs is Earth Key and Sky Key, and in order to get these he has to make a guess as to which monument they will show up at next.

He must decide correctly. If he doesn't, all could be lost.

He considers the situation carefully. The Shang has probably already killed the Nabataean, so Liu now has Earth Key and Sky Key. kepler 22b knows that the Shang loved the Mu. He knows that Liu is as sentimental as he is disturbed. Which means that if An Liu has any choice in the matter, and is resourceful enough to figure it out, he will take the keys to the Mu monument located at 24.43161, 123.01314.

kepler 22b has decided.

He shoves his free hand into the plasmastone of transpot 1 and reconfigures its connections.

He will go to the Mu monument.

He will go to the undersea temple of Yonaguni.

AN LIU, NORI KO, LITTLE ALICE CHOPRA

34.36226, 108.640262, Huzhucun, China

"Come on. Wake up."

Nori Ko nudges An with her foot. She holds her rifle in one hand and Sky Key in the other. The girl slumps over Nori Ko's shoulder, her face nestled in her neck, her arm jutting out at an odd angle. Nori Ko injected the girl with a very small dose of Demerol from her field kit. The girl was beside herself with fear and anxiety over losing the Nabataean and who knows what else.

"Wake up, An," Nori Ko repeats.

An rolls onto his side.

"There you are. Come on."

He moans. His hands rise to his face, they rub his skin and eyes. A red welt grows over his left eyebrow and cheek where Nori Ko struck him.

"Wha-what . . ."

"The Nabataean is dead."

An cranes his neck and squints at Maccabee Adlai. "How?"

Nori Ko pats her rifle. "Don't know why you bothered with the sword."

An pushes to a sit. He drapes his arms over his knees. His head hangs between them.

You should thank her, love, Chiyoko says.

SHIVERSHIVERSHIVER. His head quakes like a madman's.

SHIVERSHIVERSHIVER.

Quiet! he thinks.

You should thank her for saving the girl. You were being rash, and foolish, Chiyoko says. *Thank her.*

BlinkSHIVERblink.

An's head snaps up. "Thank you, Nori Ko." His eyes point to Sky Key. "I wasn't right in the head. You've seen me when I'm fighting. You understand."

Good, Chiyoko says.

"I couldn't have done any of this without you. I wouldn't be here without you. Thank you." He says it because he needs Nori Ko, but he also says it because it's true.

Nori Ko reaches down and offers a hand. "I understand. Players are made to kill. You most of all."

"Yes." She pulls him up. He presses a thumb into one of his nostrils, shutting one side tight. He exhales sharply through his nose, a bloody ball of phlegm smacking Maccabee's leg. "You check him?" An asks.

"He's dead."

"Is he rigged to blow if he dies?"

"No. Are you?" she asks, half joking.

"Not right now," he says seriously.

An doesn't notice Nori Ko roll her eyes. "He doesn't have any explosives of any kind," she says.

"And Earth Key?"

"Here."

Nori Ko holds out a fist. An cradles his hand underneath it. She unfurls her fingers and a stone ball drops into his palm.

"It's so . . . small."

"I'm sure that's what the others thought too."

An zips it into a pocket. He picks up Nobuyuki's sword and sheathes it, saying, "I didn't shoot him because the Maker was coming." *Blinkshiver.* "I couldn't let that happen."

"What do you mean?" Nori Ko asks urgently. "Did you *see* the Maker?"

An points at the cracked stones around the portal. "I did. He was stepping through there. It was like a doorway to wherever he is hiding. I greeted him with fire, but I don't think he was hurt."

Nori Ko reaches for him. He flinches a little when her hand comes to rest on his shoulder. "We *will* have our revenge, An."

"That's all that matters."

"Nothing else," she says.

He fingers the necklace of hair and flesh. Points his chin at the girl. "What did you do to her?"

"Drugged. She was hysterical. She seemed to . . . care for the Nabataean. She didn't want him to die."

Do not scare her again, love, Chiyoko chides.

"I'll try," he says.

Nori Ko frowns. "What's that?"

BLINKshiverSHIVER.

"Nothing. Thinking out loud. The Cahokian," he says, getting to the point. "The Olmec. They're next." Nori Ko nods. An unclips a bomb from his vest. Presses a few buttons and then places it carefully in the middle of Maccabee Adlai's stomach.

"One hour until this explodes," he explains. "No Maker will come here again." He pushes past Nori Ko and the girl and steps through the exit. "No one will ever come here again."

SARAH ALOPAY, JAGO TLALOC, SIMON ALOPAY

Famoso Airfield, Bakersfield, California, United States

"Hey there, sweetheart."

Sarah opens her eyes. Simon stands over her, kneading her shoulder gently.

"What happened?"

"You fell asleep."

She sits. "Shit." She rubs her face. "Been doing that a lot lately."

"That's what Jago said. He also said you went a few days with hardly any sleep at all in Peru, when his parents took you captive, so it's not very surprising."

"He told you about that, huh?"

"He did."

Sarah glances around the inside of the plane. "Where's Jago, anyway?"

"Outside. Trying to convince Rodney Q and Hibbert not to kill him," Simon jokes.

Sarah knows both men well. They're Cahokian trainers, one specializing in extreme survival skills and the other in metallurgy and demolitions.

Sarah rises to her feet. "So we're in Nebraska?" she asks. "We're home?" She's excited to see Olowa, to hold her hand, to tell her she that she loves her, face-to-face.

"No," Simon says. "We're in Bakersfield, California. The West Coast is a mess—earthquakes rippling up and down the San Andreas Fault since the impact—but the power grid, along with radio communications, GPS, and various satellite feeds, are working here."

Sarah frowns. "What do you mean, we're in California?"

"We couldn't risk flying home. Yellowstone's still erupting and there's too much debris to risk it. I drove to Illinois, you know."

"Then we should have driven back!" Sarah says.

"I'm sorry, Sarah. But you couldn't abandon this plane. You know that. So long as you can find fuel, it will get you anywhere in the world."

"Not anywhere," Sarah points out.

Simon squeezes her arm gently. "We're not going to stop Endgame in Nebraska, Sarah. Jago explained what's happened. All of it. He convinced me. To be honest, it wasn't that hard."

"*All* of it?"

"All of it. Including the Cahokian Rebellion."

"You sound like . . . you already knew about it."

"I've known about it for a long time, and I would have told you too after you aged out. But I couldn't while you were training. If Endgame actually happened to you then you couldn't begin with doubt in your heart. Yeah, I knew about our rebellion, but I also believed there was a chance that the prophecy was true. It was a teeny chance, but it meant you could win, and it mean that we might be able to live a long life—together. All of the Cahokians. Or, as many of us as possible . . ."

He trails off and looks at the floor. She knows he's thinking about Tate, because that's who she's thinking of too.

"Dad . . ."

Tears fill Simon's eyes. "I miss him."

Sarah's grief catches in her throat. She wipes her nose with her arm.

"Me too," she manages to say.

Pause.

"I should have told you, Sarah. I understand that now, and I'm sorry."

"It's okay, Dad. I'm sorry too."

"For what? I'm proud of you. *So* proud."

You shouldn't be, she thinks, the image of Christopher's face hanging in the air next to her father.

Simon continues, "If you'd known about the rebellion you wouldn't have been able to stop Endgame from starting, Sarah."

She shrugs. "Maybe. I could've blown myself up at the Calling, along with every other Player and maybe kepler 22b too. That might have stopped it. It would have saved him, if nothing else, the big idiot."

"What're you talking about?"

"I—" Sarah says, but is cut short as Jago bounds into the cabin.

"Sarah—Jordan's on the radio. Hilal and Shari should be on soon too. We need to talk to them." Jago holds out his hand. Her gaze lingers on her father—she wants to tell him that she killed Christopher, she *needs* to tell him, but not right now. She grips Jago's strong fingers.

"Come on," Jago says, a smile creasing his scar.

Sarah glances at her father once more as Jago pulls her away.

Simon follows, still wondering what it is that Sarah needs to say.

GREG JORDAN

Govi-Altai Province, Mongolia

“This is Charlie Echo One, on secure channel Alpha Romeo Five Seven, over. Repeat, Charlie Echo One, over.”

He clicks the transmitter and waits. Silence. He’s in the cockpit of the de-winged Bombardier, his face bruised, his nose broken. Breathing hurts. Badly. The explosion from his grenade as it met the alien’s projectile threw him at least 20 feet over the rocky Mongolian terrain. He has at least one cracked rib on his right side, and what feels like two or three on the left below his shoulder blade. He has a long abrasion up the back of his right arm and a golf ball–sized lump on the back of his head, and his neck is so strained that he can’t tuck his chin to his chest. He was unconscious well into the night of the attack, and barely able to move the whole next day. It took him an hour to get to his hands and knees and crawl the 50-odd feet to the plane. Once inside he drank water and ate some crackers and threw up and ate some more crackers and began treating his wounds. He tried hard not to fall asleep, since he was positive he’d been concussed.

Whatever. He’s the lucky one. Because he’s alive. He’s here.

“Charlie Echo One, on secure channel Alpha Romeo Five Seven, over. Repeat, Charlie Echo One, over.”

He takes a breath—or tries to—and is stopped dead by the pain stabbing his side. “Fuck,” he whispers. He spits into a paper cup from the galley. The saliva has trails of blood in it, which is an improvement. It’s a lot less than when he first came around, shivering in the twilight. His spit then was dark purple and thick. He was afraid he was bleeding internally, but since then it’s let up.

The lucky one.

A crackle on the radio. Jordan clicks his transmitter again. "Charlie Echo One, copy back, over?"

"This is Oscar Kilo Fifteen. I read you." Jago. "We have company?"

"Negative," Jordan says. "Maintain silence for third party, copy back."

"Copy that. I'll get the other," Jago says, referring to Sarah.

Jordan is glad that at least one other group lives, especially the one that had to go back to America and so close to the impact zone. He takes three tiny sips from a plastic water bottle and waits. He wonders how much he should say. What he should reveal about his situation, about Marrs and Aisling and Pop, in case the Makers are listening. They must be listening.

He doesn't have long to contemplate his options. Hilal's voice pops over the radio, crackling with urgency. "This is Tango Lima One. Is anyone there?"

"Oscar Kilo Fifteen, checking in," Sarah says.

"Charlie Echo One, checking in," Jordan says.

"Excellent," Hilal says. "Tell us your status."

Sarah says, "Objective complete. Near West Coast of US. Ready to move to the next monument."

Jordan says, "Objective complete." He pauses.

Hilal says, "Objective changed on our end, but the results are positive. We have some news regarding—"

"I gotta say something," Jordan interrupts.

Hilal says, "As do I, Charlie Echo One. Please, listen—"

"I'm sure your shit is urgent too, but my news is probably more urgent. We were attacked. By one of Them. Marrs was killed. Our plane is disabled. I should have been killed too but . . . got lucky." He spits into the cup. He hasn't spoken so much since coming around, and every word hurts. "Didn't see what happened to Aisling. She's either dead or . . . she's not here, whatever happened to her. Pop isn't either. No sign of them."

"He took them." It's Shari. "He must have. If what we learned about Sun Key is true, then he needs one of us to finish the game. He took her!"

Jordan turns his ear to the speaker and raises an eyebrow. "What do you mean? What have you learned?"

"One attacked us too," Sarah says before Shari or Hilal can explain about meeting Jenny Ulapala and her being able to read the Maker's book.

"What?" Shari asks.

"We were ambushed near our objective. The Maker nearly got us, but we . . ." Sarah pauses. "We fought back. We survived."

"How the fu—" Jordan starts, remembering the invisible and bulletproof force that waylaid them, the thing that obliterated Marrs where he stood, the giant unseen hand that caught three grenades and let them explode in its grasp as if they were popping balloons. But then he thinks better of it. If Sarah and Jago have some way of fighting the Makers, best not to talk about it over the radio.

Hilal says, "Charlie Echo One, please reconfirm: You cannot travel?"

"That's right. Might as well be on the moon. But I'm safe. Have food, water, medicine, shelter, and power. I'll be fine till you can circle back."

"And you, Oscar Kilo Fifteen?"

"Mobile and ready. We can go wherever you think we should go," Jago says. "You were going to tell us something important about Sun Key?"

"Yes," Hilal says, "but I think it better to discuss in person, in case this channel is compromised. Shari is transmitting coordinates now. I will meet you at this rendezvous ASAP. If you arrive first, please encamp at the airport. Once we are together we will move to the next monument in force."

"Roger that," Sarah says. "We'll see you there."

Hilal says, "Safe travels, Players. I will see you soon. I want to hear how you killed the Maker."

"I wanna hear that too," Jordan chimes. "But until you can tell me face-to-face, get out there and fucking kick ass, Players. For Marrs, for McCloskey, for the Harappan, for everyone. For Stella. For Aisling. Just fucking kick ass. This is Charlie Echo One, out."

AN LIU, NORI KO, LITTLE ALICE CHOPRA

Private plane holding area, Xianyang International Airport, Xi'an, China

An sits at the controls of his modified Y-12E, a laptop on his thighs, his fingers stabbing the keys. The turboprop is dormant but otherwise fueled, its course charted, its occupants ready for take off. It originally flew maritime surveillance for China Flying Dragon Aviation out of Harbin in Heilongjiang, but it has belonged to the Shang line for as long as An remembers. Of all the planes and helicopters he's flown, real or in simulation, An's logged more hours on his precious and reliable Y-12E than any other.

Over 992 hours, to be exact.

All he needs is a few more hours.

Except that he and Nori Ko and Sky Key can't take off. They can't fly to Yonaguni and to the Mu monument—which is also where the Olmec appears to be headed. When they left the Shang pyramid An checked Chiyoko's tracking watch, and there, to his delight and surprise, was the blip-blip marking Jago Tlaloc. He hadn't died. Not yet. The fool hadn't figured out that he'd been tagged way back at the Calling. Now he is over halfway across the Pacific, on a heading that will soon cross the Japanese island of Yonaguni. The place where, if they could only get airborne, the Olmec will find nothing but death.

But An and Nori Ko and Sky Key can't fly to Yonaguni because the military clearance codes An's relied on for so many years aren't working. Air traffic over China and Taiwan, which they'll have to fly over to reach Yonaguni, has been severely restricted since Abaddon.

BLINKSHIVERBLINKBLINKSHIVER.

He raps his knuckles on his temple three times. Pain shoots down the side of his head and through his jaw. The pain is good. The tics subside. He's been trying to hack through a back door of Beijing's aviation administration so they can cross China with no questions asked.

"How's it going?" Nori Ko asks from the cabin. She's working a computer too while monitoring Sky Key.

An yells, "This last encryption is challenging." *SHIVER*. "How about you?"

"I spoke with my brother Tsuro in Yonaguni," she says, her voice getting closer. She appears behind him and leans into the cockpit. "I'm glad the Mu planted him there so long ago. He's going to help us out."

"I'm glad he's there too," An says.

"Tsuro filed the request for emergency medical supplies with the trans-Asian relief agency. I sent you the doc number with our mocked-up manifest. That's the one you should use with Beijing. As far as anyone knows we're flush with gauze, iodine, and IV bags, not sniper rifles, explosives, and a nuclear suicide vest."

"Okay"—*blink*—"I"—*shiver*—"I"—*SHIVER*—"I got it. Good work."

"Thanks. I also told Tsuro that if any of the others get there before us then he needs to stall them."

"With any"—*blinkBLINK*—"with any"—*SHIVERshiver*—"with any luck that won't happen."

"Yeah. With any luck," Nori Ko says.

An shudders visibly. He holds his fingers out over the laptop, obviously trying to keep them from shaking.

"Hey, you okay?" Nori Ko asks.

"Y-"—*blink*—"Y-"—*BLINK*—"Yes."

He lowers his fingers to the keyboard and punches away.

"All right." Nori Ko points at the navigation computer. "What's the Olmec's ETA?"

"Less than six hours," An says. Nori Ko watches as windows on his computer screen open and close, open and close.

"Get us airborne, An."

"I'm trying."

Nori Ko turns back to the cabin.

Get us in the sky, love.

"I'm trying, Chiyoko."

Nori Ko freezes. "What?"

"I said, I'm trying."

SARAH ALOPAY, JAGO TLALOC, SIMON ALOPAY

Bombardier Global 8000, 590 miles northeast of Yonaguni, Japan

Sarah Alopay pinches her nose and blows out her ears. They squeak and pop but she doesn't care. They're too close for her to care.

She and Simon sit at a shiny walnut table. A bowl that's bolted to the edge of the table near the window holds the unremarkable-looking Maker weapon and a pack of Trident gum. Jago flies the plane at a level and smooth 42,000 feet. They picked up the two Cahokian trainers, Hibbert and Rodney Q, for added muscle. Both are sacked out in the plane's bedroom, sleeping in all of their gear like good soldiers always do. Sarah's injured arm is out of its sling, her elbow extended on the table. She grips a bright tennis ball, releases, grips, releases. Her arm's getting better. It's far from healed, but it can handle some light duty. She plans on keeping it out of the sling for this next mission. With any luck, their *last* mission.

Simon hits redial on his satellite phone's keypad. The phone works—he's placed random test calls to several numbers in the eastern hemisphere—but it hasn't been able to reach the Alopay compound in Nebraska. He's tried 74 times on this long flight, and 74 times he has received the automated message of a nice-sounding lady saying, "Inmarsat cannot place the call as dialed. We apologize for any inconvenience. Please try again."

But then, as Jago announces they're beginning the descent into Yonaguni, Simon's face lights up. Sarah releases the tennis ball. It makes a little spiral on the tabletop before rolling into her lap. She catches it with her thighs. "What?" she asks.

Simon hits the speakerphone button and holds up the receiver.

Ring.

Silence.

Ring.

Silence.

Ri—

"Hello?"

"Mom?" Sarah says. *"Olowa?"* her father says at the same instant.

"Sarah! Oh my goodness, Sarah! Is that really you?"

"It's me, Mom!" Her eyes meet Simon's. "It's us!"

For a few minutes they fawn over each other, talking love and loss and how Sarah and Simon found each other and what's been happening in Nebraska. Olowa and the others can't go aboveground on account of the air quality, but the bunker is warm and the power works fine. Olowa's rationing their supplies, and while she has more people to care for than she expected ("Eleven of us!"), they're good for at least five weeks. Olowa explains that she had to repair a relay to the phone's antenna and that was why they hadn't been able to get through.

"But we're fine, sweetie. How're—goodness, how're *you*?"

"She's good, Ole. She has a new boyfriend," Simon jokes.

"Dad!"

"And guess what. He's a Player!"

"Dad!"

"All right, all right," her father says.

"Who is he, Sarah?" her mother asks.

"It's not important."

"Sure it is."

Sarah shrugs. "His name's Jago. He's the Olmec."

"And he has diamond studs set in his top incisors," Simon adds.

"What?" Olowa asks.

"It's true," Simon says. "He's good for her, though. They've saved each other multiple times, apparently."

Her mother says, "Tell me as much as you can. How *are* you doing?"

Sarah sighs. "I've been better, Mom. I miss school and soccer and worrying about college. I miss being normal—or pretending to be normal. Jago and I have talked about it a lot. As he's pointed out, those days are gone. Actually, he maintains they were never really here. That I was always not normal. I still miss them, though."

"I miss all that too."

"But I'm alive. I guess, all things considered, I'm good. I can't tell you how happy I am Dad's here."

Simon takes Sarah's hand. Jago walks out of the cockpit to use the bathroom before landing, ignorant that they've been talking about him. Simon motions for Jago to wake up the Cahokian men. Jago nods and disappears to the rear of the plane.

When he passes them again a minute later, Simon joins him to help with landing the plane, and also so Sarah and Olowa can be alone. Sarah gives her mom the quick version of all that's happened, leaving out certain things intentionally in case the kepler's listening. She doesn't mention the Maker weapon, or anything about their plans to stop the aliens, but she does talk generally about how hard the road's been, and about finding Earth Key and losing it, and seeing Sky Key, and lastly about killing. "It's been so easy, Mom. Too easy. That's basically why I lost it after Stonehenge," she says, not mentioning Christopher.

She can't bring herself to say his name.

"Oh, Sarah," Olowa says. But her voice sounds strange. On their own the words mean, *I'm so sorry,* but the way Olowa says them it sounds more like, *You're strong. So* be *strong, Sarah.*

And then it spills out of her like a flood. She tells everything that happened right after leaving Omaha. She tells about how Christopher followed her and about how she fell in love with Jago as if they'd known each other for months or even years. She talks about feeling out of touch with herself, about how at her worst moments she's had no idea who she is. She tells her mother about how when she drove out of London she nearly had a nervous breakdown in the car, screaming and crying at the top of her lungs without being aware of it. She talks about how easy it's been to move and Play and kill, and to hurt people, including herself. About how easy it's been to deliver and receive pain, and bear it, except for one kind of pain that's been impossible to carry. And she still can't say what it is. She can't say the words to her mother—the woman who gave birth to her and taught her so much about life and love, and yes, also about blood and how to make it flow.

She can't say, *I killed Christopher.*

What she does say is, "Endgame's fucked me up, Mom. Really badly. I probably should have killed that little girl. Sky Key. But I couldn't. I . . . I couldn't. Not after . . ."

She can't say it.

"Stop, sweetie. Nothing could have prevented Abaddon."

"How do you know?" Sarah takes the tennis ball in her fingers. Squeezes. Releases. Squeezes. The ball caves and breaks and pops. The connection over the phone crackles. "Mom? You there?"

"I'm here."

"How do you know?" Sarah asks again, pleading.

"Listen—Abaddon's here, so there's no point in second-guessing. Nothing could have prevented it. It was too big. The Maker has too much power."

"But what if he doesn't have that much power? What if he's as desperate as we are? What if I hadn't gotten Earth Key? What if I hadn't . . ."

She can't.

"You don't have to say it, sweetie."

"Say what?"

"I know Christopher's dead. As soon as you said his name, I knew."

"Mom, I . . . I . . ."

"I know you killed him."

Silence.

"How?"

"I'm your mother, Sarah. No one knows you better than I do, whether you like it or not."

"Ten minutes to touchdown," Jago announces over the comm.

Sarah hears Hibbert say something to Rodney Q from the bedroom.

"You have to go," Olowa says.

"Yeah. But I need to tell you what happened, right now. I might not get another chance."

"I already know, sweetie."

"Mom, I'm a monster!" Sarah whispers, her lips practically pressed to the receiver.

"You're not, Sarah! Oh, honey . . . Don't you see what Christopher *really* did?"

"He didn't *do* anything, Mom. That's what's so messed up. He saw what I'd become and he wanted to die. He said he loved me, and sure, he meant it, but in the end that didn't count for shit. I still pulled the trigger. Christopher fought to stay with me after the Calling, even after he'd met Jago and seen that we were, I don't know—*together*. He fought hard to be at my side and help me. But in the end he couldn't, Mom. And I killed him for it." Sarah's ashamed over the bitterness of her words, but they ring true. Until this moment she never realized how angry she was at Christopher for following her, for loving her, for standing there and staring at her and taking it as she killed him.

For judging her.

"You're wrong, sweetie. Christopher did do something."

"What?"

"He saved your life, Sarah. And now you have to keep on living. For him."

The plane bumps through some clouds.

Olowa continues, "That's what I'm going to tell his parents, too. That he died so that you could live. That's not a lie. I'm going to tell them that you were with him when he died, and that you tried to save him but couldn't. Christopher is a hero, Sarah. You are too. If you and your friends succeed, then you'll all be heroes. Endgame could have gone a million different ways, but in *this* Endgame? Christopher, for all his faults, may be the biggest hero of all."

Several moments of silence. Sarah stares out the window at heavy clouds. The water below is dark. She does not see any land. "Jesus, Mom."

"Jesus has nothing to do with any of this."

"No. I mean I think you're right."

"Of course I'm right, sweetie. I already told you: I'm your mother."

Sarah chuckles.

"I know you don't like killing, Sarah. You're not supposed to. You're human. But you're good at it. Your friends are good at it. And before this ends, you're going to have to do it again—maybe more than once. So don't beat yourself up. Forgive yourself. Christopher saved your life. End of story. Now go out there and save what's left of our lives, before it's too late."

The plane thumps as the landing gear folds out.

"I will, Mom. Thank you."

"Thank me when you see me."

"All right. I love you."

"I love you too, sweetie. And I always will, no matter what."

HILAL IBN ISA AL-SALT

Bombardier Global 8000, 488 miles south-southwest of Yonaguni, Japan

Hilal checks the navigation system. He's got 51 minutes left. Sarah and Jago, based on their last check-in, should touch down in 10 minutes.

He works the radio controls. Gets the right channel and clicks on.

"This is Tango Lima One for Oscar Kilo Fifteen, over."

Nothing.

"Tango Lima One for Oscar Kilo Fifteen, over."

Static and then, "Tango Lima One, we read you, over." It's Jago.

"What is your ETA?"

"Nine minutes, seven seconds. Should have visual once we get under cloud cover."

"Understood. I am right behind you. A little more than forty minutes out."

"Roger, Tango Lima One. Any intel?" Jago asks.

"I spoke with the regional air director ten minutes ago. A man named Tsuro Masaka. I pretended to be an American and gave my name as Harold Dickey. He does not know we will be armed, so be prepared to subdue if you deem it appropriate. For explanation, tell him we are working on a joint US–Japanese top-secret mission in response to Abaddon."

"*Entiendo*. Anything else?"

"Yonaguni is a small island. Masaka confirmed that no one has been coming or going for the last sixty-five hours. I have checked the manifests online and can confirm that this is accurate. Masaka made it sound like the place is virtually deserted."

"So no Shang bogey?"

"Affirmative. If Liu is coming here too, then we have beat him."

"*Excelente.* Oscar Kilo Fifteen, out."

SARAH ALOPAY, JAGO TLALOC, SIMON ALOPAY

Yonaguni Airport, Yonaguni, Japan

Jago cycles down the engines. The airport outside is not much more than a few buildings pushed against a single runway, the East China Sea lapping at its long northern fringe. There's a small and empty hangar to the west and an Erector set–like radio tower to the east. A few single-engine Cessnas are mothballed nearby, their windows blocked off and dirty. The buildings are unassuming and tidy. In fact, there's no sign of anyone until a small man swings open a glass door and walks toward them. He smiles broadly, his hand raised in greeting. An orange bag is slung over his shoulder, and he wears an army-green T-shirt with a line drawing of the most venerable and loved Jedi of all time. The caption reads in English, *My Yoda Shirt, This Is.*

Jago slides open the window. "Hey there."

"Hello!" the man announces happily in English. "You are Mr. Dickey's friends?"

"That's right! Name's Feo."

"Wonderful, Feo! Welcome to Yonaguni!"

Jago claps the window shut. "That's our guy."

Simon says, "I'll send Rodney Q and Hibbert out to clear."

"Good idea," Sarah says.

They move to the cabin. The Cahokian trainers pop up from their seats, a Colt pistol snapped to each of their hips, an M4 in each of their hands. Rodney Q has a black bandanna tied loosely around his neck and Hibbert chews a big wad of pink bubble gum.

Hibbert says, "What's the word, Sarah?"

"Go out there, introduce yourself, and report back. Don't tell him why we're armed."

Hibbert nods. "Gun's the only reason he'll need," he says brusquely.

"If we're clear then start unloading. We'll move out as soon as Hilal gets here."

"Got it."

Jago throws the latch on the door and pushes it out. The stairs fold quietly to the ground. The outside temperature is warm, the air humid. The sun hides behind the clouds of ash that now cover the entire globe. Rodney Q—six foot four, 240 pounds—ducks through the opening and steps down. Hibbert, who's much shorter and lighter, follows him.

"Oh, hello," the man calls out from below. "Mr. Dickey didn't say anything about"—he swallows—"guns."

"Sorry," Rodney Q grunts, not sounding at all sorry. Masaka shuffles to the side as Rodney Q sets foot on the ground, looking this way and that.

Hibbert looks Masaka directly in the eye and says, "Don't move, please." He's not pointing his gun at Masaka, but it's clearly a threat barely concealed as an order.

Masaka stammers, "I-I'm s-sorry, sir, but—"

"And with respect, be quiet," Hibbert adds in flawless Japanese.

Masaka shuts up.

Sarah watches from the shadows inside the doorway as Rodney Q expertly skirts around the man, checking the buildings and the corners. He disappears to circle the plane. She looks past the airport. Lush trees line the road. Mount Urabe rises to the south. A white horse lazes in a field in the distance.

After a minute Rodney Q reappears. "We're good."

Masaka shifts from foot to foot, his hands joined nervously at his waist.

Hibbert moves to the side of the plane. The cargo door thumps open.

Sarah leans halfway out the door. "Thanks, Rodney. Sorry if this comes as a surprise, Mr. Masaka," she says to the unfortunate man. "We mean you no harm." He blinks but doesn't speak. She turns back inside, facing Jago and Simon. "Ready?"

"More than ready," Jago says, smiling broadly.

Sarah smiles back. "Me too."

Jago takes her arm. "You look different, Alopay. Lighter. Easier."

"I *feel* lighter, Feo. And you know? I feel confident too. I'm glad we decided to work with the others."

"Me too."

"And Dad, having you here is . . . it's good for me. Talking to Mom—that was *really* good. Thanks for making it happen."

Hibbert calls for some help with a heavy case. "I'll go," Simon says. He pushes past the Players and walks down the steps and disappears around the side of the plane.

Jago gives Sarah a full kiss on the lips. His breath is terrible. He turns aside and bounds down the stairs.

Sarah moves to the top step and inhales sharply. The air is salty and sweet and fresh. Earth is injured, but it is not destroyed or broken. Earth won't *be* broken.

It can't be.

She thinks of Christopher. Of what she did. Of what *he* did.

She's not broken, either.

She can't be.

Jago waves to her. She moves forward.

And then the air cracks, and Jago's head pops sideways, and blood and brains splatter over his shirt and the stair's handrails, and she barely makes out the suppressed hiss of a rifle's report as it slithers down from the mountainside.

"Sarah!" Simon yells.

She leaps down the remaining steps, already drawing her pistol, already running as fast as she can.

The air cracks. Her eyes don't work. Her ears don't work. Her legs don't work. The world disappears.

She was wrong.

It *is* broken.

Like Maccabee before her, she never got a chance to hear the shot.

AN LIU, NORI KO, LITTLE ALICE CHOPRA

Northern foothills of Mount Urabe, Yonaguni, Japan

A white horse bolts across the field below, the hooves like miniature thunder.

Thank you, love, Chiyoko says breathlessly.

They are the sweetest words An has ever heard.

"I told you I'd"—*blinkSHIVERblink*—"I told you I'd kill them."

Thank you.

Nori Ko peers up down right left through the range finder. Tsuro waves a hand in their direction, giving them a thumbs-up. "That was some exceptional shooting, An," she says. "Five shots, five kills. Four of them in motion." She checks the time in the range finder's HUD. "In under eight seconds."

Compliment her, Chiyoko says.

An pulls his eye from the scope and angles the rifle into the air. "I couldn't have"—*blink*—"I couldn't have done it without you, Nori Ko. Or your brother down"—*SHIVER*—"your brother down"—*BLINKSHIVER*—"your brother."

"Tsuro's been waiting a long time to help me," she says.

They'd landed less than an hour before the Cahokian and the Olmec and rushed to get their gear into a Mitsubishi Montero and up to this position south and west of the airport, leaving Tsuro to deal with An's Y-12E. While they prepared for the kill shots he single-handedly moved the plane to the back of the hangar and out of sight.

An moves from his position on top of a grassy bluff and twists to Sky Key. She's drugged and sleeping, propped against Nori Ko's pack.

Keep moving, Chiyoko says.

"I don't want"—*BLINK*—"I don't want to wait for the others, Nori Ko. Waiting for"—*BLINKBLINK*—"for this Dickey person is too"—*SHIVERblinkSHIVER*—"too unpredictable."

"Agreed." She stows the range finder in her pack, careful not to disturb the girl. "Tsuro will handle them." She taps her watch. "Besides, we have to kill 22b, and time's ticking away."

An leans his jet-black JS 7.62 rifle against a rock and checks his vest. He fumbles with his shirt buttons, his eyes blinking and blinking and blinking, his shoulder muscles twitching. He finally gets the shirt open and tugs at the vest's straps one more time, making sure they're secure. It presses into his skin, constricting his rib cage painfully. It's heavy—nearly 20 kilos—but it feels oddly comforting, like a snug blanket.

"You all right, An? Your tics are getting worse."

He's fine, Chiyoko says.

Except An is the one who speaks these words.

"What do you mean, 'he'?" Nori Ko asks.

An straightens. He buttons his shirt back up. He looks Nori Ko in the eye.

Don't tell her about me, Chiyoko says.

"I mean I'm fine," An says. "It's an old trick. When my body does this, sometimes I pretend it belongs to someone else—therefore 'he.' It helps me get a handle on everything." This is a lie, but a good one. And it works because, by luck, his body is composed and under control as he speaks.

He pushes a few buttons on a custom keypad strapped to his wrist. A light on the pad flashes three times and then glows red. "It's armed. I'm ready."

He snags the sniper rifle and an ammunition satchel and heads to the Montero, leaving Nori Ko to deal with the large pack and Sky Key. She gathers both, cradling Sky Key like a baby. The girl stirs as Nori Ko flops her into the backseat. Nori Ko takes Sky Key's chin and peels open an eyelid. Her pupils are wide and dilated. They flutter toward her nose. She's completely out. Nori Ko gets in the passenger seat and An puts the car in gear and they move.

They wind over a dirt track, heading east and south, until they link up with the main road over Mount Urabe. An drives very fast. The landscape is open and lush, with fields of hay and young wheat and dense stands of trees along the mountain's ridgelines. As they make their way back downhill toward a small marina on the southern side of the island, Nori Ko gets out her phone and makes a call.

It barely rings before she starts talking. She speaks for a few minutes in rushed Japanese. An can't understand a word of it. As soon as she hangs up An says, "Your brother again?"

"Yes. Everything's ready. We'll have to dive with tanks, but it's not deep. And we've got a full mask for the child, so we can keep her unconscious." She glances at Sky Key. "We should be inside the Mu monument within the hour." They approach a T intersection. "Go left."

He tears around the corner, the Montero fishtailing.

An presses the gas more. The car accelerates. They are nearly there.

HILAL IBN ISA AL-SALT

Bombardier Global 8000, landing at Yonaguni Airport, Yonaguni, Japan

Hilal brings the plane in smooth and easy. He watches out the right side of the cockpit window as he taxis, the plane bouncing over the tarmac. He sees the other plane, but he does not see the others.

A few minutes later, as he brings the plane to a stop, Hilal sees a small Japanese man in a T-shirt and jeans maneuvering a large and laden luggage cart to one side of the receiving area. Sarah and Jago's plane is closed up and in good shape, if a little dirty and worn for having flown through what must have been an airborne hell over Canada and the United States.

Hilal cycles down the engines. The man waves at him gleefully, and then mimes opening the window. Hilal obliges.

"Mr. Dickey?" the man yells in perfect English.

"That's right," Hilal says, maintaining his American accent. "Mr. Masaka?"

"One and the same!"

"Did my friends arrive?"

"Yes!" He points over his shoulder. "They're inside, trying to enjoy some tea. They are very impatient for you to arrive, though."

"I'm sure. I'll be right out."

Hilal unbuckles and moves to the cabin. He slings on his pack. It holds a satellite phone he can use to call Jenny and Shari back in Australia, some food and water, and a pair of night-vision goggles. He pulls on shoulder webbing with extra magazines for his rifle and slings a leather belt around his waist, his machetes on either hip. Finally he snags a matte black HK416 and turns to the door.

Hilal, merely out of habit, toggles his 416 to fire.

He releases the latch and the door swings out and the warm sea air rushes in. It is sweet and heavy, and Hilal likes it.

Masaka lets out a gasp. "Oh my," he says, clapping a hand over his mouth. Hilal knows that this is a reaction to the wounds on his head and face.

Hilal reaches the tarmac and bows. "Mr. Masaka. I apologize for my appearance. I know it is unsettling. And thank you for allowing my friends and me to land."

"Of course . . ."

"We are not here to hurt you. Quite the contrary. I am sure my friends told you something similar."

"Yes—they did."

"How long since they arrived?"

"About thirty minutes," Masaka says, unable to pry his eyes from Hilal's face.

"Good. And you say they are inside?"

"Yes, over there, behind that door." He spins and points at the nearest building. "They're eager to see you."

"And I them." Hilal starts to walk toward the building when Masaka slaps his forehead.

"Goodness! I nearly forgot my manners. Please, one moment." He takes a half step back. "Your friend Sarah asked me to do this!"

"And that is?"

"Tea! She liked my tea so much she asked me to bring you some. I have some right here!" He points at a lacquered tray resting on the edge of the luggage rack. "Please. It's tradition!"

Hilal shrugs. "All right."

Masaka shuffles to the tray and picks it up, careful not to spill anything. In seconds he's standing before Hilal. "I'm sorry if this is strange. You are visitors, and I pride myself on welcoming visitors properly." He holds up the enamel tray, a pair of jade-colored cups on it. Steam swirls above them. As he draws closer Hilal's nose is greeted with the subtle but intoxicating odor of earth, cut grass, roasted grains, and a bite of acid that tickles his nostrils.

"It does smell good," Hilal admits.

"It's my own special blend," Masaka says.

Hilal takes the cup closest to Tsuro. Masaka takes the other. The tray falls to his side. They raise their cups. A stiff breeze blows over the airport from the west, whipping around Sarah and Jago's plane. It pushes away the smell of the tea and replaces it with the smell of trees and fresh water on concrete, like after a squall.

"Kampai," Masaka says.

"Kampai," Hilal echoes, but not very enthusiastically. He slowly raises the cup to his lips.

But then Hilal notices that the concrete around the other plane is shiny and wet, while the plane itself is utterly dry.

Hilal's eyes drift to the base of the luggage cart. He freezes.

A single drop of dark liquid falls from the cart and plops onto the ground.

Blood.

Hilal drops his cup. It shatters on the concrete, the piping tea splattering his pant cuffs and shoes.

Masaka says, "What's the matter, Mr. Dickey?"

Hilal steps back and points his rifle at Masaka's neck. "What is on that cart?"

"Luggage," Masaka says nervously. "Please, have I offended you? I apologize! Your friends—I can bring them out right now. Please!"

"You will do nothing of the sort," Hilal says, dispensing with the American accent. "I warn you, and only this one time. Do not move."

But Masaka does move. He leaps directly sideways, slipping out of the rifle's line of fire. Instead of tracking him Hilal twirls the rifle and swings for Masaka's head. The strike misses as Masaka swipes the tray—its edge honed and sharp—at Hilal's neck. Hilal bends away to avoid it, simultaneously swinging a foot at Masaka's exposed rib cage. He lets out a whelp, and Hilal sidesteps him with lightning quickness and snaps the rifle across the backs of Masaka's knees. The man buckles and falls. In a quick motion Hilal takes the machete named *LOVE* and, keeping it in its sheath, brings it to Masaka's neck and holds it there, pressing it into his Adam's apple.

Hilal checks their surroundings. No other people are around, hostile or otherwise. He prays that Masaka is working alone, or Hilal may already be as good as dead.

Hilal drags Masaka to the side of the cart, and he sees what is behind the high stack of bags.

A blue tarp quickly rolled and tucked over a misshapen lump the size of a large animal.

But Hilal knows that it does not conceal an animal.

He applies more pressure to Masaka's neck. The man gasps. Using the muzzle of his rifle Hilal raises a corner of the tarp and then whips the whole thing off. It flies open on the breeze.

Five bodies. All dead courtesy of medium-caliber head shots. Three men he has never seen before, although it is hard to make out their faces on account of their wounds.

And piled on top of these figures, her right arm thrown haphazardly over the narrow part of his waist, are Sarah Alopay and Jago Tlaloc. Both killed by sniper fire. Hilal checks around one last time, concludes that Masaka simply lured the Players and their associates into the open, where they were killed from a distance, and then dealt with their bodies. Hilal reasons that if the sniper were still out there, then he would already be dead.

Meaning he is safe. At least for the moment.

Masaka tries to speak but Hilal pulls *LOVE*'s scabbard so hard into his throat that he can't breathe. Hilal needs to find something before he deals with this little man. If Sarah and Jago really do have a weapon that can kill a Maker then he needs to take it from them. Hilal quickly frisks the Olmec. He does the same to Sarah, moving up from the feet. He finds a strange object in a pocket—a lump of metal that fits perfectly in his hand. It looks completely nonthreatening, but there's something about its heft and shape that makes him think this is it. He looks at the fallen Players one last time.

Lost comrades.

Heroes.

He says a low prayer in Amharic and pulls the tarp over them.

Their Endgame is over.

He pulls Masaka to his feet and drags him back out on the tarmac and then under the wing and fuselage of the plane, giving himself some cover. He forces Masaka to his knees and unsheathes *LOVE* and points it at the man's face. "Put your hands on your head, Mr. Masaka."

He does as he is told.

Hilal can tell from how he served the tea, and from the tilt of his shoulders, that Masaka is left-handed.

"Hold out your left hand, Mr. Masaka."

He protests in Japanese.

"Your head or your hand, Mr. Masaka. Choose now."

"Okay, okay!" Masaka says. He sticks out his left arm.

"Fan your fingers."

Masaka does.

Hilal rests *LOVE*'s edge on the base of his pinkie. "Who are you working with?" he demands.

Masaka says something else in Japanese, almost certainly a string of curses.

Hilal pushes down on *LOVE* and the pinkie comes free. The man calls out and tries to pull his altered hand close to his body but Hilal quickly reaches out and grabs Masaka's ring finger. He holds the hand in place and calmly lowers the blade to the skin.

"Speak," Hilal says.

"Fuck you," Masaka says in English.

Hilal cuts off this finger too. He drops it near the pinkie and grabs the middle finger. Blood is all over both of their hands now.

"Speak," Hilal says.

"I won't," Masaka blabs.

The finger is getting slippery, Hilal can't hold on. So he takes his wrist and slides his machete up Tsuro's arm, stopping at his shoulder.

"Do not test me."

"All right, all right! It was my sister!"

"Who is your sister?"

"She is Mu."

"You are *Mu*?"

"Yes."

"Your Player died a long time ago," Hilal says, not understanding.

"Fuck you," the man says again.

"Who is your sister?" Hilal demands.

Masaka doesn't speak.

Hilal thinks he understands. "You are working for revenge, yes? This is the best explanation I can come up with."

"Fuck. You."

"Last chance," Hilal says, pressing the edge of the machete into Masaka's flesh. "Who is your sister and is she alone?"

"I am Mu. My blood is Mu. I am Mu." He spits. A ball of phlegm hits Hilal's foot.

Hilal doesn't flinch.

Instead he raises the machete a few inches and then whips it down. Blood spurts everywhere. Hilal drops the arm. Masaka screams. Hilal moves the tip of his blade to Masaka's neck. "Mr. Masaka, time is my enemy right now. Tell me if your sister is alone."

Masaka quickly goes into shock. Hilal knows he doesn't feel any pain. The adrenaline won't let him.

"Answer me."

"Sh-Shang. The Shang."

"And they are where?"

"Marina. South side of island. Please."

Shock is a wonderful truth serum, Hilal thinks.

Hilal steps back three paces. Takes up his rifle. Points it. Fires one single shot. Masaka slumps forward.

Hilal wipes his machete on Masaka's pants and sheathes it. "This was unexpected," he says out loud.

Hilal hooks his fingers under Masaka's belt and lifts him by his pelvis. He takes the severed arm. He hustles to the luggage cart and puts Masaka on top of the pile of bodies, checking his pockets first and finding his car keys.

He decides to burn all of them.

He works quickly to douse the impromptu pyre with aviation fuel and when he's done he takes a lighter and sets it off.

He leaves the airport and gets in Masaka's Toyota hatchback and takes off. As the little car winds up the mountain and away from the water he uses the phone to call Jenny. It rings once before she answers with a curt, "Yeah."

"Go to the Dreaming now," Hilal says. "Find the Mu monument and open your portal. It will happen quickly, one way or another. The Shang will be there. He has the keys. And he has an accomplice. A Mu."

"Blimey," Jenny says.

"I know. I am on my way now. Send the signal when you see me in the star chamber. Then I will move in and save Little Alice. Tell Shari I will bring her daughter."

"I will, mate," Jenny says. "Godspeed."

"And to you, Master Ulapala. Godspeed to us all."

Four and Six and Eight and Twelve and Twenty[iv]

AN LIU, NORI KO, LITTLE ALICE CHOPRA

24.43161, 123.01314, near Yonaguni, Japan

Nori Ko dives off the small fishing boat anchored directly over the sunken Mu monument. She takes her pack and a flare gun and has a bright nylon line tied to her waist. She does not wear a wetsuit. The water is warm and pleasant and bright blue. She swims down seven meters, kicks hard with her fins, her arms at her sides. She blows out her ears three times. Bubbles rise around her face and carbonate her loose hair. On her left is a sprawling stepped pyramid that's been hidden under the waves for thousands upon thousands of years, its provenance and purpose an eternal mystery to the tourists and locals who've dived it over the years.

A pyramid of Mu.

She reaches a shelf, the blue deepening into darkness on her right. She twists under an outcropping and behind a huge frond of fan coral. Yes. There, like a mouth before her, is the dark entryway. She ties off the nylon line, its other end secured to the boat bouncing on the surface. She lights a flare and holds it before her, the black stone twinkling with orange and pink and white. She hits a wall and looks up and sees the square mirror of an air pocket a meter overhead. She detaches her weight belt and kicks twice. She emerges into a dry room, its stale air trapped inside the structure for thousands of years. She tosses the flare into the room before jumping into the water and swimming back down. She tests the nylon line. It holds. She aims the flare gun at the surface, making sure to avoid the hull of the small boat, and fires.

It shoots upward in a burst of bubbles and explodes, looking like a deformed firework from under the waves.

She swims back to the room and pulls herself into it. She lights three more flares and tosses each to a different corner. The room is rectangular, and she knows from a previous Mu mission that it's three meters wide and 4.854 meters long. A slender and tall doorway sits in the western wall. This leads to a shaft that angles downward for several meters and opens into another rectangular room. This second room is as far as she got when she last came here. If she's to go any farther today—and she hopes she will—it will be into uncharted territory.

While she waits for An she unpacks the bag and checks their swords and their guns and takes what is hers.

A plume of bubbles disturbs the patch of water five minutes later. An and Sky Key appear simultaneously. The Shang Player holds up the girl and Nori Ko takes her and places her gently on top of her empty pack. She slips off the girl's specialized mask with sealed auto-equalizing ear covers and smooths Sky Key's wet face and dark hair, the skin around her chin and under her ears creased and reddened from the mask. The girl stirs and moans, but she doesn't wake.

Go easy now, love, Chiyoko tells An as he watches the other two.

He *BLINK* he slips *SHIVERSHIVERSHIVER* he slips out of his scuba gear and strips to *BLINKblinkshiver* to his underwear. He opens a large dry bag and pulls out the Chiyoko necklace and Earth Key *BLINKBLINK* and the vest and the wrist pad and a dry set of cotton clothes that are like pajamas. He brings Chiyoko over his head and smells her hair and kisses her ear. He slips Earth Key into a Velcro pocket and then puts his arms through the vest and pulls the straps extra tight against his rib cage. He slips the wrist pad over his left forearm and puts on the clothing that conceals the bulky explosive he will deliver to the kepler. He passes Nori Ko and the girl without talking, slings the strap of his ARX 160 over his shoulder. He picks up *BLINKBLINK* Nobuyuki's *SHIVERblink* Nobuyuki's katana and straps it to his back, its hilt jutting above his head.

You are ready, love.
"Ready," he says, staring at Sky Key while addressing Nori Ko.
Nori Ko stares at An in the eerie light, his deep-set eyes like black coals, his body practically glowing with vengeance, and wonders briefly if she's made a mistake.
But only briefly.
For the thing about An that frightens her most is exactly what draws her to him.
He is a killer first. And in this terrible game, killers win.
She throws An a flare. He catches it nimbly. She picks up the girl and pulls her to her chest. Sky Key's head flops onto Nori Ko's shoulder. The girl remains utterly unconscious. She will not witness her end, and Nori Ko is thankful for it.
She *is* a child, after all.
"Through there," she says, indicating the doorway. "You first."
An goes to the door and disappears through it. Nori Ko hustles after him, and after eight minutes of a corkscrewing descent they turn a sharp corner and practically stumble into the next room. Its proportions are the same as the one above, but it's twice as large. A butcher block of a table carved from the black rock, its edges straight and true, sits in the middle of the room. At the far end is another doorway, its stone door sealed shut.
The keys will open it, love, Chiyoko says.
"The keys"—*BLINKshiverBLINK*—"the keys will do it."
"Are you sure?" Nori Ko asks.
"Give me the girl," An says.
Nori Ko holds her out. An takes her in his arms. He carries her to the closed door. The girl is heavy. Earth Key is heavy in his pocket. He is heavy and getting heavier.
And then—

KEPLER 22B

24.43161, 123.01314, near Yonaguni, Japan

His eyes pop open, black slits set against his mother-of-pearl skin. A grating sound, stone sliding on stone, from not very far above.

It is time.

The old temple moves. In a few minutes its uppermost promontory will be visible to the world above the waves, a rectilinear pillar of sea-worn stone, wet and encrusted with bivalves and corals and anemones.

Like Stonehenge before it, this ancient monument has awoken.

He must prepare for the Player.

He steps from his spot and glides to the room's center. He folds in half at the waist and places the tips of his seven-fingered hands around the periphery of the gilt bowl set in the floor. The metallic surface swirls with dark colors and glimpses of the cosmos and an occasional beam of escaped light that lances to the ceiling.

He pulls his hands away, careful not to let any part of his body touch the inner bowl.

It is ready for the keys.

He moves to the portal. He places his right hand on the stone doorjamb and this liquefies and he thrusts his hand forward. He moves his fingers in the plasmastone, so cold to the touch for not having been used for thousands and thousands of years. The blank interior of the portal shimmers and blackens and he leans forward to make sure the link is open. His head appears, millions of miles away, in the teletrans room of his ship. He pulls his head back, and he is wholly in the Mu star chamber.

He swipes a finger across a sensor in the sleeve of his armor and a projectile weapon swings over his right hand. He adjusts its shot from the default wide scatter to pinpoint-thin.

He waits. The grating above continues. He scans the room one last time, moving clockwise from his left. There is the La Tène, should he need her, the living code embedded in her genes. There is the door leading up. There is the bowl in the middle of the room. The walls glow blue. But what's this? He squints. He quickly crosses the room into the farthest star point and peers down. Something he didn't see before.

A round red stone.

A stone that shouldn't be here.

He picks it up and smells it. The grating sound stops. The pebble smells distinct and he places it immediately.

It is from Australia. From near the Koori monument in the hinterland. He glances over his shoulder. The stone was exactly opposite the portal. It was thrown into the room from the Koori monument!

He drops the stone and thrusts his left hand back into the plasmastone, fine-tuning its settings. He knows that Players have moved around the world with these portals, he assumed by happenstance like when some went from Bolivia to the Himalayas, but the presence of this telltale pebble means that at least one of them has learned how to *use* the portals. This Player has not connected to this portal yet, but he assumes that he or she is trying to make a connection.

After another few moments he pulls his hand from the plasmastone and tosses the rock at the inky black of the portal. The rock bounces away and lands at his feet. Then he sticks out his hand, and it passes effortlessly through the frigid void and into his ship.

The test is satisfactory. Only he can pass now, in either direction. No one else will be able to use it to escape or to come here.

He spins back to the middle of the room and waits.

AN LIU, NORI KO, LITTLE ALICE CHOPRA

24.43161, 123.01314, near Yonaguni, Japan

An Liu and Nori Ko plant their feet as the ground shifts and turns. The sound of grinding stone is deafening, and even with no external point of reference, An senses that the room is rising through the water.

It's happening again, love, Chiyoko says. *Like when I died.*

"What's this?" Nori Ko yells. She stumbles and grabs the corner of the carved table, which is attached to the ground.

"The"—*BLINKshiver*—"the"—*SHIVERSHIVER*—"it's changing. Stonehenge did it"—*BLINKBLINKblink*—"did it too."

It means we're on the right track, love, Chiyoko says.

"I"—*BLINK*—"I know."

It means we can go the rest alone, Chiyoko says.

"I know."

Sky Key grows more restless as the room shifts and twists like a Tilt-A-Whirl, but after a few frenzied minutes it's finished.

Silence reigns.

A gust of cold air spills into the room. Sky Key's eyes flutter. She points.

"Earth Sky Sun," she says quietly.

An follows the girl's finger. The doorway is open. Another narrow passageway descending into darkness. An pushes his head into it, and his breath rises visibly around his face.

"Earth Sky Sun," Sky Key repeats.

An plops the girl onto the floor roughly.

"Hey!" Nori Ko says. "No need for—"

She's cut off as An whips his rifle into his hands and sights Nori Ko's face.

Blink.

No. Let her go! Chiyoko implores.

Except An says these words too.

BLINKBLINKBLINKBLINK.

Nori Ko raises her hands defensively.

And she finally understands.

Nori Ko says, "Listen to her, An. Chiyoko loves you."

"N-n-n-no," he says. "Thank you for"—*BLINKblinkBLINK*—"for getting me"—*SHIVERSHIVER*—"getting me here, but—"

Nori Ko cuts him off. "I can help. I'll make sure no one comes after you, An."

Let her go, Chiyoko says.

"I—I—I—I—I d-d-don't know," An stammers. "You should"—*SHIVERblinkblink*—"you should die."

Why? Chiyoko asks.

But before An can explain that it's because they all have to die and that he has to be the one to kill them, Nori Ko says, "I understand what you are, An. It's why I picked you. You're Death! Let me guard you so you can give this to the Maker, and find it for yourself. Let me help you. Let me help Chiyoko. Please!"

BLINKBLINKSHIVERshivershiverBLINK.

"Earth Sky Sun Key," the girl says.

BLINK.

Listen to her, love. Go to the kepler. Avenge me, Chiyoko says. *Now!*

BBBBBLINK. BBBBBLINK. BBBBBBBBBLINK.

His hands shake. The rifle lowers a few inches. Nori Ko considers diving behind the stone table, but while An's tics give her a chance they also show how on edge he is, how unpredictable.

She stays rooted to the spot.

SHSHSHSHSHIVER. SHIVER. SHSHSHSHShiver.

Noises echo from the passageway leading up and out of the monument. The hiss of crashing waves, a *clunk-clunk* like a metal container repeatedly bring struck like a drum, and there, right there for a moment—the sound of a man saying, "Faith."

"More are coming!" Nori Ko says urgently.

"Earth Sky Sun," the girl says loudly.

An nudges her with his thigh. "Shh."

Let her go.

BBBBBBBBBBBBLINK. SHSHSHSHSHSHSHSHSHSHIVER.

The Beretta falls to his side. "Okay. Keep me"—*BLINK*—"keep me safe, Nori Ko. Keep her"—*SHIVER*—"her"—*blinkblinkblink*—"her"—*SHIVERSHIVERBLINKblink*—"her"—*SHIVERBLINKBLINK*—"Chiyoko safe too."

Without saying another word he grabs Sky Key by the shirt collar and half carries, half drags her out of the room and into the darkness, the girl gurgling and moaning. The last thing Nori Ko sees or hears of either is the red glow from An's wrist pad, the one indicating that his nuclear vest is well and armed.

Nori Ko takes three breaths and centers herself. She draws her sword with her right hand, grips her rifle with her left. She leans against the table and drops behind it, completely hidden from whoever is coming from above.

HILAL IBN ISA AL-SALT

24.43161, 123.01314, near Yonaguni, Japan

Hilal grips a rope that's secured to his Zodiac's bow and manages to stay on the planking. The water churns as a twisting, telescoping pillar of stone rises from the waves. When it stops it juts four meters above the surface like a small lighthouse.

The dive boat that he's lashed his Zodiac to—the same boat that An and his Mu accomplice used to reach this same point—clanks against the stone rhythmically. A huge fan coral is flopped over its side, holding the boat in place. An opening large enough for a person appears on the side of the rock.

This is it.

Hilal reaches into his pocket and threads his fingers through the holes on the lump of metal. Again it does nothing. But again he is certain that somehow, some way, it will work when needed.

"I must have faith," he says.

He checks his machetes one last time and his HK416 rifle and steps off the boat and through the opening, his faith helping him take each step forward as he moves toward the end.

Reality is a dream.[v]

SHARI CHOPRA, JENNY ULAPALA

"The Dreaming," Shari says.

Their physical bodies are in Australia's Yuendumu Hinterland, but their spiritual bodies are here, in the shared void.

Shari holds Jenny's hand in both realms. In Australia they sit side by side on the red earth, knees touching. In the Dreaming they walk briskly through nothingness, have been walking for what could be fractions of a second or hours. Their arms swing with purpose, their thighs occasionally brush against each other. Shari can see forever in every direction, but wherever she looks there is nothing to see.

"When?" Shari asks.

"Soon, mum."

They are alone this time. Big Alice is not there whispering that the Harappan are at Shari's back, waving their hands, mouthing her name, pushing her forward, ever forward.

A blue glow appears in the distance. Jenny guides them toward it.

She says, "I'll stay with you when we get there, mum. But when Hilal arrives and it's time for him to bring your daughter through the portal, I'll have to leave you to signal him. Otherwise he won't know we're ready for him. You gotta stay centered and quiet in the Dreaming until Hilal's crossed with your girl, and you gotta stay calm. No matter what you see happening there, you stay calm or we could lose the connection and any chance of getting them back. You understand, yeah?"

The light grows brighter.

"I understand, Jenny."

"Good. No more talking. No more spoken thought. Silence, mental and otherwise. This is gonna be the hardest meditation you've ever done, 'cause every fiber of your being is gonna tell you to move and act on behalf of your child. You can't do none of that. Help her by being there and nothing else. If the Maker gets tipped to our presence he'll shut the door to us and we'll be good and screwed."

"I understand."

"Be nothing, like a stone on the floor, like the floor itself. You are the foundation."

To acknowledge her, Shari squeezes Jenny's hand, in this world and in that one. Here and there. Everywhere and nowhere.

They continue.

Brighter.

Brighter.

Brighter.

They see the room now, star shaped and glowing and prepared. They can't see the Maker anywhere but they can feel his presence.

He waits. He hides.

Jenny freezes near the portal. Shari does too.

Little Alice is not there yet. But—

Aisling Kopp *is* there, her unconscious face and bright-red hair peeking above the edge of a silken shroud.

Shari wants to know how this happened, but she can't speak. She can't think. She closes her eyes in the Dreaming and breathes breathes breathes.

Nothing.

Nothing.

Nothing.

Nothing is what will save them now.

NORI KO

24.43161, 123.01314, near Yonaguni, Japan

The man's voice above has been silent since she first heard it. If he's coming to her—and he must be—then he's keeping quiet. Nori Ko's repositioned herself in the passageway that An and Sky Key disappeared through, prone and propped on her elbows, her rifle covering the door on the far side of the room. The air falls around her like a frigid blanket. She mashes her teeth to keep them from chattering. The room beyond is pitch-black. She lies motionless in a void, waiting, her only window on the visible world a night vision–equipped riflescope. She keeps her eye pressed to this. She sights along the edge of the table and up to the door. Since she is a few short meters from her target she can't fit more than half the door in the field of vision. To keep sharp and ready she shifts the rifle every three seconds. Up and down and up and down and up and down.

The man—and whoever is with him, for he might not be alone—will round the final corner and appear and she will wait for the right moment and she will cut them down.

The doorway remains black and empty for four minutes.

Five.

Six.

Seven.

Eight.

This is how long it took her and An and Sky Key to get here from the room above.

Somewhere below, An is closer to meeting the Maker.

And Chiyoko too—or what is left of her. Around his neck, in his mind.

In his dark heart.

Nine minutes.

Up and down and up and down and up and down.

Up and down.

HILAL IBN ISA AL-SALT, NORI KO

24.43161, 123.01314, near Yonaguni, Japan

Hilal keeps his rifle up one-handed, the mysterious weapon ready in the other hand. His night-vision goggles are flipped over his face. He moves methodically through the dark and the cold.

After seven minutes of steady, twisting descent, Hilal stops.

The passageway ends less than a meter away. Hilal makes out the long wall of a room. If he hadn't been moving so slowly he would have poured into it. Who knows what might be waiting for him on the far side.

He moves his rifle aside and inspects the floor, looking for trip wires. Nothing. He checks the edges of the doorway for sensors. Nothing.

He stands there for several seconds, thinking about what to do.

About what he *must* do.

Faith, he says to himself.

He kneels and readies the rifle. He will roll forward and to the right, hoping to find something to hide behind.

He counts.

One.

Two.

Three.

The tip of Nori Ko's nose feels like an icicle.

She moves the rifle up and down and up and down.

Up.

Down.

Up.

A figure rolls from the doorway. She presses and holds the trigger, pushing the rifle against the recoil and adjusting to hit the target on the floor. Modified for full auto, the rifle sprays bullets into the room, muzzle flash strobe-lighting the contours of her head and shoulders and the stone walls. The figure disappears behind the end of the table. She's not sure if she scored a hit. She releases the trigger. The last few shell casings tinkle onto the floor. Her ears ring. She parks her rifle, aiming for the end of the table, painfully aware that she cannot simultaneously sight the door.

If there is more than one of them, she is done for.

She slides the gun back to the base of the door, then to the top of it, then to the table. She draws this little triangle for five full seconds, which feels like five minutes. She hears a child's wail from somewhere deep in the ancient building. She draws the triangle again. Again. Again.

Maybe she's gotten lucky. Maybe there's only one.

Movement. The figure that tumbled into the room sticks a rifle around the table's corner. They fire simultaneously. The shots being fired at her miss, but her shots hit, and a man's voice calls out in pain and his rifle drops to the floor with a clank.

She shoots this and it slides out of reach.

Then she sights the top of the door, the bottom, the table. The triangle again.

The table.

The bottom of the door.

The top.

Again.

Then she hears a sound like an arc of electricity and sees a blinding yellow light and she rolls defensively to the side, wedging between the floor and the wall. The flash zips past her in a millisecond and catches her ARX 160 right down the middle, cutting the scope and both receivers clean in half. This energy projectile burns the flesh on the back of her trigger hand, and although her eyes are shut it's so bright that all she sees is orange and red.

But the flash is gone as fast as it arrived, and the sound too. There's the smell of burned flesh and of what she swears is molten metal.

But she can't be sure because now, with the light lingering in her eyes and her night-vision scope ruined, she's completely blind.

She hops to her feet, draws a long tactical knife, steps gingerly into the room. She swings the knife here and there, here and there.

"Come on!" she blurts, defying the darkness. *"Come on!"*

Hilal twiddles the fingers of his right hand. It was rattled badly when the 416 was shot from his grip and it tingles like when a cricket batsman gets a curving pitch near the hands.

But this sensation is nothing next to what is happening in his left hand.

As soon as his rifle was hit the lump of metal came to life, as if it knew he was in imminent danger and its services were needed.

His arm went as straight as a board, locking at the elbow, as a long spike grew from the pinkie side of the piece of metal, extending for a little over a meter. As soon as this happened his hand felt as if it was joined with the metal, and his thumb found the socket, and he pressed it. His arm lit up with a jolt of energy as a bright disc flew from the tip of the spike, careening across the room in a flash and hitting his adversary.

But this shot did not kill her.

Now he takes more careful aim. He peers at this woman for a brief moment. If she had night vision before she does not now, as she stands before him swiping randomly at the air. She is undoubtedly the Mu that Masaka told him about, as she looks very much like an older version of Chiyoko Takeda. Hilal can only guess why this person is helping the Shang, and he is too pressed for time to consider it for very long.

He presses his thumb into the trigger again. The room flashes yellow once more and the weapon fires its energy disk and the air crackles

with electricity and two thumps.
Hilal looks to the far side of the room. Two halves of a person lie on the floor, the contacted flesh and innards cauterized and popping-hissing.
A child wails from deeper down in this ancient monument.
"Sky Key!" he hisses.
He stoops and runs his fingers over his 416. The magazine was knocked free and the mag well is dented and misshapen. It is useless.
He straightens. Draws *HATE* in his right hand and keeps this amazing Maker weapon ready in his left.
He steps past the cleaved body and through the doorway and slips silently into the darkness and the cold that lies below.

AN LIU, LITTLE ALICE CHOPRA

24.43161, 123.01314, near Yonaguni, Japan

Keep going, love. BlinkSHIVERSHIVERblinkblinkblinkshiverBLINKBLINK SHIVERSHIVERSHIVER BLINKSHIVERSHIVERShivershiverBLINK.

An *blink* An *blink* An drags an increasingly conscious Sky *SHIVER* Sky Key down *blink* down *SHIVER* down.

The air is cold *shiver* cold *blinkblink* cold *blink* it's freezing. A faint glow grows below. His vest feels like it weighs *shivershiver* weighs 200 kilos not *blink* not *BLINK* not 20.

Walk, love. Next foot, next foot, next foot. Move. Move!

She encourages him, speaks to him without any *blink* any hitches. No tics in her *shiver* in her voice.

She is pure. In his mind. In his heart.

The pure part of him.

SHIVERSHIVERSHIVERblinkblink. SHIVERblinkshiver.

He's so anxious *blink* so shaken *shiver* so *blinkblink* so ticking he can't *blinkblinkblink* can't talk to her *SHIVERSHIVER* either out loud or *blinkblink* or in his mind.

His mind.

His heart.

His mind.

His black heart.

Chiyoko.

Chiyoko.

BLINKSHIVERBLINK.

He tightens his grip on the girl's collar, catching a clump of *blinkshiver* a clump of hair. The follicles *blinkblink* snap-snap-snap out of her skin.

She yelps and wails and starts speaking in Hindi or Bengali, whatever it is he can't *blinkshiverSHIVERblink* he can't understand a word. She kicks and swings her arms and An gives her a hard shake but this only *blinkshiverSHIVERblink* it only makes her more upset.

She wails again.

Gunfire, and lots of it, echoes from above and beats *blink* beats *shiver* beats on his ears.

A brief silence then another burst, followed by a loud *zzzuuppp!* like a shot of electricity.

Then silence.

Sky Key cries again.

SHIVERSHIVERSHIVERBLINKBLINKSHIVER.

Keep moving, love. Don't fail now.

The child writhes and spits. Nori Ko says something above. Another *zzzzuuup!* and then silence.

Don't hurt the girl.

He can't *blinkblink* can't help himself. He shoves his rifle around to his back and yanks up Sky Key and *shivershiver* wraps both arms around her. Her back presses into his chest. He claps a hand over her mouth. She bites the web of skin between his thumb and forefinger and yells out once again.

"Ack!" he blurts. He works his fingers under her *blinkblink* under her chin and claps her mouth shut and holds it this way. He stops walking.

BLINKSHIVERBLINK.

He works his other hand over *blinkblinkSHIVERSHIVER* over the girl's nose, pinching it shut.

She needs to live, An! Don't!

Sky Key kicks her short legs into An's gut and pelvis. She gets him in the groin and he bends over to help relieve the pain, crooking her body in his. She tries to move her head side to side but she isn't strong enough. She keeps kicking, kicking.

Don't.

SHIVERSHIVERSHIVERSHIVER.

Her kicks die down. Her head stops straining. He releases her nose. Holds his hand under it.

The warmth of her breath coats the top of his hand.

She lives. She is unconscious again.

BLINKBLINKBLINK.

Good, love. Now. Go!

He cradles the girl. His vest is so heavy, and so ready, and the release of death is so near.

He is so happy.

Walk.

Next foot *SHIVER* next foot *blink* next foot. Down down down.

The blue glow gets brighter.

BLINKSHIVERBLINK.

Closer.

Brighter.

Colder.

BLINKSHIVERBLINK.

Closer.

Brighter.

Colder.

He takes one more step and stops.

The star chamber. The tics are gone. The girl shudders as if disturbed by a bad dream.

We are here, love.

SHARI CHOPRA, JENNY ULAPALA

Shari sees Little Alice's shaking body in the Shang's hands. Shari can't think she can't yell she can't call out she can't reach she can't act she can't feel she has to repress it all she is powerless she is powerless she is powerless and she has to embrace the powerlessness.

Jenny stands next to her, they both see, they both let what they see pass through them, as if each were an unthinking camera, nothing more than a lens to an observer's eye.

They both see the Shang step forward and look around and stop.

They both hear him say, "I am here, kepler 22b. I have the keys. I claim my prize as winner of Endgame. Show yourself."

AN LIU, KEPLER 22B, LITTLE ALICE CHOPRA, JENNY ULAPALA, SHARI CHOPRA

Star chamber, 24.43161, 123.01314, near Yonaguni, Japan

The Maker moves and the air shimmies and wrinkles and he appears, as if stepping from a rend in space itself.

Welcome, An Liu, Shang Player of the 377th line of humanity.

An's right hand touches the pad on his left wrist. Both are obscured from the Maker by the drape of Sky Key's clothing.

An sneers at the kepler. He would enjoy seeing him suffer, but he senses that any hesitation will make it more likely that he will not succeed in killing him.

I can almost touch you, love. Come to me, Chiyoko says.

I am, he thinks.

He smiles at the Maker. "Thank you, kepler 22b." His finger finds the detonator button. The vest feels light, airy, already like it is igniting moving in and out at the same time, taking him with it and everything around him, warming his flesh and spirit.

I am coming.

He says, "But my name is not An Liu. My name is Death."

He presses the button.

And nothing happens.

He presses it again.

Nothing.

He drops the girl. She lands awkwardly at his feet and bounces. She groans. Her mouth moves, eyes flutter.

She is in pain.

• • •

Shari closes her eyes in the Dreaming. She can't look. She will keep the connection to this place by imagining Little Alice, as she was in the yard in Gangtok, chasing Tarki through the brush, as she passed through the kitchen while Shari cooked, as she rode on Jamal's broad shoulders, as she sat in Jovinderpihainu's lap and smiled at his wrinkled face. She imagines these things without putting words to them. By filling her spirit these images help keep her rooted in the nothingness of the Dreaming. It is the practice of her meditation turned on its head and writ out as large as it can be: find timelessness *solely* by being in the present, hold nothingness *solely* by accepting everything.

Little Alice is already with her.

She always has been.

Thank you for not harming the second key, An Liu.

An desperately jams his finger onto the wrist pad. He presses the detonator, presses, presses. Nothing. He pulls back his sleeve and sees that the red arming light is extinguished.

He looks to the kepler's pale face. An is slack-jawed, eyes widened.

Oh, the bomb would kill me and stop what I am here to do. But the detonator will not work so long as I am alive and close to it. You simply cannot kill me, An Liu.

Move, love!

An drops and rolls over the girl, coming up a meter closer to the Maker, the rifle that was slung behind his back in his hands. He fires. The bullets sail into the alien and hit him and bend around his clothing and his neck and his face. The slugs bury themselves in the stone beyond the Maker, producing a cloud of blue dust as a drifting backdrop.

Although the bullets do nothing, An keeps firing. His teeth grind. Tears stream from the corners of his eyes.

The magazine is empty. The gun bolt *click-click-click-click-click*s. An releases the magazine and flips it and shoves it back in and he is about to resume shooting when the Maker raises his arm and points his fist at An. A pulse of invisible energy, like a gust of concentrated wind, lifts An from his feet into the air, throwing him against the doorway he and Sky Key entered through. He would sail through it except that now it's shut by an invisible barrier.

I said nothing will work, Shang.

An's entire body aches. He jumps to his feet and draws Nobuyuki's sword and rushes to the Maker. He leaps over the girl, who was unaffected by the Maker's blast, and arrives in front of the alien in less than three seconds, the sword driving at his long neck.

It slams into the Maker, who smiles.

Who laughs.

The sword's sharpened edge does nothing either.

Enough.

kepler 22b takes An by the neck and lifts him off his feet and holds him at arm's length. An kicks, swings the sword helplessly. The alien's hand is so cold it burns An's skin, which bunches below his jawline, turning blue and white. An tries to curse the alien but he can't make a sound. His lips turn purple. His eyes redden and bulge from their sockets. He can't breathe.

You don't need to kill him, love. Come to me anyway. Die and come to me anyway.

No! An thinks. *Death!*

I hear your thoughts, you know. I hear the thoughts of everyone in this room. You, the girl, the dead Mu who lives in your twisted mind. I hear the thoughts of the Aksumite, who will arrive at the doorway in a few seconds.

Death!

No, Shang. Not for you. I was going to kill you when I used your body to finish Endgame, but now I see that you don't deserve death. Life, Shang! That is what you despise and that is what you shall have. **That** ***is what you deserve. But . . . time is precious, so . . .***

He lifts the rail-thin Player another foot. He holds out his free hand

and opens it and one of the Shang's pockets vibrates and jostles and Earth Key strains at the cloth and shoots out, settling in the Maker's hand. Then he hurtles the Shang to the right and into one of the star-point recesses. An Liu bangs his head against the stone and crumples into it, alone and silent and completely unconscious.

We can talk about life later.

He glances at the La Tène.

I do not need your body to finish Endgame anyway, An Liu.

He drifts toward Sky Key, dropping Earth Key into the bowl in the middle of the room. It rattles and bounces and settles in the lowest part, waiting to be joined by the girl and the Player.

He reaches Sky Key and bends and picks her up. Her back goes as straight as a board as his frigid hands touch her and she screams.

She screams and screams and screams.

This noise should shake Shari Chopra from her meditation within a meditation, but it does not. Instead, when the screams drift into her awareness she sees a playful Little Alice on a swing set, pealing with shrill delight, smiling, filled with life and joy and happiness.

She sees her as she should be.

As she is, always, in Shari's heart.

HILAL IBN ISA AL-SALT, LITTLE ALICE CHOPRA, KEPLER 22B

Star chamber, 24.43161, 123.01314, near Yonaguni, Japan

Hilal stops shy of the door. The Maker stands not three meters away. He holds the girl. He stares at Hilal, black-eyed and smug.

Hello, Aksumite.

Hilal raises the weapon. "Good-bye."

He angles the weapon so that it will strike kepler 22b and not Little Alice. He drops his thumb into the trigger and squeezes. His arm lights in pain and the weapon glows and the disk shoots forward, the light consuming Hilal and the door between them and kepler 22b.

But instead of relieving the alien of his head, the blast hits the invisible shield suspended between them and it explodes and dissipates and throws Hilal violently backward into darkness.

Fool.

kepler 22b places the girl in the bowl with Earth Key. As soon as Sky Key comes in contact with the bowl she stops screaming, becoming quiet and peaceful.

The end won't hurt. kepler 22b didn't lie to the Nabataean about that.

All he needs now is the third and final key.

A Player.

All he needs is the La Tène.

JENNY ULAPALA

Very quietly, very discreetly, very gently, Jenny says, "Hell with this. I'm old anyway."

She releases Shari's hand in the Dreaming, keeps ahold of it in the physical realm back in Australia.

She drifts into the center of the star chamber, hovering over Little Alice. She watches the Maker unwrap the redheaded Player named Aisling Kopp. The Maker remains unaware of Jenny and Shari. He cannot see them. He is so sure of himself.

Too sure of himself.

Jenny turns away from the Maker and faces the limitless psychic void of the Dreaming. She leaves the room and Shari and the felled Players and moves to the great line that feeds and serves the Dreaming and which is always there just beyond perception. She gives herself to it. The world of her ancestors grows and surges and glows to life around her. She sees those she knew in the flesh and those she met in the Dreaming and those she only ever heard of. She sees the great expanse of the desert and the ancient trees and the mountains and valleys of her native land but also all of Earth, rivers of ice and pinnacles of stone and teeming jungles and voluminous life-giving seas and molten iron and nickel and black storms laced with electricity and power and windswept dunes as high as skyscrapers and deep caves dripping with mineral water and the depths of the oceans black and cold yet full of life and orange pluming vents bubbling up from the center of the ancient planet, every inch as ancient as the Maker's home world, every

inch as complete and wondrous and and and otherworldly, right here.
Earth.
Home.
Home to life and death and the Dreaming. Because Jenny knows heaven isn't up there in the stars—it's right here, on Earth and of it.
And salvation is coming.
"Hey!" she calls into the Dreaming, and the lands and seas and peaks and glaciers and drifting treetops fill and overfill with faces and shoulders and arms and fists.
"Come on now. Jenny Ulapala needs you."
And they silently raise their fists in unison, millions and billions of the dead and gone in the Dreaming. Her army. Their army. Ours. Greater than any otherwise assembled on this planet or any other at this time or any other.
She turns her back on humanity.
Not to forsake it.
But to lead it.
She takes one step back from the void and toward the Maker.
And there, next to her, comes Big Alice.
"Oi, Jenny."
"Alice," Jenny smiles.
"Baiame fucked up good, yeah?"
"How so?"
"They shouldn'ta shown us how to go walkabout in the After-After like this. It was foolish."
Jenny is so pleased. She sights the head of the Maker in the room back in the physical world. "It was."
Big Alice points at Sky Key, at the doorway blocking a stirring Hilal ibn Isa al-Salt. "Time we show him how powerful we've become."
"Quiet now, Alice."
"You got it, Gram."
Jenny marches into the star chamber. The Maker carries the La Tène, naked and pale and asleep and breathing shallowly, in his arms. Shari

remains calm and connected. She holds the connection in spite of everything. Jenny concentrates her mind to a point and aims this at the door. She could strike the Maker, but the weapon that will *definitely* kill him lies outside the room, in Hilal's hand.

Jenny is ready. Before she launches forward she whistles at the Maker.

He finally sees them.

And he is aghast.

How?

"You made a mistake. We all do."

And before he has a chance to say anything else, she carries herself forward with the psychic weight of all that's behind her and materializes in the star chamber and smashes into the barrier that seals off Hilal and the weapon that can slay their common enemy.

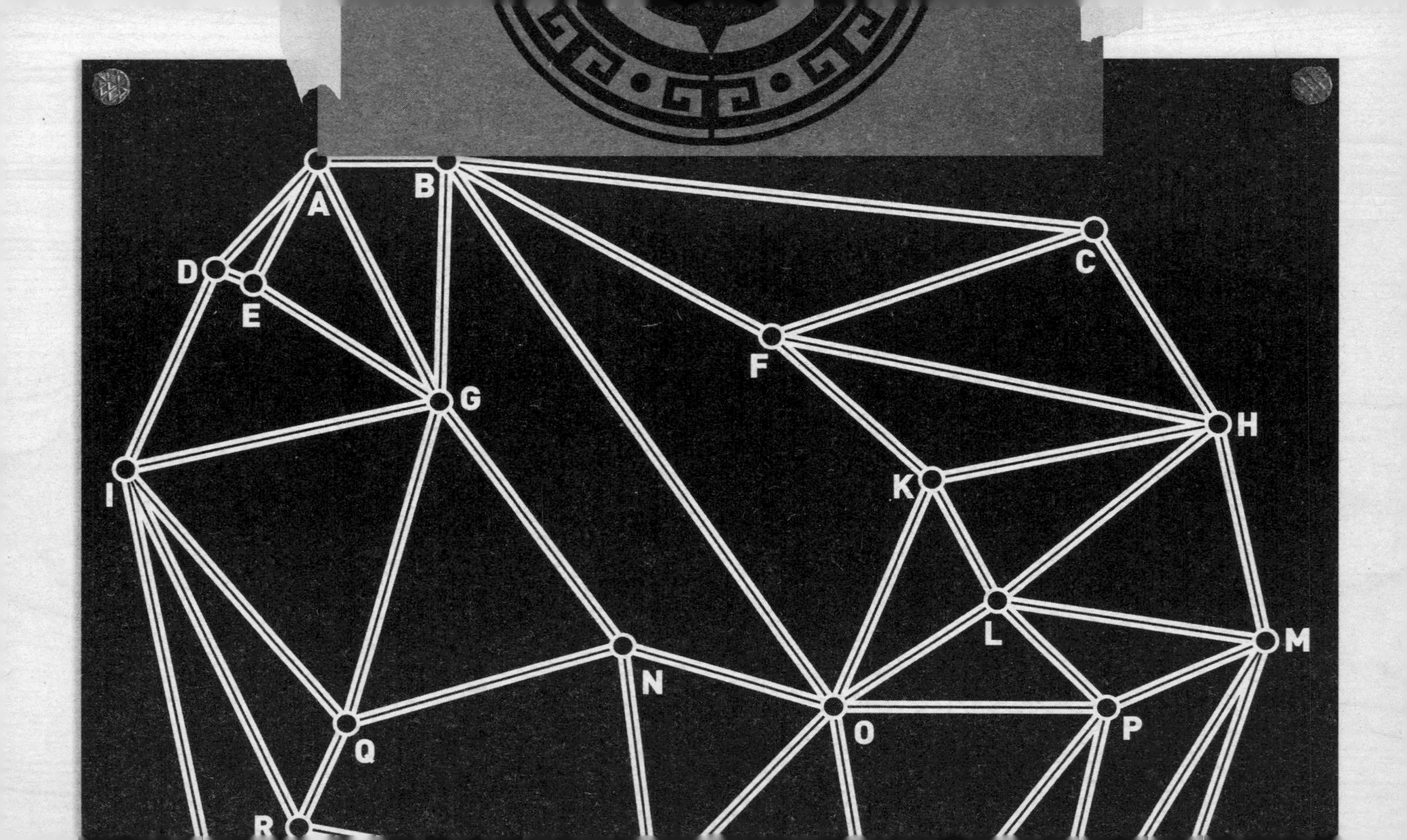
A
B
C
D
E
F
G
H
I
K
L
M
N
O
P
Q
R

HILAL IBN ISA AL-SALT, LITTLE ALICE CHOPRA, JENNY ULAPALA, KEPLER 22B, AISLING KOPP

Star chamber, 24.43161, 123.01314, near Yonaguni, Japan

"Now!" Jenny yells as she appears as if from nowhere and flies over Hilal and collapses behind him.

Hilal lies on the ground, his limbs akimbo. He twists and aims and though he's groggy and his vision is imperfect and cloudy he holds up the weapon. The Maker drops the La Tène and raises his own gun and Hilal squeezes and squeezes and squeezes and the first shot meets a shot fired by the kepler and these cancel each other out but the next shot and the next and the next all launch from Hilal's hand and fire into the room and Hilal feels the power and his arms tingle and he sees the light in his eyes and there is a loud noise and then a louder one and a deep and clamorous scream and then—

Silence.

Hilal sits bolt upright. He blinks. He is surrounded by pitch blackness. He feels around the floor and finds what he's looking for. Night vision. He slips the goggles over his head and presses the button and, thank the stars, they work.

Jenny is under him. He gently shakes her by the shoulders. She moans. She is alive. He takes her face in his hands, pinching her pockmarked cheeks, moving her head, slapping her lightly. "Master Ulapala. Master Ulapala."

"Uhn . . . Oh . . ."

"Wake up, Master Ulapala!"

"Hilal?"

"Yes," he says, full of disbelief. "How did you . . . ? You did not come through the portal . . . you just appeared in thin air . . ."

"It was a trick I never tried before. I'll tell you about it later."

"Are you all right?"

"Did we?"

"Yes. I mean, I think so."

Jenny strains to look past Hilal but winces. "Ah. My leg. I think it's broken."

Hilal pushes aside a pile of rubble. The old woman's ankle is bent at a strange angle. "This will hurt," he says, "but I have to check."

"Yeah, all right."

He runs his hand along her leg, feeling for bone or blood.

"It is not compound. You will be fine."

"Hilal. You gotta go check on . . ."

He stands. "Yes. I know. I will be right back, Master Ulapala. Do not move."

"Not going anywhere," she says.

Hilal moves into the star chamber, listening to the aches and pains of his own body.

"Uncle?" Little Alice says.

She sits cross-legged on the floor, Earth Key in her hand. Hilal rushes to her.

"Hello there. I am a friend of your mother's."

"Another?" Little Alice says. "So was Maccabee."

Hilal won't argue with her, not now. First he has to know: "Where is the Maker?"

"What?"

"The Maker."

She points directly to her left. "There, Uncle."

Hilal spins and looks and

And

Yes

The Maker is cut into at least three pieces. He is as dead as he will ever be. And Hilal looks past the Maker and sees Aisling, naked and her skin very pale in the strange green hue of the night vision, but breathing.

They did it.

They did it.

"Wait here, Alice," Hilal says.

He goes to the portal that will lead them back to Australia and to safety. It is not black and inky but bright. He pulls off the goggles and sees the red earth of the outback on the far side casting its daylight into the room. The Koori guards stand alert and shocked. They're waving their arms at him and gesturing for him to cross over. At their feet is Shari Chopra, sitting on the ground, eyes closed and entranced, holding her meditative place in the Dreaming, keeping the portal open.

He holds up a finger. "I am coming, brothers," he says. "*We* are coming."

He backtracks to Jenny. Alice says, "Uncle," but he says, "One moment. You will be with your mother soon. I promise."

"I know, Uncle, but—"

"One moment," he says, so full of joy and triumph and relief.

He reaches Jenny and pulls her arm over his broad shoulders and picks her up. "We did it," he says. "You did it."

Jenny blinks. "Really, mate?"
He laughs. "Yes, Master Ulapala. Really."
"Stop calling me that. I mean it."
He laughs again. "All right, Master Jenny," he says, his teeth gleaming in a broad smile.
"And Little Alice?"
"Come."
He puts his other arm around her waist and they walk slowly to Little Alice and stop in front of her.
"Auntie," Alice says.
"Little Alice," Jenny says quietly, holding out her hand.
Alice takes it and stands. "I'm hungry," she says.
Jenny and Hilal laugh. "I am too, sweets," Jenny says. "Starved, actually."
Together they move toward the portal.
"Uncle," Alice says.
"We're almost there."
"Auntie."
"I'll cross with you and then come back for Aisling," Hilal says.
And then they reach the doorway that will transport them away from here, but when they try to move through it they are blocked.
Jenny slaps a hand on the image of the outback in front of them, but hits what feels like a sheet of glass. She slaps it again. Hilal whispers, "No!"
Jenny punches it. Glances around the room at the Maker's body and blurts, "He sealed it!"
"Can you take us back the way you came?" Hilal asks.
"Can't. That was a one-way trip," Jenny says.
"We will have to leave the way I came then," Hilal says, thinking how long it will take and how much effort. Thinking of how distraught Shari will be to have to wait that much longer to have her child in her arms.
"Uncle," Alice says. "Auntie."

Both look at the girl. "What is it?" they ask together.

She points to her left. "Him. There."

Their heads whip to where she points. And then they see. They were so excited about the death of the kepler, and the end of Endgame, that they had forgotten.

An Liu.

He is motionless and wedged into a corner and completely nonthreatening.

Hilal says, "He cannot hurt you anymore, Little Alice."

"I know," the girl says. "But look. His arm."

Hilal squints at the Shang and there—yes—a flashing red light.

"Wait here," Hilal says, propping Jenny against the shuttered portal.

Hilal bounds to An, reaching him in seconds. He takes his arm. Sees the wrist pad, the buttons, the notations in Chinese and English.

He pats down An's body and feels the bulk and grabs his shirt and tears it open. The nylon the straps the wires the explosives.

Not C4.

Not TNT.

Not PETN.

Hilal is not sure what it is, but given what he knows about An Liu, he knows it is worse than any of these other options.

The red light flashes faster.

And faster.

He quickly inspects the wiring. There are too many for him to disarm it, and he does not have tools to work with anyway.

He stands.

"What is it?" Jenny asks.

"Bomb!" he yells, running to them. "There is no timer readout, but it is armed."

"What kind?" Jenny asks.

"I do not know. Probably a small nuclear device."

Jenny's eyes widen. "We need to get through this portal!"

"I know!"

Hilal zips around the room looking for something anything. something.

Jenny runs her hands up and down the blocked portal, tries to ignore the people on the other side, her guards and the call of the Outback, the proximity of safety.

"Auntie," Alice says.

"Not now, honey," Jenny says.

"There," Alice says, ignoring her.

She points at the stone to the side of the doorway. Jenny runs her hands up to it and—yes!—when her fingers touch it, it liquefies and she pushes her hands into the stone. She doesn't know what it is, but inside she feels buttons and switches and sliders. "Hilal, I think . . ." She moves her fingers, twists her arm, pushes it in deeper. "I think . . ." Hilal appears at her side. "This is the lock," Jenny says.

"Can you open it?"

"Maybe?" she says unconvincingly.

Hilal looks at the Shang. The red light blinks faster. "Hurry."

Jenny turns her hand again and there is a click from inside the stone and Hilal reaches for Australia but no, it is still sealed off.

"Bugger!" Jenny says.

"What?"

"I can't . . . I think it scanned my hand. And you know, I ain't got Maker mitts, so . . ." She pulls out her arm with a painful-sounding *pop*.

Hilal turns a tight circle. The light blinks faster. Faster.

"Uncle."

"Not now. I am trying to think."

Little Alice doesn't say anything else. She just tugs hard at Hilal's *HATE* machete and he actually lets it go and the small girl drags it scraping across the floor to the Maker. Hilal and Jenny watch her with perplexed looks as she stops by his pale torso and struggles to lift the blade.

"His hand, Hilal!" Jenny blurts. "Get his bloody hand!"

Hilal leaps to Alice in a single bound and snags *HATE*. He peels back the Maker's armored sleeve and lifts his blade high and snaps it down and he drops the metal and replaces this with frozen Maker flesh.

He snags the girl around the waist and bounces back to the portal, giving Jenny the limb. She jams it into the stone and it melts again and there is another click and a hiss and the warm dry Australian air hits their faces. Hilal thrusts Alice through the portal as the guards rush to them. They take the girl and help Jenny through. Hilal steps through too when he remembers Aisling. He pivots, catches sight of An's red light flashing so fast it's practically solid. He stumbles and falls over Aisling and picks her up and jumps back to the portal. He passes Aisling through to a Koori guard, the surface twinkling and snapping with electricity, and then he jumps in, through space and time and into another part of the known world.

Little Alice runs to her mother and wraps her arms around her neck, but Shari is so far away that she doesn't notice. Hilal tries to get everyone away from the portal, away from the path of the coming blast. The guards move Jenny and Aisling and themselves. Hilal comes back to pick up Shari and the girl, and as he leans over them Shari's nostrils twitch with the scent of her daughter's hair and her eyes shoot open and the portal flashes white for a fraction of a second before being snuffed out and sealed with the blackness of dark stone.

Shari is awake, free of the Dreaming. The connection is lost. The portal is closed.

They are safe.

Hilal collapses onto the ground, panting and sweating. He sits slump-backed, staring at what's in front of him.

He laughs. Deep and throaty.

He laughs at it.

At the kissing, loving, fawning, pawing, desperately grateful lives of a mother and a child, brought together for good and at last.

Come to me, love.

An blinks. He can't move. His body is broken and pain-ridden. Like it has always been, in one way or another.

Come to me.

He watches the others. The red light illuminates his face and the tattoo tear under his eye. He watches them take the Maker hand and use it in some way he can't understand. Watches the second key leave, and he doesn't care. He watches them escape.

"He's"—*blink*—"he's"—*SHIVER*—"he's"—*BLINKBLINK*—"he's gone, Chiyoko." *BLINKSHIVERSHIVERBLINK.* "He's dead."

I know. I saw it.

BLINKBLINKblink.

"I didn't kill him."

They Played for life.

"They did," An says.

In your way, you did too.

He watches Hilal almost leave and then return and trip over Aisling Kopp and then pick her up.

"No," An says.

Yes.

"No."

Hilal passes Aisling through the doorway, and then he jumps after her and is gone.

Only An is left.

He manages to bring his hand to his neck. He finds her dark hair with his fingers. He caresses it.

The red light is nearly solid.

"No."

Yes, love.

"I didn't Play for life."

Yes, you did.

He grips the necklace tightly.

"I Played for you."

And then a bright light, the brightest the whitest the hottest he has ever known.

And then nothing.

Live blindly and upon the hour. The Lord,
Who was the Future, died full long ago.
Knowledge which is the Past is folly. Go,
Poor child, and be not to thyself abhorred.
Around thine earth sun-wingèd winds do blow
And planets roll; a meteor draws his sword;
The rainbow breaks his seven-coloured chord
And the long strips of river-silver flow:
Awake! Give thyself to the lovely hours.
Drinking their lips, catch thou the dream in flight
About their fragile hairs' aërial gold.
Thou art divine, thou livest,–as of old
Apollo springing naked to the light,
And all his island shivered into flowers.

R
S
T
V
X
Y
Z
1
2
3
4
5
6
7
8
9
0

23 MONTHS, 5 DAYS LATER

Below Mercator Station, Palisades, New York, United States

Aisling and Hilal walk in the dawn twilight up a single-track dirt path. The Hudson River lies at their back, gray and flat and wide and silent but flowing powerfully toward the Atlantic Ocean, several miles to the south.

With the exception of a pair of four-inch folding knives, neither Aisling nor Hilal is armed.

Both like it that way.

They walk without urgency along the switchback trail that leads to a series of ladders and lifts plying the vertical cliff face up to the heart of Mercator Station. Their lungs and legs work against gravity. Though it's August, a summer chill is in the air and, as always in this part of the world, the sky is hung with gray clouds. These aren't very ominous, though—worldwide, but especially near the Impact Zone, the storms subsided significantly about nine weeks ago—so the two former Players haven't bothered with rain gear for their morning hike.

The basic geography of this area is mostly unchanged PA. The 200-million-year-old basalt cliffs that rise like a wall on the western shore of the river were unaffected by the impact. Being that old, and that durable, gives a thing a good measure of staying power.

These cliffs are the bones of this ancient valley—one that predates the existence of all sentient life in the Milky Way, including that of the Makers, by over 150 million years—and they loom now before Aisling and Hilal. They are dark and glistening, and while it isn't raining, the two Players still hear small gurgles of water moving all around them and under their feet, making its way down into the river and, soon enough, to the ocean itself.

But if the bones of the world survived here (and they categorically did *not* survive in the Crater Zone), the skin of the world did not.

The ecosystem here has simply been reset.

On that day nearly two years ago, everything was either burned away or torn from the ground and carried on the shock wave to the vast Debris Wall to the south and east. The force of the blast was so strong that even this wide fluvial rift did not catch any detritus, and it was laid bare. Out in the open, where Aisling and Hilal are right now, it's not much different than it was in the immediate aftermath of Abaddon. Not a single beam of direct sunlight has penetrated the clouds since then, and so the entire landscape is denuded and brown or black or gray. All that remains is dirt and rock, and all that grows are mushrooms.

Hilal stops and inspects one of these, bulbous and priapic, with a bright orange top. Aisling walked right by it without noticing. He stoops, unfolds his knife, and pokes the fungus. *"Amanita caesarea,"* he says quietly. "A young one."

Aisling stops and turns. "Hmm?"

"This mushroom." He cuts it quickly at the stem and slips it into a plastic collection bag. "Childress will like to see it, I am sure," he says.

"Childress would like to see a turd so long as it was growing out of the ground," Aisling points out.

Hilal simply smiles, tucks the bagged mushroom into a pocket, and stands back up. "Your phone is buzzing," he says.

Aisling looks left and right and pats her pockets. "Goddamn it, where—?" She finds her phone and slips it out and quizzically looks at the number display before shrugging and pressing it to her ear. "This is Aisling," she says curtly. A slight frown gives way to a smile as she says, "Oh hey, Jenny."

They talk.

At this moment Jenny is in Kazakhstan with Greg Jordan. They're preparing to board a brand-new Titan XA1 rocket carrying the final payload to an orbiting ship that will, in two weeks' time, embark on a three-year voyage to Mars. Their mission: to serve as the resident Maker and Endgame experts for an international team tasked with retrieving kepler 22b's ship for research and development purposes. And also, Aisling hopes, to retrieve the body of Pop Kopp so that he can be brought home and laid to rest.

Aisling grins broadly at some joke Jenny makes, the purple mark on Aisling's left cheek expanding as it curves from the corner of her eye down to her jaw. This is the last visible remnant of her time spent in 22b's ship, although she has no shortage of more personal and emotional remnants.

She has nightmares once a week or more. And Hilal hears about each one, writing down the details, keeping a log, trying to help Aisling understand them and get past them.

The women continue to talk. Hilal moves up the trail, patting Aisling's arm as he passes. She winks playfully. The cool air rises around his shoulders and neck from the Hudson River below. He makes three sharp turns, going higher up to Mercator, until Aisling's voice isn't more than a murmur fading into the background.

He stops. He is at least 15 meters higher than Aisling here, and the view is completely unobstructed. Boats and barges and ferries ply the water to the south. Above Manhattan, along the tops of the cliffs on the eastern bank, are newly built towers of steel topped with red blinking lights, and at their feet are lines of semipermanent buildings. Some of these are half-domed and green, others are not much more than white rectilinear trailers. These kinds of structures line the horizon to the north as far as the eye can see. Almost directly above Hilal a system of cables spans the river, and Hilal spies the sodium-orange lights illuminating the cabin of the cable car on the far side. Dark silhouettes of men or women are in it, preparing for the first crossing of the day. Above the car is the domed and pinnacled complex that is Van Houten Station, sister to Mercator, which is behind Hilal and just out of view over the lip of the Palisades.

Aisling and Hilal—and Shari and Little Alice too—live in Mercator, along with 1,845 other men and women. Shari and Aisling and Hilal are true friends now—thanks mostly to Little Alice, but also to hours of counseling and a desire to set an example for the world by healing the rift that the Makers tore between them. If the lines can come together and heal, then the people of the world can too, and while Earth and its nations have not been transformed into a nirvana, they have made great if imperfect strides toward it.

Hilal and the others are here to lend their hands at righting what was put so wrong. The mission of everyone working here is twofold. The first is to terraform this area of the ruined Impact Zone. Under each dome grows a thriving ecosystem of young forests and wetlands and meadows that will, when the sun returns, be uncovered and set free onto the land. Second is to oversee the final stages of rubble remediation of the city that was once called New York but that is now, at least unofficially, called Phoenix East. This will be the first city to rise PA, a beachhead for the New New World, one born of defiance and determination and cooperation and goodwill. And preparing the land to build it anew has required a lot of work. While most of the structures in the five boroughs of New York were torn from the ground and flung into the Debris Wall, many, many metric tons of infrastructure remained underground, all of which had to be dealt with and, in most cases, dug up and removed.

Soon, as Jenny begins her journey to the Red Planet, 58 heads of state will travel here from all corners of the world to cut a ribbon on the New Jersey side of the New George Washington Bridge. Hilal and Aisling and Shari and Little Alice will be at the US president's side, and on that day the rebuilding will begin in earnest.

The cables twang overhead. Hilal squints. The cable car dips out and moves over the water.

The clouds, usually uniformly gray like an unending blanket, are graded and defined, like a bunch of dark cotton balls.

Aisling calls for him and waves. She's done talking to Jenny. He rubs his arm below the wooden ring he wears around his bicep. The ouroboros. A symbol of violence and all that they fought against, but also a symbol of rebirth.

All that they fight *for*.

Aisling walks toward him, wending up the path.

His pocket vibrates. He retrieves his phone and looks at the display. Little Alice has texted him. *Come up, Uncle. I want to show you what I made this morning.*

He writes, *10 minutes.*

The wind picks up.

His phone buzzes again. *I can see you. Look up.*

He glances over his shoulder. Thirty meters above, leaning between the steel bars of the railings, is Little Alice. She's five years old now and taller than any child her age. She leans out farther than Hilal likes, but she is young and excitable and Hilal is certain that Shari is a few feet behind her, calm and attentive. Understandably, Shari hardly ever leaves Little Alice alone.

Little Alice waves fiercely. Hilal waves back.

The wind whistles down the valley as a bright flash, yellow and orange, slices the air. It hits the wet basalt cliff a few meters below Little Alice's feet. The girl pulls from between the railings and jumps up and down and points to the sky in the east. Hilal can't hear her, but he knows Little Alice is ecstatic, and that Shari must be ecstatic too.

Hilal swings around. Aisling is less than a meter away, and she too stares to the east, slack-shouldered and awestruck.

The clouds have broken, and there, filtering through a hole, are three long spears of dawn sunlight.

"Holy shit, Hilal," Aisling says.

"Yes," he says.

A loud air horn goes off at Mercator, and seconds later another horn answers from Van Houten, then smaller horns echo up and down the valley from substations and garden domes and mess halls and office blocks and dormitories.

Hilal bounds down to Aisling and wraps an arm around her shoulders.

The sun stays.

The wind blows.

The clouds move.

The sun disappears.

The horns blare on nonetheless.

"That was beautiful," Aisling says.

"Yes."

"We're actually going to make it, aren't we?"

Hilal looks Aisling directly in her eyes. His skin hideous and scarred. Hers porcelain and clear but marked. Both marked by Endgame.

"Yes," he says.

And then together: "Yes."

(Endnotes)

i http://goo.gl/afsgAT

ii http://goo.gl/D4hJFC

iii https://goo.gl/b1GIbn

iv http://goo.gl/SGdRu8

v http://goo.gl/jHDVwM

HUMANITY RESTS ON THE SHOULDERS OF TWELVE PLAYERS. BUT IN POST-WORLD WAR II BERLIN, A FORBIDDEN LOVE THREATENS THE FATE OF THE WORLD.

Keep reading for a sneak peek at:

CHAPTER I

Boone
December 24, 1948

"How you doing, Peterson?" Driscoll asks as we descend through the thick fog. "You look a little green. Do me a favor and try not to lose your lunch all over my plane, okay?"

The C-54, buffeted by a crosswind, shakes fiercely, rattling us like peas in a can. It's been like this the whole flight. Driscoll grins at me.

My name isn't Peterson, but he doesn't know that. He also doesn't know that I've been in far more nerve-racking situations than a rough approach. I may look like any other 19-year-old GI, but I'm far more than that.

"Last time I flew over Berlin, I was *dropping* eggs on their heads," Driscoll continues, shouting to be heard above the roar of the engines. "Now I'm bringing them eggs for their breakfast." His joke about the bombing raids that destroyed huge parts of the city during the last days of the war isn't funny. I smile anyway. I need him to think I'm just one of the guys, at least for a little longer.

The truth is, I *am* a little bit nervous. I've been training for war since I was a kid. I've been through more than Driscoll and all the other soldiers on the plane ever saw in boot camp. But this is my biggest mission yet. A lot is riding on it. And yet I don't even know exactly what it's about.

I know the basics. I've got to find a man and get him out of Berlin. I know his name and his suspected location. And I know that if he won't come with me, or if someone else gets to him first, I have to kill him.

A simple plan. That's why I know there's more to it than the council has told me. For some reason they don't want me to know the details of why this man is so important, which means they don't want anyone *else* to have that information either. If I get captured, my enemies can try as hard as they want to get me to talk, but I can't tell them what I don't know. Not that I would talk anyway. I'd never do anything to jeopardize the safety of my line. The council knows that, so it bothers me a little bit that they're taking this precaution. More than a little bit, if I'm honest. This is the first time since I became the Cahokian Player that they've kept me in the dark about something. I don't like the feeling.

I push that irritation from my mind as the Tempelhof airstrip appears—seemingly out of nowhere—and meets the wheels of the plane. The rumbling intensifies, shaking my bones, and I hang on as Driscoll applies the brakes. Through the cockpit windows I see groups of children standing on top of piles of debris that line the runway. They wave at us, grinning and clapping their hands.

"Look at that," Driscoll says. "It's like we're Santa Claus."

In a way, we are. After all, it's Christmas Eve. And along with the ten tons of eggs, milk, meat, flour, and other basic supplies in our hold, we're bringing bags of wrapped gifts to hand out to the people of the city. Chocolate bars for the kids. Cigarettes for the men. Perfume for the women. The war ended in 1945, but more than three years later, Berlin is still trying to recover. And since the Soviets cut off all sea and land access to the city's western zone earlier in the year, life has gotten even harder.

Thankfully, the airlift organized by the American, French, and British militaries has been successful in bringing supplies to the city. It's also provided me with a handy way inside. Posing as an American soldier has been easy enough. There are so many young men being assigned to the dozens of daily airlift flights coming out of Rhein-Main Air Base that no one notices one more. All I had to do was put on a uniform and start helping load the plane.

When the Skymaster comes to a stop, we reverse the process begun three hours earlier, transferring everything in our cargo area onto the trucks that pull up one after the other.

"Nobody disappear!" Driscoll shouts as we launch into action. "General Tunner's orders! We get this stuff off, turn around, and land back in Frankfurt in time for eggnog and cookies!"

The airlift is a well-oiled machine. Planes land at two-minute intervals, and the total time from unloading to takeoff is 25 minutes. Everything moves like clockwork, and everyone has a job to do. I can't make a break for the main terminal or someone is bound to notice the missing pair of hands. But when we're almost finished, one of the mobile coffee trucks arrives filled with pretty German girls who hand out drinks and smiles, and I take the opportunity to slip away while the others are distracted. I don't look back, and nobody calls Peterson's name. Even when they finally notice he's gone, it won't matter, as the United States Army has no record of him anyway.

Once I'm away from the airport, I make my way into Berlin. In an attempt to maintain a balance of power, the city has been divided into four sectors, each one controlled by one of the Allied superpowers: Great Britain, France, the United States, and the Soviet Union. In reality, though, it's become the Soviets on one side and everyone else on the other. Fortunately, Tempelhof is in the American sector, and a GI walking through the streets is a common sight. I'd prefer to be dressed like a civilian, but at least wearing a uniform means that nobody questions me. And in case they do, all my identity papers carry the name of Alan Peterson.

It's early evening, a little past seven, and already dark. A light snow is falling. And even though the streets are dotted with rubble—some of the buildings I pass have shattered windows and walls that have crumbled, so you can see into living rooms and kitchens still filled with furniture—it somehow manages to feel like Christmas. There are wreaths on some of the doors, and trees decorated with ornaments are visible in the parlors of some of the houses. The shops I pass don't have much displayed in their windows, but signs reading FRÖHLICHE WEIHNACHTEN are taped to the glass.

Bells chime, and when I turn a corner, I see people walking into a church. The inside is lit by candles, and the sound of a carol being played on an organ floats from the open doorway. This makes me think of my own family back in Illinois. It's just after noon there, and I know my mother is getting ready for the Christmas Eve gathering. She's been cooking all day. The Tom and Jerry bowl and glasses that only come out once a year are set out on the sideboard. She's probably already hung the stockings from the mantel over the fireplace, one for each kid, arranged in order from youngest to oldest: Marnie, Evan, Lily, Ella, Peter, me, and Jackson. In the morning, the stockings will all be filled to overflowing. Even mine, although I won't be there to open it. And even Jackson's, although it's been three years since he died. The people of Berlin aren't the only ones who've lost something to the war.

I hurry by the church, clearing my mind by focusing on the address the council gave me. I memorized it, as well as the best route to reach it. Writing things down is risky. As my father told me repeatedly when I started my Player training, the brain is the only notebook nobody can steal.

It takes me another 20 minutes to find the house. It's in a section of the city that was hit hard by the Allied bombing, one of a row of connected brick town homes. Most of the buildings are empty, uninhabitable because of the damage. This one looks empty too. Most of the windows are boarded up, and the front door has an official notice on it warning people not to enter due to unsafe conditions. But looks can be deceiving. Just because you can't see somebody, it doesn't mean nobody is there. Sometimes, you just have to look harder.

I don't announce myself by knocking on the front door. This isn't a social call. Instead, I go into the bombed-out house next door, climb the stairs to the third floor, and step through a shattered window onto a narrow ledge that runs along the front of the whole row of houses. I press myself against what's left of the wall and slowly move one foot at a time toward the house next door. If anyone notices me, maybe they'll just think I'm Saint Nicholas coming to deliver presents.

When I reach the closest window of the target house, I pause beside it and look inside. The bedroom behind the cracked, dirty glass is empty. When I push on the window frame, the window slides up. I slip inside, turn on the small flashlight I carry in my pocket, and look around. It's just as cold in here as it is outside, and I can see my breath. There's no heat. But coal is in short supply, and no one is supposed to be living here anyway, so this might not mean anything. More telling is that everything in the room is covered with a thick layer of dust. No one has been here in a long time.

Then I notice the footprints. They start just outside the door, run along a hallway, and disappear down a flight of stairs. A faint glow emanates from the second floor. Someone is here after all. I creep to the end of the hall and pause. I can hear voices. There are two speakers, a man and what sounds like a younger woman.

This is a problem. There's supposed to be only one person here. A man. I haven't seen him yet, but even if the man I hear talking is the one I'm after, who is the girl? Is she a wife? A daughter? Something else? I need to get a look at them.

I draw my M1911 standard-issue military pistol and walk down the stairs. It's not my weapon of choice, but it's what Private Peterson would carry, and nobody would think twice about me having it, so it's what I've got. The voices grow louder as I descend. When I reach the landing, I pause. The speakers are in a room just to my left.

"I wish Oskar and Rutger were here with us," the man says.

"You know how Oskar is," the young woman says. "He didn't want to risk anyone following us to you."

"I think everyone must have forgotten about me by now," says the man. "Still, he's right to be cautious. I worry about you making visits here."

"Perhaps it's time for you to leave," the girl says. "You've shut yourself up in here long enough. Pass the duty on to someone else. Oskar and I—"

"Lottie, please," the man interrupts. "How many times have we talked about this? I cannot leave."

"You mean you will not," says Lottie. "Do you want to spend the rest of your life here?"

"I'm already a dead man. Remember?"

The man's words chill me. What does he mean? And who is this girl? Maybe it doesn't matter. Maybe I'm better off if I don't know who Lottie is. I know from experience that it's easier to kill someone when you know nothing about her.

"Let's not discuss it further," the man says. "It's Christmas Eve. Play something for me. You know I always love to hear you play."

A moment later, I hear the sound of a piano. It's badly out of tune, but the melody is familiar. "Silent Night." The girl begins to sing, and the man joins in.

I risk moving closer and looking through the doorway. Inside the room, a scraggly pine tree stands in front of a boarded-up window, its branches hung with silver tinsel and a handful of colorful glass balls. The piano is against a wall, with the young woman seated at it. The man stands beside her. Both of them are wearing long, thick coats.

I recognize the man from the photo the council showed me. It's Evrard Sauer. I'm in the right place. But the council said nothing about the girl. Now I have to decide what to do about her. My orders were to leave no witnesses, which gives me only one option. I know what I should do—what I've agreed to do for my council and my line—but the thought of actually doing it doesn't sit right with me. The girl is simply in the wrong place at the wrong time. I hate to make her pay for that with her life.

They finish singing, and the man takes something from the pocket of his coat. It's a present wrapped in newspaper and tied with plain white string. He hands it to the girl, who carefully opens it. A happy smile spreads across her face.

"Toffees!" she says. "Wherever did you get them?"

She doesn't wait for an answer before taking one of the candies from the box and unwrapping it, the cellophane crackling in her fumbling fingers. She puts the toffee in her mouth and sucks on it, her eyes closed. I don't think I've ever seen someone enjoy a piece of candy so much.

She opens her eyes and reaches into her own pocket. She takes out a package, this one wrapped in brown butcher paper. She gives it to the man. He opens it and holds up a red knitted scarf.

"I unraveled one of my sweaters for the yarn," the girl says, sounding embarrassed. "Wool is still rationed."

"It's beautiful," the man assures her as he wraps it around his neck. "Thank you."

The girl turns back to the piano and begins to play again. This time the song is "O Tannenbaum."

I've obviously interrupted their Christmas Eve celebration. And if I do what I've been instructed to do, I'm about to make it a whole lot worse. I still feel like something is off, but there's no time to contact my council for further advice, so I have to make a choice based on the available information and what I've been told. That means completing the mission according to plan.

I accept the reality of my situation, even though I don't like it, and prepare to act. Then the sound of a door being kicked open comes from the first floor. Wood splinters. Heavy footsteps pound up the stairs. The man and the young woman stop singing and look at each other. I have just enough time to dart back to the stairwell before three figures burst onto the landing. Two of them have guns drawn.

"Evrard Sauer," one of them, a man, says. "You are under arrest for collaborating with the National Socialist German Workers' Party." He's speaking in German, but with a heavy Russian accent. And although he's used the more formal name for them, I know he's just accused Sauer of working with the Nazis.

"Who are you?" the girl asks.

"Be still, Lottie," says Sauer. "Do as you're told."

His voice is quiet, sad. As if he has feared this moment for a long time.

I huddle on the stairs, my pistol at the ready. Besides the two men, there is a woman in the room. She stands slightly behind the men, her hands in her pockets. As I lean forward for a better look, my foot presses against the floorboards, making a faint creaking sound. I see her tense. She turns her head toward the stairwell, and for a moment I think she's seen me. But I can't look away. She's younger than I thought. My age. And beautiful. She has long dark hair and dark eyes, and for a second I'm sure that I've seen her before. Then it hits me—she looks like Wonder Woman from the comic books my sister Lily loves so much. I find myself frozen in place.

Then she turns away, and it's as if a switch has been turned off and I can breathe again. I blend into the shadows, my finger on the trigger of my gun in case I need to use it. I know I *will* need to use it. I can't let these people take Sauer. I think I know who they are. MGB. Russian intelligence. And apparently they want him because of his association with the Nazis. What he did for them, I don't know. Just as I don't know why he's so important to my council. What I do know is that I can't let them leave with him.

"If you come quietly, there will be no problems," the first man says.

Sauer nods. He motions to Lottie, who stands up.

It's time. I start to raise my pistol, aiming it at one of the Soviet agents. Before I can fire, the woman draws her hand from her pocket. She's holding a Tokarev TT-33. There are two shots, and her companions collapse to the floor. She lowers the gun.

"You have a choice," she says to Sauer and Lottie. "Come with me and live, or join them."

IN THE ENDGAME SERIES, THE HUMAN PLAYERS ARE TRYING TO SAVE THE EARTH FROM BEING DESTROYED BY ALIENS. AND IN THE I AM NUMBER FOUR SERIES, DIFFERENT ALIENS ARE ALREADY HERE ON EARTH, LIVING AMONG US.

Continue reading for a preview of the first book in the *New York Times* bestselling I Am Number Four series.

THE DOOR STARTS SHAKING. IT'S A FLIMSY THING made of bamboo shoots held together with tattered lengths of twine. The shake is subtle and stops almost immediately. They lift their heads to listen, a fourteen-year-old boy and a fifty-year-old man, who everyone thinks is his father but who was born near a different jungle on a different planet hundreds of lightyears away. They are lying shirtless on opposite sides of the hut, a mosquito net over each cot. They hear a distant crash, like the sound of an animal breaking the branch of a tree, but in this case, it sounds like the entire tree has been broken.

"What was that?" the boy asks.

"Shh," the man replies.

They hear the chirp of insects, nothing more. The man brings his legs over the side of the cot when the shake starts again. A longer, firmer shake, and another crash, this time closer. The man gets to his feet and walks slowly to the door. Silence. The man takes a deep breath as he inches his hand to the latch. The boy sits up.

"No," the man whispers, and in that instant the blade of a sword, long and gleaming, made of a shining white metal that is not found on Earth, comes through the door and sinks deeply into the man's chest. It protrudes six inches out through his back, and is quickly pulled free. The man grunts. The boy gasps. The man takes a single breath, and utters one word: "Run." He falls lifeless to the floor.

The boy leaps from the cot, bursts through the rear wall. He doesn't bother with the door or a window; he literally runs through the wall, which breaks apart as if it's paper, though it's made of strong, hard African mahogany. He tears into the Congo night, leaps over trees, sprints at a speed somewhere around sixty miles per hour. His sight and hearing are beyond human. He dodges trees, rips through snarled vines, leaps small streams with a single step. Heavy footsteps are close behind him, getting closer every second. His pursuers also have gifts. And they have something with them. Something he has only heard hints of, something he never believed he would see on Earth.

The crashing nears. The boy hears a low, intense roar. He knows whatever is behind him is picking up speed. He sees a break in the jungle up ahead. When he reaches it, he sees a huge ravine, three hundred feet across and three hundred feet down, with a river at the bottom. The river's bank is covered with huge boulders. Boulders that would break him apart if he fell on them. His only chance is to get across the ravine. He'll have a short running start, and one chance. One chance to save his own life. Even for him, or for any of the others on Earth like him, it's a near impossible leap. Going back, or going down, or trying to fight them means certain death. He has one shot.

There's a deafening roar behind him. They're twenty, thirty feet away. He takes five steps back and runs—and just before the ledge, he takes off and starts flying across the ravine. He's in the air three or four seconds. He screams, his arms outstretched in front of him, waiting for either safety or the end. He hits the ground and tumbles forward, stopping at the base of a mammoth tree. He smiles. He can't believe he made it, that he's going to survive. Not wanting them to see him, and knowing he needs to get farther away from them, he stands. He'll have to keep running.

He turns towards the jungle. As he does, a huge hand wraps itself around his throat. He is lifted off the ground. He struggles, kicks, tries to pull away, but knows it's futile, that it's over. He should have expected that they'd be on both sides, that once they found him, there would be no escape. The Mogadorian lifts him so that he can see the boy's chest, see the amulet that is hanging around his neck, the amulet that only he and his kind can wear. He tears it off and puts it somewhere inside the long black cloak he is wearing, and when his hand emerges it is holding the gleaming white metal sword. The boy looks into the Mogadorian's deep, wide, emotionless black eyes, and he speaks.

"The Legacies live. They will find each other, and when they're ready, they're going to destroy you."

The Mogadarian laughs, a nasty, mocking laugh. It raises the sword, the only weapon in the universe that can break the charm that until today protected the boy, and still protects the others. The blade ignites in a silver flame as it points to the sky, as if it's coming alive, sensing its mission and grimacing in anticipation. And as it falls, an arc of light speeding through the blackness of the jungle, the boy still believes that some part of him will survive, and some part of him will make it home. He closes his eyes just before the sword strikes. And then it is over.

CHAPTER ONE

IN THE BEGINNING THERE WERE NINE OF US. We left when we were young, almost too young to remember.

Almost.

I am told the ground shook, that the skies were full of light and explosions. We were in that two-week period of the year when both moons hang on opposite sides of the horizon. It was a time of celebration, and the explosions were at first mistaken for fireworks. They were not. It was warm, a soft wind blew in from off the water. I am always told the weather: it was warm. There was a soft wind. I've never understood why that matters.

What I remember most vividly is the way my grandmother looked that day. She was frantic, and sad. There were tears in her eyes. My grandfather stood just over her shoulder. I remember the way his glasses gathered the light from the sky. There were hugs. There were words said by each of them. I don't remember what they were. Nothing haunts me more.

It took a year to get here. I was five when we arrived. We were to assimilate ourselves into the culture before returning to Lorien when it could again sustain life. The nine of us had to scatter, and go our own ways. For how long, nobody knew. We still don't. None of them know where I am, and I don't know where they are, or what they look like now. That is how we protect ourselves because of the charm that was placed upon us when we left, a charm guaranteeing that we can only be killed in the order of our numbers, so long as we stay apart. If we come together, then the charm is broken.

When one of us is found and killed, a circular scar wraps around the right ankle of those still alive. And residing on our left ankle, formed when the Loric charm was first cast, is a small scar identical to the amulet each of us wears. The circular scars are another part of the charm. A warning system so that we know where we stand with each other, and so that we know when they'll be coming for us next. The first scar came when I was nine years old. It woke me from my sleep, burning itself into my flesh. We were living in Arizona, in a small border town near Mexico. I woke screaming in the middle of the night, in agony, terrified as the scar seared itself into my flesh. It was the first sign that the Mogadorians had finally found us on Earth, and the first sign that we were in danger. Until the scar showed up, I had almost convinced myself that my memories were wrong, that what Henri told me was wrong. I wanted to be a normal kid living a normal life, but I knew then, beyond any doubt or discussion, that I wasn't. We moved to Minnesota the next day.

The second scar came when I was twelve. I was in school, in Colorado, participating in a spelling bee. As soon as the pain started I knew what was happening, what had happened to Number Two. The pain was excruciating, but bearable this time. I would have stayed on the stage, but the heat lit my sock on fire. The teacher who was conducting the bee sprayed me with a fire extinguisher and rushed me to the hospital. The doctor in the ER found the first scar and called the police. When Henri showed, they threatened to arrest him for child abuse. But because he hadn't been anywhere near me when the second scar came, they had to let him go. We got in the car and drove away, this time to Maine. We left everything we had except for the Loric Chest that Henri brought along on every move. All twenty-one of them to date.

The third scar appeared an hour ago. I was sitting on a pontoon boat. The boat belonged to the parents of the most popular kid at my school, and unbeknownst to them, he was having a party on it. I had never been invited to any of the parties at my school before. I had always, because I knew we might leave at any minute, kept to myself. But it had been quiet for two years. Henri hadn't seen anything in the news that might lead the Mogadorians to one of us, or might alert us to them. So I made a couple friends. And one of them introduced me to the kid who was having the party. Everyone met at a dock. There were three coolers, some music, girls I had admired from afar but never spoken to, even though I wanted to. We pulled out from the dock and went half a mile into the Gulf of Mexico. I was sitting on the edge of the pontoon with my feet in the water, talking to a cute, dark-haired, blue-eyed girl named Tara, when I felt it coming. The water around my leg started boiling, and my lower leg started glowing where the scar was imbedding itself. The third of the Lorien symbols, the third warning. Tara started screaming and people started crowding around me. I knew there was no way to explain it. And I knew we would have to leave immediately.

The stakes were higher now. They had found Number Three, wherever he or she was, and Number Three was dead. So I calmed Tara down and kissed her on the cheek and told her it was nice to meet her and that I hoped she had a long beautiful life. I dove off the side of the boat and started swimming, underwater the entire time, except for one breath about halfway there, as fast as I could until I reached the shore. I ran along the side of the highway, just inside of the tree line, moving at speeds as fast as any of the cars. When I got home, Henri was at the bank of scanners and monitors that he used to research news around the world, and police activity in our area. He knew without me saying a word, though he did lift my soaking pants to see the scars.

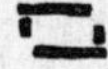

In the beginning we were a group of nine.

Three are gone, dead.

There are six of us left.

They are hunting us, and they won't stop until they've killed us all.

I am Number Four.

I know that I am next.

CHAPTER TWO

I STAND IN THE MIDDLE OF THE DRIVE AND STARE up at the house. It is light pink, almost like cake frosting, sitting ten feet above the ground on wooden stilts. A palm tree sways in the front. In the back of the house a pier extends twenty yards into the Gulf of Mexico. If the house were a mile to the south, the pier would be in the Atlantic Ocean.

Henri walks out of the house carrying the last of the boxes, some of which were never unpacked from our last move. He locks the door, then leaves the keys in the mail slot beside it. It is two o'clock in the morning. He is wearing khaki shorts and a black polo. He is very tan, with an unshaven face that seems downcast. He is also sad to be leaving. He tosses the final boxes into the back of the truck with the rest of our things.

"That's it," he says.

I nod. We stand and stare up at the house and listen

to the wind come through the palm fronds. I am holding a bag of celery in my hand.

"I'll miss this place," I say. "Even more than the others."

"Me too."

"Time for the burn?"

"Yes. You want to do it, or you want me to?"

"I'll do it."

Henri pulls out his wallet and drops it on the ground. I pull out mine and do the same. He walks to our truck and comes back with passports, birth certificates, social security cards, checkbooks, credit cards and bank cards, and drops them on the ground. All of the documents and materials related to our identities here, all of them forged and manufactured. I grab from the truck a small gas can we keep for emergencies. I pour the gas over the small pile. My current name is Daniel Jones. My story is that I grew up in California and moved here because of my dad's job as a computer programmer. Daniel Jones is about to disappear. I light a match and drop it, and the pile ignites. Another one of my lives, gone. As we always do, Henri and I stand and watch the fire. *Bye, Daniel,* I think, *it was nice knowing you.* When the fire burns down, Henri looks over at me.

"We gotta go."

"I know."

"These islands were never safe. They're too hard to

leave quickly, too hard to escape from. It was foolish of us to come here."

I nod. He is right, and I know it. But I'm still reluctant to leave. We came here because I wanted to, and for the first time, Henri let me choose where we were going. We've been here nine months, and it's the longest we have stayed in any one place since leaving Lorien. I'll miss the sun and the warmth. I'll miss the gecko that watched from the wall each morning as I ate breakfast. Though there are literally millions of geckos in south Florida, I swear this one follows me to school and seems to be everywhere I am. I'll miss the thunderstorms that seem to come from out of nowhere, the way everything is still and quiet in the early-morning hours before the terns arrive. I'll miss the dolphins that sometimes feed when the sun sets. I'll even miss the smell of sulfur from the rotting seaweed at the base of the shore, the way that it fills the house and penetrates our dreams while we sleep.

"Get rid of the celery and I'll wait in the truck," Henri says. "Then it's time."

I enter a thicket of trees off to the right of the truck. There are three Key deer already waiting. I dump the bag of celery out at their feet and crouch down and pet each of them in turn. They allow me to, having long gotten over their skittishness. One of them raises his head and looks at me. Dark, blank eyes staring back.

It almost feels as though he passes something to me. A shudder runs up my spine. He drops his head and continues eating.

"Good luck, little friends," I say, and walk to the truck and climb into the passenger seat.

We watch the house grow smaller in the side mirrors until Henri pulls onto the main road and the house disappears. It's a Saturday. I wonder what's happening at the party without me. What they're saying about the way that I left and what they'll say on Monday when I'm not at school. I wish I could have said good-bye. I'll never see anyone I knew here ever again. I'll never speak to any of them. And they'll never know what I am or why I left. After a few months, or maybe a few weeks, none of them will probably ever think of me again.

Before we get on the highway, Henri pulls over to gas up the truck. As he works the pump, I start looking through an atlas he keeps on the middle of the seat. We've had the atlas since we arrived on this planet. It has lines drawn to and from every place we've ever lived. At this point, there are lines crisscrossing all of the United States. We know we should get rid of it, but it's really the only piece of our life together that we have. Normal people have photos and videos and journals; we have the atlas. Picking it up and looking through it, I can see Henri has drawn a new line from Florida to Ohio. When I think of Ohio, I think of cows and corn and nice people. I know the license plate says THE HEART OF IT ALL. What "All" is, I don't know, but I guess I'll find out.

Henri gets back into the truck. He has bought a couple of sodas and a bag of chips. He pulls away and starts heading toward U.S. 1, which will take us north. He reaches for the atlas.

"Do you think there are people in Ohio?" I joke.

He chuckles. "I would imagine there are a few. And we might even get lucky and find cars and TV there, too."

I nod. Maybe it won't be as bad as I think.

"What do you think of the name 'John Smith'?" I ask.

"Is that what you've settled on?"

"I think so," I say. I've never been a John before, or a Smith.

"It doesn't get any more common than that. I would say it's a pleasure to meet you, Mr. Smith."

I smile. "Yeah, I think I like 'John Smith.'"

"I'll create your forms when we stop."

A mile later we are off the island and cruising across the bridge. The waters pass below us. They are calm and the moonlight is shimmering on the small waves, creating dapples of white in the crests. On the right is the ocean, on the left is the gulf; it is, in essence, the same water, but with two different names. I have the urge to cry, but I don't. It's not that

I'm necessarily sad to leave Florida, but I'm tired of running. I'm tired of dreaming up a new name every six months. Tired of new houses, new schools. I wonder if it'll ever be possible for us to stop.

BEFORE THE CALLING.
BEFORE ENDGAME.
THEY TRAINED TO BE CHOSEN.

The Training Diaries prequel novellas follow the lives of the twelve Players before they were chosen as the ones to save their ancient bloodlines—and win Endgame.

Also available as a paperback bindup *Endgame: The Complete Training Diaries.*

HARPER
An Imprint of HarperCollins*Publishers*

WWW.THISISENDGAME.COM